HERESY

The Heretics Saga: Book 1

C. A. Campbell

Paperback ISBN: 978-1-7353764-0-0

eBook ISBN: 978-1-7353764-1-7

Published by Fearless Lit

Interior design C. A. Campbell

Cover design by germancreative on Fiverr

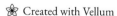 Created with Vellum

To my ride or die, Molly,
who has loved these Heretics
since Nicolette was a houseplant.

PART ONE
HERETICS

"When a man is denied the right to live the life
he believes in, he has no choice
but to become an outlaw."
—— Nelson Mandela

ONE

Rule #1. Survive. No matter the cost.

As the driverless car came to a halt, Shiloh Haven played her rules over in her head once more and checked her uniform for the twelfth time. Still perfect. She glanced back up, but the opaque car windows hid her location. She'd spent the long car ride from the Haven to the Twin Cities in darkness. Her only company had been her racing heartbeat.

When the car door jerked open, the burst of light was blinding.

A thin woman stood on the sidewalk. She wore the same white blouse—high-necked and sleeveless for summer—and dark trousers as Shiloh, like the Arcadian Codex demanded.

"Out," the attendant ordered.

Shiloh climbed out of the car and onto freshly-poured concrete, a dressing on what must have been a wounded, broken street. Before her, a massive building cast her in its long shadow. Behind her, skyscrapers interrupted blue skies. Most of the tall buildings were dark and rusted from disrepair, reminders of the civil wars that once raged here.

The attendant seized Shiloh's wrist. Every muscle coiled like a snake, but Shiloh inhaled through her teeth, forcing herself not to whip back. *Breathe in. Breathe out*

The attendant turned Shiloh's hand over and scanned the tablet over her wrist. The spiderweb marks of Shiloh's identification momentarily glowed blue. Her face appeared above the tablet in a hologram, information spinning around it.

"Haven, Shiloh?"

Shiloh didn't miss the disdain hidden beneath the required hospitality, but she was used to it. "Yes."

"Are there any other representatives from your"—the attendant paused— "family."

Shiloh swallowed the bitter taste in her mouth. She could almost hear Val's hiss when Mother had chosen her to be the representative for the Haven girls: *Of course, Starchild. You always make us proud.*

"No, just me."

"Follow me."

The attendant strode through a set of double doors. Two Protectors of the Peace stood on either side of the entrance, their blue uniforms almost as bright as the early summer sky. Shiloh's steps quickened as she passed them, their gaze feeling like pinpricks on her skin.

The attendant led her through a long hallway where lined windows in the doors allowed glances into dusty rooms with abandoned tables and chairs. What had this place been? A school? The ghost of an object long gone marked one of the walls. A cross. This had been a church back when there was such a thing—before Arcadia existed.

The attendant stopped before a door where another Protector stood and ushered Shiloh inside. "Wait here." She closed the door, and the clack of her footsteps carried her away.

A scattering of families dressed in identical uniforms to Shiloh's own sat in clusters of chairs. Mismatched paint smeared one wall. What message of heresy had been painted there? Maybe the song lyrics Hope used to sing, back when Val, Hope, and Shiloh had been little girls curled together in bed for warmth and comfort.

Amazing grace, how sweet the sound...

Shiloh dug her fingernails into her palm. *I don't remember. I don't remember.*

That was Rule #2 of a Haven girl. *We don't remember.*

Shiloh picked a chair in a corner far from everyone, but an elderly woman approached her anyway, sitting beside her and smiling graciously. "Here on your own, dear?"

"Yes."

The woman waited, but Shiloh didn't offer an explanation. "I'm Evelyn Olson." She stretched out a hand. Shiloh shook it but released quickly. "And you are?"

"Shiloh."

"Nice to meet you. Who are you here for?"

Shiloh hesitated. What word described two little girls, strangers, who'd lost everything and showed up on an unforgiving doorstep on the same day? Shiloh was only six the day she'd been taken to the Haven, but the memory was branded in her brain like a searing iron: the smell of smoke in the social worker's car, the ache of Shiloh's throat as she begged for her Mommy and Daddy, the softness of Hope's touch when she took Shiloh's trembling hand. That day, they'd formed a pact. *We're in this together.*

Until two years ago, when the Elite had arrested Hope, and Shiloh was left alone.

"Honey?" Evelyn pressed. "Who are you here for?"

"My sister," Shiloh said at last.

That was what Mother called the Haven girls, and Shiloh supposed Mother was right about this alone. They were all each other had—why Shiloh had been chosen to come.

"That's so wonderful, dear. We're here for my son." Evelyn nodded at her family, an elderly man and an adult daughter. "He's been in a prison camp for twelve years. I can't—" Her voice broke.

She cleared her throat again and smiled broadly. "But isn't it wonderful? The United Council hosting the Cleansing each year and giving us this opportunity to be reunited, for him to be forgiven."

"Yes." Shiloh's words felt robotic. "How great is the Council!"

Evelyn paused. "Dear, if you don't mind me asking, where are your parents? Shouldn't they be here with you?"

The long-familiar knife twisted in Shiloh's chest. *I don't remember.* But memories were just under the surface—flashes of screams, and fear, and gunshots.

Dead, Shiloh almost said, but she took a deep breath. "I'm a Haven."

Evelyn stiffened. "Oh. The Council is indeed generous then."

"Indeed."

Evelyn excused herself to rejoin her family, retreating quickly like Shiloh knew she would. People always did.

Heresy is contagious, don't you know?

Even though Evelyn's own son had committed heresy, Havens were still far worse, inherently bad. They were the *children* of heretics, raised in heresy. After their parents' deaths or arrests, they were placed in a Haven. There, they were stripped of their former names and given the surname Haven. There, any small sign of heresy invoked severe punishment—with canes and slaps and Repentant Closets. There, they lived by certain rules, but none more important than: *Survive. No matter the cost.*

Shiloh had worked so hard to survive. She'd played the game, obeyed the rules, perfected the mask of 'good girl' so well she'd earned a place on an Engineering Track at school. Most Havens struggled to prove that—despite their parents—they were worthy citizens, so they were stuck on the Laborer Track. All tracks were supposed to be equal, but everyone knew to be a Laborer for Arcadia was to be a slave.

But Shiloh had ensured her survival. She might even have a decent life.

But you, Hope. You had to go and break all the rules.

Shiloh could still remember the moment she knew the end was coming. Hope standing with the worn Bible pages in her hand. *Burn them,* Shiloh had pleaded. But Hope, unable to surrender the heresy of her parents, didn't. And so, the pages had been found, and she'd lost Hope. Even two years later, that could still set Shiloh's skin on fire.

Now, the Cleansing promised that Hope had a chance to be set free. Yet, Shiloh couldn't bring herself to feel excited. The Arcadian government had taken everyone she loved. She couldn't quite bring herself to believe that they would ever give someone back.

◊

"Jacob Kedric Osgood, where in Arcadia's great lands have you been?"

The great and mighty Councilor Samuel Osgood's voice ricocheted around the hotel room and drove into Jake's brain like an ice pick. *Well, froq!* Clearly, Jake was in deep trouble and should tread carefully, but then, he never really did what he *should* do.

"Shh, Dad." Jake pressed his palm to his temple. "Not so loud."

"*Not so loud!* My son disappears all night before my turn to host the Cleansing, and you say, 'not so loud'. Do you know how many Protectors I had looking for you last night?"

Jake flopped down on the couch and smiled crookedly. "Probably too few of the good ones."

Dad took a step toward Jake threateningly. *Ha!* What would his father do, really? Ground him to his room? Maybe, but then tomorrow, Dad would be halfway around the globe, Mom would have her own charity engagements, and nothing would ever be enforced.

"Relax, Dad, I'm here now," Jake said.

"We were supposed to leave for the event thirty minutes ago."

What? Jake glanced at the clock on the wall. *Peace and harmony!* He could've sworn he'd left the college dorm in time, disentangling from around the girl—*what was her name?*—and leaving behind the other passed out college kids without saying goodbye.

Last night, a friend, who'd recently graduated from their school, invited Jake to a college party. How could Jake say no? College parties were *the best*! Everyone drank and made merry like the fun ended after graduation. Which it did. It would all be *'do your duty for Arcadia, work, marry the spouse chosen for you, and have kids to repopulate the nation'*. Nightmare, really.

Jake gave Dad his best mock-sheepish look and lifted his palms. "Whoops."

Dad's face contorted in rage. Everyone told Jake he looked just like Dad. Literally *everyone*: friends, politicians, media, girls during *really* awkward moments. Same brown hair, brown eyes, and handsome face that seemed hand-designed for a nation's leader. But Jake sure hoped he didn't look like this when he was angry. It wasn't a great look.

"*Whoops?*" Dad snapped. "Is that all you have to say?"

"It's not like they can start the froqing event without you."

Dad lifted a stern finger. "Watch your *mouth*!"

Jake rolled his eyes. The Codex specifically forbid the cuss words that existed Pre-Sundering. So, of course, teenagers had invented new ones—not forbidden, but certainly frowned upon.

Dad massaged his fingers into his temples. "Why do you *always* do this?"

Because I'm sick of being a puppet in your show. Because I'm tired of your lies and all the people you've hurt. Because when I tried to be good, it was never enough anyway

Jake swallowed and looked away.

"Jake, are you listening to me?" Dad asked.

Jake forced a smile. "Not a word."

Dad growled in frustration just as Jake's mother stepped from the bathroom. Mom wore the traditional Arcadian outfit, long trousers and a shirt—hers red instead of white to mark her status. Still, with her blonde hair twisted up and her chin lifted high, she made it look elegant.

"Enough," she said firmly. "People will hear." She nodded toward the door, where bodyguards and Hazel, Dad's assistant, had gone when they'd been dismissed from the room. No doubt Hazel was eavesdropping. She always was.

Mom fixed Jake with *that* look. The *don't-try-with-me-boy* look. "Jake, get in the shower. You have ten minutes."

Jake's smile fell as he stood. "Okay, Mom."

She caught his arm as he passed. The look she gave him made Jake's gut twist into a bowtie. Dad had no power to make him feel guilty. Maybe because Dad was practically a stranger to him. Or perhaps because Dad's sins could cover a lifetime of Jake's own. But Mom was a different story. Despite her frequent travel, Jake knew he'd *always* been her priority.

"Don't you ever do that again," Mom said, even though Jake *had* done it before, and they both knew he *would* do it again. "I was worried about you."

"Mom, it's the safest nation in the world. What's there to be worried about?"

Her eyes narrowed.

Jake winced. "I'm sorry."

She released his arm. "Ten minutes."

Jake was ready with time to spare, the smell of alcohol and perfume scrubbed from his body, his hair combed, two aspirins swallowed, and his pressed clothes tucked and smoothed in the right places. But his bloodshot eyes and the pounding headache were there to stay. The bodyguards ushered them into the awaiting car, then followed behind in their own.

Cool silence fueled the short car ride. Dad buttoned and straightened his jacket at least twelve thousand times, and Mom stared out the window. Once, she caught Jake's eyes in the reflection and gave a peace offering of a smile. The *'let's-please-just-get-through-this'* type of smile.

A sudden flood of people and orb-like, hovering cameras notified Jake that they'd arrived. The Cleansing was mandatory viewing all across Arcadia: from the western border of Minnesota, as far south as Missouri, and to the coast of Maine. But first it had to be recorded, edited and approved by the United Council's media team. It was important to show the right image, even if it was a lie.

"Here," Mom said, handing him a pair of sunglasses. "Your eyes are still red."

Dad grunted and swung the door open. As the cameras hit him, his face broke into a perfect, wide smile. He waved as he exited the car.

Jake groaned. *It's showtime.*

In Arcadia, everyone had their roles to play, and this was his, whether he wanted it or not. Being the son of a Councilor, he could get away with so many things, but in the end, Jake, too, still moved to the pull of puppet strings. There were no choices in Arcadia. Not if you wanted to live.

I hate this place.

Jake straightened his collar, slipped on the sunglasses, and pasted on a smile as he exited the car. *Time to dance, puppet. Dance.*

"Let me come!"

Nicolette Howell's mother didn't even look up from where she knelt on the worn, dusty floor, shoving a first aid kit into her pack. "No, Nic."

Nic's finger curled so tightly her fingernails dug into her palms. Outside, the Mississippi River roared past the old mill—a ferocious monster that threatened to gobble up the innocent.

"Please. I can fight!" The desire to fight blazed in her blood, a fire that had been there since the day she was born—that danced to the beat of her heart. Every inch of her screamed with an internal battle cry.

Arcadia must fall.

Mom's hands froze over her bag, then she heaved a sigh, snapped the pack closed and stood to face Nic. "You're my child." Mom cupped Nic's face in her hands. "I can't do this unless I know you are safe."

Nic jerked back from the tender touch. "I'm *not* a child, Mom."

Children played with toys and went to school. Most children didn't grow up as outlaws, living in the woods and abandoned homes, hunted by Elite night and day. Nic knew more about shooting guns, physical fighting, and how to survive alone in the woods than any child would. Or really, should have to.

But a child was exactly what Mom, and the others in the Family—the rebel group she and her mother had belonged to since Nic was a toddler—treated her like. The whole time they had been planning this attack, they would only talk about it when Nic was off collecting firewood or was supposed to be sleeping. But she would only close her eyes and pretend to sleep, listening to their whispers, dreaming of war.

If this worked—*when it worked,* Nic forced herself to think—it could change everything. ROGUE had once been so powerful that the rebel organization had nearly brought Arcadia to its knees. But for over a decade, the heretics in ROGUE had only focused on survival. But not anymore. Now, they rose.

Mom groaned. "You're thirteen years old."

"Almost fourteen," Nic argued, nails grinding deep into her palms.

"Nicolette, I am not having this conversation with you anymore."

Nic winced. Even without the sharp edge in Mom's tone or the hands planted on her hips, Nic knew there was no more pushing her. Once the name Nicolette left Mom's lips, it was over, unless Nic wanted to sit in the chair position for an hour.

Still, Nic crossed her arms and huffed in defeat. She cast her eyes to look at the ten others, who were equally involved in preparation, carefully packing the weapons that would change the world, holding them as tenderly as a baby. Paul looked up from loading his gun and winked, his quick smile a flash of white against his dark skin. Nic tried to smile back, but couldn't manage to keep it on her lips.

Everyone in The Family, everyone in ROGUE, had their own reason to fight. They fought for faith, for freedom, for the hope of a different world, and for husbands, Oliver and Wyatt, for the love that Arcadia told them was wrong. They fought because they dared to be something different than what Arcadia told them to be, and that made them heretics.

And Nic had more reason than her faith to fight. She twisted the watch that dangled on her arm, meant for a much larger wrist. Her father's wrist.

Mom tapped Nic's cheek to get her attention. "Now, tell me the plan."

Nic rolled her eyes and repeated it like she had a million times before. She would wait and pray until not a minute past five p.m. today. If all went according to plan, the Family would return by then, and they would all escape together on the boat that had carried them to this abandoned mill an hour outside the Twin Cities. If they didn't, Nic would leave on her own and flee to another rebel group for safety.

But that won't happen, Nic told herself. Because they *were* coming back.

But Dad had promised to come back too, and he hadn't. After the Elite shot Dad during a supply run, Paul had returned alone and pressed Dad's antique watch into Mom's fingers. It was three years ago, and sometimes, Nic could still hear Mom screaming.

Nic gripped her wristwatch as the group swung their packs onto their backs. Nic hugged them goodbye—Mia and Oliver and even Zahid. When he pulled back, Paul pulled playfully on Nic's blonde ponytail.

"Remember," he said, "what has eyes but cannot see?"

"The eyes of our enemies when we come for them," Nic replied with a small smile as she gave the answer only a member of ROGUE would know.

"That's my soldier."

Nic turned to Mom as the others filed outside, and her Mom pulled her into a hug. Nic wanted to be stiff, to be mad, to punish her for leaving her behind—alone. But Nic found herself clinging to her instead, never wanting to let go.

Please come back, Nic wanted to plead, but that would make her a baby, and she *wasn't* a baby.

Finally, Mom released her and put up a stern finger. "Remember. Five p.m."

"Yes, Mom."

Nic watched them enter the trees, disappearing into the darkness and the fog, and kept staring, long after they were gone.

Now, hours later, Nic had paced the floor of the mill so many times she automatically leaped over the broken boards, praying for their protection, glancing at her watch every few minutes, counting down to the time when the world would change.

Finally, the long hand met the top of the hour, and Nic's heart pounded even louder.

The Cleansing should be beginning now. And if all went according to plan, it would end very soon.

Two

The trumpets flared, and the anthem played as Samuel Osgood made his way to the stage.

Make way for the king.

Jake and his mom followed close behind him, surrounded by bodyguards. The crowd rose to their feet, applauding, smiling, cheering. Only the first few rows of the huge church were filled. Later, when the mandatory 'live' viewing aired, it would look as though adoring fans were packed in every seat. But only the most trusted were here: Councilor Beck and her family, and State Advocates. People who would remain loyal to the cover story if things went awry.

The back of the stage boasted a hologram of the Arcadian flag: a blanket of red and blue with a white olive branch forming a circle around joined hand. Jake and his mom took their place side by side in front of the hologram while Dad approached the glass podium.

"My dear Arcadians." His voice boomed into the microphone, and the crowd fell silent. "In my father's time, this land we stand on was called the United States, but we were anything but united."

Son of a blight. Jake bit back a groan. *Here we go again.*

"They were torn apart by political parties, religions, race, opinions, and...sexuality." Dad gave a little shudder. "These things led to terrorism. And terrorism..."

*Led to a great civil war. Blah, blah, blah...*Jake had heard this speech so many times he could give it himself.

Before Arcadia, people couldn't get along, so they did what people did: killed each other over it. Cities were destroyed or abandoned because of chemical attacks. Some people fled the country, while many of those who stayed didn't survive. A nation was dying, hemorrhaging because they couldn't get past their own differences. Then came the devastation that ended it all—the Reckoning.

The Sons of David, a Christian terrorist group, dropped a bomb on the former capital. The initial explosion had wiped out half the government who had gathered for an emergency conference. The chemical bomb that had followed wiped out most of the rest.

Jake's grandfather—the namesake, Jacob Osgood—had been the governor of Minnesota at the time. He, with Madison Beck—the former Speaker of the House—and three other highly positioned, trusted individuals stepped up to fill the void, calling themselves the United Council. They advocated for a world devoid of differences, where true unity could be achieved. Other leaders had their own vision of the future, and to avoid more war, a treaty was made. In an event known as the Sundering, the former United States was split into three nations: Moravia, the socialists; Zy'on, the Christian nation; and Arcadia, the nation of unity, and harmony, and lies.

So, so many lies.

The United Council built the force-field walls that divided the nations. They said it would protect Arcadia—after all, Moravia and Zy'on weren't exactly pleasant either—but in reality, it was to create a cage. Because after that, the Council wrote the Codex and then oversaw the Great Excision, assembling the Elite to rid the nation of heretics who refused to conform. Hundreds of people had been placed in prison camps, working like slaves until their deaths.

Of course, Dad made it sound so much prettier than that. Jake focused just as Dad reached the crescendo of his speech.

And they named it...

"And they named it Arcadia," his father said, with just the perfect inflection of pride, "to signify that it would be a land of harmony and prosperity. Where suffering and hatred were never known."

And the only cost was freedom.

"In order to protect this peace, we must ensure the Codex is enforced. But what would peace and prosperity be without mercy? And that is why my father and the rest of the First Council created the Cleansing. Every year, five names of previously condemned heretics are drawn, and they are given the opportunity to renounce their heresy and rejoin society."

A cheer blazed through the crowd. Mom jabbed her elbow into his side, and only then did Jake remember to clap too.

Dad held up his hand for silence and moved to his list. "The name of the first heretic to be Cleansed is...Logan Olson."

On cue, two Elite—masked in their jet-black suits and helmets with dark visors—dragged a man down the aisle, a dark sack concealing his face. Pale limbs—thin as his skeleton, drowning in his brown prison suit—stumbled up the stage steps. Logan's family stepped onto the other side of the stage, clinging to each other's hands: two elderly parents, and a petite, annular blonde who was possibly his sister. The Elite stopped Logan near the podium, turned him to face the audience, and ripped the sack from his head. His face reiterated the gauntness of his body, a skull with skin, all sharp lines and bald head.

Logan's mother pressed her fingers to her lips, choking back a sob.

Don't, Jake wanted to warn. *Smile pretty. That's your role. Just smile pretty.*

"Logan Olson," Dad said, "you committed heresy against Arcadia by refusing to marry your assigned spouse, and instead, ran away with a citizen of your own gender. This neglected your explicit duty to Arcadia to ensure the repopulation of the nation and to put the United Council and Arcadia before all others."

A sour taste burned at the back of Jake's throat. He swallowed, and it went down like broken glass.

Dad continued, "Logan Olson, do you renounce your heresy and swear that you will obey the will of the Council and the law of the Codex?"

Logan spoke, but it was unintelligible. He cleared his throat. "Yes. Yes, I swear."

The crowd exploded in applause again, but Jake refused to join them. Was this really even a choice? The love that was an act of heresy had likely seemed worth it once, but after years of torture, starvation, and slavery, who could say no to mercy, even if it meant pretending an irreplaceable part of yourself wasn't real? No one had, in all the years of the Cleansing.

A wide smile carved into Dad's face. "Then, by the power of the United Council, I pardon you of your heresy."

With a swipe of the Elite's hand, the electric handcuffs disappeared from Logan's wrists. His knees nearly collapsed, and then he vaulted toward his family. They collided in a tangle of limbs and grateful sobs and kisses before being shooed off the stage by attendants.

Then the next name was called.

"Hope Haven."

Jake's back stiffened. That name... *How do I know that name?*

Jake studied the girl as she was led down the aisle, even as a soft murmur ebbed through the crowd. Jake knew what they were thinking. She was a Haven girl. A daughter of heretics. The Council was so merciful to choose her, when she'd been tainted all her life.

When Hope Haven reached the stage's steps, Jake's memory

came back to him like a slap in his face. She'd been in his grade at Ardency, his school—a girl he'd never spoken to. But he could remember her: dark curls, umber skin, a pretty smile, but mostly, the look of terror in her eyes two years ago. At only fifteen-years-old, she'd stood in front of the assembly at their mandatory boarding school, Ardency, her crimes being read over the screeching loudspeaker. He remembered how he wished he could save her as a black sack slid over her face.

Then she was gone.

Until now.

❦

"The Haven family, it's time."

Shiloh rose from the hard metal surface and started toward the attendant who stood in the doorway. Shiloh's legs wanted to wobble, but she forced them to steady.

I am calm, controlled, and obedient. That was Rule #3 of being a Haven girl. *Show Arcadia what they want to see.*

The attendant walked briskly, leading her through the maze of hallways. They arrived at the stairs backstage just as the Olson family stumbled off, a skeleton of a man between them. And then Shiloh heard the name.

"Hope Haven!"

A shudder of excitement raced down Shiloh's spine. She let herself feel it for the first time as the attendant pushed her toward the stairs. This wasn't a joke then; this was happening.

Breathe in. Shiloh climbed the stairs. *Breathe out.*

The light on the stage blinded her, the colors of the Arcadian flag bleeding onto the wooden platform. When her vision returned, she found Jacob Osgood, the Councilor's son, standing only an arm's length away, with sunglasses perched on his nose.

Shiloh nearly rolled her eyes. *Typical.*

How many times had she seen him, sitting at the back of a

classroom, wearing sunglasses to hide his red eyes and swallowing aspirins like candy? He lived up to his reputation: the Prince of Arcadia. The reckless, womanizing, party boy.

Next to him stood the Councilor's wife, Reagan Osgood, and the Councilor poised at the podium. Behind the 'royal' family, Protectors in their bright uniforms formed a line. And then, from the opposite side of the stage, two Elite appeared, someone draped between them. A chill marched down Shiloh's spine. The Elite's sole responsibility was to monitor, to prevent, and to punish acts of heresy. Their dark, reflective visors made them faceless—no one would know who they were. Anyone could be an Elite.

The Elite stopped at the center of the stage and yanked the sack from Hope's face. The first real look at Hope sucked Shiloh's air from her lungs. With bones poking like knives from her ashen skin, Hope looked as though she might fade away. Her wild hair, that Shiloh had braided a thousand times, was gone.

Finally, Hope turned toward Shiloh and smiled. And that smile was still so beautifully, wonderfully her, that it seemed to erase the distance and the time between them. For a second, time turned back to two years ago, sitting at dinner at the Haven, mouthing words to each other and reading lips so Mother and the Aunts couldn't hear what they were saying.

Hope's mouth moved. "Shi."

Shiloh took a step forward and then stopped herself. No emotion. Hope remained a heretic until she was Cleansed, and Shiloh had to pretend to reject her as such.

Instead, Shiloh mouthed. "I missed you."

Councilor Osgood spoke. "Hope Haven, you committed heresy against Arcadia by possessing pages of a religious text. This violated your duty to ensure the unity and peace of Arcadia, as well as betraying your loyalty to the United Council, which should be above all others."

Hope's smile slipped, and a fire danced in her eyes. Two years in prison and that fire still blazed.

"Hope Haven, do you renounce your heresy and swear to live according to the duties of an Arcadian citizen? Will you pledge that there is no god; there is only us?"

Hope dragged her gaze away from Shiloh and looked out to the crowd. Her chin lifted high.

Shiloh swallowed. *Please, Hope.*

Hope turned her eyes back to Shiloh and mouthed, "I'm so sorry. I love you."

Shiloh's blood turned to ice.

The Councilor cleared his throat. "Hope Haven?"

Hope jerked her head to look the Councilor straight in the eyes.

Please, Shiloh wanted to scream. *Please, don't do this!*

But she did. "No."

The Councilor recoiled. "I'm sorry. *What* did you say?"

"I said *no.*"

The whole room caught its breath. The Councilor stared mutely. This was not how the script went.

Hope took advantage of the silence. "I do not renounce my heresy. I am done—*done* conforming to Arcadia's ways. You can send me back to the prison camp or you can kill me like you—"

"Shut up!" one of the Elite barked, driving his prod into Hope's back. As the electrical current passed through her body, she jerked and fell to her knees.

Shiloh sprang forward, every inch of her screaming to come to Hope's aid. A hand seized her wrist, yanking her back. She turned, and a pair of warm, brown eyes met hers.

"Don't," Jacob Osgood hissed, low enough that only she could hear. His sunglasses must have been tossed aside, because his uncovered gaze now blazed into her with a warning. "They will kill you too."

Shiloh whipped her hand away, heart pounding in her ears, but he was right. *Rule #1.* She stayed but jerked her eyes back to Hope, who remained on her knees, gasping through the pain.

"You can kill me," Hope continued, "like you killed my parents, but you will not decide how I think or believe or who I love."

Shut up! Shiloh wanted to scream. Hot tears stung the back of her eyes, but she didn't dare let them fall. *Please, just shut up!*

But Hope's voice only grew louder. "You wanted to create a world with no differences. *Ha!*"

The stick jammed into Hope's side again. This time, she shrieked in pain, and the sound echoed in Shiloh's bones.

"Enough!" the Councilor barked. "Get her out of here."

The Elite seized Hope's arms and dragged her toward the edge of the stage, still on her knees. She refused to be silent. "You just decided which differences wouldn't be accepted. This isn't acceptance. This is intol—"

The Elite's fist slammed in her throat, and the gasp that escaped from her mouth scraped like saw blades down Shiloh's spine. Even Jacob Osgood shuddered. Hope didn't speak after that, and the Elite got her to the steps.

This can't...this can't be happening!

Shiloh couldn't be watching them take her away. Again. Within her, everything wailed in agony, but Shiloh closed her eyes, forcing herself to remain blank.

Rule #3. Rule #3. Breathe in, breathe out.

"Councilor Osgood," a voice boomed from the audience. Councilor Beck, the only other Councilor present, surged to her feet from the front row. She spoke steadily, but her eyes crackled with flames. "You know the protocol for a refusal."

The Elite froze. Hope landed, crumpled like a doll on the floor. Councilor Osgood stared at his fellow Councilor and then at the girl, with her face pressed to the wood, but didn't speak.

Councilor Beck snorted and crossed her arms. "Elite #767, do your duty."

The Elite nodded. He yanked Hope onto her knees and drew his gun from his hip.

Then Shiloh understood.

This was no longer a Cleansing.

This was an execution.

Shiloh launched herself forward, but Jacob Osgood flung his arms around her waist, holding her in place. She thrust her elbow back, hearing an *'oof'* as the sharp point connected with his ribs. But he didn't release.

"Stop," he begged against her ear, yanking her tighter against his firm chest, "I'm sorry, I'm sorry, but you have to stop."

From across the stage, Hope met Shiloh's eyes and shook her head.

Shiloh froze, a wail rising from the depths of her, but she clamped a hand over her lips to keep from making a sound.

Silence blanketed the room until only one noise became clear. Hope was singing.

"Amazing grace, how sweet the sound..."

Then the Elite pulled the trigger.

THREE

Time slowed.

Shiloh's knees surrendered, and she collapsed. Only Jacob Osgood's arms kept her upright even though he, too, trembled. A long, single tone squealed into Shiloh's ears, like every nerve in her body screamed out in pain, until she heard no other sound. Only saw a flicker of disconnected images.

Councilor Osgood clinging to the podium.

Mrs. Osgood covering her scream with her hands.

The crowd scrambling about, murmuring like rolling thunder.

And blood—so much blood—trickling toward Shiloh's feet.

Then...

Boom!

From the corner of the stage, flame exploded upward, shooting wood like bullets through the air. Shiloh flung her arms over her head. Jacob Osgood stumbled backward, toward the stage's edge, pulling her with him.

Someone screamed, "Down, down, down!"

A body hit the Councilor, another his wife, and they tumbled from the stage. A Protector started toward Jacob Osgood, but it was too late. Jacob Osgood and Shiloh fell from the edge, just as the stage exploded beneath Shiloh's feet, and the air ignited with flame.

Four

A long continuous screech played through Jake's eardrums, reverberating the sound of the explosion. Pain screamed through his body, but Jake fought against its pull and forced his eyes open. Smoke blocked his vision.

What happened?

Was that a bomb?

Froq me! That was a bomb!

A burst of light exploded through the air, a flame growing stronger. Jake's vision cleared slowly. From the ground beside him, a Protector stared back at him with unseeing eyes, his face charred beyond recognition.

Jake flung himself backward with a scream.

Move, Osgood.

He pushed himself to his hands and knees, his palms digging into splintered wood. His vision dipped and whirled and threatened to go dark.

Stay awake. Stay awake.

Somewhere, someone screamed.

"Mom! Dad!" he cried back.

No response came.

Were they dead? *Froq, please don't be dead. Please, don't—*
Pop. Pop. Pop.

Jake ducked his head, shielding it with his arms. He knew that noise. *Gunfire.*

Whatever attack had happened, still raged on. Shadows moved beyond the wall of flame and rubble: the crowd running for their lives, or murderers hunting them down. Either way, if Jake stayed here, he was a dead man. He cast one look around for his parents, seeing nothing, and then scrambled to his feet, nearly falling once again. And then—

The girl. Oh ordure, the girl!

The family member of Hope Haven, who couldn't have been any older than Hope. She'd been pressed against him as they fell from the stage seconds before the bomb went off, but they had parted in the air. He couldn't—wouldn't—just leave her.

He searched in the dark, smoldering mess of wood and metal. *There.* The smoke cleared for an instant, and an outline of singed clothes and black hair appeared a few feet away. He took two shaky steps and fell beside her. A wood beam pinned her leg to the ground, and she was still. Too still.

Don't be dead. Please don't be dead.

What had first aid class taught him? Froq, why hadn't he paid more attention? *Right, check a pulse.* But before he could touch her, she moaned.

Thank the Council!

"Wake up!" Jake shook her shoulder. "Come on, wake up!"

Her eyes opened.

"We've got to get out of here!" Jake yelled over the roar of gunfire and screams. "Can you move?"

She nodded, but when she tried to move, she cried out in pain. "I'm stuck!"

Jake shoved the beam, but the movement sent a wave of pain through his arms. Only then did he see the burns that snaked their way down the back of his arms, onto the back of his hands. He gritted his teeth against the pain and pushed again. She pushed too, but it wouldn't budge.

"L-leverage." She sucked in a breath through the pain and repeated steadily, "We need leverage."

She pointed to a long board nearby, a piece of wood from the stage that wasn't in flames. When Jake returned with the board, he followed her careful, calm directions, wedging it under the beam. He put his full weight on the slanted board, coughing with the exertion and smoke. The beam rose off her. She yelped as she pulled her foot out, just before he could no longer hold it, and the beam crashed back down.

Pop. Pop. Pop.

The gunfire ricocheted all around them.

The girl pushed herself onto her feet but buckled with a cry. Burns glowed through her tattered pants, and her leg bent into an odd angle. Crushed.

Jake reached for her, but she shoved him back. "I don't need your help."

Froq, she was feisty. In another situation, he'd have liked that. But right now, it made him grind his teeth. When she fell again, Jake barely caught her before she hit the floor.

She glared at him, her eyes slits of black. "I said—"

"Yeah, yeah, you don't need me. Everything's froqing daisies in here." Jake wrapped his arm around her slender waist. "Now, hold on to me, and let's go."

She wrapped her arm around his shoulder and hopped on her unbroken leg as they started forward. They ran blindly, unsure which way to go, dodging from bursts of flames and the sound of bullets.

"There." The girl pointed at a red glow that broke through the smoke. EXIT.

Jake steered them toward it, and a door took shape.

Pop, pop, pop. Another explosion of bullets. Closer this time.

Jake flung himself toward the door and shoved it open. Something—the door handle, perhaps—slammed into his gut, knocking the air from him. He fell forward through the doorway, collapsing onto the tile of the hallway. The girl rolled and kicked the door shut with her uninjured foot.

Jake gasped. Smoke still clogged the air in here, but he could at least get a breath.

"We have to keep going," the girl said, her voice still shockingly steady. Was she made of steel? "We can bar ourselves in one of the classrooms."

Jake started to push himself upright, but pain flared through his gut. He fell backward, clutching his stomach. The girl appeared in his vision, hovering over him with wide, dark eyes.

"Osgood, you're bleeding."

Jake lifted his wet hand from his stomach. It was soaked with crimson. It wasn't a door handle that had hit him.

It was a bullet.

Think, Shiloh, think.

The stain on the Councilor's son's stomach grew larger by the second. The bullet could have struck his pancreas or stomach, but if it had clipped his lung, he would rapidly suffocate. She needed a plan. *Now!*

She yanked at his shirt, ripping through buttons to bear his red stained chest and abdomen. She pulled off her own shirt and pressed it to his wound to slow the bleeding. That was what the first aid class at school had said. *Apply pressure. Stop the bleeding.*

But her white shirt rapidly turned red.

"If you wanted to get me naked," Osgood said through clenched teeth, "you could have just asked."

"Shut up!" Now was not the time for joking. It certainly wasn't the time for her cheeks to burn, realizing she now wore only her bra. "Froq, do you ever stop flirting?"

"Nope." He'd probably meant to say it glibly, but the word ended in a gasp of pain.

Focus, Shiloh. You need a plan.

She could drag him to a place to take cover. A classroom was only ten feet away, but it might as well have been a mile. Or, another option, she could leave him and crawl away to safety.

That was Rule #1, right? She stood a better chance of survival if she left Jacob Osgood here. And, after all the things she'd lost, wouldn't it be justice that Councilor Osgood lost something too? But when she glanced at Osgood's face—now barren of the cocky smile he always seemed to wear as he strode around campus like he owned the place—for once, she didn't see the Councilor. She only saw a boy as terrified as she was.

I'm not going to leave him.

"Hey." Osgood's breath came faster and faster. Panic? Or a collapsing lung? "What's your name? We could die in here together, and I don't even know your name."

Shiloh glared at him. "Survive, and I'll tell you my name. Now push yourself up."

With a groan, he moved up enough for her to get his shirt off. Shiloh twisted it tight and then slide it around his back like a rope, tying it over her white shirt and yanking it until he gasped from the pressure.

Somewhere in a distant hallway, feet pounded on tile.

"Listen, we have to get out of this hallway," Shiloh explained, gesturing to the classroom down the hall, "but we're going to have to get there together, okay?"

"Okay."

She used the door to pull herself to her feet and then offered her hand. Bracing himself on the wall and Shiloh's hand, Osgood dragged himself upright. Clinging to each other and the walls, they hobbled toward the classroom, leaving drops of blood like bread-crumbs behind them. Her head spun with the pain as she bore their weight on the broken leg, but she gritted her teeth and pushed forward.

A yard from the door, Osgood collapsed onto the tile, pulling Shiloh down with him. She crawled into the room on her hands and knees, and then, turning, dragged Osgood into the room by his shoulders, red smearing across the tile. Finally, Shiloh shut the door quietly, so she didn't draw attention. She locked it and found chairs and a table to barricade the door.

After, she collapsed to her knees and wretched as the pain turned her stomach inside out. She wiped bile from her mouth with the back of her hand then crawled to Osgood. All color had bled from his tanned skin. Shiloh looked around for anything: a phone, a first aid kit. *Something!*

Staring dimly at the ceiling, he caught her hand. "Hey, if something happens, can you tell my mom—"

"Froq you, Osgood." She jerked her hand away. "I'm not taking your last words, because you're not going to die on me. You got that? Don't you *froqing* die!"

Osgood gave her his legendary crooked smile. "I'll do my best."

Shiloh pulled herself to the nearest window, but nails sealed it shut. Outside the window, she could see the whirl of blue and red lights as Protectors and, hopefully, ambulances arrived. Elite streamed like black ants into the building. Help would be coming soon; they just needed to hold on.

Shiloh returned to Jake to find his eyes closed. She nudged him hard. "Stay awake."

"Yes, ma'am," he drawled, but his eyes remained closed.

Shiloh swallowed a lump in her throat as she took in the gentle slopes of his face, his eyelashes fanned on his pale cheeks. *Please, please, don't die.*

Footsteps clattered outside as two figures ran past the door, carrying rifles. But they were dressed roughly, not like any military Shiloh knew. Then...they were heretics. One, a blonde woman with a tight ponytail, glanced into the room as she ran past. A heartbeat later, she returned and rattled the doorknob.

"If you have to run..." Osgood started.

"I told you to shut up." Shiloh seized a folded metal chair, the only possible weapon. Would she even have the strength to swing it? Either way, it'd be useless against a gun.

The heretic pounded on the window. "Are you okay in there? Are you hurt?"

The second figure—a large man with dark skin—appeared at her side. "Amelia, we have to go!"

"They're kids, Paul. They need help!"

"We don't have time!"

"Then *go!*"

Paul swore but stayed.

Amelia pulled something from her pack and pressed it against the window. A first aid kit.

Shiloh looked at Osgood, and a question passed between them. Did they trust this? He nodded. There wasn't another choice.

Shiloh limped to the barrier and moved the blockade enough to open the door a few inches. The woman passed the kit to her. Did she know that she was helping the Councilor's son? Would it matter?

"There's a Quik-Clot in there to stop the bleeding," the heretic said, "and a blood loss rehydration kit. Do you know how to use them?"

Shiloh nodded.

"If not, the kit has directions." Amelia jerked her head toward the sound of a door slamming in the distance.

"Let's go!" Paul pulled on her arm.

Amelia took a step back. "I'm so sorry. We didn't want kids to get hurt. We just want a better world."

They ran and were gone before Shiloh could speak the words of heresy that threatened to leave her lips.

So do I.

Shiloh barricaded the door again. Returning to Osgood's side, she pressed the Quik-Clot into his wound, stopping the bleeding, and then took out the rehydration device. She set the square contraption in the crook of his elbow. The needle within plummeted into his vein on its own and began pumping saline into his bloodstream. Osgood didn't even wince.

Shiloh steadied her hands as she used the bandages and another bottle of saline to wrap wet dressings around Osgood and her own burns. When she was done, he grabbed her hand, his blood-stained fingers curling between her own like they were his last anchor to the world. This time, she didn't pull away.

Help finally arrived ten minutes later, the Elite bursting through Shiloh's barricade with ease. They trained their guns around the room but soon lowered them.

One Elite called into his radio, "We found Jacob Osgood. We need a medical team ASAP!"

The team came quickly, pulling Shiloh away from Osgood, even when his hand tightened on hers. Someone wrapped a blanket around her, started asking her questions she couldn't make sense of. Through the paramedics and EMTs who were frantically working on him, Shiloh could still see Osgood.

He wasn't conscious anymore.

Don't you dare die on me, Osgood. Don't you even dare.

4:58 pm

Nic watched the seconds spin around the watch.

4:59

Outside the cracked window, there was still nothing but endless trees.

Please, God, please, Nic prayed in time with her pounding heart.

5:00.

One more minute. Nic would give them *one* extra minute. Nic willed Mom to appear around the trees. For Paul, and Oliver, and Mia, and everyone. *Please come back to me.*

5:01.

A wail built in Nic's chest, and she pressed her hands to her mouth to stop the scream. She almost buckled to the ground, but she couldn't. *Run,* Mom had said, *you have to run.*

Nic took a step toward her pack, but stumbled and slumped against the wall. Her cheeks were hot and wet. She dragged her hands over the tears and gritted her teeth.

Stop crying. Don't be weak.

They weren't dead. They were only late. They would find each other later. But now, she needed to run.

Nic grabbed her pack, made sure the safety on her handgun was off, and ran for her life.

FIVE

Nic's feet pounded on the forest floor as she ran to the boat, crunching over leaves and twigs, choosing speed over stealth. Elite could already be headed this way.

Hurry, Nic!

Their little fishing boat was nothing more than a motor at the end and a windshield at the front. Or stern and bow, Oliver had said, but Nic could never keep it straight. The Family had removed all the cushioned seats, except for the driver's, to make room for all twelve of them to fit into it.

Now, she was alone.

Nic swatted at the sting of tears on her cheeks, then untied the rope from the tree. She leaped into the boat before it could drift from the shore. Dropping her duffle, she raced to the driver's seat.

Taking the key from her vest pocket, she shoved it into the ignition. Movement on the shore caught her eye. She whirled, grasping her holstered pistol, her heart thudding in warning.

There's nothing. Go!

Nic turned the key. The boat didn't start.

No, no, no, no!

Again, movement made her jerk her head toward shore. A

black orb rushed toward the boat and halted over Nic's head. *An Eye. No!*

Drawn toward body heat, the Eye was used by the Elite to seek out heretics like her. Nic jerked her gun from its holster, but not before the Eye bellowed an alarm and flashed a blinding red. Nic squinted against the light, aimed her gun, and pulled the trigger. The Eye exploded and dropped into the water. But it was too late.

The Elite had found her.

Go!

Nic turned the key again. *Please, God!* The boat finally roared to life, and she slammed the pedal to the floor.

Over the motor, she couldn't hear the gunshot. The bullet crashed into the side windshield, releasing a cloud of blue smoke. A tranquilizer bullet.

On the shore, a dozen Elite sprinted from the trees like a pack of wolves. Nic dived beneath the dashboard, dodging another bullet. Holding the bottom of the steering wheel to keep it straight, she pushed the gas pedal with her hand. The boat sped forward, water jumping over the sides.

Another cloud of blue burst over her head. Cool sweat dripped down her spine. They wanted her alive.

Somehow, that seemed worse.

Focus. Make sure you don't crash.

She exited the alcove with her gun before her, shooting blindly toward the shore, forcing the Elite to take cover. She glanced out the windshield, adjusted the wheel to keep her straight, and retreated beneath the dash again. A bullet whizzed through where she had just been and shattered the windshield in a spray of glass. Nic screamed.

That...that was a real bullet.

An Elite bellowed from the shore, "Turn your guns to Stun! Commander wants her alive!"

A few more bullets chased the boat, but eventually faded. Nic peeked her head out slowly. She could no longer see Elite on the shore. She had outrun them. For now. Soon they would be pursuing by boat. Nic jumped into the driver's seat and jerked the wheel to avoid a rock jetting out of the river.

Next step.

Heart still racing, Nic pulled the radio from her belt and quickly dialed a number. It was the first day of the month. Based on the pattern that Nic had memorized when she was little, this should be the channel ROGUE was using today. She pressed the button to talk.

"This is Freebird, seeking a safe nest to land. Repeat, this is Freebird seeking a safe nest to land."

Only static answered.

Shiloh sat in the hospital room alone, behind closed curtains. If she shut her eyes, she could see it: flame and blood and Hope crumpling like a rag doll. She didn't dare shut her eyes. Instead, she stared at her legs, which were now a mess of bandages and a splint.

The X-rays revealed that her left leg hadn't just broken. It'd shattered. She'd need surgery, the trauma doctor in the emergency room had told her. And then extensive, painful burn care.

"Knock, knock." The nurse slipped through the curtain, carrying a stack of towels and a basin of steaming water. "I thought you might like to clean up. You're covered in soot."

And blood.

The nurse set everything on the bedside table and wheeled it close. "Do you need help, or do you think you can manage?"

"I can manage."

"Keep those dressings dry and don't try to stand up without me. If you need me, you hit the button."

The nurse—Jessica, her badge said—fixed her with a look that spoke volumes of empathy. Jessica was the sort of person chosen to be a nurse. She likely had high intelligence scores and personality tests that demonstrated great depths of compassion. Unlike Shiloh's own personality tests, which revealed she should be in an occupation where she'd have minimal interactions with people. Apparently, she often seemed "cold and unfeeling".

"Are you sure that I can't call anyone?" Jessica asked.

Shiloh nodded. "The emergency room nurse already notified the Haven."

The nurse had told the Haven Shiloh had been in a terrible car accident, because that was what the Elite had told her to say. Meanwhile, a hologram of the news had played on the back wall as the nurses had bandaged Shiloh's legs.

The Cleansing canceled due to fire in building, it announced, before returning to scrolling through the list of wanted heretics. According to the media, the Cleansing simply hadn't happened.

"And they aren't going to send anyone?" Jessica asked.

Shiloh shook her head.

Of course not. The duty of Mother and the Aunts was to feed, clothe, and discipline the Haven girls. It was *not* their job to care.

What about Zyra and Willa?

With so many Haven girls, each Haven girl over the age of fifteen was assigned Littles to care for. Zyra had been Shiloh's Little for a couple of years now, while Willa had been shoved into her arms last summer, three-years-old and screaming for her mommy. Who would keep them out of trouble? Val? She already had three Littles of her own. How many hours in the Repentant Closet or bruises from Mother's cane would Shiloh's Littles earn before Shiloh made it back to protect them?

And Val. *Oh Val.* Once upon a time, it had been the three of them: Val, Hope, and Shiloh. Then Hope was arrested, and perhaps Hope had been the glue that held the three of them together, because Val had turned vile to Shiloh. But regardless of what was between them now, Val loved Hope. She deserved to know she wouldn't be coming back. That she was gone.

But Shiloh would never be able to tell her.

Jessica frowned and put her hands on her hips. "You really shouldn't be alone."

I'm always alone.

Shiloh forced a smile. "I'll be fine. Really."

"Well, if there is anything you need, you let me know." Jessica started toward the door.

"Actually..."

Jessica turned back. "Yes?"

"I know that you're not supposed to tell me, but please, Jacob Osgood..."

"I can't do that."

Shiloh's fingers curled around the stiff sheets. She didn't quite understand why Osgoqd's fate even mattered to her, but it did. So much.

"I just want to know if he's alive," Shiloh said.

Jessica hesitated.

"Please, I know the rules, but he saved my life."

Jessica smiled. "The way I heard it, *you* saved *his*."

Shiloh opened her mouth to argue, but then she realized what Jessica had done. His life was saved. He was alive.

"Thank you, Jessica."

"For what?" Jessica left the room, her giggle floating behind her.

Shiloh released a breath and then looked at her filthy, bloody hands. She picked up a washcloth and began to scrub vigorously: her hands, her neck, her face. She scrubbed until her skin was raw, and the water in the tub grew dark. But the feeling of blood never quite left her skin.

The rumble of the ship's motor echoed through the stillness of the night, matching the rhythm of Nic's racing heart. Nic laid on the damp floor of the boat, clutching her pistol and biting her tongue to silence the scream that built in her chest.

Please. Don't let them find me.

Cutting off the windshield with her electric knife, Nic had crammed the boat beneath the half-submerged deck she'd found in a swampy cove, remnants of a long-ruined hunting lodge. She hoped the broken wood and the tangles of moss would keep her from their eyes.

The boat came closer and closer, but the engine cut off where the swamp grew thick. An Eye whined as it hovered over the dock. Nic tripled checked that the survival blanket fully concealed her body. Eyes shouldn't be able to see through solid materials, but just in case, the reflective material of the blanket would reflect her own body heat back, making her invisible.

Voices murmured briefly, then the engine roared again. Nic's fingers strangled the gun so hard her knuckles ached. But the sound of the engine grew quieter and then disappeared.

Thank you, God.

Leaving the survival blanket over her head, Nic closed her aching eyes and breathed deeply, but it didn't slow the gallop of her heart.

Why did you leave me, Mom?

Nic's chest ached. She'd give anything to be back around the campfire with the Family, singing songs from all their different faiths. Because, in the end, they believed in the same freedom and the same love, and that was all that mattered.

Please. Please be alive.

Nic turned the radio on, twisted the volume to the lowest setting, changed the channel, and held it next to her ear. Static hissed like a disconcerting lullaby.

And then...

"Sparrows to Freebird. Repeat, Sparrows to Freebird."

The message which followed was a collection of nonsensical words. Nic threw the blanket off and scrambled to pull a notebook and pen from the bag. The message repeated itself, and she wrote it down. On the third and final time, she ensured it was correct. She flipped the radio off and started translating.

ROGUE's communication offered complicated layer upon complicated layer of protection. The former leaders of ROGUE had modified old army hand radios to only allow closed loop communication. That was what ROGUE was: a communication network of rebel groups. Messages would pass on and on through the web of them until it reached its intended target. In case Arcadia ever did pick up on the signals, ROGUE used patterns and codes memorized only in memory, codenames, and strange metaphors or foreign languages to send messages only soldiers of ROGUE would understand.

This message offered shelter and directions. Nic entered the coordinates into her compass, and a red "N" blinked on the screen. Nic's heart sank. She'd been traveling south like her mother had told her, but the Sparrows were almost two hundred and fifty miles in the opposite direction, deep in the northernmost part of Minnesota.

Two hundred and fifty miles of river and wood and Elite between her and safety. Nic shook off the feeling of dismay and dug her nails into her palm so hard it hurt.

I will survive this. I will.

Six

"Jake, do you understand what the doctors just said?"

Jake's mom took his hand between both of hers, careful not to disrupt his burn dressings. On Jake's other side, Dad glared at the white-coated doctors who clustered around the room like a gaggle of swans.

"Yes," Jake said. "I'm going to be stuck in this lovely place for a while."

This was the first time since the Cleansing that he wasn't so sedated that he couldn't remember his own name. Still, he struggled to focus. While the doctors had talked, he'd been distracted by images of blood and flame and a girl with dark eyes. But he'd gotten the gist of it.

His burns weren't as bad as they'd feared, but the bullet had torn his stomach apart. They'd spent hours in surgery reconstructing it, but ultimately, it would take time to heal. A lot of time consisting of lying in a hospital bed and being fed through a tube surgically placed in his gut.

Isn't that a sexy look?

But mostly the doctors told him he'd been lucky to survive. *Extremely* lucky.

"Do you have any questions, Mr. Osgood?" Dr. Rudolf asked.

His parents shook their heads, and Jake only closed his eyes. The ghost of a voice echoed in his mind.

"Don't you froqing die!"

Jake flung his eyes open. "Wait!"

The doctors paused at the door.

"What happened to the girl?"

Dr. Rudolf turned back and frowned.

"What girl, Jake?" Mom asked, squeezing his fingers.

Jake pulled his hand away. "There was a girl. She would have been with me when I was found." The memory of the girl's soft fingers laced through his burned bright now, how she'd anchored him as the world faded around him.

Dad scowled. "I didn't get any report of someone being found with you."

"Do you have a name?" the nurse asked, turning from the IV pole where she had been hanging a new bag of nutrition.

Jake sighed. "No. But her last name is probably Haven since she was Hope's—"

"Jake," Dad said lowly, warningly.

Jake choked down the truth. *That's right.* He'd been injured in a random fire. There'd been no Cleansing. No Hope.

How quickly sins can be washed away.

If only Jake could forget too, but Hope's lifeless eyes were tattooed on his brain, a haunting specter he could not escape.

Dr. Rudolf looked at the nurse then back to the Osgood family. "There was a girl with that last name brought in around the same time. She's recovering from injuries, but she'll be fine. That's the most I can tell you."

"Can I see her?" Jake asked.

"I think right now it's best if you rest," Dad said.

"You don't understand. She saved my life."

She...and the heretic who gave us the first aid kit. But Jake would go to his grave with that truth.

"Later, I promise." Mom patted his shoulder. "Right now, I need you to focus on getting yourself better."

"Thank you, doctors," Dad said. "That will be all."

The white cloud of doctors fluttered away, the nurse on their heels. Jake rolled his eyes to the ceiling.

The silence hung heavy between them. His parents had been shoved off the stage before the bomb exploded and shielded by Protectors. They'd survived with minor scratches and burns. But Mom had lost color from her face, and Dad, in the few minutes he'd been at the hospital, hadn't stopped looking at his phone. Like Arcadia was crumbling apart. And maybe it was.

"So," Jake said, still staring at the ceiling, "do either of you want to tell me who almost killed me?"

Mom's lips parted but made no sound. Dad looked up from his phone sharply and glanced at the door, but the voices outside were distant.

"Oh, I forgot," Jake continued when neither of them spoke, "it was just a fire. Apparently, flames carry froqing rifles now."

"Watch your mouth," Mom said, but her voice sounded weak.

Dad crossed to the door and shut it, before facing Jake again. "I can't share that information with you."

"Why not?"

"Because it's beyond your security clearance."

"Why? Because we're supposed to be a nation of peace, and we clearly aren't?"

Arcadia hadn't known war since the Sundering, over three decades, right? That was what the history books said. Peace was the reason for the Codex. What was the cost of freedom, if you could live in harmony?

But these heretics had to have deep connections to pull off the attack. They hadn't appeared overnight. And if there were people out there, fighting against Arcadia, that could change everything.

At least, I hope it can.

"Right now," Dad said, a bite in his voice, "all you need to know is that we *will* find the people responsible for this. And they *will* be punished."

Jake's jaw ground together.

A shadow crossed his bed as Dad returned to Jake's side and rested a hand on his shoulder. "I love you, son. I'm sorry, but I have to go."

"Whatever."

Jake didn't look up, so Dad sighed and left.

Mom let out her own heavy sigh and rose from the chair. "I need to call your Uncle Silas. He's been asking for an update. And I think I'll grab a coffee from the cafeteria. Will you be okay if I step out for a minute?"

Jake rolled his eyes. "Yes, Mom. Please go."

Her heels clacked on the tile floor as she exited the room, closing the door behind her. Jake waited for a moment to ensure she was gone, then pushed himself out of the bed.

His side cried out in protest, and he clasped onto his IV pole for support as he made his way to the door. So far, he'd only taken a few steps to and from the bathroom, but froq it all, he would do this!

Jake opened the door slowly and glanced out. A bodyguard stood at the nurses' desk, talking to the only nurse there, but the hallway held not another soul. The coast was as clear as it was going to get. He left the room and rushed around the corner before the bodyguard could see him.

One hand propped on his aching side, the other pulling the IV along, Jake began the loop around the pediatric unit, peeking in open doors.

Where is she?

Finally, he found her at the opposite end of the unit. Where his suite was massive, hers barely fit a bed and a chair. She sat alone in her bed, one leg ensnared in metal rods and bandages, another coiled in burn dressings like his own. She frowned at the thick book in the hologram floating before her.

She and Jake were surely both about to be Seniors at Ardency, but he'd never noticed her. Why would he? She wasn't Jake's type. She was too flat-chested, too pale, too lanky. But now, he studied the shine of her dark hair in the hologram's light and the sharp line of her jaw. He imagined how her voice had been so calm, her hands so steady, and her will so strong as she'd gotten them to that classroom on her shattered leg.

She was beautiful.

Or maybe that was what happened after a girl saved your life. They became all you could see.

Don't be an idiot, Osgood.

He took another step into the room, and the girl's gaze snapped up. Now, her eyes—those were extraordinary. He'd first noticed them as she gazed down at him, fighting to save his life, and they'd haunted his dreams since. They were cool and guarded and dark as night, but they seemed to shimmer endlessly, a universe you could get lost in.

Jake forced himself to breathe again and grinned crookedly. "Froq, girl, you work that hospital gown."

Shiloh snapped her head up. Jacob Osgood stood in her doorway, leaning heavily against his IV pole. His tan skin had lost some color, and a central venous line weaved into his neck, but otherwise, he looked okay. A breath of relief vibrated her lips.

What had he said? *You work that hospital gown.*

Did he *have* to hit on every girl that moved?

"Ugh, please." Shiloh rolled her eyes. "Your one-liners aren't going to work on me."

He laughed and shrugged. "That sucks. It's the only move I have."

Shiloh blinked. Of course, he was only teasing. Eleven years of school, and he'd talked to her once. He definitely wasn't going to start being interested in her now. Not that she wanted that.

Absolutely not.

Voices came from the hallway, and Osgood swiftly shut the door.

Shiloh raised her eyebrows. "What are you doing?"

"I'm a fugitive."

"From?"

"The puppet strings." Without further explanation, Osgood pulled his IV pole across the room and plopped into the chair. "Hey, I believe you owe me something."

"Do I now?"

"Yep. Turns out I didn't froqing die."

The moment rushed back to her. *Her heart screaming in her ears. His blood dripping from her fingers.*

Breathe in. Breathe out.

Only when she trusted her tone to be level did she speak. "So, it seems."

"You told me that if I survived, you would tell me your name. I did my part. So, pay up."

See. Never noticed me at all.

"Shiloh."

He extended a hand. "Nice to meet you, Shiloh."

She paused, studying the burn dressings that wrapped his arms. If those arms hadn't surrounded her, those burns would have been her own. If he hadn't pulled them off the stage seconds before the bomb went off, would they even be alive?

She shook his hand. Now that he wasn't bleeding out, his hand radiated warmth and strength against her frozen fingers. She quickly pulled her hand away and hid it beneath the sheet. "We've met before, but I doubt you remember... um... Jacob."

"It's Jake. My *grandfather* was Jacob." He made a face.

As if she needed another reminder of whose family he came from... He was only a foot away from her, and yet, millions of miles stretched between them. Haven and Osgood. There was no greater distance.

"Okay, Jake." Shiloh looked back to the book she'd borrowed. She'd been studying burn treatments and not liking what she found.

Jake cocked his head. "When did we meet before?"

"You asked me to write your biology paper during sophomore year."

He snapped his fingers. "That's right. You're the smart Haven girl."

Shiloh made fists in the sheets. The way he said that made it sound like an oxymoron.

"As I recall," he said, "you just snorted and walked away."

Shiloh nodded. She'd wanted to tell him to go froq himself, but had feared the consequences of making an Osgood angry.

Silence fell between them, thick as honey. Shiloh glared at the book, not looking at Jake. She hated silences now. In them, she could almost hear Hope singing.

"Shiloh," he said, his voice barely a whisper. She turned as he sighed and ran a hand through his messy hair. Rebellious espresso strands fell back onto his forehead, longer than the Codex allowed. "I don't know how to thank you. You saved my life."

Shiloh looked down at her hands and shrugged. "You saved mine. Twice. Once on that stage when you kept me from running to—" The name caught in Shiloh's throat, choking her, so she pressed on. "And once after the bomb, when you didn't leave me trapped there to die. So, thank you."

She didn't understand why he'd saved her, why an Osgood would care about a heretic's daughter.

"I guess we saved each other," Jake said.

"I guess so."

Again, the blasted silence came.

Amazing grace, how sweet the sound...

Shiloh's eyes stung. She pressed them closed. *Don't cry.*

Jake's hand brushed against her arm. "Hey, are you okay?"

"Yes," she said, quickly. "The doctors say if everything goes well with bone stimulation therapy and burn treatments, I'll be out of here in a month."

Jake nodded. "Yeah, I'll be here at least that long too. But that's not what I meant."

Shiloh opened her eyes. Jake's gaze met hers, and she knew what he meant.

Hope.

"I'm fine." She glared, daring him to press.

Of course, he dared.

Jake scoffed. "I call ordure."

"What makes you say that?"

"Because I'm not." He cast his eyes upon his feet and let out a shaky breath. "I'm not okay with anything that happened."

What was that on his face? Was that...shame?

"For the record," Jake said. "I'm really sorry about Hope. I'm so *froqing* sorry."

A knife slammed into Shiloh's chest. "*Don't!*" she hissed. "I don't want to talk about her. I don't even want to *think* about her."

"Okay," he said thickly and dragged a hand over his face, like he was trying not to cry. Before the Cleansing, she'd have assumed Jake was proud of his status. He'd certainly always used it to his advantage, thriving in the popularity and the ability to get almost any girl he wanted. She'd thought that, surely, he'd guzzled the bitter medicine and agreed wholeheartedly with every line of the Codex. But maybe, there was a different story altogether.

Finally, she let out a trembling breath. "You're right. I'm not okay."

Jake set his hand on the sheet above Shiloh's hand. She pulled her hand away, but the distance between them didn't seem so large now.

"Well." He picked up a pack of playing cards that sat on the bedside table. The nurse had left them for Shiloh, in case she wanted to play. "As long as you and I are both stuck here, what do you say we be 'not okay' together?"

Shiloh hesitated. Jake was the last person in the world she thought she could be friends with, but the silence and the loneliness of the hospital had been pressing into her before he entered the room. Maybe, she didn't have to be alone.

"Okay," Shiloh said.

Jake grinned, tossed the box of cards into the air and caught it with the other hand. "What's your game of choice?"

"Anything but Go Fish." Shiloh had played enough Go Fish with the Littles to last three lifetimes.

Jake slid the cards from the pack. "Egyptian Rat Screw it is."

"Egyptian what?"

Before Jake could respond, an alarm blared on the intercom overhead. "Code Pink. Seventeen-year-old male last seen in pediatric ward."

Despite herself, Shiloh's lips twitched in an almost-smile. "Well, fugitive, I think they're on to you."

SEVEN

E ven with thorough research, Shiloh wasn't prepared for the excruciating reality of the burn treatments. Before starting, Nurse Jessica gave her extra pain pills and a light sedative. Still, as the two nurses began their work, Shiloh bit her tongue to keep from screaming and threw an arm over her face

Breath in.

1...2...3...

Breathe out.

1...2...3...

"Mr. Osgood," Jessica said, interrupting the soothing noises she'd been making, "you can't be here right now."

Shiloh peeked out from beneath her arm to see Jake approach her bed, pulling his IV pole with him.

"Get out!" Shiloh yelled.

Before now, she'd been grateful for his presence. That first day —after revealing that he hadn't been kidnapped—Jake had taught her to play Egyptian Rat Screw, a fast-paced game that involved a lot of slapping the table—and accidentally each other's hands. Jake laughed like it was a habit, and the sound of it almost tempted her to smile too. Almost.

Yesterday, he'd shown up with wooden hot air balloons and paint, a craft from the pediatric playroom. As they painted the sculptures, they'd talked. About school. About favorite foods and favorite colors. About his many adventures to foreign countries, the horrors of Zy'on to the freedom of Canada. A note of envy crept into his voice as he talked about free lands, where he could be exactly who he wanted to be, where girls kissed other girls in public without fear, and no one dressed the same. Shiloh tried to imagine it, but it felt too much like a dream.

But he shouldn't be here now. With cool sweat pouring down her face, she felt too raw and vulnerable. Despite her protest, Jake dragged a chair toward the head of the bed, out of the nurses' way, and plopped down.

"I said get out!" Shiloh yelled again.

"Not a chance, tough guy," Jake said. "You're stuck with me."

"I'm fine. I don't need you." Needing someone wasn't a luxury Haven girls had.

"Look at me, Shi."

Shi? The sound of her nickname—the name only Hope and Val had called her—seemed foreign on his tongue, but soft. Sweet. A melody. Shiloh turned her head to meet Jake's eyes. They almost looked golden in this light.

"You didn't leave me in that hallway," he said, "And I'm not going to leave you now."

Shiloh fought to catch a breath, for a reason other than pain. Jessica raised an eyebrow in a silent question.

"Fine. You can stay." Shiloh groaned and slumped back into her pillow. "You're obnoxious. Has anyone ever told you that?"

"I'm *adorable.*" Jake set his hand on the mattress beside her. "And my hand is right here if you need it."

She didn't take his hand that treatment, but Jake must have gotten ahold of her treatment schedule, despite how illegal that was, because he showed up every time. She told him he didn't have to be there, but he never wavered. He sat beside her and did his best to distract her by telling her silly stories, like the time he'd picked his nose on live television when he was five, or by making her listen to some song on his phone.

Finally, in the third treatment he attended, Shiloh let out a cry and grabbed his hand so hard it must have hurt, but he didn't complain.

Just like it had the day of the Cleansing, as they waited in the room for help, his hand seemed to steady her, to hold her fast in a world that was crumbling around her.

After that, she no longer fought the urge to hold his hand.

Traveling on the boat was taking much longer than Nic had anticipated. She frequently had to change directions and take time to hide anytime she spotted a boat. Still, she'd made it a hundred and fifty miles the past few days —far faster than she would have gone on foot.

Only a hundred miles to go.

Nic stirred the boats along in the shadows cast by the trees on the shore, as the darkness grew thicker around her. She traveled only by night now, with the boat's lights turned off to avoid being seen. She reached to the cupholder where she'd placed the radio and flipped it off, dropping into total silence.

She'd been listening to the ROGUE network any chance she had, but there'd been nothing about the Cleansing. No word of Councilors' deaths. And no word about her mom. Nic had waited to hear that century old song that would signal that someone had reached safety within ROGUE. A song about wanting to come home, but being far away.

It'd be followed by an announcement. Good night, it would say, followed by the codename of that person. Nic had heard it a few times, but it was never a codename she recognized. Not Birdie or Ox or....

But they're not *dead!*

A sound pricked Nic's ears. She lifted her foot off the pedal, silencing the engine's roar. In the distance, something buzzed like an insect. Another boat.

There was nothing but flat shore around her, but the river forked just ahead. She could take one path and hope they took the other. Nic grabbed the survival blanket beside her chair, wrapped it around her, then kicked the pedal to the floor.

The boat flew across the water. Without the windshield, the water stung her face like needles. An Eye zoomed past her. Nic's stomach twisted.

The Elite.

Faster, faster.

Instead, the boat slowed. Nic lifted her foot from the pedal and slammed it down again. Nothing happened. The boat slowed and slowed, and then the engine went utterly silent.

No, no, no, no!

Nic frantically turned off the key and then twisted it again. "Come on, come on!"

It remained dead.

The Elite's black boat zoomed toward her. She had two minutes... maybe three. She only had one option.

She grabbed the radio and her compass from the cup-holders and threw them in her backpack, strapping it to her back. She reached for the duffle and the rifle, but it was too late. A bullet whizzed past her head. She flung herself to the floor. She had to jump, but she needed time, or she would never make it to shore. She reached beneath her lifejacket into her vest and clutched the one and only Sphere she had. A bomb.

Could she really throw it well enough for it to land in their boat?

She hesitated.

Never hesitate, Paul had always told her. *Hesitate, and you're dead!*

The blur orb clanked as it landed on the opposite side of the boat. A Stunner. She pushed herself to her feet and leaped from the boat heartbeats before electric, stunning bolts exploded and shot through the air like darts. The chill of the water drilled all the way to her bone. The lifejacket yanked her back to the surface. The shadow of the Elite's boat loomed near.

Now, Nic!

Fighting hard against the current, Nic activated the Sphere and flung it toward the boat. She didn't throw it high enough, and it bounced on the boat's side, landing in the water.

No!

With a scream of noise, fire and water burst through the air. The wave tossed the Elite's boat aside like a toy. The same wave slammed into Nic, carrying her further downstream. She fought against the powerful current and finally seized a tree branch near shore. When she pulled herself onto the embankment, she glanced back, finding both boats sideways and on fire.

Did I kill them?

Black suits rose to the surface of the water, and a voice yelled. Nic shoved herself upright and tore into the woods.

Nic hadn't stopped running, not for the entire day. When she felt like she couldn't run anymore, she walked only long enough to run again. The Family had done this before, the constant movement for hours at a breakneck speed to avoid the Elite. When she was little, Dad or Paul or Oliver would take turns holding her on their backs, until she was big enough to keep up with them. But now, the frantic song of her heart reminded her that she was alone.

When she finally couldn't take another step, she climbed a thick-leafed tree and settled onto a thick branch. She looked through her backpack, the only supplies she had left. Only four more days of food. Not nearly enough. A clean set of Codex-compliant clothes, in case she needed to blend in. Rope. Tiny bottles of hygiene products. A box of bullets. Pen and paper. Her radio. And her compass. Her knife, which had been stuffed into her boot, had made it, as well as her gun, which had been strapped to her hip.

But her mother's Bible was gone. She'd put it in the duffle to make more room for additional food in her pack. The loss deepened the ache of Mom's absence until it throbbed like an aching wound.

I am not a baby. I will not cry.

Nic rubbed her fists against her burning eyes and then flicked on the radio. She glanced at her father's watch for the date. She put in the channel, and the static buzzed. After forming a message in code in her notebook, she sent it through the radio.

I'm in trouble, the message said. *I can't make it to you. Please help me.*

No response came.

EIGHT

"Here we are," Jake said, bringing Shiloh's wheelchair to a stop.

Now that the metal contraption on her leg was replaced by a cast, Jake and Shiloh's nurse helped her into a wheelchair, and Jake had wheeled her out into the interior garden, right off the pediatric ward, the first time they'd been outside in days.

Jake lowered himself onto the stone bench beside her with a sigh. Small walks could still wear him out, but he supposed nearly dying and not being able to consume real food would do that.

"It feels amazing out here," Shiloh said.

It did. The sunrays broke through the surrounding floors of the hospital into the garden and brushed like soft fingertips against Jake's skin. Summer days were a priceless treasure in Minnesota, coming and going in the blink of an eye. If the Cleansing hadn't happened, he'd be at his family's house on the shores of Lake Superior, boating and water-hovering. But he didn't regret it. Not with Shiloh sitting beside him.

Shiloh lifted her face to catch the light, and the darkness of her hair seemed to absorb it, making it shine. She smiled.

Jake grinned. *Victory.*

These last several days, Jake and Shiloh had been wasting their time together: talking, watching movies, playing games, or doing the silly preschool-level crafts Jake got from the playroom. Mostly, Jake enjoyed trying to make her smile, or if he was lucky, a laugh. Getting a sincere smile was a challenge. Winning a laugh was an Olympic feat. But her smile and her soft, clear laugh made his day infinitely brighter.

No matter how many nightmares he'd had the night before or how much hatred for Arcadia he could feel boiling his blood, Shiloh's laughter, or maybe just her, felt like a beacon in a storm.

"Have you come out here before?" Shiloh asked.

"No, I wanted to come here with you." Jake took a deep breath, and his lungs flooded with the scent of fresh grass and the variety of flowers that scattered color through the garden. In the middle of the garden, a fountain sang a merry, bubbling tune.

Shiloh glanced at him, her expression guarded. She always looked so calm and collected, as though she wore a perfect porcelain mask that hid her every emotion. Sometimes, Jake wondered what had happened to her before the Cleansing. You didn't get that strong unless you had to be.

"Well, it's beautiful." Shiloh brushed a strand of hair behind her ear. Jake's fingers ached to trace the same line.

"*You're* beautiful." The response slipped from his tongue before he could stop it.

Shiloh rolled her eyes. "Really, Osgood? You're going to go with that line?"

"It is a bit trite."

"There's an understatement."

Unlike a lot of girls, Shiloh wasn't impressed by his status. She treated him like everyone else, teased him, called him out of his playboy behavior. He felt different when he was with her, or perhaps, he was just different now. How do you have the world blown up beneath your feet and come out the same?

Still, Jake only knew so many tricks. "Well, how about this

one?" He slid closer to her, so only the arm of the wheelchair separated them. "*Ma chérie, tu as de beaux yeux.*"

She raised a single eyebrow. "You speak French?"

"Don't look so surprised. I do have a brain beneath all this beautiful."

"That's not why I'm surprised. No one speaks other languages in Arcadia. Goes against the unity and conformity. Well, I guess, Val speaks Spanish, but that's only because it was her primary language before coming to the Haven. Mother tried to beat that —" Shiloh stopped short. Her perfect mask slipped into horror for a mere second. Then she cleared her throat and put her mask back into place. "Anyway, where did you learn?"

The words '*Mother beat*' hammered in Jake's brain, taking all the warmth from the summer day. Did she mean they were abused at the Haven? But, of course, they were! He'd heard the rumors about how the people who ran Havens would use any possible methods to make the children of heretics conform. Looking at Shiloh and thinking about the reality she must live with made it difficult to breathe.

There it was. What had made her so strong. And yet another reason to hate Arcadia.

"Shiloh—"

"Where did you learn?" Though Shiloh's voice was still calm, a hint of steel showed through. She didn't want to talk about it.

They didn't talk about hard things. They'd gone through the worst day of his life together, but, other than the first time they'd met in the hospital, they still hadn't talked about it. And on this subject, she wasn't just throwing up her walls and barricades. She was wheeling out the canons too.

Don't enter, or I'll shoot.

Jake sighed but answered her question. "I've had language tutors since I could babble. Then I've taken language courses every semester in school. Since I'm on a Government Track, it's allowed."

"All to learn French?"

"No. I'm fluent in six languages. English, of course. And Spanish, Mandarin, Arabic, Russian, and ordure. Some of the most common languages spoken in the world. I only know enough French to order food, find a bathroom, and flirt with girls."

There went that eyebrow again. "Seriously?"

"Oh, girls love to be seduced by French poetry."

She rolled her eyes again. "I mean, you seriously know five languages?"

She sounded impressed, but Jake wasn't. It was merely his father shaping him into the clay sculpture he wanted. Jake didn't know what Newton's theories said or the structure of a cell, but he could name all the State Advocates and their families, as well as all the key players of the foreign countries that were Arcadia's closest allies. And their closest enemies. Like he'd said he was fluent in *ordure*.

Jake forced a laugh which sounded unconvincing even to him. "Don't you know? I was bred and born for the sole purpose of being the next Councilor Osgood."

Sure, whenever a Councilor died or vacated a chair, a special election was held where every citizen in good standing could vote. It was always between a family member of the Councilor and some State Advocate who thought they could make a real change. But surprise, surprise, in all three elections that had happened in Arcadian history, the chair remained in the family. Arcadia masqueraded as a republic, but make no mistake. Arcadia was an oligarchy.

"You sound like you hate it," Shiloh said.

"I do."

He'd never admitted that to anyone before. Shiloh eyed the door uneasily. What Jake had just said wobbled a little too close to heresy, didn't it? Saying you didn't want to be what Arcadia demanded you to be.

"Okay, so what did you say to me?" Shiloh said, diverting them from dangerous territory. "In French."

Jake shrugged. "I said you're a hideous creature." He hadn't. He'd said '*Darling, you have beautiful eyes.*'

Another smile. Another victory. "Liar."

"It's true. Swamp creature, actually."

She snorted, which was almost a laugh. "You're obnoxious."

"Whatever. You know you like me."

"That hypothesis is still insufficiently supported by data."

But she gazed at him now, those glorious eyes of hers even more beautiful in the summer sunshine. A snowing of powdered sugar dusted her bottom lip, a leftover from the donut he'd stolen for her from the nurses' station. He hadn't noticed before, but now it was all he could see.

"You have something right here." Before Jake could think, he reached to brush it off with his thumb. The softness of her lips seemed to reverberate through his fingers.

Council, I want to kiss her.

He'd lost track of all the times he'd looked at her and been overwhelmed by the desire to kiss her, to touch her, to hold her. She was so different from anyone he'd ever met. She was strong, and she was smart, and even though she'd never say it, he knew that, like him, she saw Arcadia for what it was. He'd always restrained himself from the desire to kiss her, knowing that this relationship, whatever it was, was something he didn't want to froq up. His whole world seemed better with her in it.

But for the first time, she didn't pull away from his touch. And this moment seemed so right that she *had* to feel it too. So, he slid his hand from her chin to the back of her neck and kissed her.

For a moment, he felt like he'd just stepped out into the sunlight, warm and bright to his very core.

Then she shoved him away and growled, "Osgood, what do you think you're doing?"

All the warmth raced away, leaving Jake frozen. Her mask had crumbled, and he could read her clearly. She was *furious*.

Froq. "Shiloh, I—"

Her hands curled around the arms of her wheelchair, red tinting her cheeks. "You can't just go around kissing whoever you want. Unlike half the girls at Ardency, I don't care who your daddy is."

The words landed like a slap across Jake's face. His teeth ground together. "I think we both know that you care a great deal who my father is."

The truth crackled between them like lightning. Of course, she cared. How could she not? She was a Haven, and he was an Osgood. That meant, when they finally stopped pretending, not only would she not want to kiss him. She would *hate* him.

He couldn't blame her. Most days he hated himself too.

Her voice reverted to her usual placidity. "Please take me back to my room."

When they reached her room, she insisted that she would have the nurse help her get back into bed. Every step Jake took away from her hurt. The thought of losing her, even the fragile friendship, was devastating.

Froq, he was in *deep* trouble, because Shiloh was wrong. He hadn't kissed her because she was like any other girl. He'd kissed her because he *liked* her. Deeply. Intensely. In a way he'd never felt before.

And now, he'd ruined everything.

Going to steal food in town had been a mistake, but Nic hadn't had a choice. She'd managed to stretch her food out longer than the four days, but she'd run out yesterday. She hadn't been able to hit any smaller game with the handgun, which had survived the swim. Hunting large game without her rifle was out of the question. So, she'd gone to scavenge.

She'd taken her time to wash her hair in a lake she came across and wore the clean, Codex-compliant clothes in her pack. Her target had been a grocery supplier in a small Laborer town. Despite her efforts to blend in, the clerk had stared at her as she made her way down the aisle. She'd only slipped cans into her pack when he'd been distracted by a customer or a delivery. But he caught her taking bottles of water and yelled out. She threw a few into her pack and ran as fast as she could. She'd barely escaped the Protectors who had chased her on foot, but she was fast and had lost them in the trees. She hadn't heard anyone for hours now.

Still every muscle was tight with unease.

Nic shouldn't stop. The Sparrows had finally heard her distress call and agreed to send a few people to meet her partway. According to her compass, she could arrive tomorrow if she pushed it. But she needed to rest and to eat.

Using the electric knife from her boot, she pried open a can of chickpeas. While she ate, she set the radio in front of her and turned it on. There was still no word of her Mom, or anyone else, but she kept hoping.

I'm so close, Mom. I'm going to get to help, and then I'm going to find you.

Crack.

Nic jumped to her feet, her hand on the cool steel of her gun.

Silence.

Maybe it had been an animal, but Nic's heart fluttered in her chest. *Time to go.* She gathered her pack and started moving.

Crack!

A dark figure stepped out from behind a tree. An Elite.

Biting back a scream, Nic ran.

Shiloh awoke from her oxycodone-induced nap and glanced automatically to the armchair beside the bed. Since the Cleansing, she slept in fits, a couple hours here or there. Any longer and the nightmares would wake her. Jake had seemed to be following the same sleep schedule, because she often woke to find him sitting in her chair, dozing or playing some game on his phone.

He'd always smile crookedly at her and say, "Good morning, sunshine."

He really was obnoxious.

At one point, she'd even fallen asleep as they watched a movie. When she'd woken with a cry, he'd been right there, a hand on her cheek. She'd stared at him in the dim moonlight for a long moment, the warmth of his hand spreading through all of her skin, before she remembered to pull away.

Now, seeing the empty chair made her heart sink, but then she remembered the kiss, and she kicked that feeling right out of her chest. Who was she kidding? Sure, their time together had been nice, but Jacob Osgood was still Jacob I-can-have-any-girl-I-want Osgood. Jacob Love-them-and-leave-them Osgood. Everyone knew his reputation. So, why was she surprised?

But the worst thing about it? She'd almost kissed him back!

Idiot. So what if the sweet heat of his lips had drilled into her chest like a firework bursting to the sky? So what if every time he was near she found herself, somehow, both relaxing and also finding it harder to breathe? So what if she caught her rebellious eyes tracing over the shape of him over and over again? That was just physical attraction, and *of course*, she was attracted to him. He was *Jacob Osgood*. Looking solely at the objective data, the only reasonable conclusion was that he was—quite frankly—gorgeous.

But Shiloh was far from the busty, beautiful girls that normally hung all over him. Physical attraction was all it could be, unless she wanted to be yet another heartbroken girl Jake left in his wake. Besides, she'd spent years constructing walls to protect herself. Why bother falling in love, when, in the end, Arcadia would be the one to choose her spouse for her when she turned twenty-five?

Her only long-term boyfriend, Theo, she'd dated because he made sense. He, too, was on an Engineering Track. According to the guidelines of the Marriage Board, they would be well suited.

She'd dated him because it made sense, she'd had sex with him because it made sense, and when the relationship hadn't made sense anymore, she'd broken up with him.

Shiloh approached life logically, like it was a textbook. Statistics and facts: those were easy. People were hard.

"That's what you do, Starchild," Val had said more than once. *"You stick to the script."*

Jake was certainly not on the script of her life. She couldn't allow him to creep past her walls. But as she stared at the empty chair, wishing he was there, fear twisted her stomach.

What if it's already too late?

What if he'd snuck past her walls before she'd even realized he was a threat?

A knock sounded on the door. Shiloh held her breath, but it was only the food service. The nurse must have ordered for Shiloh while she napped. The woman set the covered dishes on the bedside table and left. Shiloh lifted the cover then dropped it in surprise. She wasn't sure whether she wanted to laugh or to punch Jake in the face.

On the plate beside almost-palatable looking meatloaf and mashed potatoes, ketchup had been used to spell: "Sorry."

I'm not going to forgive him that easily. But her hand was already holding the bedside phone.

Jake picked up on the first ring. "Shiloh?"

"Can't you just apologize like a normal person?" Shiloh asked.

"Sure. But where would be the fun in that?"

Silence fell between them. Shiloh stabbed at the meatloaf with her fork. What had she even called him to say?

Jake sighed deeply. "Shiloh, I really, really don't want to have froqed this thing up. It matters…it matters a lot."

"Why?"

Shiloh's fingers tightened around the archaic handheld phone. She already knew the answer, right? But deep down, she feared she was wrong. What if he did feel something for her?

What if *she* felt something for *him*?

She closed her eyes, and visions of Jake painted themselves across her eyelids. The way he'd looked at her in the garden—like he was all she could see—made her catch her breath even now.

Stop it! You're being ridiculous. You cannot have feelings for him.

All that had come from the other side of the phone was his breathing.

"Jake?" Shiloh pressed. "Why does it matter?"

"It just...does."

Well, that explained *nothing*.

"Are you going to try to kiss me again?" Shiloh said, moving on.

"Only if you want me to."

"I don't!"

"Okay."

"Then fine. I accept your apology."

"Cool. Catch you later then?"

"Yeah."

Shiloh returned the phone to the cradle and shoved a bite of meatloaf into her mouth, but it tasted like ash. The end of the phone call had been tense, something heavy lingering between them.

I think we both know that you care a great deal who my father is.

By saying those words, Jake had highlighted the chasm between them in neon lights. Shiloh should hate Jake, or at least mistrust him. But when she closed her eyes again, all she could see was the million ways he made her smile. Telling a joke. Their playful banter. Holding her hand during her worst days. Playing a game of tag in the hallway with the bald-headed children whose cancer trapped them here too.

For the first time since Hope had first been taken, when Shiloh was with Jake, she didn't feel quite so alone. And even if it was stupid and illogical, she didn't want to lose that—to lose him.

Froq it all!

Shiloh threw down her fork and grabbed her crutches. Each step required all her strength, and she gritted her teeth against the pain. A sheen of sweat dampened her forehead by the time Shiloh hammered on Jake's door. When he answered, his eyes widened, but he let her into his empty room. A jarring, party tune pounded from his phone, but when Jake pushed a button on his watch—a thin metal piece whose face hologrammed onto his wrist—the room fell silent.

Shiloh had to hop around in her crutches to face him, a movement that was awkward, and probably hysterical looking. A knot had curled into her tongue, and they stared at each other for a long moment before Shiloh managed to spit it out.

"I meant it, okay? I don't care who your father is."

Sighing, Jake sank onto the couch. "Shiloh, we can't keep pretending that it doesn't matter. Who my dad is—"

"I didn't say it didn't matter. I said I didn't care. You're not your father."

Jake stared at his feet, saying nothing.

Shiloh lowered herself to sit beside him, making sure to leave appropriate space between them. The silence hung over them, heavy as a thick winter blanket. Past the closed door, voices carried down the hall. The alarm of an IV pump wailed.

"Shi," Jake said softly, "how can you not hate me? How can you look at me and not see everything you've lost?"

A lump jumped into her throat, and it hurt to swallow it down. She couldn't look at him—see the shame that marred his face. "Jake—"

"Froq, I hate it. I *hate* being an Osgood. I get that I shouldn't. I get that in this society, I won the jackpot. But I know all these things that my dad and the Council has done, things that I wish I didn't know." He pressed the heels of his hand to his head as though the images there were physically painful. "I hate it. I hate Arcadia. I hate that people are suffering, and there is nothing I can do about it. I hate being told how to think and to behave. I hate being a puppet in my dad's show. And I hate...I hate looking at you and knowing everything you've lost. And how I wish I could give it back."

He turned his head to meet her eyes. For the first time, Shiloh felt *seen*. No one cared about Havens, what they'd lost, but somehow, Jake did care. Tales of it were written in his eyes and in his hand as he entwined his fingers with hers.

Shiloh murmured so softly she almost couldn't hear it. "Jake, I hate Arcadia too. But I don't...I can't hate you. Maybe, before all this, I did look at you like that...like you were your father. But now that I know you..." His eyes sparked with some emotion, and she jerked her eyes to the floor before he left her too breathless. "I know better now. I just see *you*. And you're not responsible for the Council's sins."

Jake's lips twitched upward for a heartbeat. His thumb brushed across her knuckles, sending goosebumps up her arm. Then reality returned. Shiloh pulled her hand away and eyed the door, her heart pounding.

"I can't afford to talk like this," Shiloh said. "This is heresy, and maybe your name can protect you, but mine can't. I have to forget. That's Rule #2 for a Haven girl. We don't remember. If you're smart, you'll forget too."

"How am I supposed to forget any of this? I see Hope every time I close my eyes."

Shiloh flinched.

"I wish there was something I could have done," Jake added, "to save her."

"Me too." And there it was...the emotion that made the grief even stronger. *Guilt.* "Hope and I were brought to the Haven on the same day."

Stop talking! she warned, but the words spilled from her lips like a sink overflowing.

"We were supposed to look after each other, but I got busy

with school, and I didn't notice her slipping until it was too late. It's not your fault." Shiloh's voice broke. "It's mine."

Her eyes blazed with heat and pinpricks. *Froq! Don't cry. Do not cry!*

Jake ran a hand across her cheek, his touch so tender it hurt. "Oh, Shi, that's just not true."

Coming here was a mistake. She had to get out before she lost control. Shiloh grabbed her crutches, but she couldn't propel herself off the couch with just one good leg.

Jake's hand caught her wrist. "Shi, please wait. You don't have to run away. I'm here for you."

Something about his voice, his gentle eyes, made her stop and slump in defeat. As her cheeks grew wet, Jake's arm slid around her. When was the last time anyone had even hugged her?

Every shred of commonsense she possessed told her that she should run, frantically throw her walls back up. She was raw and broken, open and real, and so was he. It was terrifying.

But his arms around her were firm and steady and safe, filling her with a warmth she'd never known. So she let him hold her, anyway.

"Froq you," Shiloh said into chest, breathing him in. "You're never going to leave me alone, are you?"

"Nah." He laid his cheek on the top of her head. "I've told you before. You're stuck with me."

Leaves and branches crashed as the Elite pursued Nic. She leaped over fallen logs and weaved around trees, searching frantically as she ran, because Elite never came alone. The Elite lunged and took her legs out from under her. She slid over the dirt and leaves. Hands seized her wrists. If he handcuffed her, it would be over.

She kicked back and struck the Elite hard enough that he released her. She spun on her back and drew her gun from its holster, clinging with both hands and aiming straight up at the Elite.

You hesitate, and you're dead.

She didn't hesitate. The Elite advanced toward her, and she fired, straight through the visor. With a spray of glass and blood, the Elite fell like a tree before a chainsaw. A pool of blood inked from his helmet and stained the damp leaves.

Dear God, I just killed someone.

Bile burned at the back of her throat, but she swallowed it down and leaped to her feet. Branches crashed around her. More Elite.

Faster, faster.

A whine sailed past her ear, and the bullet collided with a tree trunk to her right. Stunner bullets. They still wanted her alive.

Nic threw herself over the top of a slope and screeched to a halt, her feet stumbling at the edge of a cliff. She landed hard on the ground to keep from sailing through the air. Far below, she could see a lake, but she couldn't jump and hope to survive. She whipped back around. A line of five Elite formed a circle, blocking her escape.

She strangled her handgun in both hands and pointed it at each of their chests. Their own guns trained back at her.

"Drop the weapon," one of them, a female by her voice, barked. "Drop your weapon and get on your knees."

Nic glanced between them, and the lake far below. There was no way out. Her heart wailing in her chest, Nic dropped the gun and fell to her knees.

"Put your hands up."

Nic grabbed the radio clipped on her belt and heaved it with all her might off the cliff. An Elite slammed her to the ground, but it was too late. The radio sailed down...down...down...

At least, in the end, she'd been a true soldier of ROGUE. When capture or death was possible or even imminent, getting rid of the radio was priority #2. Priority #1 was you didn't tell

ROGUE's secrets. No matter what the Elite did to you, you never told.

She would never tell. They would have to kill her.

I'm going to die.

The Elite's electric handcuffs bit into her wrist. Pressed to the ground, Nic tried to look to the heavens and caught a momentary glance of blue sky. Then the Elite pulled a sack over her head, and the world went dark.

NINE

"You've got something here," Jake said to Shiloh, who sat beside him in his hospital bed. He gestured to his own chin.

She looked up from her paint-by-number of a brightly-colored, fall tree. His own was a kitten playing with yarn, and he dipped his small paintbrush into the blue.

Shiloh rubbed the back of her hand across her cheek. "Where?"

"Right here." Jake tapped the paintbrush on her chin, leaving a splotch of bright blue behind. He laughed as she exclaimed and jerked away.

Recovering quickly, she flicked her paintbrush toward him, splashing red across his face and down the front of his shirt.

Jake tried to school his face into a serious expression. "You *will* pay for that."

She looked down at her painting to hide her smile. "Whatever, Osgood. I'd like to see you try."

"You're talking very big for a girl who has a broken leg and can't run away."

She opened her mouth to fight back, but two bodyguards

swept into the room and began searching it systematically. Jake dropped his paintbrush. *Ordure on a stick!*

Shiloh's smile was long gone. "What are they doing?"

"The king's coming."

It'd been nearly two weeks since Dad had last visited Jake. He'd checked in periodically over the phone, but he'd been busy elsewhere. Which was just fine by Jake.

Every muscle in Shiloh's body tensed. The bodyguards stationed themselves, one talking quietly into his watch. A moment later, Dad entered the room, his phone pressed to his ear.

"Well, call me when she tells you something."

Dad hung up and slipped his phone into his pocket. His gaze flicked between Jake and Shiloh in the bed. "Hello, Jake, and..." He paused.

"Dad, this is my friend, Shiloh," Jake said.

Dad nodded his head but made no attempt to extend his hand. "Nice to meet you."

"Nice to meet you, Councilor Osgood," Shiloh mumbled. "I was just leaving."

She grabbed for her crutches and struggled toward her feet. Jake hurried to help her, but by the time he had dragged the pole that held his feeding pump around the bed, she'd managed to stand on her own.

"I'll check in later," Jake said.

She nodded and rushed from the room as fast as the crutches would carry her. When she was gone, Dad set his briefcase on the end of the bed and looked up.

"You have something here," Dad said, gesturing to his own face.

Jake grabbed a paper towel from above the sink and wiped away the red paint.

"How are you feeling?" Dad asked.

Jake forced an easy smile on his face. "Pretty good. Craving a cheeseburger, but surviving until I get this feeding tube out in a few days."

Dad looked him up and down. "You look like you've lost weight."

Jake had, understandably, but why did Dad have to say it like it was a personality flaw? Jake unlocked his jaw and tossed the paper towel toward the trash. It missed.

It was always like this between them—like sandpaper grinding against a stone. When Mom was here, she was a buffer, but she had some long-planned charity event in Arcadia's capital, Chicago. Now, a rough silence fell between them.

"What about you?" Jake asked finally. "Solved the mystery of the Cleansing yet?"

Dad ignored him, removing his jacket and draping it over the arm of the couch as he sat down. Clearly, he planned to stay awhile.

Oh, goody.

"Your bodyguard says that you've been spending a lot of time with that Haven girl," Dad said.

Jake lowered himself into the chair beside the bed, looking at his feet to hide the anger that surely crossed his face. The way Dad said Haven girl made it sound like a dirty word. "She has a name, Dad. It's *Shiloh.*"

They *had* been spending a lot of time together, even more than before. Something had changed between them since that day she'd cried in his arms. Her thick walls seemed to have taken down, not completely, but she was trusting him with things that he didn't take lightly. She'd told him about the Haven: Repentant Closets and Mother's cane, all her responsibilities, and all the rules she lived by to survive. It turned his blood to fire. When he'd wanted to report it, she'd sworn him to secrecy.

"*They know, Jake. They don't care.*"

And of course, she was right.

His dad grunted. "Do you really think that's wise?"

"Why not?" Jake said, letting sarcasm drip. "We're supposed to strive for unity between all people, right, Dad?"

Dad's eyebrows shot up into his hairline, his ears turning pink. Now, Jake had done it. Before Dad could start in on the inevitable lecture, his phone buzzed. Dad swore softly under his breath and glanced at his wrist to see the name on his watch.

"I have to take this."

He rose and hurried out of the room, before answering the phone, the bodyguards trailing after him. Jake glanced at the briefcase that Dad had left at the end of his bed. If his dad didn't give him any answers, maybe he could find some on his own. It would take Dad a while to find a private place to talk, so Jake had time. Without thinking anymore, Jake stood and kicked the door shut.

Jake pressed the thumb pad on the briefcase, and a hologram appeared above the keyhole.

Thumbprint not recognized. Please enter pin.
Think, Osgood.

His dad would use something personal but not known to the public. The Osgoods' lives were on display on every eMagazine and newspaper. What was something personal, but the media wouldn't have published?

Jake's stomach twisted as he punched in his guess 0-5-2-6. May 26.

In a nation which encouraged women to have as many children as possible to repopulate, there was a reason Jake was an only child. Mom had so many miscarriages, before and after Jake, that when Jake was five and she'd been pregnant again, his parents had kept it from the media. His mom had made it almost all the way through the forty weeks when she'd gone into labor and given birth to a baby girl who'd never taken a breath. Her birthday would have been May 26. Jake knew, because every year Mom and Dad left a teddy bear on her grave.

The hologram flashed red again, and Jake swallowed down the lump in his throat. The hologram warned him that he had one more try before the alarm sounded. He used his own phone to translate the letters into numbers.

4-9-3-6

G-W-E-N. The name of the sister who he'd never met.

The hologram flashed green, and the briefcase clicked open. There wasn't much in it: his dad's tablet, a few portable files. Jake looked at each one, reading their flashing screens. Only one caught his attention. It read: ROGUE - The Family.

Jake clicked the button to launch the hologram from the file, and he gasped. Staring back at him was the blonde woman from the Cleansing.

Amelia Howell. ROGUE - The Family. Heresy: Christian. Confirmed connection with the Cleansing attack. Current Location: Unknown.

Jake swiped his hand through the air to the next file. The black man—Paul—who'd been with the woman was next, his location unknown as well. And then there were others. Jake didn't have time to read everything, so he pulled out his phone and snapped pictures of each hologram. He returned the file to the briefcase, snapped the lock closed, and flopped casually back in the chair moments before Dad entered the room.

Jake smiled and propped his hands behind his head. "So, how was China, Dad? Or was it Australia? I can never remember."

Five minutes after Shiloh had finished her shower, or the closest she could get to a shower without getting her cast wet, Jake breezed into her room and flopped into the bed beside her. He was like clockwork, that boy. Shiloh dragged the comb through her wet hair, telling herself she didn't care that he saw her looking like a drowned rat.

"Sorry I ditched you yesterday." Jake propped his arms behind his head, his skin glancing across her own arm with the movement.

No, she yelled yourself, she wasn't aware of every inch of his flesh that brushed against hers. It absolutely *did not* give her goosebumps.

"Pops took forever to leave yesterday." He made a gagging sound.

Shiloh knew Jake and his father didn't get along, the same way cats and dogs didn't get along. Still, the complaint twisted the long-buried knife in Shiloh's chest.

"Must be hard," she said. "Having parents who love you."

Jake flinched and then groaned. "Froq, Shiloh, I'm a jerk. An absolute prig."

"You said it. Not me."

He shifted uncomfortably beside her, and Shiloh decided to put him out of his misery. She pointed to a small wooden box on the bedside table. "Jessica brought in an old poker set she found at home. Thought we might like to play."

Jake grinned crookedly. "Strip poker or nothing."

Shiloh scoffed. "In your dreams, pretty boy."

"Oh, every night."

She yanked the pillow from behind him and slapped him across the face with it, trying to distract from the heat in her cheeks.

"Just shut up and deal," Shiloh said.

Jake laughed, the sound warm and light, and Shiloh turned her attention to the cards to ignore the way sunlight bloomed in her chest at the sound.

After a tense showdown, Jake finally threw down his cards. "I fold. I only had two queens."

Shiloh laid down her hand, and Jake laughed. She had only a pair of 8s.

"You're a really good liar," Jake said good-naturedly. "The look on your face had me completely fooled."

Shiloh shrugged. "That's the point of the game, isn't it? Learning to read your opponent? Playing the hand you've been given until your opponent is forced to show their own?" She gathered the cards, shuffled them, and dealt again. "Sometimes, it's a long game. You really have to play it out to figure out your opponent, but you..." She picked up her new hand to hide her smile. "Your ears turn a little pink when you bluff."

Jake snorted. "Whatever."

The door opened. Nurse Jessica came to hook Shiloh's bone stimulation therapy to her IV. Before leaving, Jessica looked between the two of them, a twisted smile on her face, like she had a secret she hadn't let Shiloh in on.

When the door closed behind Jessica, Jake set his cards face down on the table. "Shiloh, I have something to show you."

Shiloh raised her eyebrow. He moved to sit on the bed again, and Shiloh clamped her cards to her chest. "This better not be a ploy to look at my cards, Osgood."

He shook his head, his face solemn. Shiloh's heart skipped a beat in warning.

He pulled his phone from his pocket. "I snooped in my dad's briefcase when he was here."

Shiloh sighed. "Jake—"

He ignored her tone and spoke quietly. "And I found a file called ROGUE. I think that might be the name of the organization behind the bombing. A rebel organization."

Shiloh stared at the door, willing it to stay shut.

"Here. Look at this." He passed her the phone.

"We shouldn't be talking about this." But she focused on the phone anyway, and her heart leaped into her throat. "That's—"

"Amelia," Jake whispered. "The heretic who saved me. I don't think they got her, because her location is unknown."

Shiloh shouldn't be relieved a heretic had escaped, but she was.

Jake gestured to the phone. "There's more too."

Shiloh scrolled through the phone. There was the man who

had been with Amelia, Paul Barnett. Then there were more pictures, more names, more heretics whose crimes were as varied as their skin tones, but all had one thing in common: Mia— Deceased. Oliver — Deceased. Zahid— Deceased. Oliver, Asher, Riley...so many names, all deceased. Killed during the firefight. Or executed. But the last image made Shiloh's blood run cold.

"Jake, she's just a kid."

Jake swallowed. "I know."

Shiloh studied the picture. Nicolette Howell, with her blonde hair and blue eyes, looked just like Amelia, who was surely her mother. She was only thirteen. Under her current location, it read: Captured.

Shiloh pressed her eyes closed and handed Jake back his phone. Her pulse pounded between her eyes, trying to erase away the images of that young, innocent girl.

"I hope she's okay," Jake said, his voice scarcely a whisper. Beneath the sheet, his fingers entwined with Shiloh's, and she grasped on for dear life.

"She's not," Shiloh said. "If they have her, she's not okay."

A slit of the metal door opened and shut quickly, only long enough to slide in a tray of food. Too weak to stand, Nic crawled toward it. A covered iron bowl sat in the middle of the tray. How long had it been since she'd eaten? A day? Two days? Time made no sense in this white cage the Elite kept her in. The room bore no windows, no furniture, not even any corners, just an empty circle of pure white. The white was disturbed only by spots of deep red on the floor. Blood. Her blood.

Nic's trembling fingers reached eagerly for the bowl. She hesitated. What if it was poisoned? It didn't matter. If she didn't eat what they gave her, she'd starve. Poisoning would be quicker.

She opened the lid.

It was empty.

With a scream, she threw the bowl. It clattered against the wall and then screeched across the floor, before skittering to a halt. She screamed again, rage tearing her raw throat. "Do you think that's funny?"

They probably did. They were probably sitting behind that one-way window she knew was in this room somewhere, laughing.

The door swung open, and *he* came in. Elite #767. The Commander. He'd never admitted he was, but he could direct the other Elite with a nod of his head like a puppeteer pulling a string. Nic shied to the farthest wall, because he was the worst of them all.

He set the chair he carried down with the back facing her, sat, and folded his arms over the top of it. "Nicolette, you disappoint me. Didn't you like the food?"

She said nothing. He would manipulate her with any word she gave him. She pressed herself against the wall and pulled her legs up like a shield.

"It doesn't have to be like this, you know." He drummed his fingers on the back of the chair, the metallic sound of his suit meeting metal echoing through the room. "We have food and water and a much better life waiting for you, if you could just decide to be a good girl."

They'd tried this tactic before. The first few days after they'd captured her, the Elite acted like they were kind. They'd given her food and a warm bed to sleep in, even chocolate once. But they quickly learned that sugar wasn't going to do the trick, so they switched to using torture instead.

Nic ground her fists together even though it hurt to do so. Scabs constantly opened and closed where she dug her fingernails into her palm until it bled, trying not to scream as they tortured her.

"Nicolette, we'll keep going like this until you tell us. We're not asking much. We're not asking you the location of any the groups. We just want to know how ROGUE communicates with each other. Maybe the names or locations of a few leaders, that's all."

Nic offered only silence.

He burst to his feet, kicking the chair. It screeched across the floor and crashed against the wall. She bit her tongue to keep from crying out as he closed the distance and seized her throat. Her neck already bore the imprints of his fingers like never-fading scars. Still, she instinctively clawed at his hold, but he only gripped tighter, tainting her vision with black.

"Are you ready to cooperate?" he demanded.

It took all her will, but she got it through her crushed throat. "No."

He released her with a thrust that slammed the back of her head against the wall. She gasped for air, her vision returning.

"Why don't you just kill me?" Nic asked.

He turned toward her, and though she couldn't see his face, she could hear the smile in his voice. "Because, silly girl, there are far worse things we can do to you."

TEN

At the beginning of this hospital stay, Jake had never thought that the words 'You're going home' would make his heart sink into his gut. But he'd had the surgery to repair his stomach and was tolerating food well now, so the doctors said he could go home Friday. Mom was thrilled, but Jake's smiling mask had wobbled, thinking of only one thing.

Shiloh.

Of course, she was transferring to rehab this weekend, once the cast was cut off. There, she could regain some strength before returning to that hellhole of a Haven. He hated the idea of her going back, and he hated that their little bubble was about to burst. Would she want anything to do with him after he left?

The question did cartwheels in his head as he and Shiloh crammed into his hospital bed that night, their now empty dinner trays on his bedside table. Some scientific documentary Shiloh had picked played on the ceiling above them. Beneath the sheets, their hands wove together like a beautiful tapestry. No matter how many times he'd held her hand before, her touch still left his skin vibrating. The light of the television played on her face, the slant of her lips.

And, sweet Arcadia, if she only knew how badly he wanted to kiss her.

Jake took a deep breath. "Shiloh, can I ask you something?"

She glanced at him, and as though realizing this was serious, she commanded the hologram to turn off, plunging the room into darkness. She rolled onto her side toward him, her face covered in shadow. "Okay."

He rolled to his side too, so their noses were only inches apart. "What's going to happen when we discharge?"

She sucked in a breath through her teeth and fumbled with her words. "I...um...Well, what do you want to happen?"

I want to kiss you and never stop. I want to...

A rush of heat overtook Jake, and he shoved away the mental images before he completely ignited. "My mom wants to go to the lake house and get some family time. Which means my dad will be there for twelve hours before some emergency calls him away, and it will just be us. And you know, several bodyguards." Shiloh smiled, and he went on. "And I'd really like to call you. Is that allowed in the Haven?"

She hesitated and then nodded. "It's allowed. But what about after that? When we're in school, what happens? You'll go back to your friends and to being Mr. Popularity. And I don't exactly fit into that world."

"Then I don't want to be a part of that world anymore." How could he go back to drowning Arcadia's sins in alcohol and parties and girls, when his mind was now branded with flame and Hope's innocent blood? He wanted to be different.

He wanted *Shiloh*. Froq, more than he'd wanted anything.

"Jake—" Her voice cut off as he trailed his knuckles down her arm and then laced his fingers through hers.

"I'm not going to just forget about you, Shi. If that's what you think." He met her eyes. "Froq Rule #2."

She caught her lip between her teeth, and *peace and harmony*!

That wasn't fair! He cast his eyes on the bed between them until the roar of desire silenced in his chest.

"But what do *you* want to happen, Shiloh?" Jake held his breath, knowing her answer had the power to destroy him.

She studied him a long moment, as intensely as she studied books. "You'll really call me?"

"Every day."

"Then give me your phone."

He handed it over. She tapped the number of the Haven into his phone. The grin on his face widened until it hurt.

She narrowed her eyes as she returned the phone. "I swear, Osgood, if I go back to school, and you blow me off—"

"Not a chance," Jake said. "How about this? We'll meet under the bleachers on the east side of Vigilance Stadium before the Welcoming Assembly."

"Do you promise?"

"On my own beautiful head. If I break it, may I be cursed with male-patterned baldness."

She smiled, and Jake hid whatever stupid expression was on his face by pretending to type on his phone.

"What are you doing?" Shiloh asked.

"Changing your name in my phone to Swamp Creature. Got to know who it is."

Shiloh exclaimed in protest and ripped the phone from his hand, which began a play fight of shoving, tickling and trying to smother each other with pillows. He pulled her against his chest, pinning her. Her laughter made her body shake, and he worried that, with her head pressed against his chest, she would hear how fast his heart pounded when she was this close.

"I give, I give," Shiloh said through her laughter.

Jake didn't want to let her go, but he did, and she retreated a few inches away. She looked...happy. And she was so froqing beautiful when she was happy.

"So, what other summer plans do you have?" Shiloh asked.

Jake shrugged. "Just figuring out what ROGUE is."

Shiloh's smile disappeared.

Peace and harmony, Jake! Way to kill the mood.

She looked down at the small expanse of bed between them and drew patterns with her fingers. "And what will you do if you find out about it?"

"I don't know." Jake hesitated then decided to be honest. "Maybe I'll join them."

Shiloh tensed, and he caught her hand. *Don't pull away, Shiloh. Stay with me.*

"Jake," she said, sounding breathless, "that's heresy."

"Maybe I want to be a heretic. I certainly don't want to be a puppet in my dad's show anymore."

"Jake, I know why you feel that way, but please, please be careful." Her fingers tightened around his. "I've lost everyone I've ever loved to heresy. I don't want to lose you too."

Everyone I've ever loved.

In the silence, her words pounded in his ears. It took a moment to untangle his tongue—only Shiloh had ever been able to leave him speechless. "If I didn't know better, it seems like you might kind of like me. What does your hypothesis say now, huh?"

She shrugged. "The data might support that you're okay. Maybe. I guess." Her tone was light, but she caught her bottom lip between her teeth, betraying her emotions.

Leap of faith, Jake.

"I don't need data. I know how I feel." He let his fingers trace the line of her jaw. She didn't pull away, only continued looking at him with those eternal eyes of hers. "I'm crazy about you. Certifiably insane."

"I bet you say that to all the girls," she shot back, but her voice was weak and breathless.

"No, Shi. I've never felt the way I feel about you."

Her lips parted slightly, and for several breaths, she didn't move. Then she lifted her hand to brush a strand of hair from his forehead. Her touch was as light as a butterfly, but he swore he felt her in every part of him.

He wasn't sure who moved first, but suddenly she was so close their lips were almost meeting. He pulled back just in time, even though it was torture to resist her.

"I promised I wouldn't kiss you again unless you wanted me to, Shi." Unable to breathe, he searched her face, as blank and infinite as an empty page. "So...what do you want?"

The words hovered between them. Shiloh tried to make her mind work, to weigh the pros and cons, the risks and benefits. But her head was full of only him—the feel of his fingers laced through hers, the curve of his lips, the echo of his words: *I'm crazy about you.* She knew with every thrum of her blood what she wanted. What she'd wanted all along.

"I want you to kiss me," she whispered.

His eyes flared with surprise, but he didn't hesitate, closing the distance between them like a man dying of thirst lunging for a glass of water. His lips tasted like apple juice—that he'd stolen from her dinner tray—his mouth soft and gentle, but warm. Oh, so warm. It flooded every inch of her being, thawing places within her she hadn't known existed, like he was a fire and she'd been caught in a winter storm all her life. When he tried to pull back, her hands tangled in his hair, holding him close for a few moments more. He eagerly remained, his fingertips trailing ever-so-lightly from her shoulder to her hip, leaving her flesh vibrating in their wake.

When they finally parted, she could still feel him on her lips, a permanent tattoo. His brown eyes melted into hers, and her heart skipped and twirled in her chest.

"Wow," Jake breathed, and then started toward her again, restraining himself for the last minute. He tucked a strand of her hair behind her ear, a wide grin spreading on his face.

"I'm going to walk you to your room before I do something really stupid and ruin this perfect moment."

In her room, he kissed her again, taking his time, his hands framing her face, her fingers spread across his chest so she could feel his heartbeat. It danced to the same tune as her own. He smiled against her lips, and his joy glowed in her chest.

"Good night, Shi," he said, when he finally pulled back, remaining close enough his breath teased her lips.

This is dangerous, she reminded herself. But as she drew her fingertips across the stubble on his jaw, she felt so perfectly happy that she didn't care at all. "Good night, Jake."

That night, Shiloh stayed awake for a long time, smiling like an idiot and playing the kiss over and over. When she finally convinced her heart to stop pounding, Shiloh drifted into the first peaceful sleep she'd had in a month.

Then a hand clamped around her throat.

Her arms flailed out in instant fight, but the hand squeezed tighter. She screamed, the sound weak as it passed her crushed windpipe. Another hand slammed against her mouth, suffocating the sound and thrusting her into the pillow.

"Stop," a cold voice ordered.

She froze.

The figure above her blended into the darkness. When her eyes adjusted, another scream built in her chest. The dark uniform. The visor hiding his face. An Elite.

The hand tightened on her throat. Her vision blurred and spun. He lowered his head, so his hidden mouth was close to her ear. "How stupid are you, Haven girl? You watch one of your sisters get shot like the cockroach she was, and you think it's a good idea to discuss heresy with the son of a Councilor."

Her vision vanished, his face faded into a distant echo.

"You stupid girl, you had so much promise. Engineering Track. Good little citizen. But you're a heretic, just like your parents."

He relaxed his fingers only slightly, allowing Shiloh a gasp. Her heart slammed against her chest, pleading for escape. Any moment, the Elite would stuff a sack over her face, throw her in a windowless truck and take her to a prison camp. No trial. Just gone forever.

I'm sorry, Shiloh wanted to beg, *I'm so sorry.*

"You listen to me. You are going to be discharged from this hospital tomorrow, and you are not to speak to Jacob Osgood again. Do you understand me? When you return to school, you are to pretend like this never happened. If he pursues you, you tell him you want nothing to do with him. Do you understand?"

His hands tightened once again on her throat.

Shiloh nodded.

"Good girl."

He released her. She gasped for air and scrambled back against the headboard.

He paused and turned back. "I'll be watching you," he said, and then left like a shadow blending back into night.

Shiloh buried her face into her knees. *Breathe in. Breathe out.* But her breath came in gasps and whimpers. Her eyes and cheeks burned.

Sobbing. She was sobbing.

A hand touched her shoulder. Shiloh jerked away. Jessica, the nurse, looked down upon her, face contorted with worry. "I'm so sorry. I couldn't..."

Shiloh nodded. What could she have done?

"Are you okay?"

Shiloh nodded, but she wasn't. Not at all. The bruises that swelled on her throat were nowhere near as painful as the orders she'd been given.

You are never to speak to him again.

Another sob broke through her aching throat. *Jake.*

Jake woke with a smile on his face, his mind instantly replaying what had been—without a shadow of a doubt—the best kisses of his life. After he'd left Shiloh's room last night, he'd pumped his fist in the air and whooped *"Froq yes!"*, startling some poor nurse in the hallway. This morning, he sang in the shower and practically slid across the tile floor all the way to Shiloh's room.

But when he opened her door, his blood ran cold. Her room had been stripped barren and cleaned, ready for the next patient. Only the hot-air balloon she'd painted remained on the bedside table. His was gone.

And *she* was gone.

Jake slipped the hot-air balloon into his pocket and grabbed the first nurse that he found. "Shiloh Haven? Where is she?"

"She was discharged early this morning."

Jake's world tipped. "What?"

It was too soon. And why wouldn't she have said goodbye?

"Do you have the phone number to the rehab she went to?" Jake asked. It took a lot of persuasion and a little downright begging, but finally the nurse looked it up. He tapped it into his phone.

"You didn't get this from me," she said sternly.

"Get what?"

Jake dialed the number before he made it back to his room. It still rang when he noticed his room was no longer empty.

"Mom? Dad?"

They'd been perched on the couch, but stood when he entered. Something was up. He could tell by the solemn looks on their faces. He hung up the phone and slipped it into his pocket.

"What's going on?"

Then Jake realized that his parents weren't alone. A middle-aged woman stood from the armchair, dressed in the formal Arcadian outfit, glasses set over narrow eyes.

"Jake, this is Dr. Audra Williams," Mom explained gently. She was always the one who broke hard news, because Jake would take it better from her. "She's a renowned psychologist. The best."

Jake's heart beat an unsteady rhythm. A warning. "I don't understand."

Mom wouldn't look him the eye. "We think that everything that has happened might have been a bit...traumatic for you. So we're going to check you out and take you home. The doctors are completing the paperwork now. Dr. Williams will come stay with us for a while, to help you...adjust."

Jake shook his head. "I still don't—" His voice died as clarity slammed into him like a speeding truck, plunging his heart into his stomach.

Shiloh was gone. A shrink was here. A day after he had glibly, without thinking, said he might join a suspected rebel organization. They knew. Somehow, they *knew* he'd been pulling at his puppet strings, and here they were, to yank them tighter.

The door of Nic's prison slammed open, but she didn't have the strength to move. The Elite's demanding questions and their beatings were endless. Occasionally, they would haul her from the cell to a make-shift hospital room, where a doctor, her face hidden by a mask, would pump her with fluids and medicines. But it wasn't saving her life. It was making sure she didn't die so the Elite could continue their barbaric work.

"Get up," the Elite said, prodding Nic with her foot. This was the female. Nic recognized the higher lilt of her voice.

It took all Nic's strength to push herself to her knees. The world spun.

The Elite seized her arm, yanked her to her feet, then shoved a black sack over her head. The Elite dragged her forward. Nic stumbled on her bare feet, fell and hit her knees on the cement. The Elite never slowed. Where was she taking her? The hospital room? No, this felt different.

This was it, wasn't it? The day they decided she was no use and put a gun to her head?

It was terrifying, and it was a relief.

But instead the Elite pulled her into a room. A bathroom, Nic realized when she pulled the sack from her head. The Elite made her shower, put on clean clothes, and brush her hair and teeth. Then the doctor appeared, and the Elite pinned Nic to the wall as the doctor injected two needles, one in the underside of her wrist and one in her bicep.

"What did you do to me?" Nic demanded, staring down at the pinprick in her wrist. Was this poison? Would it kill her?

Saying nothing, the Elite put the bag over her head again and led her away.

When Nic could see again, she stood in a sparse bedroom with only a couch and a bed. A soft blue coated the walls, and the color seemed ridiculously beautiful compared to the starch white of the cage. The sunlight that poured through the window almost burned her eyes. She'd been here before, at the beginning, when they were still playing nice.

A clock glowed on the wall, showing the time and the date. She'd been in that cage nearly a month. Her fourteenth birthday, July 4, had come and gone without her ever realizing.

A man lounged on the couch. He was probably close to her mom's age and handsome with short dark hair and a shadow of stubble on a strong chin. His clear blue eyes took her in.

"Hello, Nicolette."

Nic's blood froze in her veins. She knew that voice.

Elite #767.

"Come have a seat." He patted the couch beside him.

Her feet remained locked in place.

"Nicolette," he repeated, his voice laced with steel, "sit down."

Nic could already feel his hand around her throat, so she sat, pressing herself into the arm of the couch to keep as far away from him as possible.

"I think we've been going about this all wrong," Elite #767 said. "This isn't working, for either of us." He gave her a smile that should have been charming, but it sent cool sweat down Nic's spine. "So, I've decided to try something else."

Nic's fingers dug into her tender palms, waiting to hear his plan, the web he weaved to ensnare her.

"We've decided to set you free."

"What?" she cried.

"You will recover here for a while, and then, once you're feeling better, we'll let you join the Arcadian society. You've never been a part of it, and I wonder if seeing what the society has to offer will change your mind."

"I won't change my mind!" Nic snapped.

When she saw shadows consume his eyes, she inhaled, wishing she could suck the words back in.

He slid across the couch and reached for her. She winced and tucked her chin to protect her throat. But instead of strangling her, he seized her chin and wrenched her head up, forcing her to meet his eyes. The blue in them burned cold as ice.

"I hope," he said, "for your sake, you do."

Part Two
WIDER CAGES

"It is likely to make us think we are not caged.
We cannot feel the bars
unless we push against them."
—— Erin Morgenstern, *The Night Circus*

ELEVEN

B *reathe in. Breathe out.*
Shiloh yanked her long socks up to cover the hypopigmented scars that zigzagged like road maps across her legs and let her trousers fall into place. She checked herself in the mirror. Codex approved outfit pressed and clean, her hair measured and cut to the precise length, and most importantly, her calm, controlled mask fixed in place. It had slipped in the past weeks, and it wouldn't happen again.

Satisfied, she turned toward the Littles. Willa had somehow already managed to untuck her shirt again, and Zyra tugged at her braids. Her hair refused to grow to the demanded length and style of the Appearance Accords in the Codex, so they were in tight braids against her head.

"Don't tug, Zyra, or your hair will fall out again." Shiloh turned Willa in a circle, tucking her blouse back in. "Now, do you remember what you're supposed to say when the new girl comes?"

"Welcome to the Haven, sister," Willa and Zyra said in unison.

"That's right."

Yet, no welcoming feelings existed for Shiloh. She already knew the girl would come to this room—they had the only open bunk—

and she would be assigned as Shiloh's Little. Most kids were young when they came to the Haven, generally before they reached school age. As it was, Shiloh could barely keep up with Willa and Zyra, in addition to pitching in with the other Littles, saving them from Mother's wrath. Protecting another Little was going to make her life even more difficult.

"All right, girls," Shiloh said. "What's Rule #2?"

Willa frowned, but Zyra's hand shot up. "I know."

"Yes, Zyra?"

"We don't remember the past."

"That's right."

Except, you haven't been good at keeping that one, right, Shiloh? The taunting voice felt like a stab between her eyes. She pressed her eyes closed, and there it was.

Gun. Blood. Flame. Hands on her throat.

Jake.

Shiloh flung her eyes back open and sucked in a breath. *I don't remember.*

"Your new sister might want to talk about what happened before she came here," Shiloh told her Littles. "You are not to talk to her about it. You are to only tell her Rule #2. Do you understand?"

They bobbed their heads.

Shiloh pressed. "If you're caught talking about it, Mother will lock you in the Repentant Closet."

Their eyes widened. Willa's thumb crept toward her mouth, but Shiloh yanked it down. Mother's cane would get her if she was caught sucking her thumb again.

"Promise?" Shiloh said. "Not a word."

"We promise, Shiloh."

Shiloh glanced at the clock on the wall. 7:42. The new Haven girl would be there promptly at 8:00 a.m., which meant that Mother would expect them to be lined up no later than 7:50 a.m.

"You ready, Starchild?" Val asked, from her place at the door. Her three littles were already lined up.

Starchild. What had once been a term of endearment when Shiloh made it on the Engineering Track, now dripped with hate, like her success was a betrayal. Shiloh ignored her and shooed Willa and Zyra toward the door.

Most of the other almost forty Haven girls were lined up against the wall like soldiers when they arrived. Val and Shiloh steered their Littles into line and then took their own place, except Val, who leaned against the wall, her arms crossed over her chest. Heresy and rage brewed in Val's veins, likely because a part of Val couldn't be conformed, no matter how she'd once tried. If Shiloh had been forced to wager who among her friends would end up in a prison camp, it would have been Val. Not Hope.

The past few weeks the tension between Val and Shiloh had worsened. When Shiloh finally returned from rehab, Val pulled her into their bedroom alone and demanded to know the truth. Shiloh had repeated the lie orchestrated for her: she'd been in a car accident on the way to the Cleansing, and she didn't know what had happened to Hope.

"Please," Val pleaded, looking momentarily softer, like the friend Shiloh once knew. "I need to know."

"I can't," Shiloh said.

Snarling obscenities in Spanish, Val stormed from the room and slammed the door behind her, leaving Shiloh suffocating on the guilt.

Now, Val and Shiloh both double checked their Littles who looked as perfect as they could expect. And not a moment too soon.

Mother limped into the hallway, the Aunts following behind her dutifully. She seemed more hunched by the day, her body moving in a jerky three-point gait—step, limp, cane. Even Val snapped straight, as Mother's eyes fell upon the Haven girls, inspecting for every flaw.

"May, you missed a button. Demi, you should look her over better next time." She continued the critique on down the line, pointing out who had not shined their shoes or who wasn't smiling sweetly enough. Mother's eyes saw everything.

Mother stopped in front of Val and Shiloh, training her narrow eyes onto Val. "Valencia, stop smirking and stand up straighter."

"Yes, Mother," Val said, barely hiding the growl in her tone.

Mother turned her eyes on Shiloh.

Breathe in. Breathe out.

"Shiloh." Mother gave the tiniest of smiles, disconcerting on her weathered face. "You look perfect."

Shiloh swallowed, but if it was from relief, why did it taste so sour?

Mother stepped away, glaring down at Ellie, Val's Little. "Your hair is at least half an inch longer than the Codex demands."

Ellie whimpered.

Val stepped forward. "That's my fault, Mother."

"Yes, it is." Mother's dark cane flashed as it slammed into Val's knee. *Whack!*

Val stumbled and caught herself on the wall. Ellie let out a cry, and Shiloh shushed her with a hand over her mouth.

Mother continued down the line. Val stepped back into line and lifted her head high. Proud. Val had always worn Mother's punishments like purple was her favorite color.

She hates me anyway, Val would say. *I'm too brown for her taste.*

Shiloh had never argued, because she was probably right. Mother had never liked Hope or Zyra or anyone who disrupted the dream of Arcadian being a land where everyone looked the same.

When Mother finished the inspection, it was exactly 7:59 a.m. The Aunts fell into line as well. Mother opened the door. Shiloh caught a glimpse of a Protector's uniform. Why a Protector? Most of the time, social workers delivered new Haven girls.

"Welcome to the Haven," Mother said, smiling that unnerving smile.

Then Mother stepped aside to let the new Haven girl in, and all the air left Shiloh's lungs.

The Protector had one hand firmly planted on the new girl's arm, even though handcuffs held her wrists firmly behind her back. The girl's eyes swept over the line of girls, her hair wild and her eyes just as blue as they were in the picture on Jake's phone.

The Protector freed her from the bonds and left. Mother steered the girl to stand in front of the Havens and gave an introduction, but Shiloh already knew her name.

"Everyone, welcome your new sister, Nicolette."

TWELVE

Memories flickered in Shiloh's mind like a dying flame: a woman at the door, the new Haven girl, a boy pressed beside her in a hospital bed, a hand wrapped around her throat. Shiloh gritted her teeth against the rush of pain and cranked the wrench on the pipes above her.

Drop it, Shiloh.

I don't remember.

It hurts too much to remember.

Shiloh slammed the wrench against the pipe so hard it clanged, the rusted pipe finally moving into place. This was the second time this week the sink had sprung a leak. If Shiloh waited for the government to send a plumber, they would be flooded until Christmas.

Right now, Aunt Isla was showing Nicolette around, getting her settled, surely cutting her wild, blond hair. But then the new girl would be Shiloh's responsibility. Her Little. How would Shiloh help her survive here when she didn't understand why Nicolette wasn't already in a prison camp?

After more tightening and banging, Shiloh wiggled out from

beneath the sink and turned on the water. A quick glance beneath the sink told her that the leak was fixed. For now.

Ring, ring, ring.

Shiloh couldn't place the shrill noise until Aunt Morgan moved toward the phone station on the wall that so rarely made a noise. Most business was handled on Mother's personal cellphone.

"Central Minnesota Haven for Girls," Aunt Morgan said. She listened and then turned. "Shiloh, it's for you."

Shiloh hesitated. Who would be calling her?

"I think it's one of your doctors," Aunt Morgan said.

No, they'd all discharged her. Not that the Aunts or Mother had really noticed anything about her care.

Shiloh set down the knife and then took the receiver. The video screen on the wall had long since broken, leaving only grainy flashes of light instead of the face of the caller. "Hello?"

"Hi, Shi."

Shiloh's fingers tightened around the phone to keep from dropping it. That voice. *Jake's* voice. It'd almost been a month since Shiloh heard it. She'd given up hope that he'd ever call her. Now, it played in her ears like a favorite song.

And then an invisible hand clamped around her throat.

"Shi, it's me. I'm sorry I haven't called before, but I couldn't. It's complicated, and I don't have time to explain, but I never meant to break my promise. I just want to know if you're okay."

No, no, no. I'm not okay. Her throat was closing in. She couldn't breathe.

"Shiloh, are you there? Please say something."

Shiloh slammed the receiver into the hook.

Aunt Morgan turned back from her pile of potatoes. "Is everything all right?"

"They hung up," Shiloh lied. "Oh, well, if it's important, they'll call back."

To ensure Jake wouldn't, when Aunt Morgan turned back and

no one else was looking, Shiloh turned the phone station off. The grainy screen went black.

❧

From beneath the covers, Nic listened to the sounds of breathing, waiting until she was sure all the other girls were asleep in the bunk beds around her. When she was certain, she crawled out of the blanket and slipped so, so quietly from the bed. She had tried to observe earlier as the others walked around the room where the squeaky boards were. She avoided them now, tiptoeing and dancing toward her boots.

During dinner and her tour, she'd slipped a few things into her pocket and then hid them in her boot: a few pieces of bread and a couple of granola bars. The girl named Shiloh had lent Nic pajamas, which clung tight to her hips, but now she slipped back into her jeans, keeping the top. She used the long-sleeved shirt she'd come in, to make a sack that she secured to one of her belt loops with the tie from the flannel pajama pants.

Someone snorted softly. Nic froze, but there was only the sound of breathing. Still asleep. So far, so good.

She slipped on her boots, grabbed one of the girl's water bottles from the dresser, and stopped before the window. This was going to be difficult. The windows on the car had been completely black when the Protector had brought her here, so she didn't know where she was. She had no compass or radio. Even her dad's watch was gone, and its absence made her wrist feel raw and naked.

But as soon as she'd entered the Haven and seen the girls lined up like prisoners on an execution line, Nic knew: The Elite hadn't set her free. They'd simply widened her cage. She was dead if she stayed here.

Nic glanced through the window. She was on the second story, but if she hung from the seal and then dropped, she would be fine. She took a deep breath, said a prayer, and reached for the lock.

A pale hand caught hers. "Don't."

Nic jerked away, her stomach twisting. Shiloh. They'd had one brief conversation, and it'd been terse. The girl had told her that Nic was her Little, and she would be looking after her.

I can take care of myself, Nic had wanted to say, but she bit the inside of her cheek instead.

"What do you think you're doing?" Shiloh's voice hissed like a snake.

"I just...I just wanted some air."

Shiloh snorted and pointed at her make-shift sack. "Is that why you're completely dressed with water...and food, I'm assuming?"

"I—"

Come on, Nic. Think.

Shiloh crossed her arms over her chest. "If you're trying to run away, you're not going to make it far." She pointed at the window seal. A red light Nic hadn't noticed before blinked. A sensor. "An alarm will go off if this is opened. And if you get past that, there are the Protectors who are supposed to do drive-bys of the Haven at least every hour during the night. Probably more since you're here. After that, we're thirty miles from the next decent sized town. What would you do then? Hop on a bus? You have an ID now."

She tapped Nic's wrist, where she could still see the fresh puncture wound where the doctor had slid a needle into her skin. *That's what that was.*

"They would scan you," Shiloh continued, "find out you're a Haven, and immediately call the Protectors."

Nic's heart sank closer and closer to her feet with every word.

"I'm sorry, Nic," she said, using the name Nic had told them she went by. "You're a Haven girl now. There's no escaping that. That's Rule #5."

Nic's knees felt like water. She slid to the floor, her back pressed against the wall. "You don't understand. I can't stay here. They're going to kill me."

Shiloh sat on the floor before her, studying her with unreadable eyes. "They hurt you badly, didn't they?"

Nic stiffened.

"I saw your bruises. When you changed earlier."

Nic chewed her lip and didn't reply.

"But they let you come here," Shiloh said. "Which means they are giving you a chance to survive. I can help you, but you need to listen to what I'm going to tell you. There are rules you have to follow in order to survive as a Haven girl."

Nic scoffed. Help her? She knew more about surviving than this girl could possibly imagine. "What rules?"

Shiloh held up one finger. "Rule #1: Survive. No matter the cost. " She held up a second finger. "Rule #2: We don't remember the past."

Nic snorted and shook her head. "Remember? Of course, I remember."

Shiloh's eyes grew darker. "I know it sounds stupid. And I know you won't ever really forget. How could you? But you have to pretend. You can't let them realize that what they took from you mattered."

Nic gritted her teeth. "They took *everything*."

"Yeah, they *did*."

Nic stiffened as it sank it. These girls were all Havens, the children of heretics. Every girl here had had families that were murdered or sent to a prison camp. So, Shiloh probably understood all too well.

Maybe, Shiloh *could* help her.

"What's Rule #3?" Nic asked.

"We are calm, controlled, and obedient. We only show them what they want to see. We follow the Codex. We do as we're told. We never let them see how hard it is. It's all a game, Nic. If you play it well, you survive. That's it."

Survive. Nic repeated to herself. *Just survive.*

"Rule #4," Shiloh said, "Haven girls look after each other. Like I'm doing now."

"And Rule #5 was…"

"There is no escaping this." Shiloh's words came out harsh but matter-of-fact. No drama or inflection. This was just the way it was. Period. "No one is coming to save you. You are a Haven girl, and an Arcadian citizen, and you live by their rules or you lose your life. That's it. You think they can't find you? They will. You think they can't find another way to hurt you?" Her voice wavered, and she looked down at her hands. "Trust me…" She breathed slowly, in and out. "Trust me, they *will* find a way."

Nic said nothing.

"Okay?" Shiloh pressed.

"Okay." But Nic already knew. Rule #5 was one rule she was just going to have to break.

"Jake, I must say that I'm really pleased with the progress you've made this last week."

Smile. Jake told himself, and he did. Not his genuine one that he knew came out crooked. A good smile. The type you gave your grandma at Yuletide when she asked if you liked her present, and you absolutely did not.

"Thank you, Dr. Williams," Jake said. "I've really been trying hard."

Dr. Williams studied him over her glasses. "I can tell."

Jake leaned back in the couch. Even though it had been weeks since Dr. Williams had moved out of his house, and he'd started daily appointments at her office, Jake still couldn't get over how white the room was: the wall, the couch, Dr. Williams' chair. Was it supposed to be soothing? Non-stimulating? Because it made Jake feel like he was in the center of a high-volt light bulb.

Dr. Williams set her tablet aside and leaned forward in her chair, her fingers forming a triangle. "Tell me. What are you thinking?"

The question really wasn't '*What was Jake thinking?*'; it was '*What did Dr. Williams* want *him to be thinking?*'. That was the long game. To figure out what Dr. Williams and Mom and Dad wanted him to say so he no longer had to do this. It had taken him a while, but he thought he'd finally had it now: the right blend of charm and a whole lot of orduring, with just a sprinkle of truth to make it believable.

"I was thinking about how much time I wasted this summer being stupid."

"Now, Jake, you know the rules about negative self-talk."

Jake took a breath. "Sorry. But you know what I mean. I could have been having so much fun, but I let anger and fear and confusion get the best of me, and said stupid things I didn't mean."

Dr. Williams arched an eyebrow. "So, are you saying that you no longer feel rebellious and angry? That you no longer want to be a heretic?"

Jake denied the urge to grit his teeth. "I'm not sure I ever really did. It was just, like you said, choosing to process the trauma with anger, instead of a healthy way. I could have been hanging out with friends and playing sports this summer, but I wasted it."

Dr. Williams leaned back in her chair with a smile. "What are you looking forward to when you return to school? It's only, what? Three days away now."

"Soccer. Definitely soccer. I play football too, but only second string, so it's really just an excuse to hang out with friends. Which is what I'm most excited about. Seeing my friends."

"And by friends—"

"I definitely don't mean *her*." Shiloh's name had a tendency to make Dr. Williams wince, so Jake made sure to add a note of distaste to his voice. It felt like a betrayal to her, but he ignored the twist of his stomach.

Play the game, Osgood. Tell them what they want to hear.

"I just want to put that day behind me," Jake continued. "Like you've always said, I don't need any reminders."

"I'm so happy to hear you say that, Jake. I will admit that you had me concerned with the setback last week."

Jake winced. "Yeah, I'm...uh...embarrassed about that."

"It definitely wasn't a good way to repay the trust we gave you when we let you have have your phone back."

Jake schooled his features into a look of shame and looked down at his hands in his lap, studying how well the burns on his arms had healed. Almost like the burns never happened at all. That had been his parents' goal. Like a magic trick. *Poof!* The whole traumatic summer disappeared forever.

No matter how much time passed, it was never going to be enough to forget Shiloh. The memory of her was imprinted behind his eyes, on his lips, in his fingertips. If only she'd talked to him when he'd called her last week. Why hadn't she? What threats had Dad used to scare her away? At least, Jake's worst fears weren't true. She hadn't ended up in a prison camp or a Reform Home because of his recklessness.

"Yeah, I'm really sorry about that," Jake said.

"You will just have to keep earning your parents trust after you return to school. I'm going to recommend they return your phone to you after you go back to school, so you can keep in close contact with them. And with me, of course. I will be checking in frequently."

Jake's lips trembled with the effort to smile. "That would be great."

"Lastly." Dr. Williams picked up her tablet and tapped a few notes with manicured fingers. "You've been taking the medications as I prescribed, correct?"

"Every day. My mom has Ana—the housekeeper—watch me."

Ana watched him put them in his mouth, but she never checked under his tongue. So, as soon as she wasn't looking, the pills were in the toilet or down the sink drain. He had taken them the first week, when his mother was the one watching him and not easy to fool. He had felt like a zombie, like an emotionless shell. When Ana took over, she didn't press as hard. She'd been Jake's nanny as well as the housekeeper from the time he was a baby, and Jake got the impression she didn't approve of the medications. Maybe she *was* on to him and said nothing at all.

Dr. Williams looked proud—probably more of herself than anything. After all, she had done a great service to Arcadia. The son of a Councilor, a heretic? Can you imagine the scandal?

And at the beginning, Jake had made it a challenge for Dr. Williams. He'd raged. He'd locked himself in his room and refused to talk to Dr. Williams or his parents. He'd demanded to know what had happened to Shiloh and roared that he wanted to see her, which they'd absolutely forbidden. Then Jake had realized that the more he shook the chains, the tighter they yanked them. If he was going to get even the slightest freedom, he had to convince him that he was falling in line. So he started dancing to the puppet strings, even as he wanted to cut them down.

"Thank you for all your help, Dr. Williams," Jake said. "I can't imagine what would have happened if it wasn't for you. I could have lost everything."

Dr. Williams almost blushed. "It was you who did all the hard work."

When Jake was dismissed from the session, he waited until he was safely within the backseat of the car before he let his smile fall. Yet another step in the right direction. Soon, he would find his way back to Shiloh, and after that, to the truth about ROGUE—the truth he hoped could lead him to freedom.

THIRTEEN

The Haven girls almost filled an entire bus on the way to the Central Minnesota schools. Only Willa and the other girls under six stayed behind at the Haven. At the depot, they divided into groups. The younger kids boarded the buses to Goodwill, and those 7th to 12th grade headed to Ardency. This was Zyra's first year, and Shiloh had barely managed to disentangle her from her leg and hand her off to a caretaker before Shiloh's bus left without her.

Now, Shiloh rested her head against the cool glass of the bus' black window. Her heart should have felt lighter. She was returning to school for her senior year, which meant she was riding this bus for nearly the last time. She would return to the Haven for Yuletide, and then she would be eighteen in March and never have to go back.

But there was no relaxing and no celebrating.

Nic sat beside Shiloh, her hands strangled together in her lap, silent as well. The last few days Nic had asked a lot of questions about school, and Shiloh had tried to answer them, tried to teach her all she could about the Codex. Val had done the same, and between the two of them, they'd miraculous kept her out of the

Repentant Closet. But school would be an entirely different story. How could Shiloh help her survive there?

And then there was Jake.

Up until the phone call, Shiloh had thought he'd forgotten all about her. Now that she knew that wasn't the case, she'd had to form a new strategy. It might just kill her, but what choice had the Elite given her?

The bus screeched to a stop. Shiloh threw her worn satchel, which held all her possessions, over her shoulder. Beside her, Nic pulled on a backpack that was even more worn and lighter than Shiloh's bag.

"Stick with me," Shiloh said.

Nic nodded.

They joined the flow of girls and boys stepping off the bus. The parking lot was crammed with buses, teenagers milling off them like an army of ants. A long line was already snaking out the doors of the Commons, and Shiloh directed Nic there.

Shiloh took a breath and looked around her. According to the rumors, Ardency had once been an old religious college. The red bricks of the buildings were supposedly laid by the hands of the monks that once lived and taught here. Maybe it was true. The campus was like stepping into an old world, all woods and long gardens, broken only by the dorms and the halls of classrooms. It was massive and secluded, nothing but the wetlands and acres of trees for miles and miles. It served just the right purpose for separating Arcadian's children from any influence but Arcadia's own.

The line eventually led Nic and Shiloh through the four stations of check-in. First, their IDs were scanned. Then they were given their tablets, which were already loaded with schedules, textbooks, and room assignments. A stack of uniforms was collected, and lastly, they received their trackers. The slim metal circle snapped around Shiloh's wrist. Red words spun around it.

Hello, Shiloh Haven. Your next activity is Mandatory Welcoming Assembly, 7:00pm.

Nic's face grew pale as one of the women manning the station explained that it would be monitoring her location at all times, ensuring that she was where she was supposed to be. The attendant slipped the key, a small slender rod, into one of the bracelets and pressed the button on top. The tracker fell open. When Nic only stood frozen, Shiloh elbowed her in the side, and she finally offered her wrist.

As they left the Commons, Nic stared at her tracker like it was alien. "So, they track me. At all times?"

Shiloh nodded.

"Can't I take it off?"

"Absolutely not. It takes a special key to do it, and if you even try, it would send an alert straight to security."

"Where do they keep the key?"

Shiloh glared and didn't answer. Once on the lawn outside the Commons, Shiloh showed her how to use the tablet. It was evident she had never used one before.

"And finally," Shiloh said, "here's your dorm assignment. It's right there."

Shiloh pointed to a set of buildings, nearest to Lake Amity: Diligence Hall, the Laborers dorms.

"I can take you," said Val, coming up from behind. "It's my dorm too."

Nic nodded and followed her toward the dorm.

Shiloh's stomach churned. *Great.* Val and the new heretic girl. *That won't end well.*

Another perk of being an Osgood was not having to wait in the registration line. All Jake's supplies had been sent to him in advance. The car took him past the Commons, up the hill and around the Quadrangle to a set of dorms that looked like quaint, vintage homes, all ivy-covered brick. The Legacy Dorms. Private rooms given to students who had rich or powerful parents.

The car halted, and Jake scrambled out of the backseat. Maybe if he got his things quickly enough, Mom would stay in the car.

Of course, she didn't. Mom hadn't accompanied him to school since 7th grade, but here she was anyway. His dad wanted to be there, Mom assured, but he was in Zy'on...or Denmark...or somewhere. Jake didn't care. The farther Dad stayed away from him, the better.

A bodyguard grabbed boxes from the trunk and carried them inside Jake's dorm. The other bodyguard hovered a few feet away. At least, Mom and Dad had never insisted on a bodyguard at school, expecting it to be well secured and his movements tracked.

"So," Mom said, coming closer, "you'll call?"

Jake rolled his eyes. "Yes."

"Every day on weekends, and at least once during the week."

"Yes, Mom. I remember our deal."

"And you'll take your medicine?"

Jake glanced around, but except for the bodyguard, they were alone.

"Of course," Jake lied, giving her a reassuring smile. *As soon as she leaves, I'm flushing them all down the toilet.*

The bodyguard returned, took Jake's duffle and the last box, and disappeared once more into the house.

"Okay."

Mom's eyes looked sad, and she stood awkwardly, hands on her hips.

"I have to go now, Mom," Jake pressed. "I'm going to be fine."

She kissed his cheek, leaving just-the-right-shade-of-red lipstick behind. He scrubbed it off with his shoulder as she climbed into the car. She waved out the back window as the car disappeared down the road.

Jake exhaled. *Finally.*

"Hey, Jakey-boy!"

Jake jumped at the sing-song voice that came from right by his ear. He swung around. *Click!* A bright light blinded him, but he didn't need to see to know who it was.

Stefani froqing Andreou.

The girl giggled and lowered her old-fashioned camera. "Did I scare you?"

Jake pasted on a smile. "Not at all."

Stefani shook her head. Her auburn bob, that was almost too short for requirements, whipped side to side. An illegal, pink streak descended through the strands of hair near her face.

"You're gonna get a citation for your hair, Stef," Jake said. "How many will this be?"

Stefani shrugged. "I lost count after 67." Stefani shrugged. "Oh well, a little self-expression never hurt anyone."

Except it did.

But not for Stefani. She constantly defied the Appearance Accords in the Codex, dying a new color in her hair every few weeks. Even now, the shirt of her uniform was tied an inch from her waist, showing her belly button and concave stomach.

For people who were not well-connected like Jake and Stefani, the citations would have consequences. Detentions or demerits sent to the Career Board that would get them stuck on the Laborer track forever. But Stefani's mother, Reese Andreou, served as a State Advocate, and her father was some bigwig in the national media. Stefani wasn't going anywhere. She was on a Media Track, had her private room in the girl's Legacy House, and was the gossip writer for *The Ardency Times,* the school newspaper. She could get a million citations, and she would be just fine.

Stefani reached into the small silver backpack that hung from one arm and pulled out a pack of gum. "Want some?"

"No, thanks."

As Stefani slid a piece of gum between her teeth, Jake shifted his weight from his heel to his toes.

What does she want this time?

Because, of course, she wanted something. He could see that familiar glimmer in her eyes. Jake wouldn't call Stefani a friend—not when she paraded every scandalous detail of his life in her gossip column—but he knew her all too well. At school, they ran in the same social circle of the cool, popular kids—the Shiny People, as Stefani called them. But he'd also been putting up with her at state engagements and the high-society parties since kindergarten.

"You know," Stefani said, smacking her gum, the spicy smell of cinnamon drifting past her neon pink lips. "I heard about your accident. Poor guy. Horrible about the gas leak at the Cleansing. You're very fortunate you weren't injured more."

"You're very fortunate that *you* weren't there," Jake said. Her family should have been there; he didn't know why they weren't.

"I suppose." She looked him up and down. "You don't look like you were burned at all. The doctors must have done a wonderful job."

"Yeah, my parents made sure I got the best care possible."

"'Course they did, lucky boy. Except...what's curious is that I heard a rumor that you were in the hospital for a *month*. Which seems a long time for minor burns." Stefani blew a bubble with her gum and broke it with a loud *pop*. "Isn't that funny?"

Jake stiffened. What exactly did she know about the Cleansing? What had been passed on to her mother and found its way to Stefani's eavesdropping ears?

Jake forced himself to relax and shrugged. "People say crazy things. It doesn't make it true."

"It doesn't make them *not* true." Stefani brought her fist forward, like she was holding a microphone. "Would you like to make a statement about those rumors?"

"Yeah," Jake said into her fist. "*Froq you*."

She laughed. "Don't worry, Jake. I won't publish the real story, whatever it is. Truth is dangerous, didn't you know?"

Oh, believe me, I know.

"I'll tell everyone about how poor Jakey was so brave in his recovery. I'll even throw in you saving a few kittens, if you want. We can photograph a reenactment. Have you shirtless. The ladies will *love* it."

"Whatever you want." Jake forced a crooked smile as he backed away from her toward his dorm. "Just let me know how I can keep the people happy." He shot her a finger gun and a wink then turned to jog away.

"Good chat, babe! Talk more later!"

Her camera clicked again as she took a picture of his back-side—or his good side, as she liked to say. He slammed the door shut behind him. The first to arrive at the dorm, he jogged past the empty common area and up the stairs to his own private room.

It was time for some peace and quiet, where he didn't feel like he was a gorilla held captive in a tiny cage while tourists banged on the glass.

That plan fell apart as soon as he opened his door.

Because a naked girl was lying on his bed.

In the dorms, bedding was shoved into Nic's arms, and Val directed her toward her room on the second floor. Val's room was only three doors down, and Nic wasn't sure that was a good thing.

Val was a strange blend of flame and aloe. She gave kindness and protection to the Littles, and Nic too, but Shiloh only received Val's ferocity. Defiance seemed like Val's permanent nature. Once, she'd spent the entire night in a closet for talking back to Mother. The bruise still stained her cheek.

Nic stepped into her sparse dorm room. Two bunk beds and a dresser crammed into a tiny room. No one else had arrived yet, so she made her bed on a top bunk.

The door banged open, and two girls—both all red hair and

blue eyes—entered. Their laughter died in their throats as they saw Nic on the top bunk.

"Oh," one girl said. "I'm Amber, and this is Ava. We're the Mason twins. Are you—" She consulted the list on her paper-thin tablet. "Are you Eloise Sabert?"

Nicolette slid to the ground. "No."

"Oh." Amber tightened her grip on the tablet. "Then you must be Nicolette *Haven*."

The way she said Haven made it sound like something you flushed away after you used the bathroom.

Nic folded her arms over her chest. *That's not really my name, but...* "Yes."

Amber and Ava looked between each other. Whatever they were communicating silently, Nic didn't like it.

"Well, there's a problem," Ava said. "You see, Amber and I always have the top bunks."

"Oh, sorry. I didn't think the bunks were assigned."

"That's okay, Nicolette." Amber walked toward the bunk where Nic had put her things and climbed the ladder. "Rumor is you're new here. Very new. So, we'll just have to teach you how things work around here." Amber yanked Nic's bedding off and shoved it to the floor. Her worn backpack crashed to the floor.

"Oops." Amber covered her lips with her fingers. "I hope your tablet wasn't in there."

Nic's cheeks burned as Amber and Ava snickered. Nic bent, pulled her tablet from the bag, and sighed in relief. It was fine.

Ava pranced toward her own bunk, stepping on Nic's uniform on the way. They didn't even try to hide their giggles.

Nic's hands curled into fists. What would Ava do if Nic punched her straight in the nose? But the memory of her dad's soothing voice reminded her: *We don't fight unless there is no other option.*

And what had Shiloh said? Rule #3: *Calm, controlled, and obedient?*

More like: Shut up. Keep your head down. And then get out of here.

A knock came from the door as Val entered the room. Ava and Amber swallowed their laughter.

"Getting settled in okay?" Val asked, but then frowned at Nic. "Why is your stuff on the floor?"

Nic gathered her things and moved it to a lower bunk, saying nothing.

Val stepped into the room. "Nic, did your roommates throw your stuff on the floor?"

"It's fine," Nic said, fitting her sheet to the bed. "I just picked the wrong bed."

Val turned a fiery glare toward Amber and Ava. "Listen here, you little brats. You mess with her, you mess with *me*. Got it?"

Nic stared.

Amber stuck out her pointy chin. "You can't do anything to us."

"Clearly, you don't recognize me." Val advanced another step. "I'm Val Haven, *perras*. You've probably heard of me."

Ava and Amber gasped, their twin eyes turning into round saucers.

"Oh, so you *have* heard of me. Mess with her again, and you'll be sorry. On the bright side, if I break one of your noses, maybe we can finally tell you two apart." Val shrugged, like it was no big deal. Like fighting wasn't her last option. It was her *first*.

"I'm going to tell." Ava's voice was shrill—a toddlers' whine. "Threats of violence are strictly forbidden in the Codex."

"Do I look like I give a froq what the Codex says?"

No, she doesn't.

Ava and Amber stared wide-eyed at her. They were terrified, and Nic's stomach twisted with a strange mixture of delight and guilt that their terror gave her pleasure.

Val waved to Nic. "Come on, Nic. Grab your uniform. You can change in my room."

Nic hesitated then snatched her uniform from the bed and hurried down the hall after Val.

"Why are you helping me?" Nic asked.

Val stopped, smiled, and leaned in close, her voice a whisper. "Because us heretics have to stick together."

🔥

"Hi, Harper," Jake said uneasily, stepping into his bedroom and shutting the door.

Harper stretched her long limbs over his bed, her red bra and panties the only thing concealing her smooth, bronzed skin.

"Hi, Jake." Her red lips parted in that 'Come hither' smile he knew all too well. "I missed you."

Jake's tongue twisted into a knot. That was new. He'd known Harper since seventh grade, and they'd dated exclusively for a hot minute in freshman year. She'd been his first...well, everything. Even after they'd agreed they were better as friends, she was always just a text away. That had been their deal. No feelings. Just sex.

But everything was different now.

Harper cocked her head. "Didn't you miss me?"

"Sure, I did," Jake said, but truth be told, he hadn't thought about her at all. "But look, Harper..."

Harper sat up and reached forward, her fingers caressing the button of his jeans. Words died in his throat, and despite himself, heat raced through his skin. Sweet Arcadia, a part of him wanted to give in. Sex with her was pure, meaningless pleasure.

But she wasn't at all who he wanted.

Jake grabbed her arm gently and pulled her to her feet. Mistaking the gesture, Harper's lips assailed his. His lips responded instinctively, and her body melded against his chest. But in his head, it wasn't Harper he was kissing.

Shiloh.

Jake pulled away. "Listen, Harper. This is great, but I..."

Think, think. "I forgot my tablet in the car. My mom's on her way to bring it back to me."

She brushed aside the collar of his shirt and laid a trail of kisses across his collarbone. "I'll just hide in the closet. That's what I did when the bodyguard came." She giggled. "I guess he was supposed to do a sweep of the room, because he looked in there and saw me. But he just closed the door and walked away. Must know a naked girl isn't a hazard to the Councilor's son."

Fabulous.

Harper skillfully undid the first button on his shirt. Jake caught her hands.

"My mom isn't a guard. She'll *freak.*"

Harper drew back and put her hands on her wide hips. "You know, if you're seeing someone, you can just tell me."

"I'm not." *But I really wish I was.* "I just really can't do this right now. I'm sorry."

Harper swayed back a step. He'd never rejected her. Never. Jake braced himself for her anger, for her to slap him. It wouldn't be the first time, or even in the first dozen. Harper was fragile the way that a bomb was fragile. One wrong move and...*boom!*

Instead, she snatched up her clothes and dressed quickly. "Whatever, Osgood. But when you regret it later tonight, don't expect me to come running."

Her voice was light, like she couldn't care less, but when she slammed the door, the soccer trophies he'd left on the bookshelves during the summer trembled in fear.

For the first time, Jake was early to the Assembly. Normally, he stumbled in five minutes late, his tracker beeping at him angrily. But he and Shiloh had promised to meet under the bleachers. Would she still show? Had something changed in the five weeks since he'd last seen her?

It hadn't for him.

Jake shoved his hands deep in the pocket of his uniform's jacket, rocking his weight back and forth on his heels. He hoped the shadow of the bleachers hid him. No doubt his father had people watching him. If Dad saw him with Shiloh, it would be game over once again. It didn't matter though. She was worth the risk.

Jake watched the flock of students arriving. Behind him, the stadium's speaker squeaked a horrendous noise and began playing the school chant. And then...

There.

Jake's heart leaped. Shiloh trailed down the slope, alone, and the sight of her was glorious. But she wasn't walking toward the bleachers. As she started to pass him, his stomach twisted. Maybe she'd forgotten. Maybe she thought things had changed since he hadn't called.

Either way, he wasn't just letting her go. He grabbed her arm and pulled her under the bleachers.

She yelped.

"Shh, Shiloh, it's me."

Her eyes fixed on him, and his heart froze in his chest. She stared at him like he was a stranger, cool and distrusting.

"You scared me," she said.

"I know. I'm sorry. But we were supposed to meet, remember?"

Shiloh only continued to stare, her face unreadable. The dim twilight slipped through the bleachers and shone off her hair. She was so beautiful his chest ached. He wanted desperately to close the distance between them. To hold her in his arms. To kiss her. But with that look in her eyes, he didn't dare.

"I remembered," she said at last.

Jake's bloodstream morphed into a frozen river. "Shi, I'm so sorry I didn't call you like I promised. I have thought about you every single second." She stared down at her feet. "But I think my parents somehow overheard or recorded the conversation we had the night we kissed." Shiloh inhaled sharply, but Jake went on. "Because they showed up the next morning with a shrink. They took my phone, and I've basically been on house arrest. They haven't wanted me to have anything to do with you."

"Then why are you here now?"

"Because I don't care," Jake said. "It doesn't change how I feel about you."

Shiloh still stared at her feet, arms wrapped around her chest. This wasn't like her. This wasn't the fighter who argued with him, whose tongue could flow with the sharpest of wit, who was calm in the face of insanity.

Fear wrung his stomach like a rag. "Shiloh, what happened to you?"

"What do you mean?"

"I came to see you the morning after we kissed, and you were just gone. Did my dad do something? Threaten you?"

She shook her head. "No, the doctors discharged me."

"That doesn't make sense. You weren't supposed to be discharged that soon."

The volume of his voice climbed without him realizing it. Shiloh shushed him and examined the empty shadows around them. The Arcadian anthem blasted from the speakers so loudly the bleachers trembled.

When she looked back, her stone mask was fixed in place, and her eyes were ice. "You want to know the truth?"

"Yes."

Shiloh met his eyes squarely. "I realized it had all gone too far. And I had to leave before it went any farther, so I convinced the doctors I was ready to go to rehab."

The words landed like a slap in his face. *No, she doesn't mean that. She can't mean that.*

Jake stepped toward her. Shiloh reeled back like he was a wild animal.

"Shiloh, what did they *do*?"

"This is not about anyone else, Jake. This is all me. I'm sorry. I really am, but I just want to forget this summer, and everything that happened."

The words scraped like glass up his throat. "Even me?"

"*Especially* you. You would never be in my life it wasn't for what happened at the Cleansing. So, in order to move on, to forget what happened, you *can't* be in my life."

No! No! No!

Jake had spent weeks convincing himself something sinister had happened. He'd never imagined that she might not want him. But she'd said it so calmly, so logically—how could it be anything but true?

"You really mean that, don't you?" Jake asked, a knife drilling deeper into his chest.

She nodded. "Yes." She turned away and bolted a few steps.

"Shiloh, wait!"

He reached for her hand, but she yanked back. "Jake, stop pretending this was more than what it was."

Venom dripped from her words now. Jake's muscles tightened, bracing for a blow. "And what was it to you?"

To him, it was *everything*. Everything he never knew existed, and everything he wanted.

She wrapped her arms around her chest again and shrugged her shoulders. "It was just a meaningless fling to pass the time—if you can even call it that—when it was what? One kiss?"

Jake's skin ignited, and it was easier to focus on the heat of anger than the pain tearing his chest open. She turned around again, and he blocked her path.

"It wasn't meaningless to me," he growled.

"Well, it was to *me*."

She shoved past him, and Jake let her go, frozen in place, fighting to breathe past the pain. Like he'd just been shot in the gut. Again.

FOURTEEN

Shiloh ran into the locker room of the athletic complex, her leg aching, startling a couple girls on her way into a stall. She slammed the door closed, seconds before her knees buckled and she collapsed onto the toilet seat. She buried her face in her hands, her cheeks already wet.

Of all the things she'd lost, a stupid boy shouldn't even rank in the level of pain. But something clawed at her chest, and her stomach twisted and heaved like she might be sick.

And that look on his face when she'd said that terrible lie! *It's meaningless to me.* His agony had almost made her come undone right there.

Breathe, Shiloh, breathe. Rule #2. Just forget.

Shiloh pressed her eyes closed, but Jake was right behind her eyelids: his fingers entwined with hers, a laugh like a summer breeze, arms that held her and refused to let go, lips that tasted like apple juice.

How was she ever supposed to forget him?

🔥

Nic had only seen a football field once, on a television screen one of the rare nights an ally of ROGUE had let the Family stay in their basement. In person, the field seemed so much greener and so much bigger. Despite it being an open field, the noise of the crowd thundered. Nic stuck to Val's elbow, so she didn't get swept away in the tide of people, as Val shoved through the crowd.

"Where should we sit?" Nic asked.

"I'm looking for someone," Val said.

Gnawing on her lip, Val stopped and turned in a circle, careening on her tiptoes to look past heads. A second later a blur of color slammed into Val with a squeal. Val struggled, but the girl latched on tighter.

"Not so hard," Val said. "Are you trying to suffocate me, crazy girl?"

"You say such sweet things to me, Valencia," the girl said, not releasing. "How did I live all summer without you?"

"I hate you, Stef." But Val embraced her in return, hiding a smile in the girl's shoulder.

"I hate you too."

The two slowly parted. Stef's smile vanished as she studied Val's face. She lifted a hand toward the bruise on Val's sandy skin, but Val caught her wrist gently.

"Don't," Val said softly. "It's fine. I want to introduce you to someone."

Like a switch had been flicked, light flooded Stef's face again, and she turned dancing eyes to Nic.

"This is Nic," Val said.

Stef threw up her hands as though she had received the greatest surprise of her life. "Oh, *you're* the new Haven girl everyone is talking about."

"They are?" Nic's stomach twisted, but she couldn't take her eyes off the pink streak in Stef's hair. "Why?"

"Because there's a Christer in the lion's den. I'm so excited to meet you." Stefani offered her hand, not as a handshake, but like a princess in a movie. Nic squeezed her fingers awkwardly. "I'm Stefani Andreou. And I have *so* many questions."

Val elbowed Stefani so hard she yelped. "Stef, knock it off. She can't tell you anything, and you know it."

"I know, I know. My brain just runs wild." She threw an arm around Nic's shoulders and led her up the bleachers.

The three girls found a spot together. Keeping up a wave of conversation, Stefani plopped between Nicolette and Val and reached toward Nic. Nic flinched back, but Stefani only grasped Nic's red-white-and-blue tie. She undid Nic's sloppy knot and tied it with skilled fingers. Meanwhile, her mouth fluttered like a bird's wing, saying something about a 'homecoming', which was still weeks away, but it was 'never too early to start dreaming about accessories'.

Pop!

The stadium speakers exploded with sound. Like a gunshot. Nic flung her hands over her head as her heart leaped into her throat. She was running in the woods, bullets sailing past her. But no, she wasn't. She was in a crowd of people. Nic forced her arms down.

Don't be weak, Nic. Keep it together.

Everyone around Nic was now on their feet, cheering and applauding. Nic rose slowly to join them. Down on the field, a woman in a uniform just like the students' ascended onto a make-shift stage.

"That's Principal Stella Clark," Stefani explained.

Principal Clark' voice squawked through the speakers. "Young citizens of Arcadia, welcome to another year at Ardency."

Cheers roared through the crowd.

"Now let's join together in singing our anthem."

The voices of the crowd rose, singing of unquestionable loyalty, perfect conformity, and a land of harmony. Nic knew the words, but the thought of singing them made her want to vomit.

Suddenly, Stefani slipped her hand into Nic's. Nic looked at her, startled. The silly smile that had been on Stefani's face had faded, and she leaned so close that Nic could smell the cinnamon on her breath.

"For the record," Stefani said in a low voice, using the noise of the crowd to cover her words. "I'm really, really sorry that this happened to you. For everything that you lost." She encircled her arms around Nic and pulled her into her chest.

Nic stiffened. No one had hugged her in months. Since The Family left, all she had known was cruelty and pain.

"I'm so, *so* sorry," Stefani repeated.

Over Stefani's shoulder, Val gave her a soft smile.

Nic relaxed into Stefani's arm, battling against the burn in her eyes. A stubborn tear escaped, anyway, and trailed down her nose. For the first time since the day of the Cleansing, she didn't feel utterly alone.

"What did I miss?" Jake asked, as he slid onto the end of the bleacher, beside his friend, Marcus Brawler.

Marcus, of course, was not paying attention to the Assembly and, instead, was joshing with the friend on his other side. But when he heard Jake, he jerked his head up and smiled broadly. "Jake, my man." He hugged Jake in the way guys did, boisterously with lots of backslapping and little other touching. "Alive and in the flesh. Despite attempts in the contrary, the news says."

"Well, you know" —Jake smiled crookedly— "only the good die young."

"And you ain't good!" Marcus finished for him. He leaned in and whispered, "Dude, what did you do to Harper? She is *chafed*."

He gestured down the row where Harper sat. Harper stared straight into the field, but her tense shoulders demonstrated that she was aware of Jake's presence.

"Long story," Jake said. "She'll get over it."

"Can't resist the Jakester for long, am I right?"

Jake hid a wince. He and Marcus had been friends since kindergarten, when Marcus had punched Justin Hawthorne for teasing Jake for crying on live television. Jake should be used to the nicknames, but tonight they settled into his ears like a bald tire screeched against asphalt.

The Assembly mirrored all the previous years: inspiring quotes from the Codex and school chants, holograms of fireworks exploding in the air. Lastly, Principal Clark's gave a speech about striving to do the best for Arcadia: work hard, persevere and promote harmony. *Blah, blah, blah...and other garbage.*

A flask was being passed down the bleacher, through the hands of people that Jake had always considered his friends. But looking at them now, he frowned. What had he told Shiloh this summer? *They don't like me. They like my last name and what they think it can get them.*

When Marcus passed the flask to him, Jake put it to his lips automatically then hesitated. He'd promised himself he wouldn't fall back into the same patterns with the same fake friends. But a cruel voice replayed in his head.

Well, it was to me.

Jake gulped down a swig, then coughed as the bite of alcohol blazed down his throat.

Marcus slapped his back. "You've been abstaining too much this summer. Got to get you back in the swing of things."

Jake's next drink went down smoother.

How had this happened? After everything he and Shiloh had gone through together, how could she feel *nothing* for him? But here he sat in the froqing irony. He—*Jacob The-Heartbreak-Prince Osgood*—had gotten his heart ripped to shreds.

"Atta boy." Marcus leaned in close. "Hey, we're going to hit the woods after. You in?"

Jake was sure that the school officials knew about the occasional parties they threw in the woods. But they looked the other way as long as things didn't get out of hand. Better a little drinking and irresponsible teenage behavior, than heresy.

I don't want to be a part of that world anymore, remember?

But Shiloh's icy words still ricocheted in his brain like a bullet.

I mean nothing to her.

Jake drained the last of the flask. "I'm *so* in."

FIFTEEN

J ake groaned as he woke with a familiar throb between his eyes. He laid prone on his bed, horizontal with his hands hanging off the side. His tracker screamed a shrill alarm, the red words circling his wrist angrily.

YOU ARE NOT AT YOUR SCHEDULED LOCATION. PLEASE REPORT TO ROOM Q23 FOR ADVANCED TECH-NOLOGIES.

"You're not the boss of me," he mumbled weakly, sitting up and glancing at the time on his tracker.

Ordure! He'd slept straight through breakfast. Not that he felt liking eating. His stomach churned like a witch brewing a potion.

Last night came back to him in flashes. A bonfire in the woods. Enough alcohol that his throat didn't burn anymore, and then more and more. Until he too could forget like Shiloh could. And Harper—*oh, froq, Harper*. Yep, her red lacy underpants lay on his floor as a reminder. Despite what Harper had said, she'd been willing when he'd changed his mind. For a blissful window of time, he'd pretended she wasn't Harper, but a dark-eyed girl who he couldn't have. But he'd only been majorly disappointed after

Harper had left, because the silence reminded him that Shiloh was still untouchable.

Jake's stomach churned even harder. Guilt? Was he feeling guilty? He had absolutely nothing to feel guilty about. Shiloh was the one who—

Nope, not guilt!

He barely made it to the toilet before all the whiskey and tequila burned its way up his throat.

He showered quickly, threw on a uniform, put on a pair of sunglasses, and ran toward the Quadrangle. Running was definitely a mistake, even the short distance, as he had to stop and puke in the bushes before he finally made it to class.

"Thank you for finally joining us, Mr. Osgood," Professor Cooper said when he entered. "Please take a seat."

Jake normally slunk to the back of the room where the Professor wouldn't notice when he fell asleep, but the back of the room was taken. Only one seat remained available and—

Froq me!

It was right beside Shiloh Haven.

He lowered himself in the seat at the table beside her.

"Page 66," she whispered, not looking at him.

He turned to the page on the textbook in his tablet. He tried to take a breath to calm his pounding heart, but his nose only filled with a fresh spring scent—the school issued body wash—but on Shiloh's skin, it morphed into an intoxicating aroma. He clutched his fists beneath the table, trying to pretend that his hands didn't ache with the longing to touch her.

Professor Cooper read from the 3D slideshow hologrammed at the front of the room, showing computers and glowing lightbulbs and other technologies flashing steadily. "Technology is what separates humankind from all other species..."

Jake felt Shiloh's eyes upon him. It made his stomach toss even more, like all his sins were being laid out for her to judge. He didn't have any reason to care about her opinion. But if she didn't stop looking at him like that, he was going to be sick again.

Finally, he glanced over to see exactly where her eyes were directed. His neck. He raised his fingertips and felt the raised welt. A hickey he didn't remember getting.

Froq.

He looked away swiftly, yanked up the collar of his jacket and tried to pretend that he didn't hate himself.

"Why so glum?" Harper asked as she lowered herself down on the bench beside Jake. "I could see your pouty bottom lip all away across the room."

Jake looked up from pushing his lunch around his tray—a meal of mashed potatoes and — *Seriously, what kind of meat is this, anyway?* Harper leaned back against the table, arching up her chest where she'd expertly left an extra button of her shirt undone. Mission accomplished. It was very distracting.

"Didn't you have fun last night?" Harper asked.

Harper had been coming over for 'fun' every other day for a week. Jake kept thinking it would make him feel better, ease the ache in his chest—and it did for a moment—but in the morning, he'd only feel worse. What was the definition of insanity? Trying the same thing over and over and expecting to get different results?

Maybe Shiloh had the right idea with Rule #2. Maybe, he should just forget. But forgetting would be easier if Shiloh wasn't froqing everywhere. Despite Advanced Technologies being their only shared class, she seemed to be wherever he looked. Even now, she sat across the cafeteria from him, and Jake was doing his best to pretend that he didn't see her.

But she was still *all* he could see.

"Jake, Earth to Jake," Harper said, waving a hand in front of his face.

Jake dragged his eyes away from Shiloh. "What?"

"I asked did you have fun last night?"

"Yeah, sure," Jake said, though he knew it wasn't convincing.

Careful, Jake, your mask is slipping.

His skin prickled, and he turned back. Shiloh stared back at him. But why? He meant nothing, right?

Before Jake could think—because did he ever think before he did something stupid?—Jake caught Harper's face in his hands and kissed her. Harper pressed herself against him and returned the fervor. When he broke apart, Jake barely caught a last glimpse of Shiloh exiting the cafeteria.

Had she seen? Why did he care if she had? Had he been trying to prove a point? *See. You didn't hurt me. I'm just fine.* Or was he hoping he could hurt her back?

I'm such a froqing prig.

His tablet chimed in his pocket, distracting him from his self-loathing. The chime echoed through the entire hall, telling him it was a school-wide alert, probably the first edition of *The Ardency Times*. Normally, Jake would have given it a hard pass, but the picture on Harper's tablet caught his attention. He whipped his own tablet out of his pocket and unfolded it.

The picture on the front page took Jake's breath away. He knew that girl. He could picture her vividly on the hologram of his dad's file, looking so young and so fragile.

Nicolette Howell.

She was here, at Ardency.

Jake's eyes devoured the article. Nicolette had come to the Haven—*Shiloh's* Haven—only a couple of weeks before. Shiloh must have recognized her instantly too. Nicolette would have been in Elite's custody for over a month by that time.

What had Arcadia wanted from her then? What did they *do* to her? Why was she here now?

And what were the odds that she would end up here, with all the answers Jake so desperately wanted?

❧

Nic's fingers tightened around the tablet, staring down at the news article. That was her. Across the table from her, Val was sketching on her tablet. Now that they were back at school, she seemed to be drawing every chance she got.

"Val, does everyone get this *Ardency Times*?" Nic asked.

Val didn't look up. "Yeah. It's stupid. You don't have to read it."

"Stefani works on the paper, right?" Nic asked.

"Yeah."

Val's eyes trailed over to where Stefani sat in the corner of the cafeteria, giggling with a bunch of other students. Stefani seemed to know everyone, but spent most of her time with Val. Which was good, because her presence turned dark and grumpy Val into someone lighter. Happier. Best friends, Nic had concluded. *This must be what best friends look like.*

Nic frowned down at the author's name on the article; it wasn't Stefani.

"I'll have to ask her why they decided to publish an article about me later, then," Nic said, setting the tablet down.

Val finally looked up. "What?" She snatched Nic's tablet from the table. A shadow fell across her face. "I'm going to kill her."

Nic blinked. "What?"

Val shoved back from the table and stormed straight toward Stefani. Nic rushed after her.

"Stefani, what the froq?" Val snarled before she'd even reached Stefani.

The laughter and conversation of the table died in an instant.

Stefani twisted in her chair, smiling broadly. "Well, hello to you too, Valencia."

Val shoved the tablet into her face. "What were you *thinking*?"

At nearby tables, students paused eating and swiveled their heads toward the scene. Stefani's smile fell.

"Val—" Stefani started, slowly climbing to her feet and reaching out to her, but Val recoiled.

"You might as well have put a sign above her head that says 'I'm a heretic. Please kick my endsphere.'"

Oh, no.

Nic got it now. It wasn't just Ava and Amber who treated her terribly. Almost everyone said the last name Haven with disgust, but Nic felt especially hated—the new Haven girl. The girl who belonged in a prison camp. Now the whole school knew about her.

"Val," Stefani said, her voice a soothing lullaby. "Why don't we take this outside?"

Stefani took Val's arm and glanced to the side, to where a male student was approaching them. Nic stiffened as she caught sight of his Young Elite badge. Val had explained that these were students —supposedly shining examples of Arcadian citizens—had been given the authority to write students citations for Codex infringements. Though not all of them would become Elite, it was unnerving, the way Arcadia trained Elite to be monsters so young.

Stefani winked at the boy. "We were just leaving."

The boy hesitated, and Stefani dragged Val out of the Commons. Nic followed them around the corner of the building and onto the green expanse of lawn that stretched the hundred yards between the Commons and Diligence dorm.

Stefani finally stopped Val near the Commons brick wall. A group of students lounged on the grass some thirty yards off, but they were distracted, laughing and shouting at each other.

Stefani turned Val to face her. "Listen, I'm really sorry this happened, especially to you, Nic. I tried to tell everyone on the paper that it was a really bad idea, but they didn't listen to me. It was the editor's decision."

Val let out a breath, her anger leaving her with a rush. She shifted uneasily. "Sorry. I shouldn't have gone off like that."

Stefani laid a hand on her arm and smiled. "It's okay. I know

Rule #4. You're protective. It's one of the things I hate about you."
Stefani said the word hate like it was sweet candy in her mouth.

Val smiled weakly, but it tumbled quickly from her lips. "This
is still really bad."

"Well, we're going to protect her, of course."

"Would you guys stop talking about me like I'm not here?"
Nic snapped.

They turned to her in surprise.

"And I don't need you to protect me," Nic added. "I can take
care of myself."

Dead eyes and blood on fallen leaves flashed before Nic's eyes.
If they only knew what I was capable of...

Maybe they'd be impressed.

Maybe they'd think she was a monster.

"I don't think you understand the target that's been put on
your back," Val said.

Nic rolled her eyes. "They're just kids. How bad can they be?"

"I think on a scale from 0 to asteroid hits Earth and starts a
new ice age," Stefani said, "they're at least at the level of Yellow-
stone erupting."

Val let out a fresh string of Spanish curse words.

"What now?" Stefani asked.

"I forgot," Val said. "Nic got put on the running team today."

Nic's first week at Ardency had been filled with academic,
athletic, and even personality testing. Her academic scores had
been low. Nic's mother had taught her how to read and write and
do basic math, but algebra wasn't necessary for survival. However,
Nic's athletic scores had been—according to her assessors—unbe-
lievable. So, they'd placed her in a math class two years below her
grade, but also put her on the running team.

Stefani gasped. "No!"

"Yes," Val said.

"But the captain is still—" Stefani swallowed. "The Harpie
herself?"

"Yep. Harper *froqing* Martinez."

Stefani threw a hand over Val's lips. "Shh, if you speak the name of the witch, she will come." She pointed a bright yellow fingernail as two teenagers walked around the corner of the Commons.

Nic did recognize the girl that Stefani pointed toward, a tall brunette who looked and walked like a movie star. During the assessments, Nic was put in a race with her, Ardency's best runner. Harper wore such a sour look when Nic beat her.

But it wasn't Harper that made Nic tense; it was the boy beside her. As recognition flooded her, Nic's hand landed on her hip where her gun should be hanging.

"Is that Jacob Osgood, the Councilor's son?" Nic asked. You should always be able to recognize the faces of your enemies.

"In the flesh," Stefani said. "Mr. Golden Boy himself."

"He goes to school here?"

Val rolled her eyes. "Obviously."

More questions fluttered in Nic's head. *Was he at the Cleansing?* But of course, he must have been. Councilor Samuel Osgood hosted this year. His son would have been there. Which meant he knew what really happened that day.

Had he seen her Mom?

Did he know if she was alive?

Her fingernails dug into her palm until it hurt. It didn't really matter what he knew or didn't know. It wasn't like she could walk over there and demand answers. She'd have an Elite strangling her in no time.

"You should probably keep away from him," Val said.

Nic scoffed. "Duh."

Stefani fluttered her hand. "Jake is relatively harmless. He does leave a string of broken hearts behind him, but he's never been cruel. As long as you don't fall in love with him, you'll be safe."

Nic stuck out her tongue, gagging at the thought. "Gross."

Val snorted.

"Marcus Brawler, the Quarterback King, on the other hand, is not harmless." Stefani gestured to one of the boys throwing the football, who was at least a foot taller and probably twice as wide as Nic. "He's one of those kids who used to set bugs on fire just to see what would happen."

"Enough already." Nic groaned. "I'll be fine."

"Just keep your guard up," Val said. "These kids are monsters."

"No, the *Elite* are monsters," Nic snapped. "And I survived them."

Stefani's eyes widened in horror, and a shadow fell over Val's face.

Nic dragged in a breath. *I shouldn't have said that.*

"My point is," Nic said quickly, "I'm not weak, and I can take care of myself. So, unless one of you knows how to get this tracker off of me—" She raised her wrist. "—then I don't *need* your help."

Stefani and Val glanced at each other, and then Stefani rested a calming hand on Nic's shoulder. "Of course, you're not weak. And maybe you don't need us, but that's what friends do. They look after each other."

SIXTEEN

Shiloh found comfort in the demand of school. Her schedule was crammed with classes, cross-country practice, mandatory social events, and a never-ending stack of projects and assignments. Good. The busier she was, the less time she had to think about *him*.

During dinner period, Shiloh took her tray of food out to the lawn in front of Amity and laid out her jacket as a blanket. She brought up the hologram of a nuclear cell, tracing through each structure as she ate, until a face appeared behind the glow of the hologram.

Shiloh jumped. When she saw who it was, the fear washed away, but her heart didn't slow.

Jake.

"What do *you* want?" Shiloh snapped.

He flopped down in the grass beside her. "Hello to you too."

Shiloh glanced around. A hundred yards to the right a security guard strolled down the lake pathway. To her left, a Young Elite was writing a citation to a crying seventh grader. Sitting here with Jake was the exact opposite of what she had been told to do. Would the Elite monitor their trackers? Probably, but the trackers didn't necessarily show direct proximity, and there were a lot of kids here. It didn't necessarily mean they were together.

Still, Jake's presence made invisible fingers latch around Shiloh's throat. She wasn't sure if it was because of the memory of the Elite or the question crashing around in her head.

Who did he sleep with last night?

Someone new or Harper Martinez, the busty captain of the running team whose throat his tongue had been down the other day in the cafeteria?

How could she have been so stupid? She'd thought her breaking it off with him had *hurt* him. Thought that his feelings for her had been *real*. The objective data was clear as soon as he'd sat beside her in Advanced Technology, the very next morning, with a hickey on his neck.

You're a liar. You never really wanted me.

"What do you *want*?" she repeated slowly, glaring down at her tray.

"Relax." His tone was nonchalant and easy. Yep, he was *completely* over her. "I'm not here to try to woo you."

"Thank the Council for that."

"I wanted to ask you about—" He scooted a little closer, and she ignored the heat that traced through her skin. He lowered his voice. "About Nicolette."

Shiloh's spine stiffened. "What about her?"

Jake leaned even closer, so close that when she inhaled, all she could breathe in was his spicy bath wash. "You know exactly *what*."

She did. Jake knew Nic's connection to ROGUE, and whatever else had changed, Shiloh could still see that fire of rebellion raging in his eyes.

Danger.

"I'm not going to talk to you about this." Shiloh snatched her bag and jacket and shoved to her feet. Leaving her dinner, she hurried away, back toward the Commons.

"Will you just stop running away from me for two seconds?" Jake said, as he followed after her.

"Leave me alone, Jake!"

"Shiloh, just stop! Peace and harmony, this was easier when your leg was broken."

She whirled toward him. "What part of leave me alone don't you understand?"

He shrugged lightly. "I said you were stuck with me."

Her mouth went dry as those words echoed through her, bringing with it the memory of his warm arms.

Stop it! He doesn't care about you.

Jake sighed and ran a hand through his hair. "Listen, all I need you to do is introduce me."

"No." Shiloh marched away from him as a group of teenagers wandered near. She didn't want to leave the public area and make it obvious on the trackers that he and Shiloh were together. But she didn't want people hearing them either.

"What do you mean *no*?" Jake said, staying only inches behind her. "Why not?"

"I know you're not used to the word, Jake, but it means what it sounds like. *No!*"

They were near the Commons now, and the voices of students going in and out for supper made the air buzz like locusts. Shiloh stepped into the long shadows of the brick walls.

Jake caught her arm gently, but firmly, and leaned in close to her again so no one could hear over the crowd. "Shouldn't we at least tell Nicolette that her mother is alive?"

Shiloh's heart pounded in her ears. She glared at his chest. Why did his touch still have this effect on her pulse?

"We don't know that. That information is almost two months old. We don't know that she's *still* alive."

He leaned even closer. The hot summer night had cast a sheen of sweat on his face, sticking that stubborn hair—the one she used to brush away—onto his forehead. "Nicolette knows about ROGUE."

Shiloh shook her head.

"You don't understand, Shi. I need ans—"

"No, *you* don't understand," Shiloh growled, yanking her arm away him and stumbling back a step. "Are you really so reckless with everyone's lives that you have forgotten what happens to Haven girls when they don't fall into line?"

They get strangled in the middle of the night by Elite.

Jake reeled back, but she closed the distance again so she could keep her voice low. "Jake, I don't know why the Elite decided to let Nic come to the Haven, but they gave her a chance, and she's only going to get one. You saw it, just like I did. You saw them put Hope on her knees and execute her as though she was *nothing*. They might not even bother arresting Nic." Shiloh formed her fingers into a gun and placed them on her temple. "They may just pull the trigger."

"Shi." Jake's eyes gleamed with emotion. He opened his arms like he might take Shiloh into them. She almost went, knowing the warmth and comfort she'd find there. She scrambled back just in time.

Idiot.

"Promise me," Shiloh said, adding a crackle of thunder to her voice. "You'll stay away from her."

He shoved his hands into his pockets and sighed. "Yeah, I promise."

Shiloh turned her back on him, but before she could take a step, his voice came soft as a whisper, almost lost in the wind.

"Shi, I miss you."

Shiloh pressed her eyes closed. *Please don't say that. Please.*

His feet crunched on the grass until only a breath separated her spine from his chest. The crowd of students was thinning now, taking their thunderous laughter and chatter with them. In the absence, his voice reverberated, until she could feel it in her spine. "I miss you...*every day*. And I can't stop thinking about you."

Breathe in, breathe out.

Shiloh turned around to face him. Past the shadows that played on his cheekbones, he looked so sincere that, for a moment, she remembered how it felt to curl into his arms, to lace her fingers through his. To kiss him. She'd been so, so happy.

But that welt was still on his neck.

Shiloh gritted her teeth and hissed, "I'm sure whatever girl gave you that hickey will be the perfect salve to your aching soul."

His face contorted into a vicious half-smile. "Are you jealous?"

Yes.

Shiloh scoffed, shoving down the cracks and the bruises in her chest until she felt only fire. "No. I'm *angry*. I'm angry I was stupid enough to believe for one second that you cared about me."

Jake swore, paced away, and then flung himself back around. "*You're* the one who said I meant *nothing* to you, remember? This wasn't what I wanted."

"And what *did* you want?"

His mouth gaped open. A choking sound came out, but no words.

"That's what I thought." Shiloh turned her head and scowled at the Commons' brick wall. The red swam in her blurred vision.

Do.

Not.

Cry.

Shiloh reached out and clung to rage, like a lifeline in this storm of heartbreak. Without looking at him, she snarled, "I was so wrong about you. You're nothing but a spoiled, entitled little boy who's never cared about anyone but himself!"

"And you're a cold, heartless blight!"

The words slammed into her like a palm across her cheek, like a different hand crushing her throat. She bit her tongue to keep from gasping. He slapped a hand over his mouth, his eyes widening in horror.

"I'm sorry," he said quickly. "I didn't mean that."

Shaking her head, Shiloh marched away before he could see the stupid tear that snuck from her eye. This time when he called after her, repeating his apology, she didn't stop, and he didn't follow. She tried to tell herself that this didn't hurt. But that was just another lie.

Which truth was worse? Shiloh wondered later, as she sat on her bathroom's floor, her head in her knees and the shower cranked on so her roommate wouldn't hear her cry. That she'd been wrong about Jake having feelings for her, or that Jake had been so perfectly right.

Because in the end, when the Elite's hand had locked around her throat, it hadn't even crossed her mind to fight against what he wanted. She wasn't brave like Hope. She wasn't fierce like Val, and she certainly wasn't reckless like Jake. She was a good, little girl, who would choose to survive no matter the cost. Even if that cost was what could have been love.

I really am a cold, heartless blight.

Faster, Nic commanded her legs. *Run faster or they'll catch you.*

She increased her speed, even though her lungs were on fire. In the corner of her eye, she could see the other girls and boys, gaining on her. She put on one last burst of speed and crossed the finish line first.

"Time!" Coach Bradshaw said from the sideline.

Nic bent over, gasping for air. The girl in second collided into her, sending her spiraling onto her knees.

"Oops." The Harpie herself towered over Nic. "Sorry. I couldn't stop."

Nic stood and brushed off her knees. Harper wasn't sorry. She and many other students were like that, just as Stefani and Val had warned her they would be. It was nothing big. Just little violences that piled up. An elbow in the side, cutting past her in the food line, or pointing out the smallest infraction of the Codex. When Nic told Stefani and Val about the bullying, they'd been sympathetic. Val had told her to hit back and make them suffer, but Nic didn't need any more attention.

Shut up. Keep your head down. Get out.

When she'd explained that to her friends, Val said, "Okay, then *I'll* punch them."

"Absolutely not," Stefani said. "A few more citations, and you'll be on your way to a Reform Home."

Val had grunted and said nothing more, but she must have followed Stefani's advice because Val hadn't actually punched anyone. At least, Nic didn't think so.

"All right, Harper." Coach Bradshaw made her way over to them. "Nic ran a fair race. If I see anymore foolishness like that, you will be getting a citation, understood?"

Harper hung her head. "Yes, Coach."

"And you, young lady," Coach said, grinning at Nic. "What's your secret?"

Pretend you're being chased by an Elite with a gun. Nic smiled and shrugged.

"All right, girls and boys!" Coach clapped her hands. "Hit the showers!"

If there was one thing that Nic was grateful to God for—besides Val and Stefani—it was warm showers. Nic lingered in the warmth until her tracker gave her the ten-minute warning that she needed to head to dinner. She turned off the water, wrapped herself in a towel, and stepped out cautiously. For privacy, she always changed in one of the stalls, but the locker room was completely empty.

Perfect.

She opened her locker to grab her uniform, but it was gone. So were her gym clothes. She checked the other lockers nearby. Empty too. After a few minutes of searching, she found her clothes.

Submerged in the toilets.

A scream tore like knives up the back of Nic's throat. She swung her fist into the door of the stall and wished that it was Harper's nose. She yelped, but the pain in her hand was a welcome distraction from the sting in her eyes. *I'm not going to cry.*

After all she had been through, it was stupid to cry about this.

She pulled her clothes and shoes from the toilets and took them to the shower. She started the water and squeezed liquid soap onto them, scrubbing them as best as she could. And even though Nic tried hard to resist, the pressure in her chest overflowed into angry tears then turned to sobs.

I hate it here!

I want to go home!

I want my mom!

By the time she finished rinsing her clothes and had calmed her sobs, the tracker blared that she was late for dinner.

Nic stepped into the Instant Dryer in the locker room, and within three minutes, her clothing and hair were dry. She left the girls' locker room and started the long walk toward the Commons.

The braying laughter of a group of students standing near the stadium made her hair stand on edge. They shoved each other, laughing, and passing a—*Is that a cigarette?*—between them. Nic recognized Marcus Brawler and Jacob Osgood and picked up her speed, throwing glances behind her.

Osgood blew a ring of smoke, threw the rolled paper into the dirt and crushed it with his heel. Then they started away from the stadium, in her same direction, stilll tossing the football between them.

"Hey, Noah, go long!" She heard one of the boys call. Another boy ran forward, passing Nic with his hands held high.

The football slammed into Nic's head with such force that it knocked her off her feet and sent her sprawling on the grass. She pushed herself onto her knees, her vision spinning.

A fist pummeled into her face. The floor rushed up to meet her.
"Tell me, you stupid girl!"

Her eyes focused, and a boy was there, offering his hand. Jacob Osgood looked so much like his father that she yelped and leaped to her feet. Her fists rose to block an attack.

"You okay?" Osgood asked.

At the same moment, Brawler jogged up to them. A wide smile split his broad face. "Sorry about that."

"No, you're *not!*" Nic snatched the football from the ground and shoved it into his chest. He stumbled back a step. "Here's your stupid football. You'd think the quarterback would know how to throw better."

His smile disappeared. "Hey, that's not very nice."

"Neither are you."

Brawler took a step forward, but she stood her ground.

"Stay away from me," she warned. No one was going to hurt her. Not anymore.

Boots kicked into her gut. A hand squeezed her throat.

"*Marcus!*" Osgood grabbed his friend by the arm, his voice low. "Stop it!"

Brawler shook him off. "I think the Haven girl needs to be taught a lesson."

Osgood shoved his way between them. "Marcus, you're being a froqing prig!"

"Stay out of it, Jake!" Brawler shoved Osgood aside so hard that he stumbled and fell. Brawler seized Nic's wrist, his fingers grinding deep. "Girly, you're so lucky to be given the chance to be a good citizen of Arcadia. And right now you aren't being a very good citizen."

Nic trembled, but growled through her teeth, "Let go of me. I'm only going to warn you once."

"Marcus, let her go!" Osgood hollered, scrambling to his feet, but all his other friends were cheering: *"You tell her." "Stupid heretic." "Show her, Marc!"*

A pair of blue eyes—bright as sunshine, but cold as snow. A voice hissing: "Are you going to be a good girl?"

"Maybe you haven't been punished enough for your heresy," Brawler said, smiling manically. "I think a swim in the lake would do you good." He grabbed for her other wrist.

Nic whipped back and slammed the heel of her free hand into his nose. *Crack!* He released her with a cry. She swept her leg behind his and shoved her weight forward, driving into his stomach. And then somehow, he was on the ground, blood spewing from his nose and her tennis shoe pushing into his throat.

For a minute, she was the one on the ground, a black boot crushing her. *I can't breathe!* Brawler struggled, and she pressed her heel in his throat until he was still.

"You will leave me alone!" she yelled. "You got that? You mess with me again, or I will *tear your throat out!*"

Then her vision cleared, and she realized that she was crushing the windpipe of a teenage boy.

Nic stumbled away from him, just as Coach Bradshaw yelled. "Nicolette Haven, get off of him!"

Brawler gasped for air on the ground, and Osgood gaped at her. Coach marched toward them like an angry hornet coming crazed out of a hive.

Nic's stomach twisted. *So much for keeping my head down.*

"Truth or not truth?" Stefani said, grinning way more excitedly than the solemnity of the situation called for. "Did you or did you not break Marcus Brawler's nose?"

From her seat beside Nic, Val glared at Stefani and pressed the icepack closer to Nic's aching head, where the football hit.

Nic shrugged. "I think I heard it crack."

"Peace and harmony, I just wish I could write about it. I can see the headline now." Stefani spread her hands wide in the air like showing off a billboard. "Tiny, but powerful girl kicks quarterback's endsphere. How will he ever come back from this?"

The cafeteria around them was silent and dim. They were alone in a corner booth, long after dinner ended. Stefani had to beg the kitchen staff for leftovers and a bag of ice.

"I shouldn't have done that," Nic said. "I went too far. Now the assistant principal says that I will have detention every weekend for a month. What even is detention?"

"A legal version of indentured servanthood." Stefani picked a cold fry off Nic's plate and popped it into her mouth. "They'll make you mop floors or write an essay on the error of your ways or memorize passages from the Codex."

"Oh, that's not too bad."

"And don't you feel bad," Val told her. "He got what was coming to him."

But Nic could only see Brawler's face as her foot crushed against his windpipe. Add that to the list of things she felt guilty about, hung in the hall of fame next to the person she'd shot. She didn't even know if the Elite had been a man or a woman. Sometimes, she wondered who'd loved the Elite, who had been left mourning. That pain was Nic's fault.

Before she could stop herself, Nic leaned her head against Val's shoulder. She thought Val might push her away, but she only dropped the ice pack and wrapped an arm around her.

"You okay, *nina*?" Val asked.

Nic shook her head. "I miss my mom."

Val tightened beside her, and Nic thought she might scold her violating Rule #2. But Val only murmured, "Yeah, I miss my parents too. Every day."

Stefani reached across the table and took Nic's hand in one of hers and Val's in the other, giving both a comforting squeeze.

The cafeteria door banged open. Nic jerked upright. Every muscle coiled like a rattlesnake ready to strike as a figure approached.

Jacob Osgood.

❦

Jake played the fight over and over in his head: the massive Marcus being taken to the ground by a girl half his size. He had known that Nicolette had to be tough to survive, but *froq!*

"You can get yourself to the nurse, you froqing endsphere," Jake had told Marcus afterward, and then left him in the dirt with blood streaming down his face.

Now, Jake was on his way to Diligence Dorm, Room 29, where the directory had told him Nicolette lived. On the way, he caught a glimpse through the window of the cafeteria. Nic sat at a table with two other girls, one of which was Stefani Andreou.

Great. That complicated the plan.

Jake hesitated at the door to the Commons, his stomach churning. He'd promised Shiloh he'd stay away from Nicolette, and he still felt sick with guilt since his fight with Shiloh. *Cold, heartless bitch.* How could he have said that to her, when he—more than anyone—knew how deep her heart went?

Despite the days that had gone by, his and Shiloh's argument played like a song he hated getting stuck on repeat. He always came back to the same question: If he meant nothing to her, why had he caught the gleam of tears in her eyes? Why did she look...like he'd broken her heart?

If I meant something to her, why would she push me away?
Focus, Osgood. You have to find the truth.

Jake pulled open the door to the Commons.

"Jakey-boy!" Stefani called, waving at him.

When Jake stopped at the table, Nicolette was glaring down at her plate. Beside her sat a dark-haired girl with hazel skin and eyes like daggers. He'd seen Stefani with this girl often, but had no idea who she was.

"I saw you guys through the window," he explained.

"Stalker!" Stefani cried, but then she winked.

"I just wanted to make sure that you were okay." Jake turned to look at Nic. She didn't look up. "I'm really sorry. Marcus is a complete prig."

Stefani threw her arms up in agreement. "Say it louder for the people in the back!"

"I tried to stop him, but clearly, you can take care of yourself." Jake extended his hand to Nic. "I'm Jake."

Nic narrowed her eyes at his hand, but didn't take it. "Yeah, I know who you are."

Jacob's hand retreated to his pocket, away from the tone in her voice, a hiss of a cat warning a dog to stay away. And that was what he was. The Councilor's son. The enemy.

"Anyway, I really am sorry. And peace offering—" He pulled the chocolate from his pocket, a package of small spheres wrapped in colorful foil. He set it on the table next to Nic's hand. "I figured that chocolate makes everything better. And my dad sends me and my mom these foreign chocolates whenever he travels, so I always end up with—you know—*bucket loads*. Got this one today from Switzerland. Which is the king of all foreign chocolates, just so you know."

"Aww, how sweet," Stefani cooed, as she opened one of the chocolates. "It's 'I'm-sorry-I'm-a-bad-father' chocolate. That's the best kind." She popped the chocolate into her mouth. "Yep, tastes just like shame."

Jake laughed. "I'm sure it does."

Nic only glared at the chocolate. Jake rocked back and forth on his heels. This wasn't going well. Yes, he wanted the chocolate to make Nicolette feel better, but he also wanted her to trust him. Clearly, it was going to take a lot more than chocolate to do that.

"Did you get in a lot of trouble?" Jake asked.

Nic's fingers coiled around her fork, still not looking up. "A month of detention."

Jake whistled beneath his breath. "Tough break."

The dark-haired girl glared at Jake, Nic was still staring at her plate, and Stefani was busy eating another chocolate. He was making no progress here. In the silence, the memory of Shiloh's warning was loud in his ears. How much trouble could Nicolette get in, really? He didn't want to jeopardize her, but he needed answers, and there wasn't another way.

Was there?

Jake glanced at Stefani.

Oh, no, Jakey-boy. Do not *even consider.*

But he was. Other than Nicolette, Stefani was probably the only one who could get him answers. But he'd be an idiot to trust Stefani-Gossip-Girl-Andreou.

"Anyway," Jake said, breaking the uncomfortable silence. "I'm going to go. I'm really sorry, Nicolette."

She gave him the smallest glance. "Thanks."

Stefani wiggled her fingers. "Toodles."

Jake made it a few feet away and then turned around. "And Nicolette."

Finally, she looked up.

"Nice moves." Jake did a fake karate chop in the air, as ridiculously as possible. The corner of Nic's lips spasmed, like she was fighting a smile.

Stefani applauded sarcastically. "The Prince of Arcadia, everyone!"

Jake bowed with a flourish and left.

Nic stared after Jake as he left the cafeteria, unsure what to make of his kindness and his ridiculousness. Nic took a chocolate, and the richness exploded in her mouth. It was *really* good. But it didn't matter if Osgood had tried to help her or was being kind to her. Even if he had no ulterior motive, he was still the son of a Councilor.

SEVENTEEN

Nic gnawed on her bottom lip as she watched Stefani braid Val's dark hair into a crown. Val had gone to Stefani's private room to get ready for homecoming, and Nic had asked to come along. The more Nic stayed away from her room and the wretched Mason twins, the less likely she'd put them in a chokehold and get herself in even *more* trouble. She already had enough dish washing and floor scrubbing to do.

Stefani had already been dressed when they arrived, and she was nothing short of glorious. Her white dress plunged low on her back, and watercolors splashed her scandalously short skirt.

"Froq, you look gorgeous," Val had said as soon as the door opened.

It had been the first time Nic had ever seen Stefani blush.

Nic took a deep breath. "I need to ask you something."

"Shoot," Stefani said, a bobby pin between her teeth.

Nic opened her mouth, but the only sound that came out was. "I...um...oh..."

"Just spit it out, girl," Val snapped.

Nic cleared her throat. "I haven't had my, uh, period. Not last month, and not this month. And I swear, I'm not pregnant. I've never even...you know... " Heat rushed to her face.

Stefani now finished, Val grabbed her dress from where it hung on the door. "Yeah, birth control will do that to you."

"Birth control?" Nic's eyes widened. "I'm not on birth control."

Stefani's purply lips parted in surprise. "Oh, sweetie, you didn't even realize, did you?"

Val scowled. "The device. They would have put it in your arm."

Nic looked at her own arm. That doctor. Those *two* injections. One the ID. The other birth control. She shivered.

"But I'm—" Nic's face was hot. "I'm not having sex. I've never even kissed someone."

Not that there had ever been any boys her own age to kiss. The only person she'd ever had a crush on—for, like, half a second— was Oliver, and he was over four times her age. And gay.

Val snorted, pulling her dress over her head. "Arcadia thinks that all teenagers are having sex."

"They're not wrong." Stefani turned her dancing eyes on Nic. "But you really should, Nic."

"Should what?"

She zipped up Val's dress, grinning at Val in the mirror. "Kiss someone. It's pretty great."

Nic rolled her eyes. *Like that's ever going to happen.*

"Anyway," Val said, stepping away from Stefani, "all girls get the birth control devices implanted when they have their first period."

Nic recoiled. "That's awful!"

"Yep." Stefani blew a bubble with her gum, filling the air with a breath of citrus. "Centuries have passed since the woman's suffrage movement, and women still can't make decisions about their own bodies."

Now wearing her short black dress with fitted, net sleeves, Val glared at herself in the mirror. Nic had gone with Val and Stefani when Val rented the dress from the make-shift dress shop the school had put up for the event, and Nic thought she looked pretty. But Val had said she looked like a bear getting ready for hibernation.

"Stop," Stefani said, taking Val's hands. "You look beautiful, Valencia."

Stefani was the *only* one Val let call her Valencia. Nic had tried it once, and the look Val had given her had made her apologize profusely.

Val's face softened for a second, and then she glanced at Nic and pulled away. "Get your eyes checked, Stef."

"I see quite clearly, thank you very much."

"But what if a woman decides she wants children?" Nic asked, getting them back on topic.

"Oh, the implant gets taken out when you turn twenty-five, and you're given a spouse." Val patted her stomach. "You have to get that old baby factory pumping out as soon as possible."

"Well, what if you *don't* want children?"

Val grunted and slipped into her black tennis shoes, hopping awkwardly to do so. "Get with the program. This is Arcadia. It doesn't matter what you want."

"It's not fair. Not having a choice." Nic shook her head. "I think that's what I hate most about Arcadia. How Arcadia destroys love."

Nic thought about Asher and Riley, who had run away when the Marriage Board refused their application to marry each other. And Oliver and Wyatt, whose love was heresy, even though they had been together since they were Nic's age.

"To love someone," Nic continued, "Like, *really* love them, and not be able to be with them—I can't imagine what that would be like."

Val and Stefani stared at each other for a long moment.

"I imagine it hurts," Stefani said softly, taking Val's hand in her own. "It really, *really* hurts."

🔥

Well, at least the punch is good, Shiloh reasoned from her place at a table set on the balcony. Down below, Gratitude Hall had been transformed into a dance floor with a—w*hat was this? A starry night theme?* A hologram of stars played across the ceiling. Fake candles flickered in their places on the honeycomb, stained glass wall at the front of the hall, scattering colors across the dance floor like a kaleidoscope.

The older Haven girls, except Val, hadn't had dates either so they asked Shiloh to go with them as a group. Shiloh had been relieved that she wouldn't be completely alone, but one by one, they had all been asked to dance and had seemed to forget Shiloh existed. Shiloh retreated to the balcony away from the embodiment of raging, teenage hormones thriving on the dance floor.

Shiloh looked away in disgust as Jake was dragged by yet another girl onto the dance floor. Was there a girl he hadn't danced with? Shiloh gulped down the rest of her punch.

A black cloud of a girl slumped into the chair two down from her. "You look like you wish there was alcohol in that, Starchild."

Shiloh blinked in surprise. "Hello, Val." Val generally didn't talk to her at all during the school year. "Why did you choose to grace me with your presence?"

Val gestured a hand at all the other occupied tables. "You're the least vile option."

"Thanks."

"Welcome." Val glared down at the dance floor, looking as miserable as Shiloh felt.

Two years ago, at their first homecoming, Val and Shiloh had sat at almost the same table, with the rest of the Haven girls who were able to attend. Only Hope had been there too, and neither she nor Val had abandoned Shiloh, even though Hope got lots of offers to dance.

But then months later, Hope was taken. After, when Val ran from the stadium, Shiloh had raced after her. She'd caught her arm, but Val had spun and slammed her fist into Shiloh's face.

"Froq you!"

Shiloh had thought it was just the pain. Pushing people away was Val and Shiloh's specialty. Shiloh had thought in time, it would blow over. But it never had.

Reaching to her thigh, Val pulled out a flask and took a deep swig. "Want some?"

"No," Shiloh said. "Where did you even get that?"

Val snorted. "Why? Going to turn me in?"

Shiloh frowned. "Of course not. I just...worry about you. I don't want to see you..." *Dragged away. Executed.*

Val stared down at the table and took another guzzle of alcohol. Shiloh's chest ached. *I miss you, Val.* She missed the girl who made snarky jokes and threatened to murder whoever had dared hurt Shiloh's feelings. Shiloh almost told her so, but she swallowed down the words.

"Just stop," Val said at last.

"Stop what?"

"Pretending you care about anyone but yourself."

"Val—" Shiloh began, but Val pushed up from the table and stormed away.

Shiloh sighed and put her head in her hands.

Jake was grateful that the dance part of Homecoming was over, and he could move on to the mandatory Senior bonfire. His feet hurt, and he didn't know how to tell any of the girls 'no' when they came batting their eyelashes. Dancing with half the girls at Ardency was what he'd done every year at homecoming, but this year it wasn't fun. Maybe because the only girl he wanted to dance with was off limits.

Jake leaned against a tree, watching the large flames lifting past the clearing in the trees and toward the hazy sky. The crowd milled around—drinking, laughing, shoving—but Jake was content to be alone, sipping on his punch. Just punch. Dr. Williams had been riding him that he was drinking too much, which meant his parents' spies were alive and well.

A laugh rang high into the air, like a bird singing through the sky. He glanced over to where Stefani was laughing with a group of the Shiny People. Jake shifted his weight uneasily as he thought of his plan. Stefani was known for certain talents, an ability to hack past the censor wall that controlled Arcadia's internet access. Rumor was, she'd loan the services out, if you could pay enough. Arcadia could hide the truth within their walls, but they couldn't touch what was outside of it.

But there was no guarantee she'd help him, or that she wouldn't write it in her gossip section: *JACOB OSGOOD TURNS HERETIC.* He couldn't approach her unless he came armed.

So he'd been watching Stefani, trying to scoop the ultimate gossip. Tonight, Stefani had danced with different guys, but always wandered back to one person. The girl with the dagger eyes he'd seen in the cafeteria. Jake had seen the look they gave each other when they thought no one else was watching. Jake recognized that look.

The look of wanting something you couldn't have.

"Marcus." Jake tapped his friend's shoulder, interrupting his flirting with a girl. "Do you know who that girl is over there?" Jake pointed. "With Stefani Andreou."

Marcus frowned and then laughed. "Her? That's Val Haven."

"Val Haven?" Jake repeated. *Shiloh's Val.* The best friend she had lost when she lost Hope. His tie was suddenly strangling him, and he yanked the knot loose.

"Yeah, she's a Junior, so she shouldn't really be here. I

wouldn't try with her, though, mate. She'll cut your dick off. She's a bit of a heifer, anyway."

She absolutely wasn't, but Marcus had been an especially large prig since he'd had his endsphere handed to him by a little girl. Jake had been avoiding Marcus a lot since then, going to the same parties, but trying to create distance. Without fail, every time Jake was near Marcus, Jake found himself wanting to re-break Marcus's nose.

It was yet another reminder of why Jake wanted to change, why he should never have let himself fall back into this old pattern. But in order to move forward, he needed the truth.

Even though his tie was loose, Jake still felt like he was being strangled. Could he really follow through with his plan? What choice did he have, if he wanted to get the truth without involving Nicolette?

Her eyes on him were like a physical touch, and Jake turned. Through the flames of the bonfire, he saw Shiloh, the red streaks of light making her eyes spark even from this distant.

Council help me, she looks beautiful.

She wore a light blue, off the shoulder dress that ended at her knees. Jake let his eyes trace the lines of her shoulders, her collarbones, her legs that bore the scars that should have been his. Every nerve in his body hummed with electricity at the sight of her. Would he ever stop feeling this way?

She met his eyes too, and Jake stopped breathing. He could feel it, the air crackling between them like oncoming lightning. There was still something there. There had to be. And if there was even a flicker of a chance she felt something for him, then Jake had to know. Even if she broke his heart again.

So, when Shiloh walked into the woods, Jake followed.

🔥

Shiloh weaved through the trees, the laughter and hollering of the bonfire fading away, leaving behind only rustling winds and singing crickets. Then a deep sigh echoed through the air.

Shiloh ducked behind a tree. Glancing around the trunk, Shiloh saw a couple entwined together within the needles of a pine tree, curtained but still visible. They kissed with a heated passion, a white dress molding into a black dress. Shiloh's chest tightened. These reckless girls could be caught and sent to a Reform Home.

The majority of the Reform Homes—which were meant to rehabilitate citizens who'd gone astray—were filled with individuals just like these girls, condemned for loving the wrong person. For being something different. The Reform Home's methods for correcting their natural desires made Haven punishments seem mild.

The couple turned slightly, and Shiloh clamped her mouth shut against a gasp.

Val.

It'd always been so, so obvious to Shiloh that Val didn't like boys, but it'd taken Val's years to admit it even to herself. The look on Val's face—as she'd confessed to Shiloh and Hope that she was something this world would never accept—had crushed Shiloh's soul. But *this* was still reckless.

Please be careful, Val.

Shiloh hurried past them and stumbled down the hill toward the trail in her ballet flats, rocks and twigs stabbing at her heels. Whoever decided that bonfires in the woods went with girls wearing dresses and fancy shoes was insane. She followed the trail another half mile when it abruptly disappeared into the inlet of the lake.

Shiloh slipped out of her shoes and stepped into the frigid water, onto the bridge that was submerged beneath. On the other side, she slipped her shoes back on and padded up the hill. The old, brick chapel's steeple had long since crumpled, and Shiloh had to squeeze through boards that blocked the door. Stained glass windows stood like wounded guards on each wall. Gaping holes and cracks marred their beauty, except for the large circular window up front, which was intact. Its yellow star cast a magical glow around the room.

Shiloh inhaled deeply, searching for the peace she'd once known here. This was where she, Val, and Hope had felt the safest. No one really came here, so they'd felt free to just *be*.

Now she was alone.

"Hey, Shi."

Her rebel heart jumped as she turned to take Jake in. He gazed back at her in that familiar way that stole the air from her lungs: like she was all he could see.

"You look really beautiful," he said.

Shiloh struggled to breathe. It was torture looking at him, handsome in his suit, even now with his loosened tie and untucked shirt. Simultaneously, her chest flooded with warmth and a hand clamped around her throat. She and Jake were far away from public areas. If someone were to look at their trackers, they'd see them together.

"What are you doing here, Jake?" she demanded finally.

"I'm sorry." He shoved his hands deep into his pockets. "I know you've been perfectly clear that you don't want anything to do with me, but I can't let things end like they did the other day. I can't leave it with you believing that I don't care about you."

He walked toward her slowly, like trying not to startle a wild animal, but she couldn't run. She was cemented to the floor.

"And I owe you an answer," Jake continued. "The other day, you asked me what I wanted, and I hesitated, because I didn't want you to reject me again. But I need to tell you." The moonlight pouring through the windows painted blues and yellows across his cheekbones as he stopped before her. "The answer to that question is *you*."

I can't...I can't breathe.

"I want you." He brushed a lock of hair behind her ear. Oh,

how she'd missed his touch. It felt like breaking from the surface of deep water, inhaling when she thought she might drown.

"Shi, I want you more than I've wanted anything. And I am so sorry that I ever made you doubt that. I'm sorry for that horrible thing that I said to you."

Shiloh finally retreated a step, folding her arms across her chest, a barrier between them. "Jake, how am I supposed to believe that? You've had a different girl on your arm every day."

"I know. I'm such a froqing idiot." Jake threw his hands in the air. "But please, believe me, I am *so sorry*. You broke my heart that day under the bleachers, and I've never had my heart broken...ever. So I immediately jumped back into being my stupid self, who I hate. And I'm not blaming you. It's my own stupid fault. I did it because it was easy. Easier than trying to be better. Easier than facing the pain of losing you. And by doing that, I hurt you, didn't I?"

Shiloh pressed her eyes closed, and he must have taken that as a 'yes', because he inhaled so sharply it almost sounded like a sob. "I *never* wanted to hurt you."

He *had* hurt her. She'd given him that power, and no matter how she'd tried to take it back, it still hurt.

His fingers caressed against her cheek again. "Look at me."

Shiloh forced her eyes open. Even in the dark, his eyes seemed bright.

"I can't believe that what happened to us didn't mean anything to you. I don't know why you pushed me away, but I was an idiot to let you go. And I swear, if you give me another chance, I will spend every day proving how deeply I care about you."

She shouldn't believe him, but she did. The truth was written beautifully across his face.

He looked down at his feet, glancing up at her through his lashes. "But what do you want, Shi?" he asked, his voice a whisper.

Shiloh *wanted* to cry.

She *wanted* to throw her arms around Jake and never let go.

She *wanted* to not feel like the Elite's hand was still crushing her throat.

She *wanted* everything to be different.

Shiloh whirled away from him and paced toward the circular window. The yellow swirled with the surrounding blue as her cheeks grew wet.

This is killing me.

"Shiloh, please say something."

Shiloh felt the hand tighten around her throat. Well, if the lies hadn't worked to make him go away, maybe the truth would.

"Of course, it meant something." Shiloh sank onto the wide ledge of the window, facing him. It was a relief to finally say it. "*Of course,* I have feelings for you. Sometimes I wish I didn't, but I do."

Jake's mouth parted. He sat on the ledge beside her, reaching toward her. Shiloh set a hand on his chest, holding him back.

"But it doesn't matter."

"How can it not matter if we both feel this way."

"Jake, there's a reason I pushed you away. Maybe I went about this the wrong way, but think about it. Play it out in your head." Unable to look at him, she watched a moonbeam chasing across the floor, shadows from the trees outside swaying within. Though the wind that whispered through the chapel wasn't cool, Shiloh was frozen to her very core. "Your parents don't want us to be together, so how would we even make this work? And even, say we can find a way to be together. Then what? Next year we'll be sent to two different colleges halfway across Arcadia. And just for the sake of argument, if we survived long enough to apply to marry each other, do you think they would *ever* let a Haven girl marry you?"

She peeked up at him, framed by the colors of the stain glass like a prince on a glorious throne. "You...you're going to be the next Councilor."

Jake's hand tightened on hers. "You know that's *not* what I want! That's never been what I wanted."

"What *we* want?" Shiloh scoffed. "It doesn't matter what we want. We serve at the pleasure of Arcadia. We're just a piece in their games; that's it."

"No!"

The word echoed like a battle-cry across the room. Jake took a breath and lowered his voice. "If this summer taught me anything, it's that there are some things worth fighting for." Jake slid his hand to the back of her head, tenderly, lovingly. "If you're not, I don't know what is."

With the hand on the back of her head, Jake guided her mouth to his. *Pull away,* Shiloh told herself, but her stubborn lips responded to his. His arm wrapped around her, pulling her closer, until no space lingered between them. She wanted to stay here forever, wanted to memorize the way his warmth chased away the chill in her bones, the way his sweet lips sighed her name like poetry. But...no, this kiss wasn't sweet. It was salty, tainted by her tears.

He tasted like goodbye.

Shiloh pulled away with a gasp, her chest aching.

"Please, Jake. Stop. You're making this so much harder." Shiloh shoved to her feet and backed away from him. "You know I'm right. We are *impossible*. Arcadia will *never* let us be together."

Jake pressed the heels of his hands into his eyes, and when he dropped them, his eyes blared red, and his voice dripped with venom. "I've forgiven my dad for so much. But I'm not going to forgive him for this. Not for taking you away from me."

Shiloh took another step back to the door, but it still felt undone. "Jake, I need you to tell me this is over. I can't keep fighting with you. It's too hard."

He sucked in a trembling breath. From this distance, his face was concealed in darkness, but she was certain he was crying. "Okay. Okay." He buried his face in his hands, so the next words were muffled. "It's over."

A sob built in Shiloh's chest, and she rushed for the door. But something made her turn back. "Jake."

He dropped his hands.

"If you want to be different, *be different*. I've seen the guy you can be behind this playboy mask. And...he's pretty amazing."

Shiloh hurried toward the door. Before she left, he asked one more question, his voice weak.

"Shi, if things were different...if we lived in a different nation, or I wasn't an Osgood...would you be with me?"

Shiloh couldn't bring herself to look back at him. "There's a world where you and I could be together, but it's not this world."

And then she ran.

EIGHTEEN

"Okay, Jakey-boy, this better be good," Stefani said as she panted, climbing up the slope to where Jake stood near the site of last night's bonfire. "Why did you tell me to meet you all the way out in the woods? You're not going to murder me, are you?"

Jake shook his head. "Not today."

"Thank the Council, because this" —She gestured at her uniform, which she wore the correct way— "is a terrible outfit to be found murdered in. At least, my hair looks fabulous." She tossed her head to exhibit, purple strands flying.

"I'll keep that in mind if I decide to murder you in the future."

"Please do." Hands on her hip, she looked him up and down. "What happened to you? You look like a swamp creature had a love child with a dehydrated zombie."

If that meant he looked like ordure, she was probably right. His eyes ached, and his head throbbed. After the chapel, he'd gone straight to his bed, alone and sober, but he'd found no comfort there. Especially when Harper came banging on his door, and he'd told her they were over. Shiloh was right. If Jake wanted to be different, he had to choose to be different.

After Harper slapped him and stormed away, all that was left was nightmares, impossible wishes, and anger that roared in Jake's chest. He'd meant what he'd told Shiloh; he would never forgive Arcadia or his father for this. Which was why he needed to find the truth about ROGUE, a way to fight back.

"Thanks," Jake said sarcastically.

"Another bender?" Stefani clicked her tongue disapprovingly. "Jakey-boy, you are positively made of bad coping skills. Have you ever tried therapy? All those booze and girls are definitely not solving your daddy issues."

"I didn't ask you here to psychoanalyze me, Stef."

There was someone already making big money to do that. Dr. Williams had texted him just this morning, checking in, and he'd told her how he'd stayed sober at homecoming. She'd been, oh, so proud.

"Okay, okay." Stefani clapped her hands. "What do you need my assistance for?"

Jake leaned against the trunk of the tree next to him, trying to betray an easiness he didn't feel. "Rumor is that you're very handy at getting information that people want."

"Mm." Stefani twirled a strand of hair around her finger. "If that's true—*if*—I need to say up front that my services are not cheap."

"I can pay."

"I'm sure you can." She studied him for a moment. "Okay, I'll bite. What do you want?"

"I want you to get me past the censor wall in the internet."

"Why?"

Jake folded his arms over his chest. "That's for me to know."

Stefani wagged her finger, smirking. "Oh, no, no, Jakey-boy. See the way this works is that you tell me what you want to know, or you hop and skip your fine little endsphere away. Mmkay, pumpkin?"

"Fine." Jake gritted his teeth. "I want to research rebel activity in Arcadia."

Stefani let out a staccato laugh that startled a bird out of a nearby tree. "I'm *sooorryyy*. Why in Arcadia's butthole would you want to do that? And what rebel activity?"

"Don't play dumb. It's not a cute look on you. You know exactly what happened at the Cleansing. That's why you came sniffing around the first day of school."

Stefani's mask of calm cracked, and she glared at him. "Have you gone out of your froqing mind? Did you get brain damage in that fire? If the United Council is trying to keep something secret, it's dangerous to uncover it."

"Are you going to help me or not?"

Stefani scoffed. "Forget it. I don't know what game you're playing at, but I'm not getting involved in heresy with the son of a Councilor. I do *not* have a death wish." She turned around and stalked back down the slope.

Jake steeled himself, his fingernails digging into his palm. "Stefani, I know about your girlfriend."

She spun back around. "Come again?"

Jake swallowed the sour taste of self-loathing and kept his voice steady. "Your girlfriend. I saw you two together last night."

She narrowed her eyes, and a sweat beaded at the back of Jake's neck. Stefani was bubblegum and cotton candy, mixed with a little burn of whiskey. Seeing her angry was like seeing a favorite family pet turn rabid. You weren't quite sure what they were capable of.

"So what?" Stefani snapped. "The rumors about my sexuality have been going around since fifth grade. It doesn't matter. My mom wouldn't let anything happen to me based on the rumors. You know as well as I do that the rules don't apply if your parent is powerful."

"Maybe not. But it would matter for *her*."

"What do you mean?"

"Val. She's a Haven girl, isn't she? I'm pretty sure my word would be all it took to convince them about her indiscretions."

It was a bluff. Jake would *never* turn them in, but he needed to make Stefani believe he would. Still, the threat scorched his tongue like acid.

"Osgood, you son of a blight!"

Jake jumped at the bite in her words. *Froq.* He'd misjudged this. Stefani had a reputation more liberal than his. Boys. Girls. She was down for a good time. But this was different. He could read it in the blaze in her eyes. Stefani *loved* this girl. Deep, powerful, would-kill-for-if-she-had-to, *loved her.*

"Fine, I'll help you!" She stalked forward, and Jake braced himself for a punch in the throat, like he deserved. She only rammed a finger into his chest. "But I'm warning you, pretty boy. I'm going to make you regret this."

Too late. I already regret this.

After practice, Coach Bradshaw told Nic to hurry in the shower, because Principal Clark had requested to see her. Waves of dread tossed Nic's stomach as she showered and dressed. Nic stared wearily at the double doors of Principal Clark's office before finally knocking

The principal opened the door quickly. Nic had only seen Principal Clark from a distance at the weekly Assemblies, where she challenged the students to be better citizens. Up close, her face looked deceptively young, and her green eyes appeared vibrant.

"Thank you for coming, Ms. Haven," she said with an overly cheerful voice, holding the door wide. "Come in."

The office gleamed of rich mahogany wood from the bookshelves along the back wall to the massive desk. On the right, windows overlooked the rippling gray waters of Lake Harmony. On the left, hologrammed pictures showed former students who were now award-winning doctors, Olympic athletes, or State Advocates—the legacies of Ardency.

"Please have a seat."

Nic perched on the edge of a high-backed, leather chair, her muscles coiled.

"Would you like a drink?" Principal Clark asked, but she was already at the bar, popping open a colorful can that hissed as it opened. She poured the dark bubbly liquid into a glass with ice and handed it to Nic.

Nic took a careful sip and recognized the sharp, sugary taste. When was the last time she'd had pop? Her ninth birthday, maybe...

Principal Clark sat behind her desk. "I wanted to see how you are settling in."

Nic twirled her glass, the ice tinkling. "I'm fine."

The principal folded her hands on top of the desk. "I can appreciate how difficult this must all be for you, and I'm impressed with how well you are doing. I'm very sorry to hear that some students have given you a hard time. I promise you that I, and the other professors, are working to put a stop to it."

Nic resisted the urge to snort. So far, the professors had only been good at looking the other way.

Principal Clark tapped the surface of her desk, and the outline of a keyboard glowed in the surface. A hologram screen appeared in the air, but from Nic's angle, it was blank.

"Coach Bradshaw says you're quite an athlete," the principal said. "Do you enjoy running?"

"Yes."

"Good, good. Coach Bradshaw thinks you could have a bright future and recommended you for an Athletic Track. Your grades will need some improvement, of course, but nothing that we can't help you with. You could end up on this wall of mine." She swept her hand toward the holograms. "You could travel across the world competing."

Nic's heart jumped in her chest. All her life Nic had only seen one destiny: to be a soldier of ROGUE and to fight against Arcadia. But the vision of something else teased her brain like an unfamiliar lullaby. Seeing the world, running races. A life of hot showers and never wondering where her next meal was coming from. It seemed too good to be true.

Because of course, it wouldn't be true. She'd have to hide her faith and be a slave to the Council's will. A life in Arcadia was not freedom—it was a wider cage. But there were, Nic knew, far worse cages.

"Of course, incidents like what happened with Mr. Brawler can absolutely not happen again. You have shown many qualities of being a shining example of an Arcadian citizens. Hard work. Perseverance. Strength. But we must also see continued improvement in devotion. Tranquility. Cooperation."

Nic's fingers tightened on her glass. The word 'cooperation' strangled her like a noose tightening around her neck. No, not a noose. The fingers of an Elite.

"Are you ready to cooperate, Nicolette?"

Clark leaned forward and met Nic's eyes. "If you can demonstrate that your loyalty now rests with Arcadia, you can be on the Athletic Track."

Nic saw it so clearly now. What had #767 said? *"We'll show you what Arcadia has to offer."* Torture hadn't convinced Nic to give up her secrets, so maybe bribery would.

Nic sipped her pop, buying time. Saying 'no' would mean death. But all Nic could see reflected in her glass were Mom, Paul, and all the others who would be dead if she gave in.

And then Nic thought about Esther, her favorite bible story, about a queen given an impossible choice between her own survival or saving her people. *And if I perish, I perish.*

"Miss Haven?" Principal Clark pressed. "What do you think about that?"

Nic finished the rest of her drink, stood, and set the empty glass on the desk. "No, thank you."

The pleasant look on the principal's face faded.

Nic gave a sweet, little smile. "I'm not an athlete, Principal Clark. I'm a soldier."

"Miss Haven, I think you're making a—"

"Will that be all?" Nic interrupted.

Clark leaned back in her chair, a dark cloud settling over her countenance. "Yes, you're dismissed."

"Thank you for your time."

Nic walked away, making sure that her back was straight and her chin was lifted, like a queen. When Nic was outside in the empty hallway, she collapsed against the wall and hid her face in her hands.

How long would it be before the Elite came and dragged her away?

Sweat dripped down Shiloh's spine as she climbed the steps to her dorm room. Her limp had reappeared in the last mile of her cross-country run, and she ached with each step. Since her dorm had a semi-private bathroom, Shiloh always preferred it to using the locker room after practice. Her roommate, Josephine, had a demanding schedule, so Shiloh wasn't surprised when she found the room empty.

Shiloh tossed her bag on her bed and started to lift her sweaty tank top from her body.

A hand clamped over her mouth.

She screamed, the sound muffled. The hand yanked her back against a solid form, and arm cinched around her, pinning her arms to her side.

"Shh, shh, shh," hissed a voice at her ear. "I'm going to let you go, but you have to promise you won't scream."

Shiloh's blood turned to ice. She knew that voice. It had haunted her since the night she'd woken with this Elite's hand crushing her throat.

"If you scream, I'll hurt you. Do you understand?"

She nodded.

He released her, and she stumbled away, whirling around and backing up. Her hips bumped into her desk, knocking over the hot-air balloon statue that Jake had painted in the hospital. The Elite stood between her and the doorway, a faceless black figure. His dark visor reflected Shiloh's own look of terror.

He settled into Josephine's desk chair and gestured for her to sit. She didn't budge. The blood pounded in her ears as though it was crying out.

"Shiloh, sit down."

Somehow his voice portrayed gentleness and a threat all at once. She sat and gasped for breath. Even though he wasn't touching her, she still felt strangled.

The Elite held up a hand. "Relax. I'm just here to talk."

He leaned forward, and she could see the white numbers on his chest. Elite #767. *Him.*

She could see it clearly, the same gun that hung on his hip pressed into the head of her sister. Heat crackled beneath her skin; her shaking stilled. She felt a little less afraid, when she was angry.

"What—" Shiloh's voice broke. She ground her hands together, and the next time, her voice was steady. "What do you want to talk about?"

"About your ability to serve Arcadia farther." He leaned back in the chair and drummed his fingers against the desk. "You know, I'm quite impressed with you. I wasn't convinced you'd be able to pull it off."

He pulled a small disc from a pouch on his hip, next to his electric prod and his gun. He pressed the button, and a hologram of Jake and Shiloh beneath the bleachers the first day of school cast into the air. The cameras around campus were old, catching only freeze frames, but this was live action and sharp, like the Elite had installed a camera just for this.

"It wasn't meaningless to me," Jake said on the camera.

"Well, it was to me."

A wave of pain crashed over Shiloh, and she held her breath until it receded. The Elite clapped slowly.

"That boy is tenacious, but you played that well. Then there was the matter of your trackers being together at that old chapel at homecoming." The Elite cocked his head side to side and paused for a long second. He must enjoy building the suspense, watching her squirm. "But then I reviewed the cameras around campus."

The Elite clicked the button again and revealed a freeze-frame of Jake, presumably taken from the Quadrangle on his way back to the dorm. His head was bent low, his hands scrubbing at his eyes.

"The poor boy," the Elite said, with a whine of sympathy. "You must have *crushed* him. You, Shiloh, have turned out to be a loyal Arcadian, and I must say, quite the little actress. And that—" The Elite leaned forward in the chair. "—is why you're so useful to me."

Shiloh dug her nails deeper into her palm. "What do you want?"

His tone took on a more solemn note. "Nicolette has information that we want. We have tried multiple means of persuasion to get it from her."

I bet you did. Thinking of the bruises which had been painted over Nic's body, Shiloh's anger flared.

"But she's a stubborn girl. She'll never give us what we want, but she might open up to someone she trusts."

That's me.

Shiloh swallowed. "What do you need from her?"

"She has an intimate knowledge of a network of rebels called ROGUE. You and Jake heard of it, of course. It stands for Rebel Organizations against Government in United Efforts." He twirled his hand in the air, like swatting a fly. "Or something ridiculous like that."

Jake had been right all along. There were rebels fighting back, but Arcadia had buried the truth. If people knew others were fighting, perhaps they would find the courage to fight too. And Arcadia couldn't risk that.

Truth is dangerous.

"Nicolette knows things—how they communicate, leaders in the group. And let's just say I would" —the smile in his voice was clear— "*kill* for that information."

Shiloh shivered. "I've barely spoken to Nic since we got to school." She'd only checked in with her a couple times, just enough to make sure she was okay. "She isn't going to trust me."

"Then *make* her trust you." Elite #767 stood, and every muscle in Shiloh's body tensed. "You will find out all you can about what she knows about ROGUE." He took a step toward her, his shadow covering her. "Don't let me down. Do I need to explain what will happen if you do?"

Shiloh shook her head. He'd made it quite clear the last time. But this was more than breaking her heart. This was helping the Elite to bring down the people that were fighting for what was right, for freedom. This was sentencing a fourteen-year-old girl to death, because as soon as the Elite didn't need Nic anymore, they would kill her.

I won't do this.

"You'll put me on a Laborer Track?" Shiloh questioned, staring at her feet. That cost didn't seem worth it anymore.

"Maybe." He paused. "Or maybe I'll execute you like I executed your sister."

The world spun around Shiloh. *No, no, no.*

"So, I'll ask you again, Shiloh. Are you going to be a good, little girl?"

I can't do this.

But what choice did she have? Rule #1. Survive. No matter the cost. She could refuse, but then she'd die, and the Elite would probably kill Nic, anyway.

Unable to stand her own reflection in his visor, Shiloh pressed her eyes closed. *Cold, heartless blight.* "Yes."

"Yes, *sir*," he corrected.

"Yes, sir."

He patted her head, like the lapdog she was. "Good girl."

PART THREE

GOOD GIRL

"The choice that frees or imprisons us
is the choice of love or fear.
Love liberates. Fear imprisons."

- Gary Zukav

NINETEEN

It'd been five days, and so far, no Elite had come to drag Nic away. Which meant that they still had other things planned —and also, unfortunately, meant that Nic would still have to do her schoolwork. At the moment, she wasn't quite sure that was preferable.

Nic stared down at her tablet, wanting to scream in frustration. No matter how many times she worked the figures, she never got them right. Val and Stefani both shied away from math like it was the plague, so they weren't any help.

Nic attempted another problem. The tablet screen flashed red. Wrong Answer. Nic groaned and dropped her forehead onto the library table.

"You okay?"

Nic looked up to find Shiloh beside her. She did this sometimes, checked in with Nic to make sure she was okay.

"Yeah, I'm fine," Nic said. "I just hate math. Or it hates me."

"Maybe both?" Shiloh let her satchel slide to the floor and slipped into the chair across from her. "Let me see. I'm pretty good at math."

"Val said you are stupid smart." Even though Nic wasn't sure Val meant it as a compliment, Nic handed Shiloh the tablet.

Shiloh pulled her own stylus from her bag and studied her work for a second. "Here. Try it like this."

Shiloh activated the hologram so Nic could watch her as she wrote. She talked her through step-by-step and made it look easy. Nic tried a few of the next practice problems and only got half of them right. But that was better than none.

"You'll get the hang of it," Shiloh said.

Nic nodded. "Thanks."

"Are you doing okay? In your other classes?"

"Not really." Nic's heart flared with hope. "Can you help me?"

Shiloh's stared down at the table for a long moment, like she hadn't heard. Nic opened her mouth, but Shiloh finally spoke, "Yeah, I'll help you."

"You will?" Nic almost hugged her, but stopped just in time. "Thank you!"

"Please." Shiloh gave her a tight smile. "Don't even mention it."

The door of the *Ardency Times* slammed shut behind Jake, and the sound exploded in the silence of the office. Enough time had gone by since Jake had threatened Stefani in the woods, that he'd thought she was calling his bluff. But a few days ago, she'd sent him a message. Stefani needed to use an actual computer and not a tablet. The one she had access to was in the office of the *Ardency Times*. It was a busy place, but in the early Saturday morning hours, they'd have their opportunity.

Jake searched the cubicles. A hand with orange fingernails shot above one white wall. He found Stefani leaning in a chair, her feet propped up on the desk.

"Hey there, prighead."

"Hey, Stef," Jake said.

She kicked her feet off the desk and stood, gesturing for him to sit. The computer screen was already up.

"It's waiting for you," she said, as Jake sat. "Search away."

"That's it? You're through the censor wall."

"Yep." Stefani blew a bubble with her gum. "You've got thirty minutes, prighead. Make them count."

Jake began typing on the surface of the desk, using his carefully thought-out search words. An eNews website out of London had published an article on the Cleansing, but it stuck to the cover story—a mere freak fire. Other than that, he found a steaming hot pile of nothing. Searching ROGUE only brought up the dictionary definition, and 'rebels in Arcadia' took him to a porn site he really wished he could unsee.

Jake spun his chair around. Stefani was supposed to be the lookout, but instead she laid on the floor with headphones in, her hands dancing to the music.

"Have any suggestions?" Jake asked.

She pulled out an earbud. "What?"

"Do you have any suggestions?"

"Oh." She pursed her lips as though thinking, and then, "Nope." She stuck the bud back in. "Ten minutes."

With a growl of frustration, Jake kept searching. How deep was Arcadia's control that even foreign media stuck to their lies?

Stefani made a ding like a timer going off and climbed off the floor. "You have now reached your final destination. Please pay the toll and watch your step on the way out."

Froq! Jake opened his mouth to protest, but the office door banged open, and students entered, jabbering like birds. Stefani leaned around him, and with a few taps, the screen disappeared from the air.

Stefani lowered her voice as the other students wondered toward their own cubicles. "That will be 100 rations."

She hadn't been joking when she'd said her services didn't

come cheap. Gritting his teeth, Jake dragged his ration card out of his pocket, and she swept it over her personal phone. He'd have to come up with a really good lie for what he'd spent those rations on. Dad would certainly notice.

Stefani directed him to the door and followed behind him like a sentry. Something nagged at the back of his mind as she yanked the door open.

Jake kept his voice low. "Stefani, how is it possible that I found nothing? There *had* to have been something."

Stefani shrugged her shoulders as he stepped outside. "How should I know?"

But her smile widened, and Jake stiffened. *Wait...*

"And, uh," Stefani said, "don't take this personally, but I hope you get trampled by a thousand wild horses, and the buzzards feast on your corpse. Bye, babe!"

She slammed the door in his face.

Jake groaned. *Idiot!* He'd never actually *seen* her take down the censor wall. He'd bluffed her, in the most horrible of ways, but she'd done him one better.

Well played, Stef. Well played.

The tracker beeped a warning, and Nic halted. She searched the vast prairie before her, overgrown and damp. More dense woods guarded the prairie's other side. This school truly was secluded.

Since she'd completed her Saturday detentions, Nic had decided to explore the school grounds, learning the territory for when she finally escaped. She'd been out here for hours, exploring the miles of lands and woods within school boundaries. Her next activity wasn't scheduled for a while, so she had a little more time. She returned to the trail around Lake Harmony and followed it to see how far it went.

The trail ended abruptly in a narrow cove of water. On the

other side, red brick peered through thick foliage. Nic stripped off her footwear and skipped across on the submerged bridge.

Her breath caught as she took in the building, the remnants of a church. She slipped through the boards at the entrance and froze to take in the wonder. Even in its abandonment, this place was beautiful. And sacred. For the first time in a long time, a familiar peace flowed across her heart, like cool water trickling down a scorched throat.

"God, is that you?" she prayed. "It's me, Nic."

"Nope," said a voice, "just Jake."

Nic jumped. She hadn't seen the figure sitting in the far corner until she took another step into the chapel. *Idiot.* That sort of carelessness could get a soldier killed. Maybe it *would* get her killed, because Jacob Osgood had just seen her praying.

Osgood climbed to his feet. Nic's heart slammed against her rib cage, and her hand fell to her side, fingers aching for the steel of her gun.

"Are you going to report me?" Nic demanded.

Osgood smiled and shook his head. "Nope."

Nic snorted. Like she'd believe that. "Why not?" Since she had no gun, she settled for curling her hand into a fist.

He shrugged. "Because I don't believe you should be punished for what you believe in."

Nic's mouth dropped open. What was he saying? First, Osgood stood up for her, then he gave her chocolate, and now he was spewing heresy. This had to be an Elite trap. To get her to trust someone, let her guard down. But why would they use a Councilor's son, her enemy?

Her tracker beeped at her, a twenty-minute warning. If she didn't want to get a citation for being late, she'd need to leave right now and run back to campus. But she was fixed in place.

"Why are you being kind to me?"

Osgood let out a breath and ran a hand through his hair. "Maybe because you deserve kindness. Maybe, because I'm sick of all the terrible things my family has done, and I want to atone for it. Or maybe—"

He stopped, his eyes searching around the room. Sunbeams shifted in patterns on the leaf-strewn floor. The wind snuck through the cracks in the window, stirring Nic's hair, seeming to whisper ancient secrets. His fists opened and closed, opened and closed, and then he made a sound like giving in to something he shouldn't.

"Maybe," he said, "because your mom saved my life."

Nic forgot how to breathe. "What?"

"At the Cleansing." Jake fidgeted, hesitating between each sentence. "I got shot. We were hiding, and your mom, Amelia, found us and gave us a first aid kit. I would have bled out if it wasn't for that."

Nic had no words, no thoughts, just the sound of her heart hammering in her ears.

Osgood took a step toward her, and he was close. Too close. "Nicolette, listen—" He reached toward her.

Nic didn't think. She seized his wrist and twisted, jerking his arm behind his back and slamming him against the wall. He swore beneath his breath as she used her other hand to pin his head in place.

"Okay, okay, easy," he said.

"Why should I even trust you?" Nic asked through her teeth.

"You probably shouldn't. I probably wouldn't if I were you."

Nic's fingers tightened on his wrist, and he hissed in pain.

"I know you have no reason to believe me, but I just want to help you," Osgood said, "like your mother helped me."

Maybe, he was a good actor, but so far, he was only giving her information that would get him in trouble. She released him and stepped back cautiously.

He turned around, rubbing his red wrist. "Froq. Remind me never to get on your bad side."

"How do you even know who my mom is, J-" Nic struggled. What did she call him? "Jake?"

"I saw the information on one of my dad's files. I saw you too."

"When?"

"Back in June, shortly after the Cleansing. But after...after the Elite had you."

Nic shivered at the reminder. So, he'd known who she was all along. Still, he'd defended her. Still, he'd been kind.

Nic studied him, gnawing the inside of her cheek, and then her tracker wailed again. "Darn it! I've got to go."

She had so many more questions for him, but she was gaining more citations by the minute. She dragged herself to the door.

"Hey, Nicolette!"

She twisted around.

"Your mom made it out of the Cleansing alive."

A cry of relief left her lips, and she threw a hand over her mouth to silence it. "You're sure?" she mumbled behind her hand.

He nodded. "When I saw that file, her location was unknown. I don't know what has happened since, but at that time, she was alive and free."

She's alive. Nic pressed fingers to her lips to hold back a laugh. *Thank you, God! She's alive!*

"I have more that I can tell you," Jake said. "Can you meet me here? On Friday? After dinner?"

She hesitated for a moment, weighing her options, then nodded.

"And Nicolette," he continued, "this *must* stay between us."

In his eyes, she saw true worry. This wasn't an Elite trap—they would never have wanted her to know her mother was alive. This was the son of a Councilor committing heresy.

"You can call me Nic," she said, deciding to take a chance on him. "And your secret is safe with me."

TWENTY

Having a 6:30 a.m. Advanced Physics class had never bothered Shiloh before, but then she stopped sleeping. She laid awake at night, her mind spinning like a top, and when she slept, she dreamed of hands around her throat and a black sack over Nic's head. The desire to protect Nic was constantly fighting with the need to survive. There had to be a way to do both, but that would require her to be brave enough to defy the Elite. And she didn't feel brave; she felt like a coward.

A message appeared on Shiloh's tablet, interrupting her nonsensical note-taking,

WHAT INFORMATION DO YOU HAVE FOR ME?

She typed a response with unsteady fingers. *NOTHING YET.*

HOW DISAPPOINTING.

Shiloh shivered and pulled her jacket more tightly around her. She didn't have information because she hadn't really tried. The Elite made her wear an audio recorder on her bra at all times, so when she tutored Nic, she'd made sure to say the right things, but she hadn't really pressed. How long until the Elite figured that out?

Then fifteen minutes later, another message came. *MEET ME. YOUR ROOM. NOW.*

Shiloh's throat began to close. Her class wouldn't even be done for another fifteen minutes, and then she would have to rush to Advanced Technologies.

Another message: *BE A GOOD GIRL AND HURRY.*

Shiloh raised her hand.

Professor Murray paused. "Yes, Ms. Haven?"

"Professor Murray, I'm not feeling very well. May I be excused to see the nurse?"

Murray frowned. Students often made excuses to get out of class, but never her. "All right, Ms. Haven." He tapped his tablet so the tracker would know where she was going.

She grabbed her things and hurried from the classroom. The clinic was in the second floor of the Quadrangle, and her dorm was in between. When she reached the door to her room, she really did feel like she might vomit.

Her tracker was beeping a steady warning. She wasn't where she was supposed to be. Its shrill noise matched the erratic beat of her heart. *Breathe in, breathe out.* She glued her calm mask in place and entered.

The Elite was stretched out on her bed, his hands behind his head like he'd been there a while. He sat up and swung his legs off the bed. "That was fast. Good girl."

A sour taste rose in her throat. It tasted like hate.

He pulled his tablet from his pocket and hit a button. Shiloh's tracker went silent. "Sit," he said, patting the bed beside him.

Shiloh lowered herself down stiffly. Her hair stood on end, like a cat faced with a ravenous dog.

"I'm very disappointed that you've made no progress with Nic," he said. "What do you have to say for yourself?"

"I've been trying," Shiloh said, her voice flat. "You have the recordings so you know I have been. It's going to take time to win her trust."

He struck as swiftly as a snake, his open palm slamming into her cheek. She cried out, then bit her lip to cut off the sound.

"I'm not a very patient person," he said levelly.

Shiloh fought to still her trembling—this certainly wasn't the first time she'd ever been slapped—but she couldn't rid her voice of its quiver. "I just need more time. It will take a lot of time."

He seized her throat, so tightly her vision immediately tinted with black. "You must have *something* for me."

She couldn't breathe. *Don't tell him.*

"Well?"

His fingers tightened. *He's going to kill me.*

Shiloh forced words up her throat. "I saw her with Jacob Osgood."

He released so abruptly she tumbled off the edge of the bed and landed on the floor. He lifted his tablet from where he'd left it on the bed beside him. "When was this?"

Shut up! But it was already too late.

"Three days ago," Shiloh said, pushing to her feet.

She'd gone to the chapel to study, hoping to find peace there, and instead caught a glimpse of Jake and Nic through the windows. She'd ran back down the trail, before their voices could reach her—and the audio recorder could catch whatever they were talking about.

"Three days?" #767 stood. "*Why* didn't you tell me?"

Because she'd been determined that she wouldn't bring Jake into this. But her resolve had broken with a hand on her throat.

Coward.

"I didn't think it was worth mentioning," Shiloh lied. "I didn't hear anything they were saying."

Froq it, Jake! If he'd just stayed away from Nic like he'd promised...

"Well, well, well, that naughty boy." #767 clucked his tongue. "Here he made it seem like he was going to fall in line and behave, but no." He paused then shook his head. "I guess we're going to have to try something different."

"What do you mean?"

"I mean, little spy, you're going to have to keep a watchful eye on Jake too."

Shiloh's heart screamed in her chest. *No. Not him. Not Jake.* "I thought you were already doing that with all the cameras around this school."

"We need to know what's going on with him behind closed doors too. And it just so happens that we have the perfect in. Someone, he's—how did he say it?—'certifiably insane' about."

No, no, no!

Shiloh took a step back. "You wanted me to stay away from him."

"That was then. This is now. And now, you're more useful helping us to know Jake *intimately*." He chuckled at his choice of words.

Shiloh's hands coiled into fists, steam forming beneath her skin. *No, I won't do this to him.*

"Relax," the Elite said. "I merely want you to keep an eye on him so we can keep him out of trouble. Protect him. That's all."

You're a liar.

"I broke his heart," Shiloh said, gritting her teeth. "What makes you think he's even still interested in me?"

"You're a smart girl; you'll figure it out. And then you'll tell us everything that he's up to. And wear the recorder, of course. Oh, and if you get any bright ideas about telling him that you're spying—"

"You'll kill me," Shiloh snapped before she could stop herself. *Idiot.* Did she *want* to get choked again?

The Elite only chuckled. "No. I'll kill Willa."

Shiloh stumbled, sitting on the bed hard, all her air leaving her. The memory of Willa's sweet, chubby face tormented her. "She's four," Shiloh protested, but it was weak even to her own ear. "You wouldn't!"

"I would." There was a smile in his voice. "It'd be so, so easy. She's at the Haven. I could just walk right in. No one would ever care what happened to a Haven girl."

His hand might as well have been wrapped around Shiloh's throat. The threat was suffocating.

"So what do you say, Shiloh?" The Elite reached his hand forward and stroked it down her cheek. She wanted to vomit. She wanted to spit in his face. But she didn't move. "Are you going to be a good girl?"

Shiloh hesitated, visions of Jake flooding her mind, and then settling on Willa. Her responsibility. Her Little sister. Her stomach coiling into knots, she nodded. "Yes, sir."

"That's my girl." He slipped out the door.

She barely made it to the bathroom before she heaved what was left of the eggs, the black coffee, and the last of her hope into the toilet.

Shiloh wasn't in Advanced Technologies that day. Professor Cooper didn't call her name during attendance, which meant she'd been excused. Jake's stomach twisted despite himself. If Shiloh was missing class, she was probably on her deathbed.

"Okay, everyone," Cooper said. "Hard as it is to believe, we are getting close to midterm. Which means that it's time to assign partners for the final project."

A groan passed through the room.

"If you were listening on the first day of class, and I know you were *all* listening" —Cooper smiled wryly— "you know that the final project will be to design a future technology. Projects will be displayed at the end-of-semester fair."

Jake leaned back and balanced on the back legs of his chair. He *loved* group projects. He could easily bribe a partner to do all the work.

Cooper began to name off pairs. "Jacob Osgood."

Jake crossed his fingers.

The professor frowned, then said, almost a little uncertainly, "Shiloh Haven."

Jake lost his balancing act with the chair and fell backwards with a *Thunk!* The entire classroom turned to stare at him.

"Are you quite all right, Mr. Osgood?" Professor Cooper asked.

No. "Yes." Jake forced himself to laugh as he climbed to his feet and righted his chair. "But I think it might be a good idea if I had a different partner."

"Why do you think that?"

Jake opened his mouth, but said nothing. Having deep, unrequited feelings for a girl wasn't exactly a justifiable excuse. Because he *did* still have feelings for her, even if it had been over a month since homecoming. Even catching a glimpse of her slammed a sucker punch into his gut. A group project would be agony.

"I think anyone else here would be thanking the Council to have such a good partner," Professor Cooper said. "Unless you don't believe in cooperation and unity between all people."

Jake's smile pulled tight. "Of course I do."

"Then good. I'll trust you to reach out and contact Ms. Haven, since she couldn't be here today." He moved on to announce other partners.

After his morning classes, Jake pulled Shiloh's name in the directory. Luminosity Dorm. Room 23. He could have texted her on his tablet, but maybe, he wanted to see her.

I love to suffer, don't I?

It took her so long to answer the door that Jake almost assumed she wasn't there. Then the door opened slowly, her eyes peeking through a slit in the door before opening all the way

"Hello, Jake."

She really did look sick, her face colorless. She leaned against the doorframe as though it was all that held her up.

"You okay?" Jake asked. "You weren't in class."

"I'm fine. The nurse thinks that I have a stomach bug and wanted me to rest for the day. Didn't even want me logging in virtually." Shiloh rolled her eyes.

"Oh...well..." Jake rocked back and forth on his heels. Talking with Shiloh used to be as natural as breathing, but now it felt like avoiding broken glass with bare feet. "I'm sorry you're sick."

"Is that why you came? To check on me?"

"No, actually. Professor Cooper announced the partners for the group project today. He paired us together."

Her eyes widened. "Oh."

"I tried to get him to switch, but I couldn't really give him a good reason."

"Did you try 'my parents think she's evil'?"

Jake chuckled despite himself. "Didn't think of that. Might have worked."

Shiloh still clutched the doorknob, as though she might slam it into his face at any minute.

"Look, Shi, if you'd rather do the project without me...we both know you're smart enough to do it on your own."

Shiloh shook her head. "Oh no, Jake, you're not sticking me with all the work."

Froq! There went his last hope of escaping this.

Jake studied her face, but he knew by now reading her was impossible. Had she moved on any better than he had? Would he be the only one suffering through this project?

"It'll be fine," Shiloh said. "We can plan later. But I'm going to lay back down."

"Are you sure you're okay?"

She closed the door without answering.

🔥

It shouldn't be a surprise to Shiloh how quickly the Elite worked out the kinks. #767 had monitored her tracker and knew her schedule, so why wouldn't he be so ingrained in the school's computer system that he could make sure that Shiloh and Jake were paired together? It was the perfect excuse for Jake and her to spend time together. Even his parents wouldn't be able to argue.

Shiloh returned to bed and pulled the blanket over her head. Fatigue sealed an ache in every muscle, but her mind refused to give her rest. It spun in circles, desperate to find an escape from this, but how? She was just a piece on the Elite's chessboard, while he played out some strategy that Shiloh didn't know. What did he really want with Jake?

I can't do this to him.

I won't.

Being unable to be with Jake had shattered her heart, but watching him go to a prison camp? That would end her.

Thirty minutes later, a knock sounded on her door. Shiloh hesitated, afraid she might find an Elite on the other side, but when she opened it, only a cafeteria tray sat at her doorstep. Down the hall, Jake descended the stairs.

Shiloh carried the tray into her room and inspected the contents: tomato soup and grilled cheese. His favorite. The foods he'd once said made everything better. Shiloh's heart ached. If she'd questioned if Jake still had feelings for her, here—in his tender act of kindness—was her answer.

Shiloh paced across the room. *Think, Shiloh. Think.*

The names of everyone at risk sounded in her heart with every erratic beat. Jake. Nic. Willa. Herself. And then she thought of Hope, her crumpled body, the river of blood coursing toward Shiloh's feet. She hadn't protected Hope, and that had nearly destroyed her. If she lost Jake, or even Nic, without even trying to protect them, she would never survive the guilt or pain.

Rule #1: Survive. No matter the cost.

All of us. Shiloh curled her hands into determined fists. *All of us have to survive.*

It felt impossible, but maybe it wasn't. The Elite had said it himself. She *was* a smart girl. Yes, this was a dangerous game, but she'd been playing dangerous games all her life. She just had to figure out how to play the game better than him.

Twenty-One

Nic stepped nervously through the boards of the chapel to find Jake sitting against the wall. She sat in front of him on the tiled floor, crossing her legs beneath her.

Be careful, she warned herself, not for the first time. *Be very careful.*

"You said you had more information for me?" Nic asked.

Jake nodded.

Nic folded her fingers around her knees so she wouldn't grind them into her palm. "And you can tell me what happened at the Cleansing?"

He nodded again.

Nic took in a deep breath, bracing herself for whatever he had to say. Her mom had survived that day. Did anyone else?

Jake took his own steadying breath and told her everything. The bomb going off too early. Getting shot. Barely making it to a safe room with the help of someone he refused to mention by name. It was there that Nic's mom had seen them and given them the first aid kit. He'd been in the hospital for a month after that.

The timing of one bomb had meant the difference between life and death. For the Councilors and for Jake. Nic studied him. He really was handsome, like people said, and young and innocent. It would have been a tragedy for him to die, and it would have been ROGUE's fault. All this time, Nic had craved war, but she'd never once thought of all the innocent bystanders who might get hurt along the way.

Nic swallowed a lump in her throat.

Was defeating evil worth it, if you had to commit evil yourself?

"I'm glad you didn't die," Nic said.

"Me too," Jake said, with a smile. "Would've been a bummer."

"What about the rest of my Family? Did you see any of them?"

Jake hesitated, running his hand through his hair with a sigh. Nic's heart dropped to her stomach. "That file, I got from my dad's briefcase, I think it listed all of them. Paul's location was unknown, and I saw him with your mother that day."

Thank you, God. But goosebumps still spread over Nic's arms. "And everyone else?"

He didn't have to say anything. She could see it in his eyes, the way ghosts seemed to dance in them. He slowly shook his head.

"No!" She scrambled to her feet and paced away, as though maybe she could outrun the truth. "Did you see Mia or Asher or Riley or Oliver?"

Jake nodded, standing, his face contorting in sympathy. "I'm so sorry. I saw all those names. Everyone else in that file identified as The Family was dead."

The world crumbled beneath her, and Nic fell to her knees, barely noticing the pain as she hit the tile. Their faces raced through her mind, each one piercing her heart. This was worse than the prod of the Elite. This was real torture.

She screamed.

Damn them! Damn the Elite, and damn you, God! Why would you let this happen?

"I'm so sorry," Jake murmured, as he rested a hand on her shoulder.

Nic flung her arms around him. She felt like she was in a

stormy ocean of grief, and she'd surely drown if she didn't find someone to hold on to. He hesitated then wrapped his arms around her, strong and warm.

"It's going to be okay," Jake said weakly.

"No, it's not," Nic said, through her tears. "How can it be? They're gone."

"I know. I'm so, so sorry."

By the tone in his voice, she knew that he was. Any doubt she had disappeared. No, he was nothing like his father. Nothing.

The grief never faded, it never would, but eventually, Nic felt like she wasn't drowning. She forced herself to take shaky, but calming, breaths. With each inhale, her nose filled with Jake's spicy smell, like cinnamon and cedar. And suddenly, she was acutely aware that it was a boy—an actual boy—who was holding her. Warmth crawled up her neck, and she slid away.

"Sorry," she said, wiping away the remnants of her tears.

"You don't have anything to be sorry about," Jake said.

"I got your shirt wet."

He looked down at the damp splotches on his chest and shrugged. "That's all right."

Nic sniffed. Her hair stuck to her wet cheeks, and snot had dripped from her nose. She scrubbed her face on the sleeve of her jacket, hiding the heat on her cheekbones. *Fabulous.*

"Nic," Jake's voice was hardly a whisper. "Are you going to be okay?"

Nic shook her head. "No, but I'm glad I know now."

"I'm really am—" His voice broke, and he cleared his throat. "I really am sorry, Nic."

"It's not your fault."

"I'm an Osgood. It kind of feels like it is."

Nic swallowed and sniffed again, not quite sure what to say.

"Is there anything I can do?" Jake asked. "To help you?"

Nic glanced up at him. "Do you know how to get the trackers off?"

Jake shook his head. "Other than using the key? No."

Nic's heart sank a little. "Do you know where the keys are kept at least?" She'd asked Val and Stefani, but they wouldn't even answer.

Jake frowned. "They keep them locked in a safe in the principal's office."

In other words, they were untouchable. Nic sighed.

They fell silent. Outside, a bird cawed, and the wind whistled through the trembling, brightly colored leaves. The sun was setting, transforming the sunlight into glowing embers as it poured through the stained glass.

"Nic, can I ask you something?" Jake said, staring at the star in the large circular window.

Nic nodded.

"What's ROGUE?"

Nic stiffened, and he held out a hand in a calming gesture. "I promise you. I don't want any more information than that. I just want to know what it means."

The Councilors and the Elite all knew about ROGUE, so giving Jake a definition would give them no extra power. And besides, Nic really did trust him.

"ROGUE stands for the Rebel Organization against Government in United Efforts," Nic said.

A spark lit in Jake's eyes. "So there's a whole organization out there, fighting against Arcadia?"

Nic's pulse beat a little unsteadily, and she wasn't sure why. "Yes, Jake. Lots of people."

"Good." He smiled crookedly, but it was short lived. He sighed. "Look, I hate to say this, but I think after today we need to be careful about being seen together in public or having our trackers seen together in private like this. I know I have people watching me, and I don't want to bring suspicion on either of us. But I had to tell you the truth."

Nic sucked in a breath, feeling like she had been sucker

punched. Maybe because she had thought she was finding a new friend, but she understood. A Councilor's son and a heretic would raise suspicion.

She looked away. "Okay."

Jake angled himself in front of her so he could catch her eye. "But, Nic, if there is anything at all I can do to help you, I'll do it."

Nic gave a small smile. "Us heretics have to stick together, huh?"

Jake grinned. "I guess we do."

Nic's tracker beeped.

Jake's face fell. "Oh, no, what time is?" He glanced down at his own tracker and then leaped to his feet, letting out a string of curse words. "Shiloh! Froq it all!"

Nic jumped to her feet as well. "What's wrong?"

"Nothing. I was just supposed to be meeting someone...*right now*."

"Shiloh *Haven*? You know her?"

"Yeah, I...we're working on a project together." He jogged to the door before he stopped and looked back. "Look, I'm really sorry, but I need to run back."

Nic jogged after him. "I'll race you."

He spun back. "What?"

Nic smiled, feeling the now-familiar thrill she got before a race. "I'll race you back."

"You just want to see me lose epically."

Nic giggled. "Maybe."

"Okay then. Let's do this."

They crossed the water again and pulled their shoes on, before lining side by side like they were at the starting mark.

"Ready," Nic said.

Jake smiled. "Set."

"Go!"

🔥

"I'm sorry I'm late," Jake said as he stopped before Shiloh, who was waiting him on Legacy House's front steps. He panted, clutching a hand to his side. Had he run here? "I lost track of time."

"It's fine," Shiloh said, even though the twenty-minute wait had left a thin sheen of sweat down her spine, despite the chill in the growing dusk.

Jake gestured for her to follow him and led her to his room. Her nerves stood on end as she slipped into his private room. Besides the crumpled sheets of his bed, it was neater than Shiloh had imagined. Soccer trophies lined up on shelves, and a hologram picture frame rotated through pictures of his family, vacations, and a little gravestone with a teddy bear.

"Make yourself comfortable," Jake said.

His eyes on her felt like a caress down her spine, making heat rise from the depths of her. This was a mistake. She should have met him somewhere public. Not here. In his room. By his bed.

Shiloh sucked in a breath to banish the chaotic thoughts. *Focus.*

Shiloh had planned long and hard. She couldn't tell Jake what was happening. It was too big a risk. If he was reckless like he'd been at the hospital, he might ruin the whole thing. But as long as she was with him, she could protect him, keep him from doing anything to jeopardize himself, play the game until the Elite revealed his hand.

But she still didn't know how to undo the damage she'd done to their relationship.

Buying time, she took off her jacket and draped it over his desk chair. Something on his desk caught her eye, and she picked it up. Her wooden hot-air balloon, painted in stripes of black and gold. A burst of sunlight glowed in her chest. "I can't believe you kept it."

He shrugged. "You left it for me."

She had. When she'd been ushered out of the hospital like a

contagious disease, she'd left it for him to find. It was an apology and a promise. *I'll never forget you.*

"I have yours too," Shiloh said, her voice hardly a whisper. "On my desk."

Jake looked away and swallowed hard. This was torture for him too, wasn't it? Having her here?

"Maybe we should just talk about the project," he said.

Shiloh let herself really look at him for the first time since the chapel. The shape of his face, the curve of his lips, those arms she ached to be in. The brightness and warmth in her chest spread all through her until she was consumed with it.

Suddenly, she knew exactly what to do.

Be brave, Shiloh.

Shiloh shook her head. "I don't want to talk."

Jake raised his eyebrows. "What?"

Two steps closed the distance between them. Shiloh curled her fingers around his tie.

His eyes widened. "Shiloh, what are you—"

She pulled him toward her and kissed him.

He hesitated for only a heartbeat, then he kissed her back with an intensity that made her stumble until her back pressed against the wall. One of his hands rested beside her head, balancing him, and the other plunged into her hair, tilting her head back to deepen the kiss. Her every nerve cell sparked to life, and her fingers clutched desperately to his tie like he might dare pull away and leave her alone with this maddening flame that was building and building.

The kisses at the hospital had been warm and sweet, and the one in the chapel had been heart-wrenching, but this was different. This wasn't just warmth.

This was an inferno.

It took all of Shiloh's restraint to end it. She pushed Jake away with a gentle hand on his chest, feeling his heartbeat beneath her fingers, which was as erratic as her own.

Jake searched her eyes, his hands on either side of her head. "Shiloh..." He panted, catching his breath. "What the froq was that?"

$$\pmb{\delta}$$

Shiloh's face was unreadable as she stared back at Jake. One minute, he'd felt like his chest was ripping apart, having her here, next to his bed, and not being allowed to touch her. And then the next, she'd been kissing him. And froq, that kiss. It left him trembling.

"Why did you kiss me?" Jake asked. But she bit her lip, and his thin restraint broke. "Froq it! Tell me later."

Jake brought her face back to his. He kissed her deeply, fiercely, with everything in him, trying to make up for all the times he'd wanted to kiss her and couldn't. To fill the aching hole of want she'd left him with. She kissed him back just as ardently, her hands summoning goosebumps to his arms, curling into his hair. And then, they were stumbling across the room, falling into his bed.

Slow down, Osgood.

He pushed himself up, hovering above her. "Maybe we should—"

"I don't want to talk. Just kiss me."

She reclaimed his mouth, and froq, what else could he do but surrender to her? Kissing Shiloh was like nothing else. No girl had made him feel like this: like he could sense her in every nerve of his body, like he was so filled with her he might come apart at the seams, like she was *everything*.

She slipped her hands up his shirt, and he shivered as her fingertips trailed over his bare spine. More. He wanted—no, *needed*—more. He kissed Shiloh's jaw, and her sigh was an invitation, so he continued down her neck to her shoulder. It wasn't enough. It wouldn't be enough until he had kissed every inch of her.

Her voice played in his mind like an echo. *We are impossible.*

Jake shoved himself off the bed and away from her, before the reasonable side of his brain shut off again. He backed away, gasping for air. Shiloh sat up, her hair wild from his hands. And Council, she was beautiful. Every inch of him screamed to return to her.

Control yourself, Osgood.

Jake turned his back to her, hands in his hair, sucking in deep breaths.

"Jake."

He glanced back. Her knees pressed against her chest, her vulnerability raw between them.

Breathe, Osgood, breathe.

"Shiloh, we have to stop. We have to talk about this. Before this goes too far."

No matter how much he wanted to—and *froq,* he wanted to—he couldn't. He'd fallen into bed with so many girls without consequences. But Shiloh was different in every way. Sex would plunge him deeper into his feelings, and he already felt like he was drowning in her.

Jake sucked in another breath. "Shiloh, what's happening between us here? You can't tell me that we can't be together, and then a month later, kiss me like that. It's not fair to me!"

"I know." Shiloh crossed her legs beneath her, lowering her shield. "And I know what I said in the chapel, and all of those barriers are still true. But—" She paused, biting her lip. "But then we were partnered together. And I just couldn't stop thinking that we have eighty-three days."

"What?"

"We have eighty-three days before the project is due. Eighty-three days that we have a reasonable excuse to be together, that no one can question."

Jake's heart pounded so hard he couldn't think. "What are you saying?"

She stood from the bed and approached him slowly. She

brushed her cool fingers against his blazing cheek and, with her next words, stopped his heart completely. "I'm saying I want to be with you. More than anything."

Jake opened his mouth, but no sound came out. *Am I dreaming?*

At his silence, shadows fell over her face. She took a step back and wrapped her arms over her chest. "I- I mean...if you still feel the same way."

Jake finally found his voice. "*Of course*, I still feel the same way. I'm pretty sure that if I cut my heart out, it would still beat for you."

Shiloh blinked at him a moment, unreadable. Then suddenly, her mask shattered as she laughed.

"Why are you laughing?" Jake asked, but it felt so good to hear her laugh, that he laughed too.

"Really, Osgood? You're going to go with that line? That was *really* cheesy."

Jake's laugh vibrated his chest again. "Yeah, it really was."

Here she was, the girl from the hospital. He'd gotten her back. Jake pulled her into his arms, and she smiled up at him. A true smile. A victory.

"Council, this is really happening, isn't it?" Jake asked.

Shiloh nodded, then paused. "You're not seeing anyone, are you?"

He ran a strand of her hair between his fingers, still amazed that she wasn't pulling away. "No, I haven't been with anyone since before homecoming. You told me to be different, and I've been trying to be." He hadn't even gone to a party. He'd cut off all ties with Marcus and the Shiny People. He'd expected the friendships to die harder, but they'd blown away in the wind. Never really friends to begin with. "Besides, I meant what I said. All I want is you."

She smiled, even as she held up a stern finger. "But there would have to be rules."

He smiled wryly. "You know how I love rules."

"We can't be seen together. Absolutely *no* public displays of affection."

"Of course not. Just lots and lots of private ones."

Was that a blush? Yes, that was definitely a blush. Shiloh ducked her head, her hair hiding her face. Jake curled a finger beneath her chin and lifted it, so he could once against meet the intoxicating darkness of her eyes. If they did this, were really together, how would he ever be able to let her go? "Eighty-three days won't be enough, Shiloh."

Shiloh's smile fell. "No, they won't be."

"So, what will we do after that?"

Shiloh shrugged. "I don't know. Maybe you'll learn how insane I am about school projects, and you'll get sick of me."

He laughed. "That's not possible."

He kissed her again, slowly, softly. He would stop soon. He wouldn't lose control, because he was going to do this right. He didn't plan to keep her for just eighty-three days. Now that he had her, he planned to never let her go again.

TWENTY-TWO

S hiloh's heart fluttered as she knocked on Jake's door. He answered quickly and ushered her in, smiling like sunshine. The room was dim, illuminated only by the soft flickering lights of the electronic candles scattered about the room. Jake's bedspread stretched across the floor, topped with pillows. Stars and swirling clouds floated and twinkled through the air, cast from Jake's tablet. It felt like standing in a galaxy. Like she could reach out and hold the stars.

"What is this?" Shiloh asked.

"Well, it occurred to me that we haven't actually had a real date," Jake said, setting a hand in the small of her back. "And since a picnic under the stars would definitely break the rules, I thought I'd bring the stars to us."

Shiloh smiled broadly. "Jake, this is..."

She couldn't find the words, so she kissed him quickly. Or at least, she meant it to be quick until the eager response of his lips beckoned her to stay awhile. When she finally pulled back, she managed a soft "Thank you."

Jake settled down on the blanket, pulling her down to his side. He swept his arm over the glorious affair. "I have foreign chocolates and smoked almonds. And—" He reached beneath his bed. "Champagne!" He held two red cans of pop aloft. "Okay, not champagne, but it'll do."

Shiloh popped a can open and sipped the bubbles. When she looked up, Jake's eyes were dancing with the stars.

"I can't believe you're really here," he said.

Shiloh slipped her hand into his. And like that, these last months of distance and hurt unwound, falling back to that magical place they'd built in the hospital, where being together was easy and right. They teased, laughed, and ate his amazing snacks. His presence could almost erase everything else: the Elite, the audio recorder pressing into her skin.

But ever so often, it poked into the back of Shiloh's mind. A haunting reminder that being with Jake was still not uncomplicated, and of all she had to lose if she didn't play this right. Even if she did, she was bound to lose him all the same.

He'll hate me for this.

Shiloh caught her breath.

Jake's voice cut off. He frowned at her, concerned. "Is something wrong?"

Careful. Your mask is slipping.

Unable to think of an excuse, Shiloh kissed him. He hesitated for a minute, as though sensing she was using this as a distraction, but then surrendered.

They laid back on the blanket, and with every caress of his lips, he persuaded her to forget everything but how he made her body an inferno. How she craved more and more of him. Her breath came in stops-and-starts as his fingers slipped past her sweater and trailed onto the bare skin of her hip, her belly, toward...the audio recorder.

Froq.

It was probably small enough that he'd never notice, but that was beside the point. No matter how desperately she wanted to surrender to the effect Jake had on her body, she wasn't going to ruin this first, deep intimacy by worrying about an Elite listening in.

She pulled back. "Jake."

He pushed himself up on his hands, meeting her eyes. The stars shot around his head.

"I—" Shiloh started.

"Too fast." Jake sat down beside her, gulping an unsteady breath. "I'm going too fast."

Shiloh sat up and smoothed her hair with a tremulous hand. "I'm sorry."

Jake brushed his thumb across her cheek, smiling softly. "Don't be. I don't want to go too fast and ruin this. But, um—" His smile wobbled. "I'll admit, I've only ever had one speed with girls, so it's probably better if you drive."

Shiloh let out a breathless laugh. "Fair enough."

They picked a movie to watch and cast it from Jake's tablet to the ceiling, amongst the stars. Curled against Jake's side, his arm around her, Shiloh found herself instead watching the way the stars danced in his eyes.

Focus on the plan. Keep him safe.

Shiloh rolled away and grabbed her tablet from her bag beside the blanket. He watched her curiously as she wrote a message.

I thought of a new rule.

She handed him the tablet. He sat up and raised an eyebrow at her. He erased her words with a swipe of his hand and scrawled his own in a broad, flourishing script.

What's that?

I keep thinking about how your parents must have been recording us in the hospital. I think if we're going to talk about anything— She tapped the stylus on the edge of the tablet, searching for the right words. *That might get you in trouble again, we should write it. Just in case.*

Jake frowned at the message for a long time, and Shiloh held her breath. *Okay,* he wrote at last.

Shiloh held back her sigh of relief. There was one more piece she lined up in this game. This terrible, terrible game.

◊

"Jake."

"Hm?" Jake murmured, as he laid careful kisses down Shiloh's shoulder, pulling aside the collar of her oversized sweater. No matter how many times he kissed her here, it never quite lost the wonder of finding new treasure.

"We should stop."

The words splashed like cold water to Jake's face. He flipped onto his back on the bed beside her and sucked in a breath. "Sorry."

She sounded a little breathless too. "You don't have to be sorry."

Their make-out sessions always ended like this: with both of them breathless, and Jake's skin on fire. But maybe this was normal. He'd never really been the relationship type, so he didn't know the appropriate time to wait. A month? Two months? Six months? It was fine. Really. He was determined not to pressure her and froq things up, even if he was going to get citations for over-usage of water from all his long, cold showers.

Jake rolled to his side to look at Shiloh, and the smile she gave him made his heart stop. This had been the best month of his life. He and Shiloh had spent every moment together they could with her hectic schedule, under the ruse that they were working on a project together. Which they hadn't actually done. They always had good intentions but got distracted. It wasn't just the physical things. It was everything: talking, teasing, laughing, playing.

"Do you have any idea how happy I am with you?" Jake asked, trailing a finger down her shoulder.

Her eyes seemed to shimmer. "Maybe, but if you start telling me, I'm going to kiss you, and we'll never figure out this project. We only have fifty days left."

Jake groaned and buried his face in his pillow. "Don't remind me." He *would* figure out a way to buy them more time, but right now, he had no idea how. Short of running off to join ROGUE.

As wonderful as that sounded, his parents watching over him made that impossible. But one day, when he got the chance, he'd fight with them. In the meantime, he found little ways to help Nic, asking her how she was doing if they were in public or occasionally leaving a muffin on her table if she was sitting alone. Making sure she was receiving at least some small kindness.

Shiloh ran her fingers through his hair, bringing his thoughts back to her. "So, any ideas?"

He chuckled. "That's not how this relationship works. You're the brain. I'm the beauty, remember?"

She stuck out her tongue. "I can't do all the thinking. Come on! One idea. It might spark something."

"I do have one idea," Jake said with a crooked smile that made her narrow her eyes in suspicion.

"Okay, what?"

With one smooth move, Jake wrapped his hands around her hips and flipped her over, so she straddled his body. She cried in protest, pressing herself away from him, all ten fingers fanned against his chest. She glared down at him with midnight slits, but froq, this view. He could get used to this view.

Before she could scold him, he slid a strand of hair behind her ear and spoke softly, "The only thing I can think about is how I wish I could freeze this moment and hide in it forever."

Her lips twisted, and he knew what she was about to say. *Really, Osgood, you're going to go with that line?* But he was wrong.

She leaned down, her fingers curling into his shirt, and whispered against his lips, "You're trouble."

"Guilty as charged." His entire being sparked. He reached toward her to close the distance, but her eyes suddenly flung wide.

She bolted upright. "I've got it!"

"Uh...got what?"

"The project." She scrambled off him and the bed.

Jake sat up, taking a breath to coax his fiery flesh to chill out. "Okay, what's the idea?"

"Invisibility!"

"What?"

She didn't explain, only yanked her tablet from her bag and tapped on it wildly. "We're going to need to research holograms and cameras. And reserve time in the lab. Oh." She snapped her fingers. "And a belt. Do you have a spare belt?"

She paused, as though finally realizing he was gaping at her.

A faint pink touched her alabaster cheeks. "I'm sorry. I told you I get really insane about projects. Getting sick of me yet?"

"Not at all." Jake grinned. "In fact, you've never been sexier."

TWENTY-THREE

Nic daydreamed of warm pajamas in her bed as she hauled herself up the stairs. These last few weeks, she'd been running extra miles at the track during her evening free time. The physical demand eased the terror that lingered below her skin, like a scream building in her throat. Every day that passed Nic worried that today would be the day that the Elite would kill her. But days had turned into weeks, and they never came.

During tonight's run, the skies had launched a torrent of icy rain upon her head without warning. She'd been soaked through by the time she ran to her dorm. Dry clothes and a warm bed sounded like paradise.

But when Nic arrived at her room, the door wouldn't open. She pushed harder with no result.

She hammered on the door. "Hello!"

Giggles erupted from inside the room. They'd locked her out! Nic pounded again, and when no reply came, she screamed and kicked the door. It trembled in the frame, but the only reward she got was more giggling and a sore toe.

Gritting her teeth, Nic stormed down the hall. Fine! She didn't want to sleep in a room with those jerks, anyway. Nic knocked on Val's door.

One of her roommates, Ella, answered. The lights were still on in the room, each of the girls on their own bunk studying their tablets. Except for Val.

"Val isn't..." Ella shifted her weight from foot to foot. "Well, she's not here."

"What do you mean?" Nic asked. It was past curfew now. If Val wasn't here, then the tracker would send an alert to the security guards, and she'd be found and punished.

Ella shrugged. "She disappears a lot at night. But don't worry —" She added quickly. "We never tell."

The other roommates shook their heads, their eyes wide. Val had clearly put the fear of God into them.

A lot? How is that even possible?

"You okay?" Ella asked.

Nic pushed the stringy, wet hair out of her eyes. "My roommates locked me out of my room."

Ella sighed and then opened the door farther. "Okay, you can stay in here tonight. Val's drawer is the bottom one. I'm sure she won't mind you wearing some of her pajamas."

"Thanks."

At least some people could still be kind.

Val's pajamas made Nic feel like a tiny child. She clutched at the waistband so it didn't slide off her hips as she crawled into Val's bed. The other girls settled down for the night, flipping off the tablets and burying themselves in the covers.

Val's lower bunk was shoved up against the only window, and the seal displayed her collection of metalwork. She was an amazing artist. She was always drawing or painting, but playing with fire to create beauty seemed to be Val's favorite. A metal, female warrior held up a spear, and an elephant reared its trunk. Nothing new since Nic had last been here.

Nic rested her head on the pillow; something hard lay beneath.

When she lifted the pillow, Nic's heart exploded in her chest. On the bed lay Val's tracker. She dropped the pillow, before the other girls could see.

A strange mixture of hope and anger clenched Nic's stomach. It *was* possible to get the trackers off, and Val had known it all along.

But then...why did Val lie?

The time on Nic's tracker said 2:32 a.m. when she felt the mattress shift.

"Scoot over," Val hissed quietly, as she squeezed into the bed next to her.

Nic pressed herself close to the wall. Still clothed in jeans and a t-shirt, Val slipped beneath the covers. The rain must have stopped, because she wasn't wet at all.

"Why are you here?" Val whispered.

"My roommates locked me out."

Val grunted.

"I borrowed pajamas. I hope that's okay."

"Whatever. Just go to sleep."

Val buried her face in the corner of the pillow, leaving Nic the other corner. She smelled weird—smoke blended with an exotic, flowery scent. It was familiar, but Nic couldn't quite place it.

"Val," Nic whispered.

Val groaned.

Nic shook her shoulder. "Val."

Val pulled the blanket over her head and mumbled, "Shut up and go to sleep."

"How did you get the tracker off?"

Val flung the blanket off her face and rolled toward Nic, her eyes narrowed. Despite how quiet she spoke, Val's voice snapped like fangs. "I'm not telling you."

The words landed like a slap on Nic's cheek. "Val, *please.*"

"Not a chance."

"Val, you don't understand. I can't stay here."

Val shoved herself up on her elbow, so she could look down on Nic. "And where will you go?"

Nic pressed her lips together. She hadn't thought that far ahead. She had no idea how she'd get connected with ROGUE again. She only knew that she was dead if she stayed.

"Nic, I'm sorry, but you're stuck here." Val's words stabbed in Nic's chest like poisoned blades. "You better get used to it."

"I thought" —Nic took a shaky breath— "I thought you said you were going to help me."

"I'm not going to help you get killed." Val rolled to her side, turning her back on Nic.

"Val—"

"Shut the froq up, and go to sleep."

Judging by that tone, Nic was liable to end up sleeping in the hallway if she didn't drop it. Heat welled up in her throat, trying to morph into a scream. She'd never had friends before Val, but she was certain that this was not what friends did.

Nic didn't sleep for a long time. She forced her aching eyes to remain open. Val *had* to put the tracker back on at some point. But a long hour dragged by, and she didn't stir. Nic stumbled into an unwilling sleep, and when she awoke to her tracker's alarm, Val wore her tracker once more.

"Anytime you want to stop glaring at me, that would be great," Val said, not looking up from her sketching.

Nic hadn't realized she'd been glaring, so instead she glowered down at the soupy eggs on her tray. Val had to have gotten ahold of some kind of key. Did she hide it on her person or in her room? Nic had to get it from her, even if it meant stealing it.

"If it isn't my two favorite ladies."

Stefani appeared at their side, looking as flawless as always, the streaks in her hair bright orange today. She sat and threw an arm around Nic's shoulder. Nic stiffened as she inhaled a flowery scent clinging to Stefani's clothes—the same scent Val had worn tattooed on her skin. Val had been with Stefani. Which meant that Stefani, too, knew how to get the tracker off.

"Can I talk to you?" Nic said, her voice a growl.

Stefani raised her eyebrows. "Sure."

"Outside."

Stefani's eyes flicked to Val, hesitating. Nic grabbed Stefani's wrist and stood, pulling her from her seat.

"Nic, hold on—"

But Nic only continued to drag Stefani toward the door. Finally, Stefani stopped resisting, and Nic pulled her outside of the cafeteria, Val following on their heels. Outside, the lawn was empty. The cold bit through her sweater and coat and made the damp grass crunch beneath her feet like crackling ice.

Once they were away from the entrance of the cafeteria, Nic released Stefani's wrist and spun to face her. "You know how to get the tracker off."

Stefani's mouth dropped open. "What?"

"Her roommates locked her out of the room last night," Val explained, crossing her arms over her chest, "so she slept in my bed...which I wasn't in."

"Oh." Stefani leaned against the brick wall, looking at the ground. She, at least, had the decency to look guilty.

Nic took a breath. "Please tell me, Stef. Please."

Stefani caught her lip between her teeth.

"*Don't*, Stef," Val said. "If you tell her, she'll run and—"

"Shut up!" Nic barked, her hands curling into fists. She softened her voice as she turned back to Stefani. "*Please*. I have to get out of here. I am dead if I don't."

Stefani finally lifted her gaze, twisting her hands together.

"What is going on with you, Nic?" Stefani spoke with that tone she often used to talk to Val—like she was calming a crazed tiger. "Why are you so scared? You're not causing problems. You're doing just fine."

Nic wrapped her arms around herself, the cold piercing down to her bones. "You don't understand."

Stefani straightened and rested a hand on Nic's shoulder. "Then help us to. If you tell me, I can help you."

Nic shook her off. Telling them would reveal ROGUE, and she'd never do that.

"You can help me by telling me how to get this tracker off," Nic said through her teeth.

Stefani shook her head sadly. "No, Nic. I'm sorry."

Nic drove her nails into her palm so she could focus on the physical pain, instead of the ache in her chest. "I thought you were my friends. But I guess I was wrong."

Stefani pressed a hand to her lips, looking hurt. Val glared. Nic bolted away from them and didn't stop when Stefani yelled. She ran until she couldn't breathe, and then she collapsed to the ground, still gasping from their betrayal.

TWENTY-FOUR

"You're disappointing me, girl."

Shiloh's breath froze in the air as it left her cold lips. The Elite paced in the snow before her, black boots crunching into the deep layers. The first snow of the season had fallen five days ago, and it hadn't stopped dumping since. It'd grown so deep that the professors were already forced to commute on snowmobiles from their homes just outside school property, and it had driven everyone to stay indoors more often, including Josephine. Her roommate's presence had made Shiloh feel safer until #767 had told her to start meeting him in the snowy woods where no one would venture.

"I am doing everything you asked," Shiloh said, proud that her voice was learning how to be calm in his presence.

He checked in on her in person every few weeks, never having gained anything from the audio recording. Which meant her plan was working.

Shiloh shoved her hands deeper in her pockets, but she still couldn't feel her fingertips. "I'm wearing the audio recorder. I'm keeping Jake out of trouble. I'm working on gaining Nic's trust.

And it's not my fault that Nic won't talk. You've heard how much I've tried to bring up her past. She won't talk about it."

It was a careful game with Nic, saying the things that would make it seem like Shiloh was trying to pry without pushing too hard. It was obvious that Nic would never give up ROGUE's secrets, which made Shiloh's job easier. And as for Jake, he *had* said things that would have gotten him in trouble—admitting to Shiloh that he'd talked to Nic and what he'd learned about ROGUE—but he'd always used the tablet.

#767 stopped in his tracks and whirled toward her. A shiver passed through Shiloh, like he ripped her coat from her body and left her exposed to the biting cold.

"You've had *weeks* to gain her trust," the Elite growled, "and still you fail me. Why should I even bother with you, if you're not going to be useful?"

Shiloh's heart pounded in her ears, but he'd been making these threats every few days. It was a bluff. She *hoped* it was a bluff.

She looked squarely at her own reflection in his visor, meeting the eyes that were surely behind it. "Because you have no other plan. You have no one else who can keep a close eye on both Nic and Jake. You *need* me."

His hand curled around the electric prod on his side, and Shiloh took a step back. He'd slapped her a few more times, left bruises on her arms from how tightly he'd grabbed her. But he hadn't used that on her...yet.

"For now," he admitted. "But not forever, unless you can prove how useful you can be."

Shiloh gritted her teeth. *Be brave.* "Are we done now? Because if I'm late for another class, people are going to start getting suspicious."

His fist worked around his electrical prod. Shiloh held her breath as the wind wailed in the silence, stirring clouds of dusty snow into the air.

At last, he gave a jerk of his head. "Run along."

❦

"You okay, Shi?" Jake asked.

Shiloh looked up from the jumble of tools that rested on the laboratory table in the science center. It was Saturday and another snowstorm raged outside, threatening to dump another several inches to the already thick blanket. Because of that, the laboratory was empty and the perfect place to work on the project.

Jake lounged on the stool beside her, leaning against the counter, dark safety glasses hiding his eyes.

"I'm fine." Shiloh set the small welding knife back in its assigned place. "Why do you ask?"

Now that she wasn't using heat, Jake slid his eye wear off and tossed it on the counter. "I don't know. I just feel like there is something off with you."

Shiloh forced herself not to take a sharp breath. She thought she'd been concealing the anxiety she often felt after a visit from the Elite, when the guilt of her own web of lies threatened to strangle her. When the fear that she'd fail, and they'd all end up dead, made her feel like she'd never be warm again.

Just be the good little actress you are, Shiloh thought, but it didn't sound like her own voice. It sounded like #767.

Shiloh shrugged, picked up her tablet and scrolled through the coding. "There's just stuff on my mind."

"Hey." When she didn't look at him, he took the tablet from her hands gently and set it aside. He pulled her to him and lifted her safety glasses to her forehead so he could see her eyes. "Talk to me. What type of stuff?"

She could read tales of caring and affection—and maybe even something deeper—in the intensity of his warm brown eyes. It made her breath catch in her chest, a knife of pain driving deep beneath her ribs.

He's going to hate me.

Shiloh forced herself to breathe. "The end of the semester

always gets really busy with finals, so it's always stressful. And your parents are coming next week. What if they find out?"

Jake laced his fingers through hers. "That's not going to happen." He brought her knuckles to his lips, leaving a kiss like he was sealing a promise. "My parents will be here for three hours tops on Friday for the Unity Dinner, and then they'll be gone. And my dad probably won't even come."

"Even if they don't...we only have thirty-four days left."

Jake's hand tightened on hers. "I've told you before, and I mean it. Whatever it takes, I'm not letting you go. Not again."

Shiloh looked down to the ground. "I just don't want to lose you."

But that inevitability was the only thing she was certain of.

"You kind of like me, huh?" Jake asked with his classic crooked grin.

Shiloh shrugged. "The data was found to be statistically significant, and the hypothesis was accepted."

Jake laughed. "I'm going to assume that's a yes."

When she didn't return his smile, he pulled her against his chest. Despite everything, her shoulders relaxed as he held her.

"I'm not going anywhere," Jake whispered against her hair. "I promise. They'll have to haul me away in a body bag to get me away from you."

To hide her wince, Shiloh kissed him. *That's exactly what I'm afraid of.*

"Dad, you made it!" Jake said in surprise as his dad stepped out of the car.

"Of course, I did," Dad said with a smile. "Wouldn't have missed it."

You missed the last two.

Jake's mother closed the distance between them swiftly and

gracefully, even wearing high heels on the icy cement. He embraced her tightly. "Hi, Mom."

"Happy Unity Day!" She took his face in her hands and looked him over carefully. "You look great. Feeling almost back to your old self?"

"Yeah." Jake forced a smile, even though he felt nothing like his old self, and he preferred it that way. "Let's go eat."

Stick to the mission. Perform to the puppet strings then get them out.

He led them toward the Commons, ignoring the three bodyguards who trailed after them. Students and their families packed the cafeteria to its seams. Unity Day had replaced an old American holiday on the last Thursday of November, but Ardency turned it into a weeklong celebration so parents could attend meals with their children. This week held a lighter load of classes for the students, and the only decent food they would eat all year.

Even though other families crammed together at tables, Jake and his family had one designated by itself, separated from the crowd so that the bodyguards could form a barricade. The Osgoods still had to go through the line in the cafeteria like all the other common folk, getting their helpings of turkey, mashed potatoes, and pie.

When Jake turned from the line, he nearly collided with Stefani Andreou, who was clutching her camera and smiling widely. Jake's stomach tied itself into a sailor's knot. They hadn't even exchanged words since the blackmail, and the unusual radio silence confirmed that she was still very, *very* angry with him.

Stefani looked around him to his parents and waved. "Councilor and Mrs. Osgood, welcome to Ardency!"

Dad smiled at her. "Well, thank you, Ms.—" He paused, trying to place the familiar face, his smile wavering at the sight of the orange streaks through her hair.

"Andreou," Stefani said.

"Oh yes, how is your mother? I haven't seen her since the state meeting last month."

"She's great. Thanks for asking." Stefani lifted the camera that was around her neck. "Can I take a picture for the *Ardency Times*?"

"Of course," Mom said.

Jake posed with his family, pasting on his TV-ready smile. Stefani snapped the picture and stepped out of the way.

"You should check out today's issue of the *Times*," Stefani said as they walked by. "It'll be launching any minute. The gossip section should be very...*tantalizing*." Stefani winked at Jake.

Oh, great! Jake thought, as he settled around the table with his parents. *What did she do now?*

Mom began catching him up on the happenings of Uncle Silas, Aunt Aubrey, and Jake's three cousins. Jake wished, as he often did, that his cousins didn't live in another school district, so that Unity Day would include them too. His uncle, Silas, effortlessly eased the tension with his humor and didn't make Jake feel like his every word was somehow wrong. But then Silas had been around a lot in Jake's early childhood, filling holes that Dad left empty. So perhaps it was only natural that Jake wished Silas was here...and Dad wasn't.

Jake had barely taken a bite when he heard an alert that echoed through the cafeteria. The *Ardency Times* coming through like Stefani said.

Jake didn't move to pull his tablet out of his pocket, but Dad glanced at his phone, even when Mom shot him a glance that clearly said that they'd already talked about turning his phone off. Jake had forgotten that parents could subscribe to *Ardency Times* as well.

"Anyway," Mom said. "They think your cousin, Claire, will be placed on an Art Track. She's so talented."

Having a Councilor as an uncle probably helps too... "That's great, Mom."

"Jacob," Dad said. The use of his full name made Jake's spine tighten. A dark shadow crossed Dad's face. "Do you care to explain this to me?"

Dad turned the phone to show the *Ardency Times* article, and Jake's heart stopped in his chest.

In Stefani's column was a picture of Shiloh and him in the laboratory last Saturday, her glasses perched on her head, his arms around her, kissing. The headline read:

AN OSGOOD AND A HAVEN:
OPPOSITES ATTRACT, BUT CAN THEY SURVIVE?

Rage branded every line of Dad's face. It was over. It was *all* over. Then Jake's heart didn't just stop.

It tore completely in two.

Twenty-Five

Shiloh stepped out of the gym shower, wrapped in her towel. She hated showering in the gym, but she no longer felt safe in her room. She no longer felt safe *anywhere*, but the Elite couldn't approach her when she wasn't alone.

Since winter had fallen, cross-country practice had turned to running drills with the running team. Today, the physical demand had been a welcome distraction from the fact that, right now, Jake was having dinner with his parents.

A series of pings from tablets went off—the *Ardency Times* weekly edition. Shiloh grabbed her uniform from her locker and glanced around. Harper lounged on a bench nearby, running fingers through her damp hair and staring down at her tablet. Shiloh couldn't look at her without remembering Jake kissing her perfect, ruby mouth.

Shiloh swallowed and started toward the stalls to change in private. Feet sounded on the floor behind her, and before she turned, a hand shoved her. She stumbled, dropped her uniform, and clutched her towel just before it fell too.

Harper stood behind her, easily a head taller than Shiloh. With her teeth bared, she looked like a lioness about to pounce.

"It's *you*?" Harper snarled.

"I'm sorry?" Shiloh said, her heart thrumming in her ears.

Around the room, girls in various stages of undressing twisted toward Shiloh and Harper. Harper looked Shiloh up and down, and she wrinkled her nose, like Shiloh smelled like ordure.

"I knew it! I knew he was seeing someone. But *you*?" She let out a bitter laugh. "You've *got* to be kidding me!" Harper shoved her tablet into Shiloh's face.

Shiloh's skin, once warm from the shower, turned to ice at the headline. *An Osgood and a Haven.*

No, no, no.

A murmur rose from the girls in the room, but the noise was lost behind wailing in Shiloh's chest. *This can't be happening.* Everyone would know. His *parents* would know. Her ability to protect him would be lost.

"He chose *you*?" Harper said, from somewhere far away. "Over me?"

When Shiloh didn't respond, Harper shoved her again. Shiloh's feet slipped on the slick tile, and she fell hard, dropping her towel. Harper brayed with laughter, a laugh that was echoed by other girls. Shiloh scrambled to cover herself, her cheeks blazing. Her imperfections suddenly felt massive: the flatness of her chest versus Harper's abundant one, the scars that trailed up Shiloh's legs compared to Harper's flawless skin.

"Has he seen you naked yet?" Harper asked. "Because I'm sure once he does, he'll come crawling back."

"Leave her alone!"

Nic charged toward them, her face contorted with rage, her fists at her sides.

Enough was enough. Screw Harper for thinking she could be cruel to whoever she wanted without consequences! Nic had tolerated it for months, but now Nic was done being the nice girl, the good girl, the keep-your-head-down girl. *No one* went after her friend.

"Leave her alone!" Nic folded her hands into fists.

As Harper swung to face her, Nic wasn't sure what her plan was. But this ended today.

Harper scoffed. "And what are you going to do about it, pipsqueak?"

Nic closed the rest of the distance between them. *Don't hit her.* As much as she wanted to break Harper's perfect nose, she didn't think it would be effective, but words might.

"You think I'm scared of all of you, don't you?" Nic stopped in front of Harper. Only inches separated them now. "You think that's why I've just been taking your...your *ordure*. Well, you've got me all wrong."

Nic could feel all of their eyes on her. Shiloh leaned against the wall, still clutching her towel, and that made Nic's anger blaze in her chest.

"I'm a heretic. I survived things you can't possibly imagine. I've been taught to fight and defend from the time I could stand upright—with my hands, knives, guns, with anything. In this room, there at least twenty-three items I could use to kill you."

Nic had just made up a number, but they didn't know that. Harper scrambled back, and several other girls shied away like spooked horses.

"Do you know when the Elite finally came for me, I was alone, and it *still* took six of them to bring me down. I killed one of them. Shot straight through the visor." Nic formed her fingers into a gun and aimed it at Harper's chest. "*Bang!*"

Harper jumped back another inch, and a smile crawled over Nic's face. "I'm not scared of you, Harper. No, I'm scared of what *I* might do to *you* when I finally lose control."

"You're lying," Harper said, but her voice trembled.

"Look at me." Nic drew herself to her full height and met Harper's eyes. "Do I *look* like I'm lying?"

Harper looked at Nic then dropped her gaze to her feet.

"I am done with you." Nic spun around to look at all the other girls, who followed Harper's bullying like mindless ants. They stepped back, like she was a loose tiger. "I am done with *all* of you. You leave me—and Shiloh—alone, or I promise you, you won't like what happens. Now, get out!"

No one moved.

Nic took a step toward them and raised her voice. "I said, *get out!*"

Harper and the rest of them scrambled to pull on clothes and hurry out of the locker room. There was a rush of noise, like a stampede, and then the only sound was the drip of a leaking showerhead.

Nic couldn't stop the grin that crossed her face. *I win.* But then she caught Shiloh in the corner of her eye, and her smile fell.

Nic touched Shiloh's shoulder. "Are you okay?"

"Yes," Shiloh said quickly, too quickly, stooping to pick up her clothes.

"No, you're not. Shiloh, what Harper said...she was just being cruel. You're really pretty."

Shiloh drew in a trembling breath and pinched the bridge of her nose. "Thanks, Nic."

She stood, frozen in place, until Nic took her elbow and steered her toward a bathroom stall. As Shiloh dressed, Nic stood in front of the door, in case any of the other girls tried to come back. She pulled her tablet from the pocket of her uniform's jacket and unfolded it.

As Nic read the *Times* article, her chest ached. It was mindless drivel, comparing Shiloh and Jake to Romeo and Juliet because she was a Haven and he was an Osgood. The author made it seem scandalous, even stupid for them to be together. The author's signature was a flourish at the end. *Stefani Andreou.*

Nic gritted her teeth. Why would Stefani write this?

Nic had been avoiding her and Val for a couple weeks now.

They both kept attempting to get her to talk to them, but it didn't matter, because they wouldn't change their minds about the trackers. But as soon as Nic got the chance, she was going to sneak into Val's room and take whatever key Val had.

Nic dragged her attention back to the picture of Jake and Shiloh kissing. A knife twisted in her chest, but she wasn't sure why. Jake only spoke to her briefly in public, but sometimes, he'd discreetly leave chocolate or a snack on her table. He, without fail, always made her smile.

Nic folded her tablet and slipped it into her jacket.

A lock clicked, and Shiloh stepped out of the stall, looking back to her usual composed self.

"Is it true then?" Nic asked.

"Is what true?" Shiloh replied, as she walked to the sink and turned the water on.

"You and Jake?"

Shiloh glanced up so Nic could see her reflection in the mirror, but her face was unreadable. "Yes." She cupped water in her hands and splashed it onto her face.

Nic didn't want to talk about it, but she also wanted to know everything. How long had they dated? Were they in love? Why, in their dozens of tutoring sessions, hadn't Shiloh ever mentioned it?

Shiloh dried her face with a paper towel and turned off the sink. "Thank you for what you did."

"Rule #4, right? Haven girls look after each other."

Shiloh nodded. "I have to go find Jake."

Nic nodded, and Shiloh headed toward the door. Halfway, Shiloh turned around. "Is it true? You killed an Elite?"

Nic blinked against the image of blood on leaves and swallowed down a painful lump. "Yes."

Shiloh nodded once again and started toward the door. She said it so quietly, Nic almost missed it.

"Good."

❧

"Jake, how could you?"

The hurt on Mom's face stabbed Jake deeper than the anger and disgust of his father. They now stood in Jake's room. Dad had forced them to finish the meal in the cafeteria—to not make a scene—and Jake wasn't sure how he'd managed not to choke on his food.

Now, Jake perched on his bed, his head in his hands, while Dad paced the floor and Mom stared at him numbly.

"You told Dr. Williams that you two were just working on a science project together," Mom said.

Jake groaned. "I know."

He looked down at the floor, where Shiloh and he had their first official date, the stars playing in Shiloh's eyes. He could feel her presence there even now: her head on his chest, her fingertips on his back, the sound of her laughter.

It can't be over. It can't be.

"Jake, look at me!" Mom snapped. She'd been talking, and Jake hadn't heard. He looked up. "You said that you no longer wanted anything to do with her."

Jake threw his hands in the air. "Mom, I know! What do you want me to say? I lied, okay? I'm not over her. I've *never* been over her."

I'll never be over her.

Dad turned toward him. "So, this has been going on the *whole* time?"

"Not the whole time. Just since the project started. We knew you wouldn't get reports about our trackers being together if we had a reason to be together."

Twenty-eight more days. Jake was supposed to get twenty-eight more days to be with her and to figure out how to keep her for all the days after.

This isn't fair!

"You're coming home with us for the weekend," Dad said. "We can figure out the next step."

"You have to at least let me talk to her," Jake said.

"Absolutely not!" Dad snapped.

Jake jumped to his feet. "Look, I'm sorry that I almost died, okay? I'm sorry that I watched a girl get shot and that a stage blew up with me on it, and that I was so messed up from that that I said something stupid. But none of it had to do with Shiloh. Yes, we talked about it—we processed it together—but she's the one who warned me not to press it further. If you heard us that night, you *know* that! Please, *please*, don't take her away from me." His hands were pressed together, like he was begging, but he didn't care.

Jake looked between his parents, but Mom still looked dazed, and his father was a wall of stone. "Mom? Dad? Please, I'll do anything. I'll keep in line. I won't drink or party." Which he wasn't doing, anyway. "Whatever it is that you want me to do, I'll do it. Just please let me keep seeing her. She means *everything* to me."

Mom wiped a tear from the corner of her eye and glanced to Dad.

"I suggest you pack your bag quickly, Jake," Dad said, his voice merciless.

The rage boiled like a fire in Jake's chest, a volcano ready to explode, rumbling his whole being. "I hate you," he growled, meeting Dad's eyes. "I *really* hate you."

If the words hurt, it didn't show. Dad only folded his arms over his chest and glared.

"Jake," Mom murmured, reaching toward him.

Jake jerked away.

"Fine. Hate me." Dad marched to the door and yanked it open. "But you *will* be in the car in ten minutes."

Shiloh made it through the snow to Jake's dorm, just in time to see a bodyguard throw a bag into a car's trunk. Jake stood by the open back door, about to climb in, when he saw her from across the hood of the car. His face contorted. An invisible hand clenched Shiloh's heart.

"I'm so sorry," he mouthed.

Councilor Osgood had been standing with his back to her, but he turned. His eyes narrowed, and his lip curled like she was vile, disgusting, *worthless*. After all, she *was* a Haven girl.

"Get in the car," Councilor Osgood snapped to Jake before ducking in himself.

Jake mouthed something else before he too disappeared into the car, but Shiloh wasn't sure what it was.

Maybe it was just another apology.

Maybe it was *I love you*.

Either way, it didn't matter now. Because it was over. It was all over.

Stefani answered her phone on the third ring. "You've got Stef!"

"Stefani, how *dare* you!"

Jake paced in his room, back at home. He'd bolted there before his parents decided to take his phone away. He'd wanted to call Shiloh, but school tablets only talked to each other. So he'd dialed Stefani's number instead.

The hologram of Stefani didn't look up as she painted her fingernails. "Oh, Jakey-boy. I saw your parents sweep you off in a hurry. Have any fun weekend plans?"

"Froq you! You have *no* idea what you've done."

Her head snapped up, and a cold smile sprawled across her face. "Oh, no, make no mistake. I know quite well what I've done." She put the brush back into the bottle of nail polish and screwed it shut. "I may not know why you wanted to keep your relationship a secret, but I know that you did. You were never seen publicly with anyone, but Harper wouldn't shut up about how different you were acting and how she just *knew* you were seeing someone. It just took me a little time to figure out who it was."

Harper, you blight! Jake kicked a soccer ball that had rolled from his closet. It slammed against his wall with a *Thud!*

"You don't understand, Stefani. My parents are never going to let me see her again."

Stefani popped a bubble of gum. "We all have our reasons to hide things, Jakey boy. And it doesn't feel good when people expose them, does it?" She smiled again and then blew on her nails. They were a bright, don't-froq-with-me shade of red.

Realization dawned. Jake sank onto his bed. *Oh, froq.*

"It's kind of funny, if you think about it. And by funny, I mean not funny *at all*. We both had our own Haven girls we wanted to keep a secret. That's how you knew how vulnerable Val was. It's just too bad you didn't protect your own Haven girl better."

"Stefani—"

She leaned forward so that he could see her face more clearly. When she spoke, she sounded like a cat, hissing at a mouse it had cornered. "Jakey-boy, you *froqed* with my girl, so I froqed with yours. And now, we're even."

She hung up, and her image disappeared from the air. Jake's hand tightened around his phone, using all his willpower not to scream and throw the phone against the wall. *He* had done this. He had blackmailed Stefani, knowing that he would face consequences. And this consequence was more than he could bear.

TWENTY-SIX

Nic rubbed at her stinging eyes, slipped into her snow boots and wrapped herself in careful layers. Last Unity Day—or Thanksgiving, as her Family called it—Nic had sat around the fire in the abandoned cabin with her Family. They'd cooked a special meal, meatless chili and cornbread, and Nic had devoured it, pressed close to her mother's side for warmth. This year, she'd be celebrating with the rest of the Haven girls, who —besides Val and Shiloh—were strangers. But Shiloh had assured her the food, at least, would be good.

Nic stepped into the hallway. Down the hall, a door slammed.

Nic's heart exploded in her chest, and for a moment, all she saw was white. *It's fine. It's not the cage.* It was only Val, exiting her room. Her scowl looked deeper than usual.

Nic approached her tentatively. They were going to the same place. There wasn't any reason they couldn't walk together.

"You ready for this?" Val asked, pulling her stocking cap over her ears.

The way she said it made it sound like they were embarking on a glorious expedition into hell. Nic nodded. They exited Diligence Dorm together and found Stefani standing on the doorstep. She wore a rainbow scarf wrapped around her neck, dusted with the fine snow that was falling, and her red coat, much was much brighter than the Codex-compliant hunter green that Val and Nic wore. She wasn't wearing even a spot of makeup, and her eyes looked puffy. Like she'd been crying.

"Hi," Stefani said, her voice croaking.

Val didn't return the greeting, only shoved past her.

Stefani grabbed her arm. "Val, wait!"

Val jerked away with a hiss—a cobra rearing its head to strike.

"Val, please talk to me."

Nic froze with her feet deep in the snow.

"I don't want to talk," Val said, whirling around and walking off so briskly that Nic had to jog to keep up with her.

Stefani hurried after them, feet crunching in the snow

"You *know* why I published the story, Val!" Stefani pleaded. "He had it coming."

Nic's frown deepened. Why would Jake have it coming?

"But *Shiloh* didn't!" Val growled.

Stefani threw up her hands. "Peace and harmony, Val! That's kind of like the pig calling the goat a smelly farm animal. We both know that you haven't said a kind word to her in two years. Why do you find it necessary to defend her now?"

Val spun around, fists at her side. Stefani stopped so quickly she nearly slipped. "Haven girls are off limits, Stef. And you know it! You put a target on Shiloh's back!"

"It was collateral damage," Stefani whined.

"Shiloh is *not* collateral damage!" Nic snapped.

Val and Stefani jerked their head toward her, as though they'd forgotten she was there.

"You don't know what Harper did to her yesterday," Nic said.

Val's glare narrowed even farther. "What did that Harpie do?"

Nic's mouth went dry. She didn't know if she could actually repeat the terrible things that Harper had said to Shiloh.

Val stepped toward her. "Tell me." When Nic stiffened, she added more softly, "Please."

For someone who acted like she hated Shiloh, Val clearly cared deeply. How could you hate someone and love them at the same time?

Nic took a breath and explained what had happened. "They humiliated her," she said at the end, ignoring her tracker's beep as it gave a two-minute warning. "I think I basically threatened to murder Harper if she didn't leave her alone."

Nic had tried the same speech on her roommates last night. By the looks on their faces, Nic thought that they, too, would be leaving her alone. She should have done that a long time ago.

Val's brown eyes had morphed to a deeper black. Stefani buried her face in her scarf, trying and failing to hide her tears.

"I told you," Val said to Stefani.

"I never meant for that to happen," Stefani whimpered.

Val scoffed. "I don't care what you *meant*."

Val threw open the door to the Commons and stomped inside. Stefani watched her go, her tears turning from a drizzle to a flood. She looked so miserable that Nic's hand reached toward her shoulder on its own accord, and then she whipped it back and followed Val into the cafeteria.

Shiloh dragged her fork through the gravy, smearing it across the tray. Generally, the Unity Day meal was the best of the year, but the thought of putting a single bite into her mouth made her want to puke.

Of course, Mother and the Aunts couldn't—and wouldn't—attend the Unity Day, so it was just the Haven girls of Ardency. According to tradition, they each stated their gratitude for living in the 'great nation of Arcadia' and what they would do the coming year to promote unity. Shiloh had barely been able to force an answer out. Nic had struggled too, and Val had said what she said every year: "Pass."

When they were done with the mandatory pandering to Arcadia, Demi was, of course, the first to speak. They would be lucky if she let anyone else talk.

"What I want to know is about Shiloh's boyfriend! You and Jacob Osgood!"

Shiloh's fingers tightened on her fork, and she looked across the table at Demi. The sophomore squealed and clapped her hands in excitement. "Girl, spill! I must know *all* the details."

So many people, girls Shiloh knew and girls she didn't, had demanded details from Shiloh since the article came out. And the last thing Shiloh wanted to do was talk about Jake or think about Jake, which was really all she was doing. It made her chest feel raw and empty.

How am I supposed to protect him now? But it was more than that.

I don't want to lose him.

Before Shiloh could fake an excuse, Val threw her fork down on the table with a clatter. "Seriously, guys? We're supposed to pretend like this is a good thing. This is *Jacob Osgood* we're talking about. The Man-Whore of Ardency." She shook her head and narrowed her eyes at Shiloh. "Starchild, you're supposed to be the smart one. Why would you do something so stupid?"

"It's complicated, Val," Shiloh said, swallowing the taste of bile that rose in her throat.

"Why? Because you *lllooovvve* him." Val faked a gagging sound. "Don't give me that lovesick ordure. You've always thought with your head first. You must know that he doesn't deserve you."

Shiloh's mouth parted, but no words came out. Of all the objections that she thought that Val would have, this was not one of them.

"He's going to chew you up, use you, and once he gets bored, toss you aside like you're *nothing*."

The other girls stared down at their plates, trying to pretend this wasn't happening.

Shiloh opened her mouth, but from beside her, Nic snapped, "That's not true. Jake isn't like that."

Shiloh's blood ran cold. Surely, they weren't hanging out again, having more than the brief run-ins Jake had told her about. And if Nic was going to reveal it, Shiloh had to think quickly to keep it from being caught on the audio recorder.

"And how would you know?" Val asked, glaring at Nic now.

Nic's mouth opened and closed a few times. "I met him a couple of times, months ago. He was nice to me. He brought us the chocolates, remember?"

Shiloh began breathing again.

Val rolled her eyes. "It's an act, Nic. He could charm the panties off of anything."

Nic turned the exact shade of the cranberry sauce.

Anger lit up Shiloh's chest. "Shut up, Val! You don't know what you're talking about."

"Really? I know he's an Osgood, and that's enough. He doesn't care who gets hurt, as long as he gets what he wants in the end."

"You don't know him."

"Don't believe me? Ask your boyfriend why Stefani wrote that piece. It was revenge, and he knows it."

"What are you talking about?"

"Ask him!" Val jammed her knife into the turkey on her plate, like she might kill it all over again. "Shiloh, he's going to break your heart."

Shiloh threw down her fork. "I don't even know why you care!"

Val glared down at her plate. "I don't."

"Then stay out of it." Shiloh shoved up from the table and stormed away. "Have a happy Unity Day!"

❧

Jake sat on his bed, leaning against his headboard, when he heard the voices. Today had been ordure in a handbasket with an all-day emergency session with Dr. Williams. She'd told him how very disappointed she was, and he'd told her to blow it up her endsphere. Ultimately, Mom fired Dr. Williams, because if she could be manipulated by a seventeen-year-old, she clearly wasn't as good as they thought.

The voices grew louder. Jake disentangled himself from the sheets and padded across the heated wood floors to the vent below the window. Dad had never figured out sounds floated from his office, which was directly below Jake's bedroom.

"I think we made a mistake keeping them apart, Sam," Mom said.

"We made that decision together, Reagan," Dad said. "We thought it was the best thing."

"I know, but that's when we thought it was just a crush, and it would blow over. But, Sam, you didn't pay attention to the way that he looked at her when he was getting into the car. This isn't a crush. He is *in love* with her."

Jake jerked in surprise. Mom always did see straight through him, didn't she? He hadn't even had the courage to admit it to himself, but balancing on the edge of losing Shiloh, the truth screamed in the silence.

I love her.

I deeply, irrevocably, and recklessly love *her.*

"I couldn't care less how he feels for her," Dad barked. Jake heard a jangle of bottles as Dad poured himself a drink from the bar in his office. "He's acting spoiled and entitled, and he needs to grow up."

Jake's jaw tightened.

"Well, I care how he feels about her," Mom said.

"You know, this might not be a bad thing," said a third voice which Jake recognized as Hazel, Dad's personal assistant. She handled everything from his agenda to publicity. "If he continued to see the Haven girl, we could control the story in the media. Use it to show how deeply your family believes in unity, by overlooking the differences in statuses."

Jake gritted his teeth. Yeah, that was just what he wanted. For Shiloh to be a publicity stunt.

"Hazel," Mom said levelly.

"Yes, Mrs. Osgood?"

"Get. Out."

"Yes, Mrs. Osgood." There was a scramble of heels on wood, and a door opened and shut.

"Listen to me, Sam," Mom said. "You know how your son is. You tell him not to do something, and he wants to do it ten times more. I think by forbidding this relationship, we made his feelings even stronger. Maybe if we just let this relationship run its course, it'll fizzle out. How many high school romances really last? And more than that..." She paused. "You think he rebelled this summer? What do you think he'll do if we take this girl away now?"

Jake slid down to sit beside the vent, his back against the wall.

"You heard what they talked about in the hospital," Dad protested. "She's a bad influence. She will ruin him."

"I went back and listened to the recording. Shiloh never once encouraged Jake. In fact, she told him to be careful and not pursue it."

Bang! His dad had surely slapped his hand on the desk. "Reagan, she is still a Haven girl. Her parents were heretics."

"And mine were monsters too!" Mom shouted back. "Or have you forgotten that?"

Jake winced. He often forgot that his strong, kind Mom came from a hard place—an alcoholic mom who'd left Mom and Uncle Silas with an abusive father. Then they'd bounced through the foster care system, before finding a home with an elderly woman who'd supported them through their teen and college years. They'd been lucky, Mom had told Jake. One adult to protect a kid could make all the difference. Prior to Dad being crowned king, she'd had a successful career as a family lawyer, protecting kids. Now she ran multiple charities.

Silence hovered in the air, feeling thick and foggy with tension.

Finally, Dad said softly. "No. Reagan, I haven't forgotten. But you're different."

"I'm *not* different. If I'm not my parents, then *she* is not her parents. Froq, she's on an Engineering Track. She didn't get there by being a heretic."

Another long pause stretched on and on.

"Sam, we almost lost our son this summer. I'm not going to risk losing him again."

Dad grumbled something Jake couldn't hear.

"No, Samuel. We tell him he gets to see the Haven girl. That's my decision. I need you to decide how you're going to be okay with that."

In any other room in Arcadia, Samuel Osgood was the most powerful man by far. But in that room, against his wife, about their son, he knew he was outmatched.

"Okay," Dad said heavily.

Jake pressed his hand to his mouth. He could have laughed. He could have run down the stairs and twirled his mother around in a circle. But he only buried his face in his knees, feeling the relief wash over him like a flood.

Thirty minutes before curfew, Shiloh was curled in her bed, wrapped in two blankets but still not able to warm the chill inside of her. Josephine soft snores filled the air but were interrupted when someone began pounding on the door.

"Make it stop," Josephine whined, pulling the blanket over her head.

Shiloh padded to the door and opened it. Jake stood on the other side, bouncing from one foot to the other and grinning. *Well, that's promising.*

"Can we talk?" he asked.

Shiloh nodded. "Let me grab my coat."

She knew the common area would still be full of late-night study groups, so she slipped her coat on over her pajamas and pulled on snow boots.

"My professional opinion," Josephine said, peeking out from beneath her blanket, "is that you lock that down. That boy is *fine.*"

"Thanks, Jo," Shiloh said dryly, leaving the room.

Jake grabbed her hand and pulled her down the stairs and out of Luminosity. This was not at all what she'd expected. She'd thought that, when he returned, it would be to end it, but he almost bounced as they walked down the slope toward Lake Harmony. The thick layer of ice over the lake gleamed in the moonlight.

"What's going on, Jake?"

"My parents wanted me to give you something."

He pulled an envelope from his pocket and handed it to her. She had to slide her gloves off in order to break the fancy seal. Light burst from within, casting a hologram into the night air. Snow fell and Yuletide lights twinkled as gold letters scrawled through the sky like an invisible hand was writing it. She had to stare at it a long time before her brain could make sense of it.

"It's an invitation to the Osgood's Yuletide Eve Ball," Shiloh said at last.

He grinned. "Yes, it is!"

"I don't understand. I thought they were never going to let you see me again."

"I thought so too." He pulled her into his arms then spun her around, laughing. "But they decided to not stand in our way anymore. They think if our relationship isn't forbidden, it won't be as exciting and will just burn out."

Shiloh should be excited too, but she felt...cold.

This was too neat. It felt wrong. And...

Ask your boyfriend. He knows.

Shiloh had been putting the facts together. Stefani Andreou had written the article, and when Shiloh had looked her up in the school directory, she recognized her instantly as the girl Val had been kissing in the woods at homecoming. The girl Shiloh had seen with Val a lot over the past year or two. Her girlfriend, surely. And that had clicked the last chilling piece together.

Jake leaned to kiss her, but Shiloh backed out of his arms.

"Jake, what did you do that made Stefani Andreou publish that article?" Shiloh asked. "And what does it have to do with Val?"

The joy completely drained from his face, and Shiloh knew Val was right. Whatever he'd done, she wasn't going to like it.

"Shiloh, you have to understand..." he started.

"Just tell me the truth," Shiloh snapped.

He sighed, shoved his hand deep into his coat pockets and stared at his feet. "I wanted Stefani to help me hack through the internet censor wall so I could research ROGUE."

"What?"

Thank goodness Shiloh had stripped off her bra, and the audio recorder, when she'd put on her pajamas. She hadn't taken the time to put it back on when she left the room.

Jake cringed and looked around him. They were still alone, so he went on, each word hesitant and pained. "And so, I told her that if she didn't help me, that I would tell... that Val is her...girlfriend."

An invisible fist slammed into Shiloh gut. For a second, she couldn't breathe. She barely managed two words. "You...*what*?"

"Shiloh, I'm so sorry." Jake reached toward her, but she jerked away. "It was a bluff. I would never have actually done it. Never."

"Then why even threaten to? She's my *sister*, Jake!"

Jake dropped his face into his hands. "I know. I should never have done it. I've regretted it ever since."

"How could you have done this when you know what she means to me? When even was this?"

Jake glanced toward the lake, his jaw tight. "Right after homecoming."

That horrible night came back to her. The chapel. Their tears. Shiloh pinched the bridge of her nose. "So you did it because you were mad at me?"

He spun to face her. "Froq, no! I just..." He searched around them again. They were still alone except for the trees, their leafless branches clawing at the sky. "I was so angry. I would have done anything to get back at Arcadia for keeping us apart. Even though I knew it was the worst thing I'd ever done."

Shiloh turned her back to him and stared at the moonbeams crawling on the lake, her vision blurring.

He took another tentative step toward her, his feet crunching in the snow. She didn't turn around. "You have to believe me. I never intended to follow through on my threat. If Stefani had said no, I would have just found another way. In fact, she didn't even let me through the censor wall. She lied and took my rations, and I still didn't tell. But I'm still so, so sorry."

Shiloh pressed her eyes closed, unable to look at him. "Even if it was a bluff, that was a terrible game to play with Val's life."

"I know."

Terrible game. Shiloh's own words jabbed back, landing a solid blow to her stomach. Yes, Jake had played a terrible game, but it was *Go Fish* compared to the game that Shiloh was playing with Jake's life. All the lies she told, the bruises she hid, the gamble that could end in ruin.

People play such terrible, terrible games when they're trying to survive.

But none more terrible than hers.

Shiloh slowly turned back to face him. The shadows on his face preached of his regret. "Do you *promise* me that it was a bluff?"

He nodded. "I promise."

Shiloh released a trembling breath, breathing out some of the fire in her veins. "Okay."

"Okay?" Jake repeated, his shoulders still tense.

"Okay, I believe you."

Jake let out a breath like he'd held it this whole time and reached toward her. Shiloh shook her head, and his hands dropped.

"I'm still mad at you," Shiloh said. "But I trust you. I believe you."

Jake winced, but nodded. "Fair enough. Take as long as you need, just...let me know when you're done being angry, okay?"

Shiloh nodded, pulling her coat tighter to her. "So..." Shiloh cleared her throat. "Tell me about this ball."

TWENTY-SEVEN

Finally. Nic found her opportunity to sneak into Val's room. She peeked into the room to confirm no one was there, and then she slipped in and quietly closed the door.

Nic shuffled through dresser drawers, pulled off bed sheets, and checked under the mattresses, then put everything back into its proper place. She got down on her knees and ran her hands over the floors and walls, checking for loose boards or hidden seams. She found something wedged behind the frame of the window, close to Val's bed, but it was only a lighter. She was slipping it back, when she heard the door open. Without thinking, she hit the ground and rolled beneath the nearest bunk.

"So how are we going to tell her?" The voice was deep and familiar. Val.

"I think the question is how are we going to get her to trust us again." This was Stefani's trilling voice. She sighed and lowered herself on the bunk. "I should have done more digging months ago. So much for being the best snoop at Ardency!"

"Well, we've figured it out now." Val sat beside her in the bed. "It's no use worrying your beautiful head about it."

Stefani's voice crept higher, like she was singing. "Oh, so you think I'm beautiful?"

Val groaned. "Oh, shut up!"

"Make me."

The mattress whined as they moved, and Stefani made a sound in her throat, almost a purr of pleasure. Then there was nothing, but the sound of lips gliding together.

Oh. My. Gosh!

Nic inhaled sharply and then clamped a hand over her mouth. How had she missed this? Val and Stefani weren't best friends; they were *girlfriends*! It should have been obvious. The fights. The way they looked at each other. The sadness in Stefani's eyes when Nic talked about Arcadia killing love.

I imagine it hurts. It really, really hurts.

Nic's heart sank for them. That's why they'd taken their trackers off—to be together, where no one would know or see.

"Stef, did you hear something?"

Oh, no!

The bunk groaned as Val stood and then kneeled, looking right under the bed to meet Nic's eyes. Nic scrambled out of the front of the bed and bolted toward the door.

Val and Stefani jumped to their feet.

"Nic, stop!" Val yelled.

Nic yanked open the door.

"Freebird!" Stefani snapped. "You stop *right* there!"

Nic's heart slammed against her chest. She whirled around to face them, clutching the doorknob to steady herself. "What...what did you call me?"

No one would know her codename. No one...except someone in ROGUE.

Stefani and Val took a step closer, and Nic shut the door slowly.

"You were trying to find a key, weren't you?" Val asked, her voice scarcely a whisper.

Nic nodded stiffly.

"And you heard us kissing," Stefani said, her voice no louder, "didn't you?"

Nic swallowed and nodded again. "I won't tell anyone."

"We know," Stefani said. "We trust you. And I'm going to tell you something so that you'll trust us." She came closer and put her lips next to Nic's ear, so only she would hear. Her next words pound in Nic's veins. "What has an eye, but cannot see?"

Nic gaped at Stefani and barely managed to finish the ROGUE greeting. "Our enemies when we come for them."

Somehow, someway, Stefani was ROGUE.

"Do you trust us now?" Stefani asked, her eyes dancing. "Are you going to let us help you get out of here?"

"You're...you're going to help me?"

Stefani nodded. "Yes. We can't explain everything here. But we can tonight. Someplace safe. Can you trust us?"

Nic flung her arms around Stefani, feeling hope once more. "Yes!"

Nic lay awake, watching the minutes slowly pass on her tracker. Right at midnight, the door creeped open, and a shadowy figure slipped in and kneeled beside Nic's bed. A scarf wrapped around Val's face, and her hood was pulled up, so only her murky eyes were visible.

"Give me your wrist," Val whispered.

Nic held out her tracker. From her pocket, Val pulled a lighter and a slender piece of metal that Nic recognized as the toothpick-thin spear on Val's small, iron warrior. She flicked the lighter and stuck the tip of the metal into the flame. When it glowed a hot orange, Val stuck the metal into the keyhole of Nic's tracker. It popped off without a sound.

She was free.

Val pulled it free of Nic's wrist and then snapped it together. It reactivated quickly.

"You can't leave it undone for longer than a few seconds," Val whispered. "It'd alert the security guards that it had gone offline."

Nic slipped her tracker under her pillow and then hurriedly put on her boots and coats. She pulled up her hood and coiled her scarf around her face. Nic followed Val out of the room, remembering the directions they had discussed earlier.

"When we get outside, follow right behind me," Val had said. "Go exactly where I go. There are cameras, but most of the ones outside are super old and only catch a picture every few seconds. But you have to know exactly where they are."

Together, they slipped out of the Diligence dorm. A new layer of snow fell, fluttering in beams of moonlight. Val led them in zigzag patterns across campus between the buildings, flattening against the brick beneath the cameras. The journey took a while, but finally, Val led her around the corner of the Quadrangle. This corner boasted two raised small towers, like it had once been a grand entrance, but the front was completely boarded up. Val grasped one of the boards and moved it to the side.

"Hurry," Val said.

Nic slid through the narrow space between the boards, and Val squeezed in after her. The small room held nothing but the rubble of stone and wood scattered on the floor. In one corner of the room, Val began to move the rubble, revealing stone tiles. Val pressed down a stone; it indented, and then another, and a portion of the floor slid away. A trapdoor.

Val smiled mischievously. "Come along." She disappeared below the floor.

Nic followed her down the ladder, jumping from a few rungs down, and landing with knees bent. Nic blinked in the darkness until Val flicked on a small flashlight she pulled from her pocket. A long stone tunnel stretched before them.

"Where are we?" Nic asked. It was warmer down here, and she pulled down her hood.

"You'll see."

Val led her down the long tunnel, finally explaining the key as they went. "The real tracker keys work by creating a small impulse of heat that signals the clasp to release. The same thing can be replicated by heating the metal and slipping it in. Stefani figured it out when she was in seventh grade. She must have set off a million alarms before she finally figured it out."

The tunnel opened into a massive round room. Nic flung her hands to her mouth in surprise. Treasures filled the room. Paintings of bible scenes leaned against the wall, and old books were stuffed in bookshelves, cobwebs crawling over every surface. A statue of St. Mary stood watch over everything from its place in the corner.

"It's beautiful," Nic said, breathlessly. She hadn't known that relics like these still existed in Arcadia. "What is this place?"

"We think that the monks who used to live here must have known what was coming, so they hid a lot of their precious artwork and books down here, before they were arrested in the Great Excision. Arcadia must not have found it when they set up the school. I don't even know how Stefani knew about it."

"Did someone say Stefani Andreou?" Stefani said, as she swept in behind them, pulling her dark scarf from around her face. She gave Nic's shoulder a brief squeeze and greeted Val with a kiss. Val pulled away, glancing at Nic uneasily.

"For the record," Nic said, smiling, "I think you two make a really cute couple."

Stefani smiled, and Val looked away. Was she blushing?

"But I do have a question," Nic continued. "Why do you guys say 'I hate you' to each other so much?"

"Oh." Stefani smiled. "We can't exactly say 'I love you' in public, can we?"

Val's smile went all the way to her eyes, making them glow with a completely different type of fire. Love was beautiful.

Releasing Val, Stefani took a blanket out of her bag and spread it out on the floor. They sat down in a tight circle, leaning in close.

"Listen," Stefani said, "what I'm about to tell you goes to the grave with you? Do you understand? An army of flying monkey ninjas should not be able to tear it from your lips, all right?"

Nic nodded.

"My mom is Minnesota."

Nic's heart stopped in her chest. That codename had been muttered often as The Family planned the Cleansing attack. Nic hadn't known who it was, but knew it was someone powerful, who could tell them where the Cleansing was and get them access to the building to set the bombs.

"You—your mother is an ally of ROGUE?" Nic asked.

Stefani nodded. "So is my dad."

Nic's mind spun. "W-why didn't you tell me sooner?"

Stefani shifted uncomfortably, and Val laced her fingers through hers. "I just didn't know for sure you were connected with ROGUE or the Cleansing. I should have guessed, but—"

"I get it," Nic said. "You don't talk about ROGUE unless you know for sure."

Stefani tucked her hair behind her ear. "Anyway, after you got so upset, I decided to ask my parents about you at the Unity Day dinner. My dad has heard messages on the network looking for a Freebird. By the little hidden clues they gave, he thought that might be you."

"It is." Nic let out a breath. "Did he say who was looking?"

"Not all the messages specified, but one message said, 'Birdie is seeking Freebird'."

A sob of relief broke through Nic's lips. She covered her face with her hands, her cheeks growing wet. "She's alive! My mom's alive."

Stefani wrapped an arm around Nic's shoulder, and Nic used her own scarf to wipe away the tears.

"Wait." Val frowned. "What about the Cleansing?" She cocked her head at Stefani. "You didn't mention the Cleansing earlier."

Stefani winced. "Oh."

Val's hand tightened on Stefani's. "What happened at the Cleansing?"

Stefani still hesitated, but now that they were here, Nic trusted Val with her life.

"My Family set off a bomb beneath the stage in an attempt to assassinate Councilors Osgood and Beck," Nic said.

Val made a sound, like she couldn't breathe, then burst to her feet, "No, no, no, no!" She paced wildly across the stone, pulling at her hair with both hands, her protests never stopping. "No, no, no, no!"

Stefani jumped to her feet and rushed over to her. "Council, Val, what's wrong?"

"Hope," Val croaked through her hands.

Stefani frowned. "What about Hope?"

Nic slowly got to her feet, watching in confusion. Val continued to pace, not answering, until Stefani took her hands gently and pulled them from Val's face. Only then did Nic realize she was crying.

"Hope was there," Val choked through her sobs.

Color drained from Stefani's face. "Oh froq, Val. Why didn't you tell me?"

Val shook her head, saying nothing, as Stefani pulled her into her arms, cradling her against her chest.

"Who's Hope?" Nic asked Stefani.

"Her Haven sister," Stefani explained, over Val's head. "They were very close. She was arrested two years ago."

Nic's heart wrenched in her chest.

"I'm so, so sorry, Val." Nic laid a hand on her shoulder. Jake who had almost died. Hope. How much sacrifice was freedom really worth?

"Val, you don't know that she was killed," Stefani reasoned, leaning back to look in Val's eyes. She trailed her fingers across Val's cheeks, caressing away her tears. "You don't know she was on that stage when the bomb went off."

Val pulled away, gulping in breaths to calm her sobs. "Yes, I do. Because Shiloh was."

Nic inhaled so sharply her throat stung. "*Shiloh* was at the Cleansing?"

"Mother sent her as the family representative." Val wrapped her arms around herself and stared at her feet. "Shiloh was in the hospital for a month...and she was burned so badly. She had to have been on that stage."

Nic had seen the spiderweb of scars that weaved across Shiloh's legs. They'd seemed recent, but she'd never asked. Other pieces connected. There had been someone with Jake, a name he wouldn't mention because he'd never put her at risk. A girl he was now dating.

That was when they met.

Val swore in Spanish. "I wish Shiloh had told me."

"To be fair," Stefani said, tucking a damp strand of hair behind Val's ear, "Shiloh probably couldn't tell you anything. Arcadia has terrible ways of keeping people's mouths shut."

Val nodded and sniffed. "At least, I know." She wiped away the last of her tears, returned to the blanket on the floor, and put her usual tough expression back on like she was adjusting a mask. "Okay, what happened to you after the Cleansing?"

Nic hesitated. "Are you sure you're—"

"I'm fine," Val said in that tone that warned Nic not to press.

So Nic told them about being left behind in the old mill, and how she'd had to run. Those weeks she'd survived on her own. About shooting the Elite when they'd captured her. But when she got to the part of the cage, Nic couldn't make the words come out of her throat.

Stefani caught her hands in both of hers, and Nic realized she'd been trembling. "It's okay. You don't have to talk about it. We can figure out the rest."

Val nodded. "I'm so sorry, Nic. I saw your bruises. I can't even imagine."

Nic sucked in a trembling breath. "They wanted me to give them information on ROGUE. Which, even if that person were my best friend, I'd never tell them. I think they sent me to school because they thought they could bribe me. Principal Clark offered me an Athletic Track. I don't know why they've let me stay so long after that. They must be working on another plan."

"Then we need to get you out of here before they can complete it," Stefani said. "My parents are willing to help, but it'll take time to make sure we do this right."

A thrill raced down Nic's spine. For the first time, she could see something in her future other than death. And she was incredibly grateful that she'd met Val and Stefani. Maybe, no matter how it felt, Nic's God hadn't abandoned her after all.

"Here take these," Val said, handing her a lighter and a metal piece. A tracker key. "Just in case there is an emergency and you have to leave quickly." Val folded her fingers over the gift and then grinned at her, her eyes dancing mischievously. "Now, let's commit some heresy and get you back to your mom."

They began discussing plans. How Stefani's dad would get the message out. How Nic would get enough of a head start before the Elite discovered she was missing. How to ensure no one knew Val and Stefani were involved. It began to set in with Nic how difficult this task would be, and how much easier it would be if she had someone on her side who was beyond suspect. Who could go where he pleased without being questioned.

The only question was: Was Jacob Osgood willing to keep his promise to help her?

❦

Jake dragged his heavy eyes open, not quite sure what had woken him. But there it was again.

Tap, tap, tap.

Jake stumbled out from the tangle of blankets and across the floor to the window. Maybe it was the large tree that grew outside. Sometimes, when the wind howled, its branches scratched against the glass. But this seemed too rhythmic, too insistent.

Tap, tap, tap.

He looked out the window and jumped. Someone was perched on the branch near his window, face concealed with a hood and scarf. Jake's heart slammed against his ribcage, and then the person lowered the scarf.

Nic.

He opened the window, a burst of the frigid night air blowing the curtains. "What in Arcadia are you doing out there?"

Nic carefully slid in through the window, onto his desk, and sat on the edge of it. She smiled. "Hi!" And then her cheeks flushed bright red, wide eyes staring at Jake's bare chest.

Froq! Jake snatched his sweater from the end of his bed and yanked it on.

"Nic, are you crazy? There will be a security guard here any minute."

"No, they won't." She held up her left wrist—her *bare* left wrist.

"How did you get it off?"

"I'll show you."

She pulled a sliver of metal and a lighter from her pocket and gestured for him to give his wrist. Jake stretched his arm out hesitantly. She flicked the lighter and heated the end of the metal, before sliding it into the tracker's lock. The tracker unlatched and fell from his wrist. She snapped it together and tossed it on his bed. Jake rubbed his bare wrist.

"Where did you learn that from?"

"That's a secret," Nic said.

"Okay, but that still doesn't explain what you're even doing here?"

Nic lowered her voice even farther and whispered, "I need your help, like you promised. But I can't tell you here."

Jake's spine tensed, but he *had* promised. "Okay."

He grabbed his snow boots and pulled on his coat.

"Grab your scarf and put up your hood," Nic said, adjusting her scarf back over her face.

Jake did as directed. Nic was already sliding out the window, and he followed behind her, not as gracefully as she did. He almost fell from the icy branches more than once.

When they were finally on the ground, Nic said, "Go only where I go. There are cameras everywhere, but I think I figured out where they are between your dorm and there."

She darted across the road and pressed her back against the Quadrangle. Jake copied her. He could see the box of the ancient security camera above their heads. She stayed close to the wall as she went around the corner. Jake caught a flash of light in the corner of his eye, a moment before Nic pulled him down behind the bushes. His heart sounded unnaturally loud in the quiet as the security guard slowly walked by.

At last, Nic held the board as he slipped through a crack into the boarded-up corner of the Quadrangle. Nic pushed aside rubble and then stepped on stones that compressed downward. And then part of the floor opened.

Well, peace and harmony.

He followed Nic down the ladder. She flicked on a flashlight, highlighting the stones all around them. The tunnel ended in a room, full of crosses and books and statues—relics of a religion long forbidden.

"Wow," Jake said beneath his breath.

"Wonderful, isn't it?" Nic asked.

Jake nodded. He didn't know anything about God or Christianity, but he knew that these things must mean something to the heretics who did. He was glad that some of it had survived.

Nic lowered herself on the cool stone, and Jake sat beside her. She shifted uneasily, and he waited for her to reveal why'd she brought him here.

"Soo...you and Shiloh, huh?" Nic said instead, catching Jake off guard.

"Um...yeah."

Nic elbowed him in the side. "Do you *looovvve* her?"

Jake snorted. The way Nic said that made him feel like he was back in grade school, and his answer would be immediately followed by, *"Eeewwww!"*

But there was only one honest answer.

"Yeah, I do," he said.

He hadn't said those exact words to Shiloh yet, even though he'd wanted to a million times over the last month. It took several days for her not to be mad at him—not that he blamed her—but since then, they'd fallen back into their peaceful bubble. Now that Shiloh and he weren't forced to hide their relationship, they'd had a dozen perfect moments he could have said those words. But, to be honest, he was terrified. What if she didn't say them back?

Jake yanked his thoughts away from Shiloh. "Nic, just tell me what's going on. You didn't ask me here to talk to me about my girlfriend."

Nic drew in a breath and said it on the exhale, like a prayer. "I need your help."

"What do you need?"

"It's a big ask."

Jake waited patiently for her to go on.

"I need you to help me escape. I can't stay here. The Elite want something from me, information on ROGUE, and it's only a matter of time before they realize I'll never give it to them. And then, I'm dead. I've made connections to ROGUE through another student. But I need someone to go with me when I get off campus. And if we're caught, at least you're—"

"I'm a Councilor's son," he finished for her.

"Please, Jake."

Her tone was pleading, but she didn't need to beg. There'd been so many other heretics, like Hope, who Jake had wanted desperately to save. Innocent people whose only sin was to be themselves. What was heresy anyway, other than daring to be different from what the world tried to conform you to be?

Jake couldn't turn back time and save them. But *this* he could do. He could save *this* girl. He could take away something that Arcadia wanted and keep ROGUE safe.

At long last, he could fight.

"Yeah, Nic. I'll help you."

Twenty-Eight

"**R**elax," Jake said, massaging his thumbs into Shiloh's shoulder as he stood behind her. "You're going to get an A, and if they had a higher grade, I'm sure they would give you that."

Their project was set up on the table beside them, his tablet casting a hologram of information and a tablecloth covering the prototype. The indoor gym had been transformed into a science fair. Some abhorrent music played over the speakers as students wandered from station to station—because it was either attending this or studying for tomorrow's finals.

Jake felt Shiloh's deep breaths rise and fall against his chest. In and out, the way she did when she was trying to remain collected. "Jake, you do know that the least helpful thing you can tell an anxious person is to relax, right?"

He turned her around to look at him. "Shi, you're a genius. They're going to love it."

Her lips twitched a little, but every muscle still seemed tight. Jake couldn't shake the feeling that something was off, but every time he asked, she said it was just the stress of finals. So instead of asking again, he stroked his thumb across her wrist, over the small purply bruises there. She'd fallen on the ice, she'd said. Again. She'd gotten so many bruises this winter, he thought he might need to put her in a bubble for her own protection.

Professor Cooper and the rest of the judges made their way to their table. Shiloh straightened the sheet for the millionth time, and Jake sighed in relief. *Finally.*

Professor Cooper read off his tablet. "We have Jacob Osgood and Shiloh Haven with... *The Cloak?*"

Jake gave a bow. "Ladies and gentlemen."

The judges chuckled. The prototype had been all Shiloh, but showing off their project, giving a speech, winning the judges over —that was his specialty.

"Humankind has daydreamed about the power of invisibility for years. It's been the power of many superheroes and legends, but it's always been impossible. As my lovely partner told me—" He gestured at Shiloh. "True invisibility would require transparency on a cellular level, which is, of course, impossible. But in nature, animals have been managing to hide themselves to an impressive level." Behind him the hologram showed a chameleon, changing colors. "From studying nature and utilizing existing technologies of holograms and cameras, it is possible to create a camouflage so convincing it would render the user nearly invisible. Let us demonstrate."

Shiloh whisked the tablecloth off the table. Underneath was one of Jake's belts, with tiny circular screens embedded in the leather. Jake set one of his soccer trophies in the center of the belt, and Shiloh pushed a button. Instantly, the belt and the trophy vanished.

The judges gasped.

"The cameras are embedded in the belt 360 degrees," Shiloh explained. "It captures the environment in real time, and then projects it as a hologram on the opposite side. The human eye only picks up the environment, and how it flows seamlessly together. Not invisible, but fully cloaked."

Demonstrating, Jake grabbed the trophy and pulled it away from the belt. It reappeared. He put it back, and it disappeared again.

The judges applauded. Shiloh smiled, and that made Jake feel a little lighter.

"The current prototype will need continued work," Shiloh explained. "We have not been successful in making a human invisible, which would be the ultimate goal."

"It's amazing," Professor Cooper said. "I knew your project would be outstanding, Ms. Haven."

Jake felt a rush of warmth, of pride, of love as he looked at Shiloh. Her smile had climbed all the way to her eyes, making them gleam like starlight. She was magnificent.

"I must say," Professor Derby, another one of the judges, said, "we may want to tell the Elite about this one. It would be quite useful in hunting heretics, don't you think?"

Shiloh's smile tumbled off her lips, and Jake's stomach jerked into his throat. The judges moved on. Shiloh turned away from him and tucked the Cloak under the sheet. Her lightness from moments ago had vanished, leaving behind a thick gloom.

Jake squeezed her shoulder. "Shi..."

She held up a finger to stop him, grabbed her tablet and wrote a message to him.

Did I make a terrible mistake? I don't want this in the hands of the Elite.

Jake took the tablet and wrote. *We haven't turned the coding in. Can you change it, so it won't work? Then the secret is safe with you.*

Shiloh read the message, and her shoulders relaxed a little. She slipped her arms around him and buried her face into his chest.

"Are you okay?" Jake asked. If he didn't know any better, he'd think she was shaking.

"Fine," she said.

Liar.

❧

"I'm worried about you," Jake told Shiloh as they walked through the thick snow on the trail around Lake Harmony.

Shiloh studied him from the corner of her eye. Was this why he'd asked her to go on a walk into the forest, in deep snow, the morning of departing on Yuletide break? She'd told him he was crazy, but she'd bundled herself and gone with him anyway.

"Why are you worried?"

Jake kicked at the snow, sending up a fine mist that fluttered like fairies in the grey air. "I just hate the idea of you going back to the Haven."

"I'll be fine, Jake," Shiloh said. "You don't have to worry about me."

Jake stopped and turned toward her. Despite the scarf that was wrapped around his mouth, his frown was evident in the lines between his eyes. "How can I not worry about you?"

Shiloh paused and faced him. "I really will be okay. I'm Mother's favorite. I know how to stay out of trouble."

Jake took a deep breath, looking past her into the trees, his eyes shadowed. Shiloh closed the distance and laid a hand on his chest.

"I promise. It's a little over a week, and then I'll never have to go back."

His voice hardened. "Just the very idea of someone hurting you makes me—" He stopped, but his gloved hands coiled at his side.

Shiloh swallowed. Jake didn't know that, right now, she was likely to be safer at the Haven than she was here. #767 was getting increasingly agitated, and she wore the bruises on her neck and arms from his frustrations. She'd been sleeping less and less, knowing it was only a matter of time before the Elite figured out her defiance. Then what would she do?

Honestly, it was a relief to leave. Before she got on the bus, she'd be taking the audio recorder off and leaving it in her dorm. She'd probably pay consequences for it later, but she didn't care.

Shiloh slid down her scarf and smiled. "It's pretty nice."

Jake arched an eyebrow. "What is?"

"Having you care about me." Shiloh pulled down his scarf as well and stood on her toes to kiss him. He smiled against her lips and kissed her in return. Even though both their lips were frozen, she felt warmth spread to her fingertips.

When they parted, Jake twirled a piece of hair that had escaped from her hat around his finger. "I need to tell you something."

Shiloh's heart thumped in warning at the seriousness in his tone. "Okay."

He let out a breath, and it formed a cloud before his lips. "About Nic."

Shiloh's stomach lurched into her chest. *No, no, no.* Whatever he was going to say, the Elite shouldn't hear. They didn't have the tablet. But why would he think they needed it, when he'd brought her into the middle of nowhere? What could she do? If she yelled out to interrupt him, it'd be game over. The Elite would know.

It was too late, because Jake was already talking. "I'm going to help her escape."

The world spun around Shiloh. The audio recorder felt like it was searing her chest. *I can't breathe. I can't...*

"Jake, that's dangerous," Shiloh managed. Maybe, it wasn't too late. Maybe she could talk him out of this. No matter what the Elite really wanted, he'd told her to keep Jake out of danger. "You can't do that."

"I have to," Jake said. "If I can do something to help her, if I can save someone after all my family has done, then I have to do it."

Of course, he did! He was wonderful like that. He wasn't going to watch a kid die if he could help it, but if he did this, she'd lose him. She might have already lost him.

"I know you're worried about me, but I'll be fine." Jake

caressed a thumb across her eyebrow, a half-smile on his face. "I don't want to tell you any more than that. The less you know, the safer you'll be, but I'm not going to hide anything from you."

A sob was building in Shiloh's throat, and she swallowed it down. *Be a good girl, Shiloh.* She forced a smile, even as she died inside. Even as the same words spun over and over in her head.

Game over.

TWENTY-NINE

"You have arrived at your destination."

Shiloh pushed the button on the car that the Osgoods had sent for her, making the darkened windows transparent again. The car traversed a long driveway, lined with trees wrapped in white Yuletide lights. Shiloh had seen Jake's house on television before, but it didn't do it justice. It was massive, with peaked roofs and stone that made it look like a fairy-tale cottage.

And maybe it was a fairytale. After Jake's confession, Shiloh had suspected that the Elite would drag her into the woods before she made it onto the bus leaving Ardency. When she made it back to the Haven, she was surprised he hadn't walked in and held a gun to her head. But the time had passed, and she was still breathing.

When Shiloh stepped out of the car, Jake bounded down the stairs toward her, without a coat, and she let out a breath that had been trapped in her chest. Of course, if the Osgoods had sent the car, Shiloh knew he hadn't been arrested, but the carefree smile on his face told her all was well. Shiloh met him halfway, and he pulled her into his arms, swinging her around and almost bringing them both down as he slipped on the ice. Shiloh laughed, but the sound was cut off by his lips.

Not today, Shiloh promised herself during that kiss. *I'm not going to worry today.*

If the Elite hadn't arrested Jake, maybe it'd take more than words for the Councilor's son to be arrested. Maybe the Elite really was supposed to keep him safe. So today, it would just be her and Jake. No Elite. Just him and her.

"I missed you," he breathed against her lips.

"Jake, it's been two days."

"I know, it's been *forever.*" He grabbed her bag from the car, wrapped his arm around her waist, and led her to the door. "Don't lie. I know you missed me too."

Stupid as it was, she had. Still, she teased, "You were gone?"

He faked a laugh then kissed her again, before leading her through the double doors which bore glorious, silvery Yuletide wreaths. The foyer was as grand as the outside, all white tile and a crystal chandelier looming far above her head.

Jake kicked off his snow boots, and Shiloh followed suit, tucking them in a closet beside Jake's.

"Come on. Mom's waiting on us for brunch."

Shiloh swallowed, and Jake squeezed her hand reassuringly. "She's really excited to meet you."

"The heretic they think will ruin her son?" Shiloh whispered.

"No." He tucked a strand of hair behind her ear. "The crazy smart, amazing girl that her son adores."

"That's how I know you're the son of a politician," Shiloh teased, so she wouldn't blush. "You always know exactly the right thing to say to get what you want."

"I already have what I want." He kissed her knuckles and then pulled her down the hallway.

Every inch of the house was manicured, decorated, and cleaned to perfection. The perfect painting to fit each space. The gleaming wood. It seemed a dizzyingly long time before Jake was leading her through what she swore must be the third seating room and out onto an enclosed porch. Floor to ceiling windows gave a view of the snowy backyard that seemed to expand forever until it met with the banks of the frozen Mississippi River. Despite the glorious winter just through the glass, the room was as warm as Jake's touch.

His mother sat at a large round glass table, but she rose to meet them. She seemed to float toward Shiloh, elegant and timeless and breathtakingly beautiful. Next to her, Shiloh felt positively drab in her massive white sweater—the winter variant of the Arcadian uniform.

"Hello, Shiloh." Mrs. Osgood extended her hand.

Shiloh shook it. "Hello, Mrs. Osgood. Thank you for your kindness in inviting me to your home."

Mrs. Osgood gestured for them to sit, and they did. "I believe I should be the one thanking you. I never came to meet you at the hospital as I should have. I know what you did for my son, and I am very grateful."

Jake squeezed her hand beneath the table. Shiloh hoped he didn't notice the sweat on her palm.

"He saved me too," Shiloh said.

Dishes jingled as a woman with graying hair and amber skin pushed a cart onto the porch and began setting plates on the table before them. Breakfast was a masterpiece of eggs, bacon and French toast covered with a snowing of powdered sugar.

At school, it was so easy to forget how different Jake's and Shiloh's lives were, but being in this house and being waited on by staff made the differences stand out like blaring, neon lights.

"Thank you, Ana," Jake said with a smile. "Ana, this is my girl-friend, Shiloh."

Ana—who must have been the nanny Jake had talked about, the one he'd spent so much of his childhood with—smiled at her. "Wonderful to meet you."

"Nice to meet you," Shiloh said.

Ana touched Jake's shoulder lightly and said something in Spanish. Shiloh only recognized the word '*hermosa*'—beautiful—from the sweet nothings Jake often whispered in her ear, taking turns between all his different languages. Turns out, Jake was right. Girls did love French poetry. At least, she did when it came out of Jake's sultry mouth.

"*Gracias*, Ana," Jake said, smiling.

"Yes, thank you, Ana," Mrs. Osgood said, something pointed in her words.

Ana must have understood, because she smiled and left.

"I apologize that my husband isn't here to greet you," Mrs. Osgood said, taking a sip of her orange juice. "He was called away yesterday. He'll be flying in this afternoon in time for the ball, so you'll meet him there."

"That's all right." More than all right. If Shiloh could avoid Councilor Osgood for the rest of her life, that'd be just fine.

As they ate, Mrs. Osgood asked Shiloh about her Engineering Track, about what sports she played, and their group project. Despite her politeness, Shiloh was relieved when Mrs. Osgood's cellphone gave a delicate ring. "I'm afraid I must get this. It was so lovely to meet you." She picked up the phone and left, and Shiloh felt like she could finally breathe again.

"See? Not so bad," Jake said.

Mrs. Osgood was much kinder than Shiloh would have thought, but she didn't trust it. Jake's mother was putting up a show while waiting and hoping for an inevitable breakup. But if that didn't happen, Shiloh was sure his parents would find another way to get rid of her.

"How about a tour?" Jake asked.

I'm not worrying, not today, Shiloh reminded herself and took his hand.

🔥

It was undoubtedly the best Yuletide Eve of her life. After the tour, Jake took Shiloh on a snowmobile ride. She clung to his back as they flew through the snow, charging over hills and catching air. He laughed and whooped each time, and despite being slightly terrified, Shiloh laughed too.

They ate a late lunch of grilled turkey and cheese, which Jake prepared himself. Apparently, Ana had taught him more than Spanish. Afterward, Shiloh had picked an actual physical book from their massive library, and they'd snuggled in Jake's bed— reading, talking, and kissing. She'd taken a long, dreamless nap, safe in the cradle of his arms.

It was as though a magical bubble had formed around them, like in those easy simple days at the hospital, and nothing mattered except this day, this moment, this breath.

But of course, it was all an illusion, and despite her attempts to forget, she knew it was only a matter of time before it faded.

Shiloh stared at her reflection in the full-length mirror in the guest room where she'd been sent to get ready for the ball. Here, she'd found not just one dress waiting for her, but three. She spun in the mirror, eyeing the dress she'd chosen. Black lace and tulle flowed in layers to her feet, formed flowers around the rouched bodice and climbed up one shoulder, leaving the other bare. The rations for this dress could probably have fed all the Haven girls for a week.

A soft knock tapped on the door.

"Shiloh." It was Mrs. Osgood's voice. "Can I come in?"

Shiloh opened the door for her. Mrs. Osgood looked ravishing in an off-the-shoulder, Yuletide-red gown fit for a queen. A majestic crown of hair graced her head.

"I wanted to see how you were getting on."

"Fine, Mrs. Osgood," Shiloh said. "Thank you for the dress."

"Not a problem. Do you need help with your hair? Or your makeup?"

Shiloh began to shake her head, but then stopped. "I don't own any makeup."

"Oh," Mrs. Osgood said, softly. "Just a minute."

She returned shortly with a kit of make-up and hair supplies. "My foundation is too dark for you, but I think we'll do fine without it." She gestured for Shiloh to sit on the bed and started sweeping brushes across Shiloh's cheek. "I can tell you're overwhelmed. You know, if you want to be in my son's life, there will be lots of these. Appearances, fancy parties, big houses. You're going to have to learn how to deal with it."

Shiloh took a breath. "I guess I am."

"Hm," Mrs. Osgood hummed, as she swept eyeshadow across Shiloh's eyelids. Shiloh felt like she'd just failed a test.

"Mrs. Osgood, I hope you know that I'm not with Jake for his status. I don't want fancy houses or dresses or parties. I only want him. And if this is what comes with being with him, then you're right. I'm going to have to figure it out."

Mrs. Osgood smiled, but Shiloh couldn't tell if it was genuine. The Osgoods were the greatest of performers.

When Mrs. Osgood finished with the makeup, she began to work on Shiloh's hair, her touch gentle. Shiloh wondered with a twist of her stomach, if this was what having a mother would have been like.

"Take a look," Mrs. Osgood said, when she was done, nodding toward the mirror.

The makeup was light but brought color to Shiloh's pale face and made her eyes seem bigger. A comb shaped like a rose pinned her dark hair to her head. Reagan offered a pair of simple earrings for Shiloh's ears, which were only pierced because, in a terrible lapse of judgment, she'd let Val pierce them with a needle in the Haven bathroom. After carefully applying a red lip gloss, Shiloh stared at her reflection, barely recognizing herself.

"Thank you, Mrs. Osgood," Shiloh said, even though she almost wanted to take it all off. She didn't know what to make of this Shiloh in the mirror.

Shiloh slipped on the black ballet flats waiting for her. Mrs. Osgood approached the door, but she paused and then turned around.

"Shiloh?"

"Yes, Mrs. Osgood?"

Mrs. Osgood met Shiloh's eyes. "I'll tell you what Sam's mother told me at my first event. Don't be fooled. Women are not sugar and spice. They are roses and steel. So, chin up. Don't let the crown slip and show them what you're made of." Mrs. Osgood slipped out the door without a goodbye.

This offering, a genuine kindness, startled Shiloh, but then again, Jake had to get his kindness somewhere. Shiloh lifted her chin and stepped into the hallway where Jake waited, leaning casually against the wall.

When he saw her, he stood up straight, his eyes trailing over her like he didn't want to miss a detail. "Wow, Shi. You look amazing."

And Shiloh felt suddenly beautiful, not because of the dress or makeup, but rather, the way he looked at her. She was pretty sure that she could be covered in mud from head to toe, and if he looked at her like that, she'd still feel beautiful.

"Thanks, your mom did it. I was pretty hopeless." She looked Jake up and down. "You don't look too bad yourself."

That was a gross understatement. He was glorious. This was the Jacob Osgood of TV, wearing a tuxedo like a second skin and his unruly hair perfectly styled. But then, he was always gorgeous.

"May I?" Jake offered the crook of his arm.

Shiloh took it. "You may."

❧

Jake led Shiloh in through one of the side doors. Stepping into the ballroom was like stepping into a winter wonderland. Wreaths hung in the windows, and red and gold ribbons and ornaments adorned the multiple Yuletide trees scattered about. Individuals, dressed in the richest of clothes, milled the room, taking drinks from waiters' trays. Cameras in the shape of snowflakes zoomed around the room, picking up shots for the media. A grand piano played itself in the corner, an Arcadian Yuletide song, while Ashia Springstein, a famous Arcadian pop singer, belted out the lyrics.

"Oh, come, all ye Citizens.
Loyal and obedient.
Oh, follow ye, oh follow ye, the Codex."

"You do this every year?" Shiloh asked, even though she already knew. She'd seen the magazine spreads and the news reports, but it had never fully captured it.

Jake nodded, leading her around the outskirts of the room.

Shiloh looked around her again, losing the wonder and seeing only expense. *Everyone equal,* the Codex said. *Everyone according to their duty.* But here, the truth was laid out in bright technicolor.

Occasionally, people would stop Jake and say hello to the Councilor's son. There were State Advocates and other important political figures from as far away as India. Jake called them by name, asked about family, told the right jokes to get them laughing, and sometimes spoke fluently in their native language. He was a master at this puppet show. Jake proudly introduced her as his girlfriend to everyone he met, and she'd struggle with a smile and a handshake.

"I'm really bad at this," Shiloh said, when there was a break in the deluge.

"No, you're not."

"Liar."

He grinned and opened his mouth. But something in the crowd caught his attention. "I see my Uncle Silas. Come on! I want to introduce you." He grabbed her hand and pulled her through the clusters of people.

Jake had previously mentioned his uncle, Silas Petrovic, and Jake's affection for him was clear. Jake had told her about how Silas had taught him to play soccer, taken him on camping adventures, and had never *once* missed a birthday party or Yuletide, a better 'Dad' than his own was.

"Uncle Silas!" Jake called as he slowed to a halt.

A man turned from his other conversation, and a smile as wide as Jake's split his face. "Jake, my boy!"

Jake threw his arms around him, laughing. After a period of back slapping, they parted, and Jake steered Silas toward Shiloh. "I want you to meet my girlfriend, Shiloh."

Everyone in this family, Shiloh decided when she got a look at Silas, *is beautiful.*

In a dark suit and bowtie, Silas seemed just as regal as his sister, Mrs. Osgood, but in coloring, he was the opposite, dark hair where she was light. Only their eyes were the same—that penetrating clear blue.

And then he spoke again, and the earth opened and swallowed Shiloh whole.

"It's lovely to meet you at last, Shiloh."

She would have known that voice anywhere. It made her skin crawl, and her heart race. Elite #767. The one who'd killed Hope. The one who'd tortured Nic. The one who had left bruises all over Shiloh's body that still hadn't quite healed.

He was Jake's *uncle.*

THIRTY

Am I breathing?
I'm not breathing.

Jake had introduced Silas to her, and she hadn't even heard him. A little belated, she forced out a breathless, "Hi. Nice to meet you."

Jake frowned at her in concern. "Are you okay?"

"Yes, Shiloh, are you okay?" Silas repeated, a wry smile curling at the edges of his lips. *He knows that I know.* "You look a little flushed."

Shiloh forced a smile. "I'm fine."

He offered a hand in introduction, and Shiloh barely contained the tremor as she extended her hand. Instead of a handshake, he dramatically bowed and lifted her knuckles to his lips, a hot brand against her skin. Shiloh gritted her teeth to keep from yanking away.

"I must say when I heard Jake was bringing his girlfriend," Silas said, "I was very excited to see who he could be so smitten with. It makes perfect sense, seeing you. You look ravishing."

Glaring? Was Shiloh glaring? This froqing son of a blight had known she'd be here. He'd heard it a million times on the audio recorder. That was why he hadn't shown up after Jake's confession. He knew the ball would give him the perfect opportunity. She'd thought she was safe here.

She was wrong.

Jake frowned at her again. She still hadn't spoken.

Stick to the script.

"Thank you." The words felt like gravel in her throat.

"I must find my seat, but let's catch up more tonight," Silas said to Jake. He winked and elbowed Jake playfully. "I'll have to steal a dance from your date later. Get to know the girl who managed to steal your heart."

Jake laughed, and Silas went to join a table where there were three young kids and a brunette who greeted him with a kiss. His wife. Aubrey. Did she, too, wear bruises that she buried like secrets?

"Are you sure you're okay?" Jake asked.

Shiloh's very core was shaking, but she forced another smile. "Yeah, I'm great."

Jake gave her a sideways glance, but steered them to their seats, right before someone announced the entrance of Councilor and Mrs. Osgood. They swept in elegantly; Councilor Osgood said a few words, but Shiloh couldn't get her mind to absorb them. Her eyes drifted over to Silas.

When Jake had talked about his uncle, he'd painted grand images of a kind man—a *good* man. Shiloh couldn't reconcile those stories with the feeling of Silas's hand crushing her throat.

The Councilor and Mrs. Osgood joined them at the table.

"Shiloh," Councilor Osgood said, looking over at her. "It's nice to meet you again."

"Nice to meet you too, Councilor Osgood," she said, not looking straight at him. She was afraid if she looked at him, all she would hear were Hope's screams. "Thank you for the invitation."

He graced her with a smile, but quickly sipped his wine to hide his strain.

Then it was time for dinner. Shiloh could feel Silas's eyes on her now like daggers trailing across her skin. The food, an array of salmon, potatoes, and fresh vegetables—an otherwise delicious meal—tasted like sawdust in her mouth, but she made herself eat it all.

After dinner, the three of the five Councilors who were in attendance—Osgood, Beck, and Bennett—opened the dance floor with their spouses. When the Councilors returned to their seats, the individual controlling the music announced, "And now for the time-honored tradition. Will the children of the Councilors please come to the floor?"

Jake took Shiloh's hand, but she didn't stand.

I can't do this.

Jake had been apologetic when he'd told her about this stupid tradition. She'd mentally prepared, but now, going in front of all these people—in front of *Silas*—felt like she'd be stepping on stage naked.

Shiloh glanced around, looking for an escape, and her eyes fell on Mrs. Osgood. She tapped one finger against her chin.

Chin up. Show them what you're made of.

Shiloh lifted her chin and let Jake lead her to the dance floor. Others were gathering, ranging from young teens to adult children. One girl a little older than Shiloh age eyed her from across the dance floor. Shiloh recognized her from magazines as well: Katerina Beck, the gorgeous granddaughter of Councilor Beck who Jake had been forced to dance with all the years before, much to his dismay. Shiloh ignored her and faced Jake, going through the mental checklist. *Arms like this. Feet like that.* Just like they'd practiced a million times.

The announcer read off names. "Jacob Osgood is joined by his girlfriend, Shiloh..." The announcer paused and said uncertainly, "Haven?"

A murmur passed through the tables, and eyes drilled into her spine. Jake's smile never wavered, but a dark shadow crossed his eyes. She realized he'd never mentioned Shiloh's last name when introducing her. Perhaps because he wanted to avoid subjecting her to this very reaction. Now, she didn't feel just naked. She felt vile as well.

The music started, a melody from centuries past, but Shiloh's feet were bolted to the floor. A snowflake camera fluttered by her head.

"Shi," Jake whispered, "I'm sorry, but don't look at them. Look at me."

She met his eyes.

"I've got you. Just follow my lead."

His hand tightened on her side, strong and steady, and he made her feel brave.

As he pulled her into the waltz, her thoughts were consumed with the next step, with not stepping on her dress, with the way Silas' eyes followed her around the dance floor. When Jake dipped her, Silas applauded and smiled. A sick, frightening smile that sent shivers crawling down her spine. Jake twirled her, and Shiloh wasn't ready. She stepped on her skirt and stumbled, but Jake caught her.

"You're okay. I've got you," he breathed, and somehow, she managed to survive the rest with no incident. The music ended, and polite applause filled the air.

Jake pulled her close and laid his forehead on hers. "Thank you."

"You owe me," she said

"Big time."

During the next dance, almost everyone moved onto the dance floor, which meant that she and Jake were no longer actors on a stage. Shiloh rested her head on his shoulder, taking shelter in him, as they swayed around the dance floor.

A hand tapped Jake's shoulder. He turned to face Silas, who stood behind him, smiling again. The warmth Shiloh had found being in Jake's arms vanished.

"May I cut in?" Silas asked.

Jake glanced at Shiloh. "Can he?"

How was she supposed to say no? Shiloh nodded.

Jake walked away. Silas took one of her hands and set his other hand on her waist. She attempted to keep as much distance between him as arms would allow. But still, when she breathed, she inhaled his expensive, spicy cologne and almost wretched.

"I must say," Silas said in a low whisper as he steered her in a circle. He no longer sounded like the jovial uncle from earlier; he sounded like the monster she'd always known. "I could never quite tell how deep my nephew was in from the recordings, but now that I see him in person, I know. You have him completely under your spell, don't you?"

Chin up. Shiloh forced her jaw higher.

"But you are much harder to read," Silas continued. "Do you really care about my nephew or is it all an act?"

Over Silas's shoulder, Shiloh could see Jake swaying his youngest cousin around the dance floor, both laughing. Silas's daughter looked to be the same age as Willa, who Silas had so callously threatened.

Silas twirled Shiloh around so quickly her head spun, then pulled her close so his lips pressed near her ear. "Do you know what I think?"

Shiloh shook her head.

"I think you've gone and done something stupid. You've fallen in love with him, and you're going to throw your life away, aren't you?" He chuckled. "It'll be a pity when I have to kill you."

Shiloh yanked back, but Silas tightened his grasp on her hand until her bones cried in protest. "Now, now. Be a good girl. People are watching."

Shiloh swallowed down the bile at the back of her throat. When the last note played, she whipped away from him. *Run,* every beat of her heart cried. She pushed through the door that led to the veranda outside and stumbled forward to cling to the snowy railing, welcoming the burn of the cold, gasping for air.

A shadow cast in the snow before her. She whirled around. Silas had followed. He pulled a small device from his pocket and stuck it in a camera above his head, disabling it so it wouldn't capture him stepping into view.

Mistake. She'd made a terrible mistake. With the windows covered and only one door, no one would see her out here with him.

He approached her with a smile on his face. "Are you going to be honest with me at last, Shiloh?"

Shiloh took a step back, but her hips hit the railing. Trapped.

He stopped, only inches from her. "Are you going to apologize for being such a bad girl?"

Shiloh's mouth opened, but her words caught at the back of her throat. Her arms trembled with more than the biting wind.

Breathe in, breathe out, she tried, but...

I can't...I can't breathe.

"You must think that somehow you can protect them," Silas continued, "but maybe, I need to explain the situation better."

He seized her arm and ripped her away from the rail, his fingers grinding down to her bone. She tried to drag her feet, but they slipped on the smooth stone of the veranda. He pulled her to the top of the short staircase and then released her with a shove. She spiraled backward, slammed into the middle of the stairs, and rolled down the rest, before landing sprawled in the snow. The cold stung her rapidly bruising flesh.

She shoved herself to her knees, but Silas had already crouched beside her. He struck out like a snake, his fingers biting into her neck. He loosened his hold carefully, so not to leave bruises, but he held her in place, forcing her to meet his eyes.

"Let me make something perfectly clear. You're going to stop playing this silly little game with me. You're going to do as you're told from here on out, or I'm going to kill you. And you'll die in vain, because your precious Nic will still die. And Jake will still pay for his heresy."

Shiloh's throat ached like her words were knives. "But...but he's your nephew."

"No, he's a *heretic*!" Silas's voice raised for the first time, and his fist tightened, cutting off her air for a moment before he released. "Which means he's a cockroach ready to be squashed." Silas glared at her then shoved her back into the snow and stood. He glowered down at her, his lip curling in disgust. "And *you*? You're nothing but a pathetic, little Haven girl. You think you can save them?" He laughed bitterly. "You'll be lucky if you can save yourself."

A scream built in her throat. For help. For someone to save her. Save Jake. Save Nic.

Please!

"Get up!" he barked.

Shiloh scrambled to her feet, but stepped out of arms' reach. Her damp dress clung to her skin, but she was so numb she barely felt it.

"Are you ready to listen to me now?"

Shiloh nodded, wrapping her arms tightly around herself, but that didn't calm her shivering.

"This is what we're going to do now. Nicolette is going to try to escape. Jake is going to help her. And you are going to help them too. Once you know their plan, you're going to tell me."

"I thought you wanted information out of her," Shiloh said.

"I do, but if she won't give it, the next best thing is following the little birdie back to her nest."

"And Jake?"

Silas rolled his eyes. "I just told you. He'll end up in a prison camp where he belongs."

Shiloh pressed her eyes closed, her chest cracking open. *No, no, no.*

"If you're going to arrest him, why haven't you done it?" Shiloh asked. "You have the recording."

"I have a reckless boy saying reckless things," Silas said, pacing a short line back and forth in front of her, like a caged tiger. "That won't work for the Councilor's son. Samuel will always disgustingly choose to protect his heretic brat just like he did this summer. Jake needs to *commit* heresy. When he helps Nicolette, he'll be caught aiding and abetting a known heretic. Aiding ROGUE. Not even his dad can save him from that."

Here it was. Silas's grand plan. His hand of cards that she'd been waiting for him to reveal. He'd been waiting for her, his little spy, to catch proof of Jake's heresy. Waiting for Nic to lead him right back to ROGUE. That was why he'd given Shiloh so much time. He'd played the long game.

And all Shiloh could see was Jake. His eyes. His warmth. His goodness.

I can't do this. I won't.

But what choice did she have? She'd failed. Silas had won this terrible game. How could she possibly save them now?

Silas stepped toward her until only inches separated them once more. Shiloh forced herself to stand in place. "Do you understand what you have to do?"

Shiloh nodded, self-hatred rising in her throat like bile, but he'd kill her here and now if she gave him the smallest hesitation.

"And you understand what will happen if you refuse?"

Shiloh nodded again.

"What was that?" Silas said, with a sickening sweet smile.

"Yes."

"Yes, *what*?"

"Yes, sir."

"Good girl."

THIRTY-ONE

J ake's eyes wandered around the ballroom one more time, even though he'd already walked around it twice. Still no sign of Shiloh. He tapped Mom's shoulder, interrupting her conversation with an ambassador from Moravia.

"Hey, Mom, have you seen Shiloh?"

She glanced around and shook her head. "Not since she was dancing with Silas."

Frog. That'd been at least thirty minutes ago. He hadn't seen her since either.

Jake hurried out the front doors of the ballroom, searching the hallway outside. Empty. He slipped past the security in the hallway and went down another hall. The clack of heels sounded behind him like galloping hooves. He turned and stiffened.

Stefani Andreou, wearing a long golden dress that sparkled like the sun, charged toward him. Before he could react, she seized the front of his jacket, yanked open the closet door next to him, and shoved him inside. She slammed the door behind them.

Jake's heart blazed a warning in his throat. Rabid-dog Stefani was back. Even though the utility closet was actually somewhat spacious, it felt like being dropped into a cobra's den. Well, if she attacked him, at least there was a mop in here to defend himself with.

"You know, Stef," he said, forcing his voice to remain calm. "There are cameras all over this house. If you murder me in this closet, they will know it was you."

"I'm not going to murder you. Not that the thought hadn't crossed my mind. Besides, the security guards watching the hallway right now will probably just think we came in here to make out."

"Gross."

Stefani made a gagging sound. "Like I actually want to suck face with you. Who knows where your mouth has been."

Jake folded his arms over his chest. "So, what's on your heart, Stef?"

Stefani put a sharp fingernail, painted with red and gold sparkles, into his face. "Listen here, you crossbred mongrel. Just because Nic has some crazy crush on you and thinks you're trustworthy, doesn't mean I trust you."

"What are you talking about? Nic doesn't have a crush on me."

Stefani snorted and dropped her voice low. "You're about as bright as a burned-out lightbulb. I'm talking about the mission."

"The what?"

"The escape plan."

Jake's eyes widened as it clicked. "*You're* the one with connections to ROGUE?"

Stefani dropped her voice to a hiss. "I can't believe Nic told you. I swear on my grandmother's bald head, that if you utter one word about my parents being allies of ROGUE, I'll let Val skin you alive. It'll be like a Yuletide present for her."

"Wait." Jake leaned back against the shelves in the closet to steady himself. "Your parents are a part of ROGUE?"

Greyson and Reese Andreou? Right now they were in the ballroom, rubbing elbows with the Councilors like they were old friends. Because they were.

But, *of course*, ROGUE had to have connections to someone

higher up to know the Cleansing's location. Advocate Andreou had conveniently been unable to attend the Cleansing, though she must have had an amazing alibi to avoid suspicion.

Stefani froze, her lips parting in horror. "Wait? Nic *didn't* tell you?"

"No, I didn't even know *you* were helping her. She said a student had connections with ROGUE, but never said who."

Stefani groaned and put her face in her hands. "*Froqety froq on a froqing sandwich!*"

"Stefani, I'm not going to tell anyone."

She dropped her hands. "Give me one reason I should believe you. You, who was willing to throw my girlfriend's life away like it was *nothing*."

An invisible punch landed in Jake's stomach, and he pressed his eyes closed. "I know. And I'm sorry. It was a terrible thing to do, but it was a bluff."

Stefani snorted.

"Stefani, I'm not an idiot. I know you never took down the censor wall and took my rations, anyway." Which made all the more sense now. Stefani hadn't been froqing him over; she'd been protecting ROGUE. "If I'd wanted to push the threat farther, don't you think I'd have done it then?"

Stefani folded her arms over her chest. "What's your motivation for helping Nic, then, huh?"

Jake took a breath. He needed to make Stefani trust him, but how? She'd only known him for the prig he'd always been before. But all he had was the truth in a world of lies, and she would have to choose to believe it.

"Because I hate Arcadia, okay?" Jake kept his volume low, but the words quickened as he went, gaining speed and heat. "I hate this puppet show that I have to perform in. I hate that every choice is made for us. I hate that Nic is a kid, and they tortured her. I hate that you and Val have to live in secret, when it's utter ordure and hypocrisy. I hate that my girlfriend has suffered more than anyone should have to. And mostly, I hate that I love Shiloh more than I've ever loved anything, and sooner or later, I know they're going to try to take her from me."

Stefani stared at him, her ruby lips parted.

"Oh. And Nic's mom saved my life, so yeah, add that to the list of motivations." Jake folded his arms over his chest. "There. You can put that in your gossip column. *Jacob Osgood Speaks Heresy.* The readers will love it."

Stefani sucked a breath in through her teeth. "Whoa. Plot twist."

They stood in silence for a few minutes. Far off, holly jolly Yuletide music played, and laughter chimed, but all other sound muffled in comparison to Jake's blood rushing in his veins.

At last, Stefani smiled grimly. "I guess we're going to have to trust each other, aren't we?"

Jake nodded. "I guess so."

"That's scary."

"Terrifying."

Stefani held up a hand. "But wait. Rewind a little. Did Jacob Osgood just say he was in *love*? Like with someone other than himself?"

Jake cringed. He definitely shouldn't have given her that ammunition.

"Huh," Stefani said, cocking her head like he was a strange, new creature.

"Look, I have to go," Jake said. "I need to find Shiloh. Have you seen her or not?"

"Not."

Jake swore under his breath and ran a hand through his hair, probably ruining the gelled perfection, but not caring. He stepped toward the door with a mumbled goodbye.

"Jake."

He looked back.

Stefani met his eyes. "If you really love Shiloh...don't let them take her from you."

Jake swallowed as he took in the gleam of emotion in Stefani's eyes, one he understood too well. In this, he and Stefani were utterly the same: Loving people Arcadia would never let them have.

He nodded and opened the closet door. Light flooded in. "I don't intend to."

Shiloh somehow managed to find her way back to Jake's bedroom and stumbled in, collapsing on the end of his bed. She pulled a velvety throw blanket from the coiled sheets and wrapped it around herself, but it couldn't touch her chill.

She should go back down. Jake would be worried. But her dress was still damp, and she didn't know how she could look him in the eyes.

What am I supposed to do?

Surviving and saving them. That was what she'd wanted. But she couldn't have both. If she chose to risk her life, would she even be able to save them?

Her mind ran in endless circles. Tears burned in her eyes, and pressure built in her chest until she felt she might have to scream to release it.

Then she heard Silas's voice again. "I think it's going quite well, don't you?"

Shiloh jerked her head up, but the room was still empty.

"I really don't like this game you're playing, Silas." Another voice. Councilor Osgood.

Shiloh's eyes fixed on the floor vent, where the voices were coming from. Clutching the blanket around her shoulders, she lowered herself down on the floor next to it, leaning against the wall.

"I have it perfectly under control," Silas said. "You were the one who wanted Jake to be watched closely."

"Yes, but I didn't think you would get his *girlfriend* to do it."

"Two birds, one stone, Sam."

That confirmed Shiloh's suspicion. Councilor Osgood did know what was happening. Why else would he allow Jake to keep seeing her?

"And she's cooperating?" Councilor Osgood asked. "Willingly?"

"Of course. She does seem to care about him. She's doing a decent job keeping him out of trouble."

"And the other girl. Have you gotten any closer to finding out what she knows about ROGUE?"

"No, but I will."

"That better be it, Silas. That better be exactly the plan. I know you. You're a dog with a freakin' bone. If I find out that somehow you're taking advantage of Jake's vulnerability because of what happened this summer, in order to get you closer to ROGUE, there will be hell to pay. You are to protect my son. Do you understand?"

"Yes, of course. I love the boy."

Liar.

"And I know how bad it would look for you if your son was labeled a heretic," Silas continued. "I wouldn't do anything to jeopardize you or the Council. My duty is to serve you."

Liar. But if he didn't want to protect Councilor Osgood, what did he want?

Suddenly, Silas laughed. Shiloh shivered.

"What's so funny?" the Councilor demanded.

"I'm just thinking about how Alec and Elaine Sanders would react if they could see their daughter now."

There was the sound of sputtering, and Councilor Osgood coughed, like he'd been drinking at the wrong moment. "Wait...

I'm sorry. Shiloh is *their* daughter? My son is dating *their* daughter!"

Shiloh's heart hammered against her ribs. She'd never remembered her parents' names, but Shiloh's middle name was Elaine. *Shiloh Elaine Sanders.* It twirled in her mind like an old lullaby, bringing with it faint memories of a man who sang sweet as a bird and a woman who smelled like crushed pine needles.

"That's not possible," Councilor Osgood said, the same horror in his voice. "I pulled her records. Read about her parents. She can't be their daughter."

"You told me to make sure no one knew we let their daughter live. And I did."

Councilor Osgood let out a string of curse words that were forbidden in the Codex. "Are you *absolutely* sure?"

"Of course, I'm sure. Consider it a victory, Sam, and enjoy it. I certainly have. The daughter of our greatest enemies completely under our control."

Greatest enemy? What were they talking about?

Who were her parents?

Who am I?

Before Shiloh could hear more, the door to the bedroom opened, and Jake walked in. "There you are."

Shiloh slid her thumb along the switch that closed the vent so no more voices would come up. She pulled the blanket more tightly around her to hide the discolored flesh that would lay her sins bare.

"I was looking all over for you," Jake said, closing the distance between them and lowering himself on his knees before her. "Are you okay?"

No, I'm not okay. They're coming for you, and I don't know how to save you.

Save him? *Ha!* Silas wanted her to be the one to pull the trigger, and she could see no way out.

Shiloh started to say she was fine, but he wouldn't believe her. "All these people. These fancy dresses. I don't belong here."

He kissed the top of her head. "You belong with me."

"Jake, I—"

"Hold that thought."

Jake jumped to his feet, retrieved something from his closet, and sat back down next to her. In his hands, he held a rectangular box, wrapped in gold paper and a red ribbon.

"Happy Yuletide, Shiloh."

Shiloh's heart twisted as she took it. "You shouldn't have done that. I didn't get you anything."

Jake smirked and opened his mouth, but Shiloh cut him off.

"Jacob Osgood, if you say something stupid like 'You're the only thing I want for Yuletide', I'll strangle you with this ribbon."

He laughed. "Just swallow your pride and open it."

She pulled away the ribbon and the golden paper, opened the box, and gasped. A set of tools, like the ones she'd used on their project, sat carefully tucked into a leather case.

"For when you're a world-famous engineer one day," Jake said.

"Jake..." She ran her fingers over the smooth leather, struggling to find words. To breathe past the guilt that was choking her.

He doesn't deserve you, Shiloh, Val had said, but she'd gotten it backward.

"Jake, you're so good to me," Shiloh said, ducking her head to hide her face. Her mask was crumbling. "I don't deserve you."

"That's not true."

"It really is."

Jake brushed the hair out of her face, and his face contorted with worry. "Hey, why are you crying?"

Shiloh hadn't felt them before, but now, she was aware of the hot drops that crawled down her cheeks. She looked at him, at those eyes she adored. The question replayed in her mind. Survive or save him?

I can't... I can't lose him.

She'd lost everyone she'd ever loved. How could she possibly survive losing him?

"Shiloh, please talk to me. What's going on?"

She couldn't answer that question, so she kissed him with everything in her. The sadness. The guilt. The anger. The depth of her passion for him.

Jake pulled away, frowning, "Shiloh, I know you're trying to distract me. Why won't you—"

Shiloh covered his lips with a finger and straddled his lap, pulling up her dress to do so.

"Shiloh..."

His words died in his throat as her fingers landed on the buttons of his shirt, slowly undoing them. She slipped her hands across his bare chest, feeling his heartbeat beneath her palm.

"Shi—" He tried once more, but a fire had sparked in his eyes that matched the shimmering heat beneath her skin.

"Shh," she breathed into the curve of his neck. She laid a path of kisses down his throat, his collarbone.

At last, he gave in. Letting out a sound that was half groan of defeat, half sigh of desire, his lips urgently claimed hers. One arm wrapped around her back, pressing her closer to his chest, knocking the blanket from her shoulders. His other hand slid past the slit in her skirt and trailed up the delicate skin of her thigh. Her nerves picked up a now-familiar song.

As Jake's lips moved from her mouth to her bare shoulder, Shiloh traced the lines of his chest, etching his every detail into her memory. Who knew the next time she would be able to touch him like this without being spied on? Who knew how long it would be before she lost him forever?

Save him, her heart begged. *Save him.*

She found his mouth with hers again, just as his fingers discovered the zipper of her dress. It went down with a sigh. The simmer of heat beneath Shiloh's skin intensified until it threatened to consume her.

"Shiloh?" Jake pulled away to search her eyes. There was a question, a desire, in her name. But before Shiloh could open her mouth, a voice called from the hallway outside.

"Jake!"

Mrs. Osgood.

Jake swore as he pulled away from her. His absence felt like she'd plunged through the ice of Lake Harmony and into the frigid water beneath. He scrambled to his feet, buttoning his shirt and straightening his hair and bowtie. Shiloh slowly climbed onto trembling legs, and he turned to zip her dress back up. He pressed a gentle kiss on the back of her neck.

"I'll go," he said. "Follow in five minutes once we're downstairs."

She turned to face him and nodded.

He cradled her face in his hands, eyes intense. "I know there is something going on with you. I can feel it. Please, don't pull away from me." He kissed her quickly, sweetly, and she could taste her own tears on his lips again.

"I love you," he said as he turned to leave.

He'd said it like a habit, as though he'd said it a million times before, like it was a truth so blatantly obvious he didn't even notice that he'd said it. It echoed in her ears long after he left.

Shiloh pressed a hand over her lips to silence a scream building in her heart. She struggled against the tears that threatened to destroy what was left of her makeup-painted mask. It was a losing battle.

I think you've gone and done something stupid, Silas's voice floated through her mind. *You've fallen in love with him, and you're going to throw your life away, aren't you?*

But the memory of Hope came on its heels, her knees on the stage, swearing she'd die before she was a slave, before she submitted to being anything but herself. And died for it, she had.

Well, Shiloh, she asked herself. *What would you die for?*

❧

It wasn't until Jake made it down the stairs that he'd realized what he'd done. *I love you.*

Idiot. He'd meant to say it carefully, when he was sure she'd say it back. And of course, she hadn't said it back. Granted, he'd left the room immediately after. Maybe, she'd been too stunned to say anything.

Or maybe she just didn't want to say it.

Shiloh finally returned downstairs, much later than five minutes and wearing her school jacket like she couldn't get warm. She smiled and chatted with his mom and danced with him a few more times. But he could tell. She was moving to the puppet strings.

As Jake walked her to the car amongst all the other departing guests, his chest ached. Something was wrong, but he couldn't help her if she wouldn't tell him.

Jake opened the car door for her and bent to kiss her goodbye, but her words halted him.

"Jake, I need to tell you something."

Jake swallowed. "Okay."

She gestured for him to follow her into the backseat, and he closed the door to give them privacy. He pushed a button on the door to delay the car's journey, before twisting toward her. The Yuletide lights that hung on his home shone in the whites of her wide eyes.

Jake's stomach churned. "What's going on?"

She looked away, staring out the opposite window as cars drove past, temporarily illuminating the backseat. Each flash of light highlighted her porcelain mask, the walls that—even after all this time—made her untouchable.

"You told me that you knew there was something wrong," she said at last. "That I was pulling away. And you're right. I was."

"Okay."

She stared down at her hands. "You know, I was getting along with everything just fine. I had these rules, and I just had to follow them. That's it. And then I met you, and *you*..." Her voice broke like glass. She took a deep breath—in and out—then continued. "You completely changed the rules of the game. You turned my life upside down. And Arcadia be froqed, sometimes I am *so* mad at you about that."

"Shiloh—"

"Stop!" She finally looked at him, but the intensity in her eyes made him wish she hadn't. "Just let me say this. You're right. I was distant tonight, because I knew I had to make a choice I haven't wanted to make. But now I need to be honest with you, because you deserve the truth."

She's going to break up with me. He was certain of it. Tonight, she'd realized how different they were, what it meant to be his girlfriend. And then the confession of love had been too serious. She was going to shove him away and run.

The words were razor blades in his throat. "And what's the truth, Shiloh?"

She slid closer to him, so only a breath separated them, and looked up. In the Yuletide lights, her eyes shimmered like a million stars.

"I love you, Jacob Osgood."

All Jake's air left his lungs. "What?"

She smiled. "Did I stutter?"

Shiloh watched his eyes, the light in them growing so bright that she thought she could feel it in her chest. This world so often seemed like only lies and chains until it felt like there was no truth. No choices. But there *was* truth here. And there *was* a choice, an impossible one, but a choice all the same.

Me or Jake? Nic or me?

Fear or love?

And the truth?

Well, the truth was dangerous. It could set people free or destroy them. It could end lives and save them. It could build up kingdoms and tear them down. And this truth—how she felt about him—might just be the most powerful and most dangerous truth of all.

He was still searching her eyes, dumbfounded, so she took his face in her hands and said it again. "I love you, Jake. It scares me to death, but I *love* you."

And I choose you. Not me.

You.

What was survival if she lost everyone she loved? If she had to live with the monster she was? They couldn't all make it out of this alive, but Silas was wrong. There was a way to save both Nic and Jake.

Shiloh was a smart girl, and if Silas thought she was done playing this game against him, he was wrong. She had a plan. She'd been running it over and over in her head since Jake had told her he loved her.

Jake's smile was pure and wonderful and made his eyes shine. "I love you too."

She kissed him, and with that kiss, she changed all the rules. She was done being the good girl. The Haven girl Silas could kick around because she didn't matter. The girl who survived even if she'd never truly lived.

New Rule #1: Save Nic and Jake.

No matter the cost.

Part Four
GAME OVER

"We cannot change the cards we are dealt.
But we can change how we play the game."
—Randy Pausch, *The Last Lecture*

THIRTY-TWO

On the first day back at school, Shiloh told Jake the plan to help Nic escape, spelling it out on the tablet—at least the portion of the plan she could tell him. She wanted so badly to tell him the whole truth, but she feared that if Jake knew Shiloh was signing her own death warrant, he would choose to save her, not Nic. And that would break Rule #1.

Jake filled her in on what he knew of the plan and then arranged a meeting. Jake gave her a tracker key and explained how it worked and where to go. As Shiloh returned to the dorms for the evening, she looked for and memorized the locations of the cameras. The far entrance of her dorm stood only a few feet from that corner of the Quadrangle, so it would be easy.

Later that night, Shiloh waited until Josephine fell asleep and then unlocked the tracker. She placed it under the pillow next to the audio recorder. She pulled up the hood of her coat and wrapped the scarf around her face, then bolted the few feet to the Quadrangle. She slipped through the boards and found Jake there already. His eyes danced as soon as he saw her. Her heart warmed.

Shiloh could still hear Willa and Zyra's delighted squeals when they walked into the common area of the Haven Yuletide morning. Instead of seeing socks tied with old cord around their pathetic little tree, there had been piles of brightly colored packages. Donated, apparently, by a charity called Foster United run by Mrs. Reagan Osgood. There'd been a toy for each Little, packages of makeup and jewelry for the older girls, and games and art supplies for all to share. The delight in all the Littles had been the greatest sight Shiloh had seen. For one Yuletide morning, they got to feel as though they were as important as every other little girl.

"I know it was you," Shiloh had said to Jake when he called later that day, but he'd denied it and said it was all his mother. Maybe Mrs. Osgood had a lot to do with this kindness, but Jake had certainly played a part.

It'd been reconfirmation that she'd made the right choice. Him. She'd always choose him.

Jake showed her how to open the trapdoor, and they submerged themselves in darkness. Using the light of his phone, Jake led them down the dark tunnel. At the end there was a room filled with wonders, but Shiloh had barely registered them and who was standing in the room, before she heard a familiar growl.

"Why the froq would you let *her* come here?"

Shiloh's heart stopped as she turned to face Val. *No, no, no.* Val couldn't be a part of this—in danger—too. Shiloh glanced to Jake, but he shook his head. He hadn't known.

Save her. I'll have to save her too.

"Stefani?" Val snapped, looking over at where Stefani stood, gnawing on a fingernail. Shiloh did know about Stefani's involvement.

Nic sighed in exasperation. "Val, I trust everyone in this room."

"But you can't trust *her*." Val stabbed a finger at Shiloh.

Shiloh's hand curled into fists. Enough was enough. She had let Val and Silas and all of Arcadia beat her down for too long. Shiloh was done.

"Really, Val?" Shiloh marched toward Val so only a foot separated them. "You can't trust me? Remember when you kissed Demi, and she was going to tell Mother, until Hope and I threatened to put spiders in her bed every night until she left the Haven? You trusted me then."

"That was *before*!" Val's voice echoed against the stone walls.

"Val," Stefani said softly, reaching for Val's arm, but she shook her off.

"Before what?" Shiloh demanded.

"You know exactly what!" Val shoved her, and Shiloh stumbled back a step.

"Hey! Don't touch her!" Jake leaped toward them, but Shiloh held up a hand.

"I'm fine, Jake."

He stopped but watched with worried eyes.

Shiloh turned back to Val. "Why don't you enlighten me."

"Because Hope would still be here if it wasn't for you," Val said, speaking through her teeth.

Shiloh's breath hitched. "What does that mean?"

"You told them! You told them about the bible pages!"

"*What?*" If Val had slammed her fist into Shiloh's gut, it wouldn't have hurt like this. Shiloh's voice came out strangled. "That's what you think? That's what you've thought this *whole* time?"

"We were the only two who knew, and I didn't tell."

"How could you think that...How..." Shiloh's voice shattered, and her chest ripped opened. How cold of a person could she have been that her own best friend had assumed that of her? *Cold, heartless blight.* "You really think it's my fault?"

Val turned her head and glared at the wall.

"Maybe it is." Shiloh wrapped her arms around herself. "I should have burned those bible pages as soon as I saw them. I should have protected her better." She gritted her teeth, forcing fire behind the next words. "But I *didn't* tell anyone. I would have died before I told them."

Tears burned at the back of her eyes, and Shiloh pressed them close. She stood on that stage at the Cleansing, watching Silas put Hope on her knees. Only this time, Shiloh ran to Hope—saved her —or at least held her hand at the very end. Shiloh didn't know when her coldness had turned to heat, when her helplessness had turned to power, but Shiloh knew there was no going back.

Never again. She would never again let Arcadia take away someone she loved. She would die first.

Val's mouth moved, open and shut. The shadows cast by the flashlights in the room danced about her face.

Shiloh braved a step forward. "Val, we have always protected each other. That's what you and I do. You were still trying to protect me on Unity Day, when you were scared I was going to get my heart broken. And I will always protect you, Val." *Always.*

Val searched her over, studying her face. Her mask of anger was slipping, replaced by the softness and love she hid beneath.

"Do you want to know what the worst part of losing Hope was?" Shiloh asked. "What nearly killed me? That when she was gone, I didn't just lose her, I lost you too."

Val glared down at her feet, silent for a long moment. When she spoke again, her voice was barely a whisper. "Hope died at the Cleansing, didn't she? Nic told me about the bomb. And I just... need to hear it for sure."

An invisible knife slipped through Shiloh's ribs, taking her breath away.

Jake laid a hand on the curve of Shiloh's back. "Do you want me to tell her?" he asked, his own voice thick.

Shiloh shook her head and swallowed the lump in her throat. "She didn't die in the bomb, Val. She...she said no. When Councilor Osgood asked her to renounce her heresy, Hope said no. So they..." Shiloh forced the words out, choking on their edge. "They executed her."

Val groaned and sagged against the wall as though her knees were giving out. Stefani's hands flew to her lips, and Nic gasped.

Shiloh tried to fight against the tide of grief, but warm tears descended down her cold cheeks anyway. Grief was a funny thing; It had been seven months since Hope died, and sometimes, Shiloh didn't think about Hope, but other times—like now—she thought she might drown beneath the waves of grief.

"I'm so sorry, Val," Shiloh said, sweeping at her tears with her coat sleeve. "I wanted to save her...but I couldn't."

Val, at last, met her eyes, and she was crying too. "You watched her die, and you've been living with it all this time."

Shiloh nodded.

Val stared at her for a long moment, the only sound in the stillness was hollowed breath echoing against stone. Then she lunged at Shiloh, throwing her arms around her. She hugged her so tightly that Shiloh couldn't breathe.

"I'm so sorry, Shiloh," Val said into her shoulder. "I'm so sorry for everything."

And with those words, the two years that separated them seemed to fade. Shiloh embraced her in return, grateful that—even if Shiloh's end was near—she'd at least gotten her sister back.

Stefani let out a loud breath. "Oh, thank the stars this moment is finally over with. I knew you two would eventually either reconcile or kill each other, and I wasn't sure which one."

Val pushed Shiloh away as suddenly as she'd hugged her, but that was just how Val ended hugs.

"All right, all right," Val said, "enough with all these feelings. We need to get down to business."

Shiloh nodded and looked at Nic with a smile

"Let's do this." She felt a thrill of excitement that startled her. But maybe it was because the idea that a Haven girl would get her mother back felt like the stuff of fairytales.

"So, Starchild," Val said, and this time the name was a compliment. "What exactly are you going to do?"

Shiloh glanced up at Jake, who grinned crookedly in return, and then back at Val. Whatever happened in the future, they were all united in this moment. United by something forbidden. Something different, but something real.

Maybe everyone had a little heresy in them.

Shiloh's own smile turned crooked as she reached into her bag and pulled out hers and Jake's science project. "I'm going to make Nic invisible."

"This isn't going to, like" —Nic flicked her eyes to Jake uncertainly as she slipped her arms in the jacket, which was the upgraded design of the Cloak— "burn my skin off?"

Jake smirked. "Probably."

Shiloh sent him a warning glance over her shoulder. "It went just fine when I tried it on me." She did a circle around Nic, making sure it all looked good.

It had been a lot of long sleepless nights this week as Shiloh tried to get the Cloak functioning. Shiloh had quickly realized that the belt wouldn't work for a human. The arms frequently got in the way of the cameras. So Shiloh had taken the cameras from the belt and put it into one of Jake's old jackets, embedding them across the front and back and the sleeves. After discussions with Nic, she'd also lined the jacket with the material from a survival blanket. Invisible from human eyes, and the heat-sensing Eyes as well.

Shiloh had urged them to move the plan along as quickly as possible. They'd wasted enough time getting her out as it was. Every day Silas sent threatening messages asking if Jake had told her more of the plan. Every day, she lied and said Jake wouldn't tell her anything, because he was determined to keep her safe. It was only a matter of time before Silas called her bluff.

Shiloh stepped back and rubbed a hand over her eyes, that ached from lack of sleep. "Okay, Nic, now hit the button on the side, and let's see what happens."

❦

Nic took a breath, did as Shiloh directed, and heard a soft gasp by Stefani. "Did it work? Can you see me?"

Stefani clapped her hands to answer. "Jakey-boy, your girl-friend is froqing brilliant!"

Jake grinned, his eyes shining. "Yeah, she is."

Nic swallowed, grateful they couldn't see her face.

Shiloh only nodded solemnly. "All right, Nic, I need you to walk for me, so I can see how adaptive it's being with movement."

Nic walked several feet down the tunnel and then back toward them. The jacket was one of Jake's and massive on her. The collar bunched close to her nose, smelling of his sweet, woodsy scent.

"There's still a little more lag than I would like," Shiloh said, her eyes flickering around the room. "But unless someone is looking directly at you, I don't think it should be a problem. So, if you're close to someone, try to be as still as possible."

Nic pushed the button, visible once again. Hopefully.

"How's everything else going?" Shiloh asked.

"I think I have everything I need," Nic said. She, Stefani, and Val had been saving up any packaged rations they were given at mealtime. Jake had used his rations to purchase water bottles over the last week. And Val had somehow managed to get her a knife from the kitchen. It wasn't a gun, but it would have to do. All of it was hidden in the tunnels in a backpack, ready for whenever they would leave.

"Good," Jake said. "Then Saturday?"

Nic nodded, but her heart twisted in her chest. She was finally going to be back with her mom, but the thought of leaving behind her friends was painful. The five of them had grown strangely close in the last few nights while they had been planning in the tunnel.

"I can't thank all of you enough," Nic said, a lump rising in her throat. "I'd...I'd never had friends before all of you, and I—"

"Nic," Val snapped, "no waterworks. If you start crying, Stef's going to start crying, and I'm going to have two wet shoulders, and it'll all be unpleasant."

Nic laughed and rubbed her fists over her eyes. "I'm going to miss you, that's all."

Stefani hugged her tightly, and with a grunt, Val joined in. Nic wished that Jake would join in too, but he only stood, his arms wrapped around Shiloh as she rested her tired head against his chest.

THIRTY-THREE

Escape day.

Shiloh watched Nic run drills between the two basketball posts. She was fast, tagging the next girl into the relay several seconds before anyone else did. Hope blazed in Shiloh's chest. They could actually do this. Everything was laid out carefully. Jake and Nic would leave from the tunnels tonight and, by the time that anyone noticed Nic was not in bed with her tracker, Jake should be back in his own.

Shiloh was barely managing to keep Silas's suspicion at bay. She wore fresh bruises across her wrist to prove it. It was only a matter of time before the entire game board upset, but by this time tomorrow, it wouldn't matter. Because Nic would be gone, and Silas would be without proof that Jake was involved.

And I'll be dead.

Shiloh forced back the thought, locking it behind a door in her mind. It would do no good to let fear control her now. She would face the consequences tomorrow, knowing she'd saved the people she loved.

Coach Bradshaw blew her whistle. "All right, girls. Hit the showers."

The girls quickly filed out. In the commotion, Nic's hand slid into Shiloh's. Nic squeezed it and gave her a smile that said 'thank you' and 'goodbye' all at once.

"Be safe," Shiloh mouthed, and Nic nodded.

Shiloh was halfway down the hallway when she realized she'd left her coat in the gym. When she returned to grab it from the bleachers, the gym's lights had gone dark. She walked back to the door, her sneakers squeaking in the silence. The door didn't budge. Shiloh frowned and pushed harder with the same results. She'd just come through this door. It couldn't be locked.

The hair at the back of her neck prickled, before she even heard his voice. "Hello, Shiloh."

She whirled around. Silas stood by the basketball post. Her eyes hadn't quite adjusted to the thick blackness of the gym, but the tightness in his voice made icy drips of sweat form on the back of her neck.

"Here I thought you were a smart girl, Shiloh," Silas said. "That you were going to finally be good. But you're a cockroach, a disgusting infestation that only deserves the heel of a boot. Just like your parents."

"I don't know what you're—" Shiloh began, but he seized her hair and hauled her forward.

"Don't lie to me!"

He slammed her head into the post of the basketball hoop. Pain screamed through Shiloh's head, and the world tipped on its side. She collapsed to the tile. Blood pooled in her mouth from her bitten tongue, and the same hot stickiness dripped down her forehead.

"I knew you weren't being honest with me," Silas sneered, towering above her. "So, I did a little investigating in your room and found this."

He threw something on the floor in front of her face. Unable to see through the darkness of gym and the black in her vision,

Shiloh stretched her fingers forward to feel them. The lighter and a thin piece of metal. *The tracker key.*

Oh, Council, he's going to kill me.

"You've been helping them. This whole time!"

He pressed something hard to the back of her neck, and Shiloh's vision collapsed upon itself. That scream. It couldn't belong to her. It sounded shrill and bottomless, like the wail of a dying animal. The electricity from his prod coursed through her body, blazing like fire, making her limbs jerk. When she thought she'd pass out from the lack of air, he pulled away.

Shiloh gasped, choking on the blood in her mouth. His hand seized her ponytail, yanking her to her knees.

His face was only an inch from hers, so close she could see the rage in his eyes. "What are they planning?"

Shiloh spat, spraying blood over his face. "*Froq you!*"

Again his prod. Again the pain, ripping her apart.

"When is she going to try to escape?"

Shiloh said nothing. His boot slammed into her ribs. She collapsed back to the tile, biting her tongue to keep from screaming.

"I will kill you. Do you understand?"

Another kick. A crack shuddered through her entire body, shrieking in her ears. This time, she couldn't hold back her scream.

"This is not a game!" Silas roared.

It took all of Shiloh's strength to push herself to her knees. "That's all it has ever been. A game. Are you mad—that I'm beating you at your own game?" Grabbing the goal post, she pulled herself to her feet. All of her was shaking, but she forced her chin up. "I'm not going to tell you, Silas, which means... *I win!*"

The words were suicide, but she was dead anyway. He seized her throat and shoved her back against the pole. "I will kill you. It's you or them. That's the choice."

Shiloh dragged enough breath through his fist's grip to speak. "Them."

His fingers tightened, and he growled. "*What?*"

"Them," she repeated, with the last of her breath. Her head spun, but she said it over and over again to herself. *Them. Them. Jake. Val. Nic. Stefani. Them. Them.*

It came in an onslaught. The punches, the kicks, the waves of electricity coursing through her body. She curled in as small a ball as possible, arms shielding her face, biting her tongue to minimize her screams and his satisfaction.

She didn't know how long it went on before he stopped. Everything hurt. Everything.

"Did you forget that this choice doesn't just impact you?" Silas said, pacing. His boots clicked against the basketball court. "What about Willa?"

Shiloh's heart wailed. *No.*

She imagined the Littles, standing in the yard and waving as the other Havens returned to school after Yuletide break. Willa and Zyra had bawled when Shiloh explained she wouldn't be coming back to the Haven, and Shiloh had barely held back tears of her own.

He couldn't really do this. He had a daughter Willa's age!

He pulled his phone from his pocket and put it by her ear. A little girl was screaming.

No, no, no.

"You're a monster!" Shiloh screamed.

"*You* are the monsters," Silas said. "*I* am the monster-catcher. The exterminator. You want to play games with me? *It's your move!*"

The girl screamed again.

No, no, Willa.

Shiloh screamed, rage and grief and frustration. She'd made the choice to trade her life for Jake and Nic and ROGUE, but this was a price she'd forgotten to calculate. A price she couldn't pay.

"One..." Silas counted. "Two..."

"They're leaving tonight," Shiloh said, and the words

destroyed her. "Nic and Jake are leaving from the old chapel across the lake and leaving through the woods tonight. At eleven."

"What else?"

"That's all," Shiloh said.

"I don't believe you."

Another scream from the phone.

Shiloh pushed herself to her knees, and she was begging, like the pathetic, disgusting thing she was. "I swear to you, Silas. Please. Please. Jake wanted me to know as little as possible. To protect me. *Please.*"

Silas stared down at her.

"Please."

"You better not be lying," he growled, and then kicked her in the stomach one last time.

Shiloh spat up more blood as she heard the door to the gym open and then bang shut. She was still alive, but she wished...she wished she wasn't.

It wasn't until the third time that Jake called from his tablet that Shiloh answered. She hadn't come to dinner, but instead sent a text. *Don't feel well. Sorry.*

Only silence came from the other end of the line, but he could hear her breathing softly. She'd turned off her camera, so he couldn't see her face.

Jake's stomach churned. "Shiloh? Are you okay?"

"Yeah," she said at last.

"Why don't I believe you?"

"I just feel sick, that's all."

Something was wrong. Jake could feel it in his bones, but he didn't have the time to do the mental and emotional effort it would take to get her to be honest. Not tonight, with the escape hours away.

Jake sighed in frustration. "Do you want me to bring you dinner?"

"No."

There was a long silence.

"Jake, I—" She paused.

Jake's hands tightened into fists. "Yes?" *Please, just talk to me.*

She let out a trembling breath. "Whatever happens tonight, remember that I love you. More than anything."

The vulnerability in her voice was tangible. Jake's stomach twisted. She was afraid. "Everything's going to be fine. You're stuck with me, remember?"

She said nothing.

Jake ran his hand through his hair. Tomorrow. He'd press more tomorrow. "And I love you too, Shiloh. More than anything. I'll see you in the morning."

He hung up.

❦

The few phones the school offered for student use had a long wait on Saturdays. Shiloh spent an hour waiting in line to call the Haven. Her head throbbed. She'd told the nurse practitioner who staffed the school's medical clinic that she slipped on ice and hit her head on the stairs. If the provider doubted her, she'd said nothing as she sutured her up then warned her to return if she developed symptoms of a concussion.

When Shiloh finally got to the front of the phone line, she dialed with shaking fingers.

"Central Minnesotan Haven for Girls."

Shiloh's fingers tightened over the receiver. "Aunt Morgan, it's Shiloh."

Aunt Morgan was surprised. "Shiloh, how are you?"

"Is everyone okay there?" Shiloh asked. "Willa...the other girls."

"Yes, of course."

"And there haven't been any strange men there? No....Elite."

Aunt Morgan gasped. "No! Why would there be? Shiloh, are you okay?"

Shiloh hung up the phone and pressed the heel of her hand to her forehead. Of course, it'd been a bluff. This was a game.

And she was still playing, too.

Jake listened carefully as Stefani went over the plan one more time.

"Got it?" Nic asked him.

Jake nodded.

Nic turned to face Val and Stefani, who'd come to the tunnels to see them off, her eyes glossy. "I don't know how to say goodbye. I'd never have survived here if it wasn't for you." She hugged Val and Stefani hard, a hug that went on for a long time.

When she pulled back, Stefani looked a little misty eyed too. "We love you, kid."

"Yeah, you're all right," said Val.

They exchanged one last hug, and then Nic took a deep breath and stepped toward Jake.

Jake steeled himself for what was to come. "Ready?"

Nic nodded. "Ready."

"Stop!"

Shiloh? Jake turned as Shiloh came running down the tunnel, her feet pounding on the stone.

"Stop. You can't go," she said through gasps.

"Shiloh, what are you doing here?" Jake demanded. She wasn't supposed to be here. She was supposed to be safe. He swung toward her, and the flashlight in his hand cast on her face. Jake's heart stopped.

"Froq, Shiloh!" Jake closed the distance between them. A stunning mixture of purple and green painted the left side of her face, her eye so swollen it barely opened. A laceration ran from her eyebrow back into her hairline, closed with a few stitches. "What happened to you?" He reached for her, but she stepped away from him.

"You can't go," she said again. "The Elite. They know you're leaving tonight."

"Shiloh," Nic said, "what are you talking about? How could they know?"

Shiloh glanced at Jake, and there was no mask on her face anymore. Her emotions were on clear display: sorrow and guilt. So much guilt.

She looked down at her feet and answered. An answer that destroyed him.

"Because I told them."

Thirty-Four

The words seemed to drain all the air from the room, leaving Nic breathless. Val and Stefani gasped, but Jake didn't make a sound; he only stared, his face frozen in an expression of horror.

No, no, this couldn't be happening! Shiloh was their friend. She wouldn't betray them like this. But one look at her purple face, and Nic knew it was true. How many times had Nic almost broken in that cage?

Shiloh was shaking, and she leaned hard against the wall. "This whole time I've tried to keep you safe, but I..." she said, through puffy lips. "I failed..."

Nic took a step closer.

"The Elite did this to you?" Jake asked, his voice crackling, his face contorting like he was in physical pain. "They tortured you?" He reached toward Shiloh, and she jerked away from him again.

Jake stared at her with wide eyes, looking hurt. Nic tentatively approached Shiloh.

"Can I see?" Nic asked, reaching for the bottom of Shiloh's shirt. Shiloh stiffened, but let her lift the sweater up.

Val let out a string of angry Spanish beneath her breath. Jake swore aggressively, then marched away with his hands in his hair.

The bruises covered both sides of her ribs, and most of her lower belly. Finger-shaped bruises and a prod's burn marks were tattooed on both sides of her throat. Nic was sure if she looked at Shiloh's arms and legs, they too would be a glorious display of cruelty. Nic knew all those wounds intimately.

Shiloh finally met her eyes, and Nic could see the depth of her shame. "I'm so sorry. I'm not as strong as you. But he...he threatened the other Haven girls, the Littles. Willa. I was willing to let him kill me, but I couldn't risk them. He was bluffing, but I didn't know..."

Maybe, Nic should have been mad at the betrayal, but all she could see reflected in Shiloh's eyes was herself, sitting in a white cage. She knew what the Elite were like, what they would do to you to get what they wanted. And now, Shiloh was here, warning them at infinite risk for herself.

So instead, Nic carefully slipped her arms around her. "It's okay."

Shiloh jerked in surprise as Nic hugged her. Why? Why was she being kind to her? Shiloh didn't deserve it. She had played a deadly game with their lives, and she had failed.

"It's not okay!" Shiloh snapped. She yanked away from Nic so quickly her head spun. She caught herself on the wall. "You don't understand. The Elite have been using me to spy on you." Shiloh gestured to both Nic and Jake. "Both of you. For months."

"*Spying*?" Jake repeated, choking on the word. "You were spying on me? Since when?"

The confession burned Shiloh's throat. "Since September."

"September?" He made a choking sound. "But that was when..."

He trailed off, but Shiloh could hear the unasked question. *Did we start dating because you had to spy on me?* Shiloh looked away, and that was the only answer that he needed. He swore and turned away from her, pacing once more.

I'm so... I'm so sorry, she wanted to say, but those words would never be enough. Here it was, the inevitable. This was when Jake stopped loving her.

Stefani marched forward, the rage Shiloh deserved crackling in her eyes. "What did you tell them?"

"I—"

"Shiloh, did you tell them about *my parents*?"

"No," Shiloh said. "I didn't tell him anything about you or Val being involved. He made me wear an audio recorder, but I haven't worn it down here in the tunnels. I've been lying to him the whole time, trying to keep Jake and Nic safe. I pretended I didn't know anything about the escape plan. I thought I could get Nic out of here before he figured that out, but he searched my room and found the tracker key, so he knew I'd been helping you. The only thing I told him was you were leaving tonight from the chapel."

Stefani took a step back. "But the plan was always to leave from the tunnels. You lied to him?"

Shiloh nodded. "But you still can't leave. He probably has Elite stationed all over the woods."

Shiloh looked at Val, who stood in the shadows, her expression unreadable. This hurt almost the worst. She'd just gotten her best friend back. These last days in the tunnel had almost been like before Hope, but that too would be gone now.

I'm so sorry, Shiloh mouthed, but Val only looked at her feet, her arms folded over her chest.

"What are we going to do now?" Stefani asked, her hands flying through the air like a startled bird. "Nic can't stay here."

"If you go, the Elite will follow her straight back to ROGUE," Shiloh said. "They will either slaughter them or torture them to get the information they couldn't get from Nic. Jake, they're going to arrest you; that's been his plan the whole time. You have to stay. You have to think of a different plan."

Nic shook her head. "I'm still going."

"Did you hear what I just said?" Shiloh snapped.

"Yes," said Nic calmly, "but I'm still going. I can lead them to a different location. Jake can stay. I won't meet up with Stefani's dad. I'll just run until they catch me."

"Don't be stupid," Val growled. "That's suicide."

"If I don't go, they will know that Shiloh warned us. And they'll kill her." Nic looked sharply at Shiloh. "Won't they?"

Shiloh gritted her teeth; she could still taste blood in her mouth. "Then let him kill me!"

"*No!*" Jake cried.

"Let him! Because I am done. I am done being his...*froqing* good girl."

"No," Jake growled, fists at his side. "Absolutely froqing not. We'll figure something out."

"Me or you two. That's the choice. That has *always* been the choice." She met Jake's eyes, and the anguish and the anger there made her almost crumble.. "And I have always chosen *you*."

"Would you all just shut up?!" Val stormed toward them. Shiloh thought Val might hit her, which she absolutely deserved, but Val just stopped in front of her, shaking with rage. "Because you know what's *not* happening? I'm not losing another friend. Got that? So, you dying or Nic dying—those aren't options."

Shiloh shook her head. "Those are the options we have. If they survive, he'll kill me. He made that perfectly clear on Yuletide eve."

Jake jerked to a halt and spun toward Shiloh. "*What* did you say?"

Jake's eyes went dim, like a light being flicked off. A shiver passed through Shiloh. Jake was warmth and golden sunlight, but now his eyes were as cold as the air outside.

He stepped toward her, his voice turning to a growl. "What about Yuletide?"

Shiloh bit her lip. She hadn't meant to tell him like this. He'd already been hurt so much. She'd betrayed him, and his entire family had too.

He stopped in front of her, his fists at his side. "Shiloh, why did you really disappear at the ball? Was the son of a blight there?"

Shiloh nodded. "Yes."

"Who?" Jake demanded.

"Jake, listen—"

"Shiloh, *who*?"

Shiloh took in a breath and exhaled the truth, "Silas."

Jake gave a short bark of laughter, utterly humorless, while Stefani's hands flew to her mouth.

"You mean, Silas Petrovic, Councilor Osgood's brother-in-law?" Stefani asked. "Jake's uncle?"

Shiloh nodded.

"Silas isn't an Elite," Jake said, shaking his head. "He's...I don't know, some big business guy or something."

"That's the point of the Elite, Jake," Shiloh said. "They could be anyone, and you'd never know. And I *know*. I recognized his voice as soon you introduced us."

Jake gave her an icy stare that chilled her to her bones. When the disbelief finally faded, he swore and paced away.

"My mom told me that, for someone not in politics, Petrovic is uncomfortably close to all the members of the United Council," Stefani said, drumming her fingers against her chin. "Of course, that makes sense, if he's an Elite."

"But why?" Jake slumped against the wall as though he could no longer stand. "Why would my own uncle want to have me arrested?"

Shiloh shrugged. "Because he has no sympathy for heretics. Even if it's his nephew."

The last of disbelief fled Jake, and he sank to the floor, his head in his hands.

Shiloh ached to go to him, but she'd seen the cold way he had looked at her—the affection that used to overflow in his eyes completely gone. She swallowed the sob growing in her throat.

Nic went to Jake's side, setting a hand on his shoulder and sitting next to him, her eyes sad and distant. Shiloh looked away.

"Well, that's good then, right?" Val said. "If we know him, then we can figure out his weakness. And then we can figure out a different plan."

Shiloh sighed and dropped her head. "Val—"

Val stepped forward and grasped her shoulders. There wasn't hate in her eyes, only love and determination. "Starchild, you are the most brilliant person in this whole school, and you're going to think of a different plan."

"I don't understand. Why do you even care what happens to me? I've lied. I've failed you. I've put all your lives at risk."

Val dropped her hands. "Shiloh, look at you." She gestured up and down, at the black and blue masterpiece Silas had left on her skin. "You've been protecting us with your life. Now, it's our turn to protect you. So, stop being a froqing martyr and think of a new plan."

Shiloh looked around, at Stefani who gave her a small smile and at Nic who nodded. But Jake—the one who mattered most— kept his head in his hands and wouldn't even look at her.

"I don't..." Shiloh started.

"What if Jake went to his father?" Stefani asked, pacing a few steps. "Tell him what Silas is doing to you. You're a law-abiding citizen, Shiloh. He can't torture you."

Shiloh scoffed. Stefani was smart, but she was the daughter of people whose status protected her, not condemned her. "No one is going to care what an Elite did to a Haven girl. Besides—" *Don't say it. Don't hurt Jake anymore.* But it was the truth, and he deserved it. "Councilor Osgood already knows."

Jake's head jerked out of his hands. "My dad knows about this?" His face contorted—pain—and then it flashed into something else, his hands making fists on his knees. Rage.

Stefani took a step back, pulling her coat tighter against her. "The Councilor is trying to get Jake arrested? That's not possible. Everyone with even a shred of power in this country knows that Samuel Osgood loves his family. It's his greatest weakness."

"No. He knows that Silas is using me to spy on Jake." Shiloh bit her lip. "But he only thinks that I'm keeping him *out* of trouble."

Silas, you're like a dog with a bone.

Shiloh heart skittered in her chest, with something other than pain and fear. Hope.

That was it. Councilor Osgood *loved* Jake. Everything he had done to cover up Jake's heresy proved that. Stefani had said it right —anyone with a shred of power recognized Councilor Osgood's weakness. And Silas was powerful.

I would never do anything to jeopardize you.

And finally, finally, Shiloh knew the hand of cards Silas had been hiding. A plan took form in Shiloh's mind. So much could go wrong. But it was the one chance to save Nic and Jake...and maybe herself too.

"I have an idea," Shiloh said.

Because everybody had a little heresy in them.

Even Silas.

THIRTY-FIVE

"**J**ake, please talk to me."

Jake didn't turn to Shiloh who sat a few feet from him, leaning against the tunnel wall.

The first part of the plan was for Nic to go to the chapel, alone. She would wait awhile and then she'd go back to her dorm. It'd look like Jake had stood her up, and she'd abandoned the attempt tonight. Saving Jake right before he actually committed heresy. They'd wait in the tunnels awhile, in case the Elite followed Nic back to campus.

Val and Stefani had retreated to a different corner, while Shiloh sat only a few feet away from Jake. He sat, unable to look at her, unable to think. Feeling as though his world had crumbled, and he had plunged into darkness.

He couldn't grasp this new reality—reconcile the uncle he knew with the monster who had left bruises on Shiloh's body that made Jake feel like he'd been tortured too. With the Elite who'd used Shiloh as a piece in a sick game, even as she tried to protect him and Nic. And Jake knew that she had. If she'd truly wanted to betray him, why make him use the tablet?

But her willingness to protect him didn't change the truth that clawed Jake's chest open. Shiloh didn't want to be with him; she'd *been forced* to be with him. Everything else after that—the kisses, the *I love you*'s—had all just been playing the game.

Jake wanted to scream. To punch something or someone. To cry.

"Jake," Shiloh tried again, "please."

The tornado of emotion swirling within him settled on anger and exploded to his chest, sending him to his feet. He whirled toward her. "You want to talk?" The sharpness in his voice echoed back to him from the stone walls. "Fine. Let's talk."

Shiloh used the wall to help herself to her feet, rising slowly. Jake couldn't look at her bruised face without his chest caving in, so he glared at the stone instead.

"Let's get this straight," Jake said. "The only reason you changed your mind about dating me was because an Elite made you?"

Shiloh winced and shook her head. "I didn't change my mind. The night we first kissed, I woke up with his hand on my throat." Shiloh touched the base of her throat, where the same hand had left the same bruises. "He told me to stay away from you."

Jake had known something had happened that night. He'd been right all along. *Froq my father!*

But if Shiloh's lies had started that very first night, under the bleachers, had anything at all been truth?

"Jake," Shiloh said softly, taking a tentative step forward. "I know you're angry. And you have every right to be, but—"

Jake threw up his hands and growled. "Of course, I'm angry! I'm angry with Silas and my dad and myself, and this whole froqing country."

"At yourself? Why?"

Jake could feel Stefani and Val's eyes upon them, and he hated that this too had to be performed like a depressing third act of a terrible play.

"Because you've been getting hurt for months!" Hadn't he

sensed something was wrong this whole time? He'd seen the random bruises she wore, but he'd believed her dumb excuses—because he'd never imagined this. "And I didn't notice."

Idiot, idiot, idiot!

"Jake, that's not your fault. I hid it from you."

"But why?" His voice cracked, and he forced that away, clinging to the anger so he didn't drown in the pain. "Why didn't you tell me? I could have helped you. I could have *protected* you."

She wrapped her arms over her chest and looked down to her feet, her hair forming a curtain over her face. "I just wanted to keep you safe."

"That doesn't explain why you couldn't tell me?"

She paused for a long moment, a sure sign she was going to lie again. "He threatened me. I was—"

But Jake had already figured it out. He could feel it deep in his gut, like a knife had been buried there.

"Scared because you didn't trust me," Jake finished. "I was the one who said what I did and got us in trouble in the hospital. I'm the one who took you into the woods to tell you about helping with Nic's escape instead of using the tablet like you already told me. What am I to you? Just some useless, reckless, pathetic boy you were obligated to pretend to love, so he didn't get himself killed?"

"Jake," Shiloh gasped, but he had already spun away from her and refused to look back.

The truth. That was all he'd ever wanted, and here it was, illuminated in glaring lights. He'd loved her with everything he was, but she didn't love him.

Her hand brushed against his, and he jerked away. He whirled to meet her eyes. Those beautiful, dark eyes that he adored so much, now swimming with tears. *Froq those eyes.*

"Jake, I know it's all froqed up."

Jake could barely hear her. He could only hear the echo, building like a wail in his chest. *She doesn't want me. She doesn't love me. She never did.*

"But I need you to know—"

"Shiloh, *don't*!" It burst out of him, halting her words. "Just don't. I was so stupid. I actually believed that in Arcadia, a country of lies, I had finally found something real. That *you* were real. But I was wrong. You're just another one of Arcadia's lies."

She flung a hand over her lips and pressed her eyes closed, fighting against the sobs now shaking her frame. Jake swallowed the guilt that rose like hot bile in his throat and turned away. He put his back to the wall and slid to the ground.

"Jake."

"I said *don't*! I don't want to play this game with you anymore. It's over." He scrubbed his hands against his burning eyes. He wasn't going to cry. At least, he wouldn't if he could just spend the next hour pretending she didn't exist. Pretending that his heart wasn't lying in a million pieces on the stone floor.

It's really over.

"I thought a lot about what you said," Jake told Shiloh, as they both sat, cross-legged on his bed the next day. "And I just couldn't do it. You were right. It was a really big risk, and so I told Nic I couldn't do it anymore. I couldn't help her."

He's a good actor, Shiloh thought. But then Jake had starred in his own puppet show as the son of a Councilor all his life. Jake had given her stationary in class, and she'd written the script out for him. He held it in his lap, but barely glanced at it. The audio recorder was pinned to Shiloh's chest. Hopefully, Silas would believe the story they were feeding in.

"Part of me wanted to, but—" Jake hung his head, even though no one would actually see his performance. "But in the end, she's a heretic, and I have too much to lose. Like you."

He said that last part with so much affection in his tone, that Shiloh's heart gave a jolt of hope. But she forcefully reminded herself that this wasn't real. She'd heard him loud and clear last night.

It was over.

Her heart hadn't stopped breaking since.

"Do you think I'm a coward?" Jake asked, sprinkling just a little self-loathing into his tone.

"No," Shiloh said. "I think you made the right choice."

Shiloh strangled her hands together in her lap, so she wouldn't give into the desire to touch him. With all she'd lost, Shiloh considered herself an expert in pain, but this was entirely new level of suffering.

Maybe, he'd been right. Maybe, she should have had the courage to trust him. But it was far too late now.

"What will Nic do?" Shiloh asked. "She didn't leave last night because I saw her at practice today."

Jake shrugged. "I don't know. Try again on her own, I guess." He blew out a big breath through tight lips, like blowing a raspberry. "Anyway, I have a Calculus test tomorrow so I should probably study for that. And don't you have something back at your dorm tonight?"

That...wasn't part of the script. Shiloh didn't have anything back at her dorm, but she understood loud and clear. He didn't want her here. "No," she said, since Silas knew her schedule. "But I'll leave you to study."

She got up to leave. Unlike all the times before, Jake didn't follow her, stealing as many kisses as he could before she got to the door. She hoped that Silas didn't notice that or notice Jake, who'd never missed an opportunity since Yuletide, didn't tell her 'I love you' when she left.

Because she'd certainly noticed.

A few hours later, Shiloh received a message on her tablet that woke her from sleep and confirmed that the act had worked: *JAKE IS LUCKY HE SAW SENSE. YOU BETTER FIND OUT*

WHEN NICOLETTE IS LEAVING NEXT. YOU KNOW THE
CONSEQUENCES IF NOT.

Yes, Shiloh knew the consequences of playing this game all too well.

A few days later, the plan was ready.

Shiloh sent Silas the message, *SHE'S LEAVING TOMORROW NIGHT FROM THE CHAPEL. MIDNIGHT.*

Silas responded quickly, *THAT'S MY GIRL.*

Silas's phone pinged, and he looked at it. One of the security guards from the school was calling.

"What?" Silas answered.

"Commander, we got an alert from Nicolette Haven's tracker," the security guard said, his voice uneasy. "She crossed the boundary line at the school."

"*What?*"

"Should we pursue?" the guard asked.

"No," Silas snapped. "We'll take care of this."

Within minutes, Silas's team piled into trucks and raced toward the spot where he could see the tracker moving on his tablet. Silas strangled his prod with a gloved hand as they drove. That little cockroach, Shiloh, had told him it would be tonight. Had she lied, or had something changed that had made Nicolette bolt, without even stopping to take her tracker off?

The location of Nic's tracker had been in one place for the last ten minutes. They got as close as they could on the back roads around Ardency, and then Silas climbed on one of the snowmobiles they'd hauled on the back of the trucks. Two other Elite's zoomed after him, while the others pursued on foot. When he converged on the area of the tracker, the large valley a mile from the campus, they found the bracelet on the ground. It was snowing again, great big snowflakes that threatened to turn into a real blizzard, and the red letters glowed through a layer of snow.

Silas signaled toward the other Elite and gunned the snowmobile to follow the set of footprints that led from the tracker. It was stupid for her to have left in winter. Her footprints would lead straight to her. But then, a half-mile from where they'd found the tracker, there were two sets of footprints—one continuing straight while the other veered west.

Silas gritted his teeth. So, Nicolette wasn't alone, after all. He sent one Elite to follow the diverging path and followed the one going straight. That path, too, split into two separate paths. The Elite split again. The three sets of footprints zig-zagged in different directions, going back into the woods, doubling back, crossing over one another. Whoever had done this had known that they would be followed. Maybe they'd even wanted to be followed.

This is a distraction. Had this ever been Nicolette at all, or someone else purposely leading them astray?

Each of the footprints ended on the same stretch of asphalt, each almost a half mile apart, and no tracks appeared on the other side.

Silas swore and kicked the snow, sending it flying. "Where is she?"

If Shiloh had anything to do with this, I will strangle her with my bare hands.

Silas logged into the school tracking system and looked for Shiloh and Jake, but their trackers remained in Jake's room. He put in his ear-piece, the one that connected to the recorder that Shiloh wore. Two voices came across.

"Ugh, I hate calculus."

"You're making it harder than it really is."

So, if Shiloh and Jake weren't the ones helping Nicolette, who was? When he figured it out—and he *would* figure it out—they were going to regret the day that they had ever met that filthy little heretic.

THIRTY-SIX

Nic and Jake laid flat against the ground, hiding behind the large snow pile as a professor drove up the hill on a snowmobile, headed toward campus. Across the road, a cluster of townhomes in bright colors stood in sharp contrast to the white backdrop—a small neighborhood of professors' homes just off Ardency's campus. Jake peeked over the drift and locked eyes on the next step of the plan: the snowmobile sitting in Professor Vida's driveway.

Stefani had somehow—Jake didn't ask—snatched the keys out of the eccentric art professor's pocket, and Val had made a copy of it in the metal workshop. The professor had found the key in his drawer the next day and thought he'd simply misplaced it.

Jake glanced at Nic and reached to adjust her hood, pulling it forward to hide the blonde hair that had escaped. Just like him, her scarf was tied so only her eyes were visible.

"Ready?" he asked, fingering the key in his pocket.

She nodded.

Jake glanced over the snowbank one last time. No one. "Now."

They leaped over the snow, sliding on the ice of the road, and then bounded to the snowmobile. Jake leaped on front and felt

Nic's arms surround him. He shoved the key into the ignition and almost laughed in relief when the snowmobile roared to life. He gunned it so quickly its tail spun before thrusting forward.

The snow stung his eyes as they sped through the valleys. They had ten miles to travel to where Greyson Andreou picked Nic up, and they had to do it without being seen. He used the cover of the trees, weaving hazardously around the trunks, jumping and catching air over steep banks.

Behind him, he could hear Nic laughing.

Shiloh was the last one to step from the snowy path and into the car, pulling the survival blanket she'd worn over her head with her. Stefani and Val were already in the backseat, ducking way down low so they couldn't be seen through the windows, and Shiloh squashed in with them. The car peeled away before Shiloh even had a chance to shut the door.

From the driver's seat, Stefani's mother, Reese Andreou, looked back at them. She didn't look anything like her daughter. Where Stefani had sharp, pixie-like features, hers were soft and round, surrounded by ashen brown hair. It was the kind of face that seemed to be instinctively trustworthy. Perhaps that was part of the reason Advocate Andreou was so good at being close to the Council *and* to ROGUE.

"All of you okay?" she asked, steering them down the road.

"Yes," the girls said.

Most cars were driverless, but this ancient car couldn't be as easily tracked, since it didn't have the navigation center. The plan was for Mrs. Andreou to drive them around for a little while, give the Elite time to clear out, and then drop them as close to campus as they could get without the car being seen. Then the girls would sneak back.

Shiloh pulled the scarf from her face and breathed in a deep breath. Doing so made her ribs ache—Silas had probably broken some. But luckily, Shiloh's bruises would fade, and the concussion from the head wound had only left her with some mild dizziness and the occasional headache.

"Mama," Stefani said, "I want you to meet my girlfriend, Valencia Haven." She took Val's hand and held it up proudly, while Val shot one of her dagger-glares. "Don't call her Valencia though. She hates it; therefore, *I'm* the only one who can call her that."

Reese glanced in the rearview mirror and smiled. "It's so nice to meet the girl my daughter is so in love with."

Color rushed to Val's face, but her eyes were shining. Stefani brushed a kiss on her cheek. Val looked momentarily so happy that Shiloh felt her heart rejoice for her—yet ache at the same time. Ache because these moments, when Stefani and Val didn't have to hide how they felt about each other, were so few and far between. And also ache from jealously. Which was selfish and stupid.

Shiloh dared to glance out at the surrounding farmlands, before ducking back down. Jake and Nic were out there somewhere. Safe, hopefully.

Please let them be safe.

Please let him come back to me.

Stefani laid a hand on Shiloh's back. "Jake's going to be fine, Shi. I'm certain of it."

Shiloh gritted her teeth and nodded.

"And he's going to get over himself and forgive you," Stefani said.

Val growled and said something beneath her breath in Spanish, no doubt something about cutting Jake up in pieces too small for fishes to eat.

Shiloh ignored Val and leaned back into the seat with a sigh. If only she could believe that Jake would forgive her, but some things were unforgivable. Besides, Jake had made so many excuses not to see her this last week. He wanted nothing to do with her.

"I mean," Stefani said, "is that what you want?"

"Yes. I love him, Stef. So much."

Stefani squeezed her hand. "Then tell him."

Shiloh shook her head. "He won't believe me."

"Then you do what I had to do with Val," Stefani said, smiling at her girlfriend. "You keep telling them you love them, over and over, until one day, they believe it."

Nic clung to Jake, hiding her face in his back in order to avoid the sting of the snow. Even through his coat, his warmth eased the chill from her body. He maneuvered the snowmobile with ease. He gunned it up a bank, and they caught air from the top. Despite the circumstances, Nic couldn't help but laugh at the exhilaration.

A while later, they exited the woods to the road and found Mr. Andreou standing by an old sedan. Nic knew she should feel relief, but a wave of sadness crept over her. It really was time to say goodbye.

When they neared, Jake didn't turn off the engine. He was stiff as he studied the man, who was just as covered as they were, only his eyes and the strong arch of his nose visible.

"What has one eye but cannot see?" Greyson Andreou called, and Nic gave the appropriate response.

Jake finally cut the engine and jumped off. Nic followed.

Greyson opened the trunk. "It'll be safest for you to ride in here."

Nic nodded but turned back to Jake, pulling down her scarf so her face was visible. He did the same.

"Be safe," he said, pulling her into a quick embrace.

Nic's pulse beat erratically in her throat, his spicy, woodsy scent tantalizing her nose.

Jake released her. "Goodbye, Nic."

She wasn't sure why she did it. Perhaps because she felt so

deeply grateful to him. Perhaps because she'd never felt this heat in her skin before, or maybe because she could hear Stefani's voice say, *'You should try it'*. But probably, mostly, because she knew she'd never see him again. Before she could think better of it, she stood on her toes and kissed him. It was brief, and Jake didn't move at all, but his lips were warm and sweet.

Jake stared at her, his mouth opening but no sound coming out.

"Goodbye, Jake," she said, and ran to the car without looking back. She climbed into the trunk and Greyson slammed it shut, leaving her in darkness.

Jake abandoned the snowmobile a mile from campus near a path where he could get through the woods without being seen. Hopefully, when the vehicle was found, they would assume some hooligan took it for a joy ride. He adjusted his hood and scarf and moved as quickly as he could through the deep snow.

As he hurried, he thought briefly about Nic kissing him goodbye. He'd never seen that coming. He remembered what Stefani had said on Yuletide Eve: *'just because Nic has some crazy crush on you'*. Jake had completely blown it off.

How am I going to explain this to Shiloh?

The question came unbidden to his mind, and it brought with it razors to reopen the wounds on his heart. He shook his head and gritted his teeth. Shiloh wasn't his concern anymore. He could kiss anyone he wanted.

But unfairly, all he still wanted was her.

Shiloh sat in complete silence on Jake's bed. Her tablet laid before her with the audio recorder next to that. Jake and her voice streamed from the tablet in intermittent conversation, and then pauses, as though they were studying side by side. Jake and she had recorded four hours of conversation in the tunnels a couple of nights before, somehow making their conversation not seem forced or awkward. It would create the perfect alibi. Silas knew they could take their trackers off and be in a different location, but it would be impossible for him to prove that when there was an audio recording at the same time.

Shiloh gnawed on the inside of her cheek, waiting. Each second seemed to stretch for an eternity, but finally, the door opened, slowly, soundlessly, and Jake slipped in. He closed the door just as quietly, so the lock couldn't be heard on the recording.

He was drenched with snow, his cheeks scarlet from the cold, but Shiloh swore he'd never looked more amazing.

He came back to me.

A wealth of emotion welled up inside her, and before she could stop herself, she stood and rushed a step toward him. But his eyes, cool as the wind outside, made her stop.

Shiloh winced as her heart cracked a little deeper, but it didn't matter the condition of her heart. He was safe. She had saved him. Whatever happened now, that was all she cared about.

"Everything okay?" Shiloh mouthed.

He nodded as he put his tracker back on. "She's with Greyson," he replied without making a sound.

He was barely looking at her again, but for the brief moment that he did, she could see his face contort. What emotion was this? Sadness? Anger? Disgust? She couldn't tell.

Shiloh waited until there was a natural break in the recorded conversation then stopped the recording. She slipped the audio recorder beneath her shirt, pinning it back to her bra. "Well, I should probably go. There's a trivia night and all academic tracks are required to go."

Jake nodded. As Shiloh passed him, it took all her willpower not to touch him. She stared down at her feet as she slipped through the door.

"Shiloh," he said.

Shiloh turned around, her blood rushing in her ears.

He met her eyes for the first time in days. "Be careful, okay? It's slick out there."

He wasn't talking about ice. Her next task wasn't going to be easy. So, he still cared for her a little. Which meant, maybe, there was hope.

Tell him, Stefani's voice urged in her memory. But would Shiloh survive if he rejected her again?

Jake started to close the door.

If you're not worth fighting for, what is?

Shiloh's foot shot forward, blocking the door from closing.

He raised his eyebrows and opened his mouth. She put a finger to her nose, hushing him, and then pulled her tablet from her bag. She wrote the message quickly, pouring all her heart into the words.

She held it up for him to read.

I need you to know that loving you was never a game. It is the truest thing I have ever known.

Jake looked down at the tablet and then at her, and his face, generally so alive with emotion, was utterly unreadable. He took the tablet, wrote a message, and handled it back. Then he shut the door in her face.

The message read: *I don't believe you.*

When Shiloh left, Jake told the wail in his chest to just *shut up.* As desperately as he still loved her, how—how was he ever supposed to trust her again? How was he supposed to look at her without seeing her betrayal? He shoved the thought away and moved on to the next phase in the plan. He picked up his phone and hesitated a moment, before dialing.

It took four long rings before he picked up the phone.

"Jake?" His father sounded confused and concerned. Jake never called him.

Jake swallowed down the disgust that rose in his throat and forced out the words.

"Dad, I need your help."

When the trunk opened again, night had fallen. Greyson offered his hand, and Nic climbed out of the trunk and into the snow on the shoulder of the road. Dark, towering trees rose on either side of the back road where they'd parked. Greyson handed Nic a bag of supplies. A glance inside showed her what Stefani said he'd have for her: a compass, a ROGUE-issue radio and some extra food. Nic slipped the compass into her pocket, clipped the radio to her belt, and added the food into the backpack.

"Thank you for everything, Mr. Andreou," Nic said. "Your daughter is amazing."

"She gets it from her mother," he said, and then grimaced. "Now, this isn't going to be pleasant, but we have to take out your ID."

They moved into the path of the car's headlights. Greyson carefully cleaned her wrist with an alcohol wipe and took the scalpel from its sterile case. The sharp tip glinted in the light.

"Ready?" he asked.

Of course not. But she bit her lip and nodded. She looked away as the sharp tip broke her skin. Her fingers curled, and she bit her tongue to keep from crying out. A few deft moves, and he flicked the ID out and crushed it under his heel. He'd clearly done this before. He wrapped a pressure dressing onto the wound.

"It would heal better with a suture," Greyson said. "But I'm a reporter, not a doctor."

Nic nodded. "Thank you again."

He squeezed her shoulder. "Best of luck to you, Freebird."

He got back into the car, and she watched him drive away. Nic studied the compass, already programed with the coordinates. The group—the Sparrows who'd tried to shelter her before—sheltered in a long-abandoned ski-lodge on a mount deep in northern Minnesota. They planned to meet her at the base of it. Ten miles still separated her from them, through deep, deep snow.

Nic squared her jaw, activated the Cloak, and started forward determinedly.

Ten miles and she would home.

Silas seized the first thing within reach—a mug sitting on his desk in their makeshift headquarters just off-campus—and threw it against the wall with a scream. He watched it shatter, but it wasn't nearly satisfying enough.

At 8 p.m., the Elite had raided the campus, but Nicolette was gone. There was no question about it. She'd gotten away, and Silas had no idea how or where she could have gone.

That loss had cost him everything.

And Shiloh Sanders would pay the price.

THIRTY-SEVEN

Thirty minutes before curfew, Shiloh got the message that she knew was coming.

MEET ME IN THE QUADRANGLE BASEMENT. NOW.

A fierce snowstorm raged outside. He couldn't meet her outdoors, and Shiloh suspected that the basement offered the most private. And he would want it private for what he planned to do to her. A shiver ran down her spine as she checked the recorder she had attached to her bra. This one didn't belong to Silas.

She sent a message to Jake. *QUADRANGLE BASEMENT. IT'S TIME.*

A quick response. *WE'LL BE THERE.*

Breathe in. She forced in the air and let the pain in her broken ribs flood her with rage. It made her feel brave.

Nic couldn't feel her feet, or her fingers, or her toes, but she had made it through a small Laborer town—unseen, thanks to the Cloak—and she only had one more mile. One more.

She sunk even deeper into the snow, coming up past her knees., making progress slow and each step difficult. She wanted to stop and rest, to lie down and maybe shut her eyes awhile, but that would be the death of her. So, she propelled herself forward, driven by the memories.

Val and Stefani, being her friends through all those months.

Shiloh, willing to die for her.

And Jake...sweet, handsome Jake, leaving muffins on her table, holding her when she'd cried. Kissing him.

And Nic pressed on.

She half walked, half slid down a hill toward a great level expanse. At the end of it, she thought she could see the shadow of the mount. She stepped onto the flat, and the snow wasn't as deep, only coming to her ankle. Her stomach twisted in warning, and she bent, sweeping the layer of snow aside to find a solid layer of ice. A lake. Did she dare cross over it? But who knew how long it would take if she tried to go around? She was so close.

She shot a prayer upward and started across. Movement easier now, a burst of energy propelled her forward. The base of the mountain grew clearer and clearer. Nic turned off the Cloak, so whoever waited on the other side would see her. She was almost to the opposite bank when she heard it: someone calling her name.

Mom!

Nic broke into a run, slipping and sliding.

Thank you, God. Thank—

CRACK!

Nic froze. Even her blood seemed to stand still. Spiderwebs of cracks appeared beneath her feet, rapidly growing in a circle around her. Her pulse thrummed to the time of a ticking bomb—waiting for it to explode.

If she moved, she might die, but if she stayed, she was certainly dead. She took a tentative step forward. The whine of the ice increased to a wail.

Oh, God help me.

In the distance, dark figures raced toward her, still calling her name.

Then she plunged through the ice into the dark waters below.

❧

Silas slammed his fist down on the steel table between him and Shiloh. "I don't believe you!"

He'd picked a small cramped room in the basement with only a steel table scattered with a variety of rusted tools—the janitors' workshop, probably. The only light came from a single bulb that flickered and swayed, casting shadows like lurking monsters around the room.

"I'm telling you the truth," Shiloh said. "I can't help what you believe. Nic told me she was leaving at midnight. I don't know why she left earlier."

"You're lying to me," Silas yelled, as he paced the floor.

"I'm not."

"Then who helped her? I know someone helped her."

"I don't know."

Silas screamed and kicked his chair. The metal chair slammed against the wall, clattering. Shiloh's fingers made fists around the seat of her chair, using the frigid metal to ease her shaking.

Breathe in. Breathe out.

He leaned over the table and put a finger in her face. "I know you helped her somehow. Jake, too."

"We were in his room this entire afternoon." Shiloh spoke steadily and slowly, like explaining something to Willa.

Silas returned to pacing, back and forth, back and forth. "You faked it, somehow. And I'm going to figure it out, and then I'm going to throw you both in a prison camp."

"You could, Silas, but you don't have proof. And if you say that *Jake* was involved, Councilor Osgood is going to want proof."

He leaned across the table until his face hovered inches from hers. "I don't need proof to throw *you* away."

"Maybe." Shiloh shrugged. "But think it through. What will the politicians think? They all saw me with Jake at that Yuletide ball; they all know he's dating a Haven girl. You can tell the outside world whatever you want, but the other Councilors and the State Advocates are going to want to know what I did, how badly the Councilor was compromised, what the evidence was against me. And the only proof you have is the location of our trackers and the audio recorders—which say that we were in his room all afternoon."

He stalked around the table toward her. Without the barrier, Shiloh's heart picked up speed, but she pressed on.

"If you say all this is falsified, then they won't just suspect me, they will also suspect Jake. And then what happens? I don't know how this is going to come back on Councilor Osgood, but it likely won't look good. The politicians might raise quite a ruckus if they think that a Councilor is associated with heresy."

That was the thing about power. You only had it for as long as people gave it to you. And maybe it didn't matter if one person rebelled, or even two, but when they rose together... that was when the world changed, and kingdoms fell. It was a delicate balance. And Silas knew it.

He seized her hair, yanking back her head. She refused to flinch. "Listen here, you filthy cockroach. I'm going to take down ROGUE, and I don't care who has to burn to get there."

"Even the Councilor?" she asked.

He released her. "Yes, even the Councilor."

"I'm a smart girl, remember, Silas?" Shiloh stood and met Silas' eyes levelly. She made her voice cool as ice, as strong as rolling thunder. "I heard you and the Councilor at the Yuletide ball. You were only supposed to spy on Jake to keep an eye on him, to keep him safe. *That's* what you promised the Councilor you were doing. But you'd already told me that you wanted me to help you get Jake arrested. That you wanted me to manipulate him into helping Nicolette, so he too would be found guilty. You knew how badly that would reflect on the Councilor. You *had* to have known."

Silas's fists opened and closed, opened and closed.

"But that's exactly what you wanted, isn't it?"

"Watch it, little girl," he hissed.

Shiloh slammed her hand down on the table, the sound echoing in the tiny room. "Everything that happened with Jake this summer...it dawned on you that you had an opportunity. You're the commander of the Elite. You're well respected and well aligned. Councilor Osgood has no other blood relatives except Jake to follow in his footsteps. So, if there was suddenly an opening in the Council, you might just get the Council's support. Especially if you'd just brought down ROGUE. Your nephew gave you this little window of vulnerability, and you knew that if you could take down Jake, you could take down the Councilor too, didn't you?" Silas didn't react, so she pushed the final button. "That was your plan all along, and I, a pathetic little Haven girl, ruined that for you, didn't I?"

His hand seized her throat and slammed into the wall. "Yes, you little bitch. You ruined everything. And I'm going to make you—"

The door opened, and a voice barked, "Silas, that is quite enough!"

Councilor Osgood.

Silas froze, his stand still crushing her throat.

Another voice growled, "Let her go!"

Jake.

Silas loosened his hold, and she managed to gasp a breath, but he didn't release her. Councilor Osgood stood in the doorway, flanked by at least half a dozen Elite.

"Silas Petrovic," the Councilor said, "you are under arrest for heresy and conspiracy against the Council."

Silas's eyes flicked around the room, looking desperately for escape, but the only door to the room was the one behind Councilor Osgood and his small army.

"Step away from Shiloh and submit to the Elite," Councilor Osgood commanded.

Something flashed in Silas's eyes, and Shiloh's heart stopped. He'd found his escape route. He drew the gun at his side, pinned her against his chest, and pressed the gun to her temple.

"Shiloh!" Jake sprang forward, but an Elite yanked him back.

Councilor Osgood held out a hand. His voice was calm, but Shiloh could read it as clearly in his eyes as she could in his son's: fear for her life. "Silas, don't make this worse for yourself than it already is. Put down the gun."

"You're going to let me leave," Silas said calmly. "Or I'm going to kill her. At least I'll get to take one more heretic with me." He dug the gun's cold muzzle into Shiloh's temple.

Jake lunged toward her again, and Silas aimed the gun at Jake's chest. "Don't be stupid, boy. I don't think you'll survive another bullet."

The Elite moved to shield the Councilor and Jake with their bodies. But rage had exploded in Shiloh's chest, seeing that gun pointed at Jake. The same gun that had been on Hope's head. Held by the same hand that had left bruises on Nic's body and tortured Shiloh for months

Enough!

Shiloh steeled herself. What had Nic taught her about defense and fighting these last few days, just in case? *You don't have to be stronger. You just had to know how to throw your weight.*

Shiloh seized Silas's gun hand and shoved it upward, just as she slid her foot behind his leg and thrust her entire weight backward. *Boom!* Water exploded from a pipe on the ceiling as a bullet burst through it, and Silas tripped backward over her leg. Shiloh slammed down on top of him. *Boom!* The gun fired one more time, her ears ringing. Jake screamed her name. Shiloh rolled onto Silas's arm, pinning it and the gun to ground, and kept rolling away from him. As soon as she was free, the Elite fell upon him, driving their fists into his face.

Shiloh stumbled to her feet, standing over Silas as they wrestled him into handcuffs.

"Game, set, match," she said, as water streamed into her eyes from above. "I win, you son of a blight!"

Silas smiled as the Elite jerked him upright. "Did you?"

Jake's hand alighted on Shiloh's shoulder. Panic edged his voice. "Shiloh, you're bleeding."

Shiloh looked down. Her white shirt bloomed red over her shoulder, growing faster and faster. She remembered the gun, exploding near her ear, but she'd never felt the bullet. Until now.

The world spun, and her legs collapsed. Jake caught her before she hit the ground, and his warmth, his arms, felt like home.

"Someone call an ambulance!"

Thirty-Eight

Nic fought against the pull of the water. The backpack yanked her down like an anchor. She wrestled free of it and kicked her legs wildly. *Up, up.* Her head broke the surface of the water. She could hear frantic yelling.

"Nic, hold on!"

Paul?

Her hand found its way over the edge of the ice, but her soaked hands slid off, and she slipped under the water again. The next time she made it to the surface, she only found ice above her. She pounded her fist against, but it was as solid as bulletproof glass. She swam backward, searching for the hole she fell through, but she could only find more ice.

She couldn't breathe!

Oh God, please.

Her vision tainted black as she began to sink.

Shiloh's eyes were so heavy; she closed them for a second.

"No, no," Jake begged. His hands pressed into her shoulder, trying to slow the bleeding. "Stay with me."

Shiloh wanted to, but the bullet could have hit her subclavian artery or her lung. "Listen," she said through gasps. "I'm not going to make it...until the...ambulance gets here. It's too...far."

"Shut up," Jake growled.

One of the Elite leaned over her, bringing a first aid kit, applying a Quik-Clot. That would stop the bleeding outside, but wouldn't help the internal bleeding, nor her lung that was surely crumpling like a ball of paper.

"She's right," said the Elite. "We have to take her now."

She was weightless, being carried in Jake's arms. She heard car doors, felt the jostle as the car sped forward, wheels squealing on ice and the newly fallen snow.

"We can meet the ambulance," someone said. "Tell them we're coming."

"Hold on."

There was a sting in her elbow, the taste of salt in her mouth.

"How's she doing?"

"Don't you die. Don't you froqing die."

She could feel herself falling, so she clutched onto Jake's shirt. She needed to say something first, something...It took her a long time to figure it out because her mind faded in and out. And then it flowed from her lips.

"I love you. Please...believe me."

Even if he didn't believe her, that was the truth. And the truth was dangerous she knew, but it was also so, so beautiful.

Then she let herself fall, not into darkness, but into light. It felt weightless, like flying. Like her bonds, Arcadia's chains, were finally cut. She heard someone whisper "I love you". And for the first time, she felt worthy of it.

♪

Shiloh was limp and unconscious, but still breathing, when they squealed to a halt next to the air-ambulance parked in the road with its jets humming. Jake lifted her from the car, the rehydration kit the Elite had placed dangling in her arm. He laid her on the waiting gurney. Her pale skin blended into the white sheets. It took all of him to let her go, to watch them wheel her into the ambulance, the paramedics already frantically working to save her.

"Come back to me," he begged, as the ambulance lifted from the ground with a roar of jets and a blare of red and blue lights.

A hand touched his shoulder, and he whirled around to see his father. Before he could stop himself, the anger boiled over and burst forth. He shoved his dad. Hard. With hands covered in Shiloh's blood. Dad stumbled back, slipping in the snow.

"This is your fault!" Jake shoved him again.

A bodyguard stepped forward, but Dad held up a hand.

"Jake..."

"You knew! You knew that Silas was using her."

Dad winced. "I didn't want this. I only wanted to keep you safe."

Jake shoved him once again. It wasn't enough. Jake wanted to punch him, to hurt him, to make him feel what losing Shiloh felt like. And it felt like *dying*.

"No, you wanted to keep *you* safe! Did you see what he did to her in there? He was doing that *for months*. He was hurting her, and she couldn't even tell me! And now she is *dying* because she still chose to save us."

"I'm sorry, Jake. I didn't know that he was hurting her, I swear. I'm so sorry."

"You're sorry? *You're sorry*?" Another shove, and Dad only continued to take it. "Why? Why can't, just once, you be my dad before you're the Councilor?"

"Jake, *stop*!"

Jake went to shove him again, but this time Dad caught his wrists and roughly pulled Jake against his chest. Jake wanted to pull back, but instead found himself collapsing against his dad's shoulder. Crying.

Froq, he was so stupid. He'd spent these last few days furious, pushing her away to ease his pain. She'd told him their love was the truest thing she'd ever known, and he hadn't believed her. Then she'd said it again, bleeding in his arms, dying because she'd saved him *again,* and he knew what an idiot he'd been. Regardless of the games they had to play, she was real. *They* were real.

"Dad, I can't lose her," Jake said, against his shoulder.

"I know, son. And I'm going to do everything in my power to save her."

"Wake up, baby. Please wake up."

Nic slowly became aware of the breath between her cold lips, of the hard chill of the ice pressed into her back. She was breathing; she wasn't dead. Memories returned in flashes: arms grabbing her in the water, getting her head above the surface. More hands, pulling her out. Coughing, gagging, spitting out water, and then falling unconscious. Now, she felt gentle hands, pushing away the hair that clung to her face.

Nic forced her eyes open. A face hovered above her, one as familiar as breathing. A sob broke from Nic's lips. "Mom?"

"Yes, baby, I'm here."

Nic flung herself upright, throwing her arms around Mom. Nic sobbed, with joy and relief and the sadness that they'd been apart for so long. Her mother was crying too, kissing her cheeks. Behind Mom, Paul rested on his knees on the ice, water dripping from his face and clothes. Nic held out a hand to him, and he crawled forward, wrapping his arms around them both.

I'm home.

THIRTY-NINE

"Can I get you anything?"

Jake lifted his head from where it rested on the edge of Shiloh's hospital bed and blinked his aching eyes at Jessica, Shiloh's nurse. He recognized her from this summer, and from the gasp she gave when Shiloh was wheeled into this room after surgery, she'd recognized them too.

"No." Jake's voice croaked, and he cleared his throat. "Thank you."

"You should probably try to get some sleep, or at least eat something. She's very stable, and you've had a long night."

There's an understatement.

The night had felt like a small eternity. Shiloh had been flown to the hospital in the Twin Cities, where Jake's dad had arranged for esteemed surgeons to be waiting to operate. Jake's two-hour drive to the hospital and the wait during the long surgery had felt worse than physical torture, but at last, a doctor had updated them.

Shiloh would be fine. She had a chest tube, a broken clavicle, and multiple broken ribs, which had likely occurred prior to being shot. But the bullet had missed major arteries. She'd woken long enough in the recovery room for her breathing tube to be removed, but now, she lay in the hospital bed, sleeping, oxygen tubing curving across her face.

Jake tightened his hold on Shiloh's hand. "I'll sleep when she wakes up."

Jessica nodded, patted his shoulder, and left. In her absence, she left silence so deep he could hear the hiss of oxygen flowing into Shiloh's nose.

Mom and Dad had waited with him during the surgery, but left as soon as Shiloh was pronounced stable. Silas's arrest would be an ordure-storm, both for the country and for Jake's family. Jake should be worried about his aunt, his mom, and his cousins—they were losing so much—but his biggest concern right now was Shiloh.

Jake watched the rise and fall of Shiloh's chest, trying to let it soothe the fear, the pain, and the guilt. But it all felt too raw. Flashes of Silas's hand wrapped around her throat, and the feel of her blood on Jake's hand, lit his skin ablaze.

I almost lost her.

They almost took her from me.

One day, they'll try to take her again.

Jake gritted his teeth. No. Whatever he had to do, whatever heresy he had to commit, he'd never lose her or let her go again.

Shiloh's hand twitched in his grasp, and she groaned softly. Jake stood quickly, hovering over her. "Shiloh?" He brushed her hair back, revealing the bruises that still painted her face, the purple faded into a mixture of yellow and green. The sight still slammed a knife into his chest.

She blinked her eyes open, and a cry of relief escaped Jake's lips. There was so much he wanted to tell her, but all that came out was, "Hey."

Her mouth moved, her voice faint, but he read it from her lips. "What happened?"

"You're in the hospital. In Minneapolis."

Her eyes flicked like dolls' eyes around the room, Jake's large suite. She groaned and tried to push herself upright, but Jake set a hand on her shoulder. "Easy there, tough guy. You've got a chest tube in your side."

Her eyes flew wide, unfocused, frightened. The monitor blared as her heart rate rose. "Silas."

Liquid hate burned in Jake's gut, but he sat on the edge of the bed gingerly and made his voice calm, "He was arrested. You're safe now."

Shiloh let out a breath; her heart rate slowed.

Summoned by the monitor, Jessica breezed into the room and fussed over Shiloh, making sure she wasn't in any pain, taking off her oxygen, helping her sit up, checking vitals. Meanwhile, Jake slipped his hand into Shiloh's. She stared at it like it was foreign.

When Jessica finally left, Shiloh's eyes looked more alert. She brought her lips close to Jake's ears, enough that her breath sent a shiver down his spine. He'd missed her being this close.

"Nic?" she asked.

Jake shook his head, his own voice barely a whisper. "Nothing yet. But Stefani will let me know. I've been giving them updates every hour. She and Val have been worried about you."

Shiloh nodded and leaned away. Her eyes traced the chest tube from where it trailed from beneath her gown to over the side of the bed.

"It's okay if you want to go now," she said, not looking up at him.

Jake's back tensed. "What?"

She drew patterns into the stiff hospital sheets with her fingers. "I know you're only here out of obligation." Her voice cracked, and she cleared her throat before continuing. "But I'm going to be fine."

Jake swallowed the acrid taste of guilt. He'd truly made her believe he no longer cared about her. How could he have been so stupid? She'd risked everything for him, and he'd listened to anger and cast her aside like she was nothing.

He shook his head and tucked a strand of her hair behind her ear. "When are you going to get it through your head that you're stuck with me?"

A fine line formed between her eyebrows. "You said it was over."

"It's not over. It'll never be over."

Before Jake realized what he was doing, he was kissing her, wanting desperately to erase the distance that he'd forced between them. She hesitated then kissed him in return. The familiarity of her lips was exquisitely sweet, and his fingers plunged into her hair, pulling her closer. He ached to touch her everywhere, memorize every piece of her in case he'd forgotten, but he didn't dare.

She broke away with a gasp. "Can't breathe," she said, clutching the side where her chest tube was.

Jake cringed. "Sorry."

When she was breathing normally again, she hesitantly reached a hand to his cheek. He caught her hand in his, pressing her closer to his cheek, so she wouldn't pull away.

"Does this...does this mean you forgive me?"

"Yes. And that I'm sorry too. I was such a prig. I'm sorry I pushed you away and I'm so, so sorry that I ever made you believe for a minute that I didn't love you."

"You love me?"

She stared at him as though she couldn't quite believe it. That was okay. He'd keep telling her until she did.

Jake laid a kiss on her forehead and breathed, "I love you." He moved his lips to her unbruised cheek. "I love you." He hovered close to her mouth, so when Jake smiled, he was sure she'd feel it against her lips. "I love you."

Finally, he claimed her mouth again. He kissed her slowly, tenderly, pausing to allow for breath. He hoped that this kiss, and this truth, had the power to wash away the lies, and the pain, and the darkness that had nearly torn them apart and, in its place, leave nothing but love.

"Do you believe me now?" Jake asked, when he finally pulled back.

She smiled. *Victory.* "Hypothesis accepted."

🔥

Nic sat by the fireplace, now in dry clothes, blankets wrapped around her. The warm red flames cast a golden hue on her mother's face, who sat across from her, wrapped in her own blanket. They had spent the hours since arriving at the lodge discussing everything that had happened. Nic already knew that Paul and her mom were the only ones to survive, but when Mom told her, the grief felt fresh and raw all over again. Mom and she had both cried, clinging to each other.

After the attack, the Twin Cities were overrun with Elite, and Paul and her mother had to hide. That was why they hadn't made it back in time. Their radio had been damaged during the attack, so they couldn't contact her. They'd tried to catch up with Nic on the river, but the boat they'd taken was attacked by Elite, and they'd barely escaped. By the time her mother had gotten reconnected to the ROGUE network through the Sparrows, it was too late. The Elites already had Nic in custody. Mom had never stopped looking, but until she had heard from Greyson Andreou, she hadn't even known Nic was alive.

Then it was Nic's turn to share. Nic tried to tell her about the cage, but the words got stuck in her throat, so she glossed over it and told her about everything else. The Haven. The school. Stef and Val. Jake, and his dream for a better world, and how he'd helped her. Shiloh, and how smart she was, and how brave.

"Wait." Mom held up a hand, frowning. "Did you really just say Jacob Osgood? Councilor Osgood's son."

Nic nodded.

"He was the Lion Cub?"

Nic nodded again. Stefani had come up with the codename. It made sense, since ROGUE referred to Councilor Osgood as the Lion, a great devourer.

Mom glanced at Paul and shook her head, smiling softly. A 'can-you-believe-it' sort of smile. But Paul was gazing deeply into the dancing flames in the fireplace and didn't notice.

"What did you say the girl's name was?" Paul asked after a long moment. "The Haven girl who made the Cloak."

Nic narrowed her eyes as she studied him. Something peculiar rang in his voice, and his dark eyes that reflected the firelight seemed like he was a million miles away.

"Shiloh," Nic said at last. "Why?"

Paul stroked the long stubble on his face, still not looking at her. "How old was she?"

"She'll be eighteen in March. *Why?*" Nic asked again.

"No reason," Paul said, but he finally met Mom's eyes. "The name just sounded familiar, that's all."

Something wordless passed between them, and Mom's mouth parted, a strange emotion flickering in her eyes. Nic couldn't quite place it.

Paul chuckled hollowly and scrubbed a hand over his face, shedding whatever expression had been there. "But it's not possible. She died a long time ago."

Nic opened her mouth, but Mom laid a hand on Nic's knee and changed the subject. "I'm so sorry I couldn't find you sooner. That you've been through so much."

Nic sighed. She'd make them tell her tomorrow. She was much too tired now.

"Yeah." Nic stretched her fingers toward the flame to warm them. "Some was pretty awful, but some...some was pretty wonderful too."

Mom cocked her head. "What was wonderful?"

Nic thought, wondering how best to explain it. "Friendship.

Hope." Tears pricked the back of Nic's eyes, but not all the tears were sad. "And love."

That was what Nic would choose to remember: the deep, deep love she'd found. How Shiloh loved Jake, and Stefani and Val loved each other: the kind of love you risked everything for. How they'd all known Nic for such a short period, and yet they'd risked everything for her.

Love, in all its different forms, was so real and so powerful. Love was God in action. Love, not exclusion, was the key to a better world and to unity. All-encompassing, overwhelming love that covered all differences and all hurts and all opinions and left only hope, peace, and joy.

Love.

That was the only thing in this world worth dying for.

When Shiloh awoke again, she found Jake sitting in the chair beside the bed, looking out the window, earbuds in his ears. Deep lines sculpted around his eyes.

I love you.

Her head had been filled with clouds and stars the first time she'd awoken from surgery, but he was still here so what he'd said couldn't have been a dream.

A tear slipped from the corner of Jake's eyes, and he reached to sweep it away with a knuckle.

Shiloh's stomach clenched. "Jake, are you okay?"

Jake jerked his head toward her then smiled crookedly, but it didn't reach the shadows of his eyes. "Good morning, sunshine." He stood and lowered himself on the edge of her bed. "Here. Stefani sent me this."

He took an earbud from his ear and fit it into hers, before pushing play on his phone. The song was somehow foreign and familiar at the same time, the song about home that Nic had told them to listen for. Its final words vibrated in Shiloh's heart. "*I'm coming back home.*"

Then a deep voice, like syrup and honey, "Good night, Freebird."

She'd made it. *She made it!* A sob of relief burst from Shiloh's lips, and Jake moved to slip an arm around her, pulling her against his chest. She turned her face into him, breathed him in. Strong. Safe. Home.

He whispered in her ear, so no one would hear, even if they'd hidden a recorder in the mattress. "You did it, Shi. You saved us."

Somehow, she had. She'd won this terrible game.

Her fingers curled into fists of their own accord, and she leaned close to Jake's ear. "Promise me, Jake. We won't play their games anymore."

"I promise," he breathed, trailing a hand down her back, bare beneath the hospital gown. "No more lies. No more puppet strings."

She rested her head against his chest, listening to the steady rhythm of his heart. When she glanced up, shadows and cold still warred in his eyes, overtaking his golden warmth. She missed the way his eyes blazed brighter than the sun.

"What's wrong, Jake?"

"Nothing." He gave another fake smile.

"Jake." She turned his face toward her with gentle fingers. "We just said no more lies, remember?"

He sighed, pulled her closer, and talked lowly into the top of her head. "I keep thinking about how I almost lost you and about what you said in the chapel. 'There's a world where we can be together, but it's not this world'."

Shiloh swallowed the lump in her throat. She remembered those words well. They resonated with truth as deeply now as they did then.

"They're going to try to take you from me again," Jake said, with a shuddering breath. "They will never let a Haven and an

Osgood be together. Whether tomorrow or when we're assigned spouses at twenty-five. It's only a matter of time."

Shiloh tilted her head up to him, studying every line of his face. Once upon a time, she was a good, little girl who followed strict rules, but that girl no longer existed. She'd died the day she'd watched her sister be executed, and a bomb had blown up beneath her feet. Shiloh didn't quite know the girl who had taken her place, but she knew she wasn't calm and controlled and obedient.

She was fury and strength and rebellion. A bomb, in her own right, about to set the world on fire.

"Well, I know what I'll have to do then," Shiloh said, with a crooked smile of her own.

Jake lifted an eyebrow.

"If this world won't let me have you, I'll burn it down and create a world that will."

A spark ignited in his eyes. There it was, what she'd always seen there before, the heresy that had once scared her, but now made her feel more alive than she ever had. The revolution in his eyes was breathtaking.

"Careful, Shi," he said. "That sounds an awful lot like heresy."

Yes, it did. Because *everyone* had heresy in them.

That was what made them great.

"Good," Shiloh whispered against his lips. "Let's be heretics."

WELCOME, HERETICS!

If you liked this book, please review it on Amazon, Goodreads, or whatever platform you purchased on! Reviews are gold to an indie author. It doesn't just let us know that there are people who like our work, but it helps us with our future career in tangible ways, such as the success of future books.

Want to keep up with updates, sneak peeks, cover/date reveals, giveaways, and chances for ARC copies, and more? Follow C. A. Campbell on Instagram or subscribe to her newsletter.

Website: https://cacampbellwriter.com/subscribe
Instagram: https://www.instagram.com/cacampbellwriter

Acknowledgments

As the saying goes, it takes a village to raise a child. Well, I think this applies for books as well, especially a book that has been my baby for over a decade. I could not have gotten here without the help of some amazing people. It's time to give a million thanks to the following rock stars:

To my husband, for putting up with the tip-tapping of my computer at all hours, for not having me committed when I practice dialogue in the shower, and for supporting my dreams like they are your own. I love you more than anything.

To my writing bestie, Molly, for being with me from the very beginning, for keeping my dreams alive when I almost let them die, and for pulling me out of the self-doubt spiral. You are my cheerleader/proofreader/plot hole fixer/writer block buster. Without you, there would be no book. Oh, and tag! You're it! Time to get that book published!

To my mom, for being the first to push me toward writing. To my sister, Joselyn, for being the first to tell me that I was her favorite author (But then...maybe you're biased).

To my beta readers, particularly Andrea and Casey, for giving me invaluable feedback that helped shape my story to what it is now. To my editor, Kelsey, for her stunning work (Really, I should buy you Starbucks for a lifetime, but I'm poor). To my final proofreader, Sarah, for your invaluable support, positive spirit, and error catching-eyes.

To all my Fearless Writers, for giving me support, feedback, advice, and above all, just being really awesome friends. Especially

Kristina—girl, you're the greatest. Don't you ever forget. And of course, Derek too! Hey, dude, I think I have another question!

To the Author of Life, whose Spirit has taught me what real love is and that every person—no matter what religion or sexuality or race or if they have a horn growing out of their head—is worthy of love, acceptance, and social justice. I hope that this kind of love is reflected in all that I write—no, in all that I *do*.

To YOU, my reader, for picking up, purchasing, and spending hours reading this book. I've been dreaming about sharing these characters and this story with you since some of you weren't old enough to read. I hope that you will love them as much as I do. But more than that, I hope it will teach you that, no matter what anyone says, who you are—who you choose to love, what you choose to be, and how you believe/think/dress/dance/smile/wrinkle your nose/all the little things that make you up—is valid, important, and worthy of infinite love and acceptance. And most importantly, I wish that one day you will live in a world where you don't have be afraid to be who you are. Until then, be courageously, unapologetically you. BE A HERETIC!

And last, but not least, to me, for all my hard work, dedication, and never-say-die attitude. Because in the end, only I can make my dreams come true.

Ya'll, I froqing did it!

About the Author

C. A. Campbell hails from Kansas City (The Missouri side, if you please), where she shares her writing space with her husband, three ridiculous dogs, and her rambunctious toddler. She splits her time between writing, saving lives, and teaching students how not to kill people as a family nurse practitioner and nursing professor. When she's not working, she can be found (likely, in her pajamas) spending time with family, listening to a true crime podcast, or yelling at medical errors in television shows. *Heresy* is her debut novel.

Made in the USA
Monee, IL
22 December 2022

23374762R00213